The Warrior's Bride

Lisa Samson

HARVEST HOUSE PUBLISHERS
Eugene, Oregon 97402

Cover by Terry Dugan Design, Minneapolis, Minnesota

THE WARRIOR'S BRIDE

Copyright © 1997 by Lisa Samson
Published by Harvest House Publishers
Eugene, Oregon 97402

Library of Congress Cataloging-in-Publication Data

Samson, Lisa, 1964–
    The warrior's bride / Lisa Samson
        p.   cm.
    ISBN 1-56507-636-2
    I. Title
PS3569.A46673W37 1997
813'.54—dc21   97-2664
                                                                                CIP

All rights reserved. No portion of this book may be reproduced in any form without the written permission of the Publisher.

Printed in the United States of America.

97   98   99   00   01   02   / BC /   10   9   8   7   6   5   4   3   2   1

For Mrs. Gloria Danaher,
my "second mom,"
with thankfulness and
love for the countless hours you
spent with the little girl who
lived on the next street over.
Thanks for always
being home.

Acknowledgments

Many thanks are due the following people: Bill Jensen, still crazy after all these years. Betty Fletcher and Margie Brown of Harvest House. James Byron Huggins for his unique perspective, much appreciated. Lanissa Spivy, the internship coordinator at Lynchburg College. Alicia Williams, my terrific intern who never blinked at any research request. The special folks of "The Sedalia Writers Group," especially Marcia Opitz, Tony Spivy, and our fearless leader and seasoned veteran of the pen, Darrell Laurant—I value your encouragement tremendously.

Many more thanks to family and friends who help me keep it all going with their love and encouragement: Mom, Lori, Miss Gloria, Jennifer, Heather, and Chris. To my readers: I would like to say thank you as well for your support. I always enjoy hearing from you.

To my own family: Will, Tyler, Jake, and Gwynneth . . . you are the sunshine of my life. Thanks for giving me a lot more than writing to think about and care about. I love you all so much it hurts.

To Keith Skillicorn, I say thank you for all the information on leprosy you sent via e-mail. To the good people at the American Leprosy Mission, especially Susan Renault, who provided me with invaluable literature, my gratitude is immense. Many people are still victims of leprosy. If you would like to help fight this disease, I encourage you to send a contribution to:

American Leprosy Mission
1 ALM Way
Greenville, SC 29601
1-800-543-3135

Thanks be to God who gives us the victory through Jesus Christ our Lord, who heals our hearts as well as our bodies, and showers us with His grace.

❧ PROLOGUE ❧

Spring 1478

A pretty girl, dark and small, sat closely beside her great-grandmother. A battered wooden box lay open before them—a box containing history itself. The contrast between the splintered planks and the silken gowns the two wore made the contents twice as interesting, for their gowns were new and the box was very old.

The dignified old woman, with hair of white and knuckles enlarged by arthritis, unwound a length of tapestry, about 18 inches high and 15 feet in length. "See here, Maggie, what this depicts. This begins the life of Edward, the Black Prince."

Margaret Durwin's eyes were wide at the picture of a swaddled babe with a crown on his head. A king and a queen looked on in what appeared to be a nativity arrangement, only halos were missing. " 'Tis a lovely thing. I don't believe I can work such a fine needle, Grandmama."

"Not many can. But this was begun by my grandmother over a hundred years ago when she was even younger than you are now."

"Did she look like me?"

"She was pretty like you are and small. But she wasn't as serious a soul as you're turning out to be, Maggie. And she was blessed with long, blond hair, as white as the clouds and nearly as full."

Maggie fingered the first several feet of the tapestry. "Why did she decide to depict the life of the prince?"

"She told me that she loved him with a youthful passion, like young girls will do."

Excitement tickled Maggie's brain. Whenever she came to Durwin Manor, her great-grandmother's ancestral home, she always learned something new about her family. Most likely the tale began because of the box, the contents of which her great-grandmother, Lady Mary Durwin, had taken upon herself to gather and preserve. "You must tell me all about her, Grandmama. Please?"

"That's exactly what I had in mind. And while I talk, dear Maggie, gaze upon the little figures of men and women now departed, feel the intricate stitches, the woven threads, and remember that your life is intertwined with theirs, that you are who you are now because of who they were then."

Margaret closely examined the delicate tapestry as her great-grandmother began to speak, her voice a unique ocean-going vessel, carrying Maggie on seas of fancy back to the distant past.

❧ ❧ ❧

Oxfordshire, England—Spring 1370

"*Sometimes our lives are forever changed by that which we have long forgotten. I count that as a blessing. That my earthly hell is not of my own choosing.*" The words, scratched on a tattered fragment of parchment in undisciplined handwriting, thick and careless, were read aloud softly by the girl who propped up the scrap between her finger and thumb. The rosy glow of youth still blushed over her fingertips, the shine of childhood rested undisturbed upon the moist surface of her pale-blue eyes. The dimness of the small hut in summer did little to dampen the dazzling shade of her white-blond hair.

She was 12.

The splendid purple gown she wore contrasted rudely with the pitiful dwelling into which she had wandered as dusk was stealing over the hills and into the shadowy weald. Searching for sights never yet beheld by her perpetually inquisitive eyes and employed by no other means of worthwhile distraction, she had entered the lonely abode without reservation.

Poorly furnished with only a straw pallet for sleeping, a table, and a stool—all battered and worn—the hut was pathetically tidy. A wooden bucket from which she had taken a drink upon entering sat in the corner, and a small pile of kindling wood was arranged nearby. The table held more scraps of parchment anchored down by a large, smooth, egg-shaped brook stone, formed thus by centuries of rushing waters. An inkwell and two quills rested upon the marred surface as well, in silent defiance against the inferior surroundings.

Advantaged by a privileged upbringing, the girl was already more educated than most noble boys her age. Thus it was with confident fingers that she set aside the rock and began to read the rest of the scraps. Such pride amid such obvious poverty, seen closely and in private, intrigued her already over-stimulated intellect. The thought of this obviously educated man living in such rudimentary conditions somehow reached up to her—or perhaps down. For although she had been taught to believe in an inherent, higher value to the upper class into which she was born, this man's pen was far more noble, insightful, and melancholy than hers would ever be. Pain was found in his words, clawing introspection, and an utter disregard—a loathing even—for the outer man. "A worm's repast." He kept referring to himself as such, insistently so, and almost with a pleasure to be able to so regard his body.

And yet I know that the flesh which shall see God will not be that which mars the body He gave to me, the body formed 30 years ago in the womb of she who bore me. Curse this frail state of being man, when a greater, more heavenly form awaits. But when? How long until the very voices of the angels cover this flesh with a cloak of the heavenly kind, a covering of newborn flesh filled with the radiance of the Son of God Himself?

His journey to such revulsion for the flesh has been one fraught with many difficulties, the girl surmised as the light of the dying day retreated too quickly for her liking. Rapid speculation naturally began regarding who had written these words of pain and promise. A hermit, most likely. A holy man whom God had not called to the communal brotherhood of monastic service, but a man whom God consecrated for His glory in some lonely, isolated hut. Penning great truths. Relying only upon divine substance.

Such a life was incomprehensible to her.

Such a God was even more obscure.

Her name was called in the distance. *Back to the carriage,* she sighed, wanting to read more of these thoughtful expressions. But her family was traveling home from London, and Mother needed to rest a bit without the knocking movement of the lavish pleasure vehicle her father had purchased years before. He would come looking for her soon, wanting to finish the journey now that the cool of the evening was spreading over the land.

One last, adoring sweep. Her fingers caressed the parchment scraps. She considered taking them with her, but knew somehow that to steal this man's sole source of self-expression would be a sacrilege. The words thrilled her strangely enough for all their spiritual content, and before placing the smooth, oblong stone on top of the pile, she held the final page to her lips and closed her eyes.

A sudden shadow dissolved the light in the doorway.

"What mean you, girl!" an abrasive masculine voice cried, and a wooden clapper violently shook in his hand, the small wooden plates resounding their clacks in quick, erratic succession against her eardrums as her eyes sprang open. She stood rooted to the spot, mouth opened in horror. Her conclusion about this man's circumstances had been correct. He was indeed a hermit. But not by his own choosing.

"Get out!" he yelled, shaking the warning rattle yet louder with clawed hands. She opened her mouth to scream as he drew closer, wanting not to see the face beneath the peculiar, yet well-recognized hood that people of his ilk were forced by the church to don after taking their vows of . . .

"Leprosy!" he shouted, louder this time. "Are you deaf, girl? Get out! Hasten! Leprosy! Run as fast as you can!"

The noble maid was returned her faculties forthwith, fear accelerating her now-hammering pulsebeat. Obeying his final command, she ran out of the hut and back down the path her feet had trod an hour before. The dense forest consumed her small form as she tried to escape more than just the hermit's wrath. Her family was not a devout flock, considering themselves above the superstitions of the church; nevertheless, she frantically prayed that she was returning to the carriage exactly as she had left it.

The fragment of parchment was still clutched tightly in her hand.

ONE

Six years later, 1376

Lightning splashed in brilliant display against the fused clouds of the storm. Drops of June rain barraged the Gothic windows of Durwin Manor. Crofters in the surrounding fields pulled the oxen and asses to shelter when the hail began to fall. Mothers shouted for their children from the doorways of huts and cottages to hurry to shelter. Denizens of field and wood sought their dens, holes, and nests. Once secure inside their homes, all life paused for the storm in awe, homage, and a bit of fear as the lightning drew closer—the upright fork of an angry god piercing the earth with its astonishing fire.

Thunder shook the wind.

"One...two...three..." Lady Johanna Durwin counted evenly after the streak of white flame which shocked the sky. "Three miles away," she reported after hearing the answering thunder, carefully unraveling a length of black embroidery silk to thread inside the waiting needle's eye.

"Yes, my lady," answered Margery Chandler, Lady Johanna's lady's maid. She plied her own needle with as much expertise as her mistress—more, actually—and whereas Johanna was working on an embroidered tapestry depicting the Battle of Aquitain fought 20 years before, Margery lovingly decorated an altar cloth for the family chapel. Grapevines intertwined with leaves and heavy, ripened grapes that appeared ready to burst from their deep-red jackets.

In contrast to the tempest outside the stately walls of Durwin Manor, inside the great hall the only daughter and servants of Johanna's father, Sir Gordon Durwin, entitled Lord Clifton, were saturated by a calm warmth. Except perhaps Margery, who never particularly enjoyed a thunderstorm. Lady Johanna and Margery perched on stools before the massive wall fireplace, and the family bard was plucking absentmindedly on his lyre. He wasn't a very good bard, but he was good-looking, and Johanna's mother liked having comely people around her to dispel the natural gloom carried by stone walls. The steward and several house servants sat at one of the many tables which surrounded the hall. Busily polishing the silver plate, which normally inhabited the carven cupboards near the fireplace, their conversation formed a low hum, melodically blending with the bard's tune, the drumming of the rain upon the roof and windows, and the crackling of the fire.

Lightning flashed again. "It draws nearer, my lady," Margery remarked with bridled consternation.

Johanna's eyes sparkled. "I know." Nevertheless, she bowed her head and resumed her concentration. She was working diligently on the figure of Edward, the Prince of Wales, sword raised in the air as his horse reared on its hind legs. Known affectionately by all Englishmen as "the Black Prince," he was a worthy figure for all boys to emulate, the ideal medieval man. And Johanna, through many years of girlish devotion and hours of stitching a linen shrine in homage to the brave, courtly military genius, had firmly placed him on the alabaster pedestal of her heart and decidedly crowned him her ideal.

"Your tapestry grows more fine each day, my lady," Margery complimented, jumping a little at the next crash of thunder.

"You are a fine teacher," Lady Johanna replied to her faithful servant. Knowing the woman had never doled out a frivolous compliment in her life, Lady Johanna received Margery's words with great pleasure, for she had worked hard at perfecting the movements of her needle.

Margery Chandler had been with the Durwins for three years, having come from London and the household of the illustrious Buckinghams. Her mother had been a lady's maid before her, and her grandmother before that. She was well-schooled in the art of gentle, gracious servitude and realized well that her position was great as far as servants went. Her garments were of nearly as fine a cloth and cut as those of her mistress, although not so lavishly adorned. She bathed quite regularly and could wield a needle with great skill, offering valuable suggestions to her superior. Practically speaking, Margery was every inch the lady that Johanna was, save the noble background. But what separated her even more from most of the servants at Durwin Manor was her ability to understand Johanna as completely as one human being can understand another. Margery could hear the cries of her lady's heart—cries that Johanna seldom heard herself. As the only child of Lord and Lady Clifton, Johanna knew great loneliness at times, and had tried valiantly to overcome it when it became unbearable. It was then that Margery stepped in and tried to be more than just a servant.

Margery saw it all.

She knew that her powers of observation—those sharp eyes which missed nothing—were something she had been given from the womb. An uncanny intuition had settled in fully when she attained womanhood, and all of it was tied together by a commitment to prayer. The Chandlers, descended as their name suggested from a family of candle makers, had been people of a strong, lively faith for generations. And Margery was no exception.

Margery furtively studied her mistress. Johanna was an interesting creature, to say the least. Beautiful by most standards, her features were still somewhat irregular: high brow, prominent nose, and full lips, somehow redeemed by the thick, straight hair, so light in its blond shading that it appeared white in full daylight. But the ropelike braids held the silver light of the moon among their strands, and not the golden light of the sun. The pale-blue eyes, icy in color, yet glowing with the fires of a vibrant soul beneath their arctic surface, counterbalanced the fact that they were too widely set. And though her lips were fuller than the court beauties of the day boasted of, the straight teeth beneath them—healthy, strong, and white—were some of the finest in the kingdom. Men found her beautiful; women found fault.

Johanna was of diminutive stature, and Margery often marveled that a fiery, vibrant spirit such as her lady possessed could be contained in what looked like the body of a 14-year-old. Lady Johanna Durwin, however, was 18 that very day. And, despite many offers, not a bit closer to marriage than she was at 14, and stubbornly so.

"Do you know what Father is doing today?" she asked her maid nonchalantly.

"I believe he is in Oxford, my lady. And since you're asking, I don't know what present he's planning to give you this year."

"I asked no such thing, Margery Chandler! Shame on you for your impertinence!"

"Forgive me, my lady." Margery bowed her head contritely, but smiled broadly with her heart. Moments such as these made her job that much more enjoyable.

Johanna primly continued her reprimand. "Your job is to serve me, Margery, not to read my mind. And the fact that you are so sure about what you think is inside my head, and so smug when you give voice to your suspicions, is really quite beyond your place."

"Would you rather have a simpering idiot at your side all day long?"

Lady Johanna eyed the tall, dark-haired woman sitting beside her. "Of course not!"

They glared at each other momentarily, then slowly grinned, their eyes betraying that they were both lovers of friendly conflict. Johanna wouldn't care to openly admit how much she had grown to rely on the woman beside her. Margery was a dark, ordinary backdrop against which the flamboyant Johanna could dazzle the world. Her raven hair was always dressed most severely, and her lips were as pale as her skin. Long arms, long legs, large hands and feet. Hardly graceful. Yet somehow she moved about with a bustling, lively dignity, which plainly showed in her luminous black eyes. In them danced an unmistakable serenity, a celebration of peace. Johanna loved Margery's eyes.

Lightning flashed and Johanna counted again but barely made it to one before the thunder cracked the air around the house. " 'Tis upon us!"

The bard began to play more loudly, competing with the din. Even so, when the heavy door to the outside stairs was shoved open by a broad shoulder, its hinges were barely able to absorb the shock as it caught the wind and slammed against the wall. Everyone jumped somewhat off their seats. The fire danced wildly in the sudden breeze.

"Great Father in heaven!" Margery crossed herself fervently.

"Papa!" Johanna threw her work down into the basket beside her and jumped to her feet. " 'Twas a suspicion of mine that you had begun to lose your faculties, and I now have proof that my assumptions were well-founded! What mean you traveling back from Oxford in such a storm as this?"

Lord Clifton, aged yet vibrant, good-natured yet a force to be reckoned with, took little account of his daughter's consternation. He was always in some sort of trouble with the ladies of Durwin Manor. Instead, he reached into the leather pouch he had slung over his shoulder and pulled out a leather-bound volume. Most precious.

" 'Tis no worthy manner in which you hail your sire, good daughter, especially when I rode most hastily to celebrate with you the day you arrived in our family!"

Johanna's smile was echoed by her father's, strong teeth and all. He was an intelligent, convivial man, given to excess of wit and mirth, if not food, which he sparingly consumed. His tallish frame, still in excellent condition, reminded all those around him that he had been a knight of the highest order in his younger days. Gordon Durwin walked for miles each day, a kindly lord, visiting his tenants and inquiring after their well-being.

He was possessed of massive hands, the right pinkie finger now just a memory, which brought to mind the Battle of Crecy and the swift sweep of a Frenchman's sword. The many nights, collecting into years, spent sleeping in the damp out-doors seemed to have gathered in the joints of his knees, causing him to limp a bit now that age had settled down to stay. His hair, once the color of Johanna's and now a pure silver, hung just below his earlobes, and his eyes were an even paler blue than his daughter's, or perhaps they appeared that way due to the deeply tanned, leather skin which surrounded him in pleasingly weathered folds.

He showed her the book.

"Papa, is that for me?"

"Yes, Johanna. All the way from Florence."

By this time, Johanna was at his side, but Lord Clifton held the volume high in the air. It was quite large and quite heavy, but he took no notice of the bulk. How could he, when his revered daughter, who had returned springtime to his days, laughed up at him with such enchantment in her eyes? She jumped futilely beside him, reaching in vain for her gift.

15

"Tell me, Papa. At least douse my curiosity. Tell me what it is!"

He lowered the book and handed it to her saying, "Perhaps God is laughing yet."

She gasped. *"The Divine Comedy!"*

"Yes, child. Anything for your pleasure, my Lady Johanna."

Johanna put her arms around his waist and laid her cheek against his upper chest, hugging him tightly. "Thank you, Papa. Thank you for remembering."

He kissed the top of her head. "There is only one requirement I have in regard to this venerable work of the master Dante, and it is that we read it together."

Johanna pulled him toward the fireplace. "Then we'll begin now. Shall I read or shall you?"

" 'Tis your decision—after all, today is your birthday. But I must say, I'm most weary from my day out and about."

"You weary? Impossible. Nevertheless, I'll read, as I do believe my Italian has now surpassed yours."

"Indeed?" He loved her pluck. "That's not laying claim to a great deal. I've never pretended to be the linguist you are, Daughter."

She shrugged her small shoulders in a most womanly manner, the movement coming as a surprise to him, as if the fact that it was her birthday had not held its true meaning to him until that very moment.

"Then do as you will, my lady," he bowed, as though genuflecting to King Edward himself and, throwing his drenched cloak over a bench near the fire, sat down in his chair and stretched his booted feet toward the blaze. A young servant boy immediately ran forward to remove the sopping footgear.

"Inferno, Canto One," she began, moistening her lips with the pink tip of her tongue. Her excitement did little to keep her voice from shaking or her hands from sweating on the precious manuscript. Margery laid a firm hand on her

16

lady's arm, engaged Johanna's eyes firmly with her own, and nodded serenely. It was all Johanna needed.

Halfway along the road we have to go,
I found myself obscured in a great forest,
Bewildered, I knew I had lost the way.

Her father interrupted her. "Translating as we go? Impressive."

Johanna cocked her head to one side and assumed the haughty expression of any one of the many Oxford dons who came regularly to instruct her. "Naturally, Papa."

But Margery knew Johanna was doing the translating for the benefit of her maid-in-waiting and all those who cared to listen to the words of one of Europe's greatest poets. But soon Lord Clifton was barely listening, his mind burdened with weightier matters. He had something to tell his daughter, most grievous news, but he hadn't the heart to spoil her birthday.

Tomorrow would do little to drive the news away, most unfortunately, for if he could have made it go away for her sake, he would have.

᯽ ᯽ ᯽

Johanna began the third canto some time later, the hall more widely populated than before. Henry, the head cook, and some of his staff sat quietly mincing garlic and onions or grinding the spice in a mortar. The laundresses folded the warm linens which had been hung to dry in the overheated kitchen due to the storm, and all were enraptured at Lady Johanna's words. It wasn't only what she read which captivated them, but how she read. Her perfect timing and most appropriate use of inflection enabled them to more easily understand the meaning.

Through me you go into the city of weeping;
Through me you go into eternal pain;
Through me you go among the lost people . . .

"I see I've come in just as it was getting sentimental." A dry female voice pulled everyone from Dante's world.

Johanna immediately set down her book. "Maman!" She had always called her mother by the French word and not the English.

"Back from my sojourn with repose," Lady Rosamunde Durwin said as her faithful servant Ned carried her crippled body in from the solar.

"From the land of the dying to the land of the dead," Ned, a lumbering brute of a man with arms the size of oak trees and calves just the same, said as he gently deposited her on her special chair and lifted the useless legs to rest on a softly padded footstool.

She rapped him on the arms sharply. "I would hardly call my naps the land of the dying, Ned. The land of the befuddled perhaps, but not the land of the dying!"

"More strange dreams, mon amour?" Lord Clifton took her hand and kissed the back of it lingeringly, in a most gentlemanly, yet husbandly manner.

"Yes. But no matter, Gordon. 'Tis a blessing that I forget about them almost as soon as I open my eyes."

"There was a great storm which passed through. Perhaps that attributed to your colorful slumber, Maman."

At Rosamunde's arrival, the servants scattered. The lady of the manor didn't like to wait long for her dinner. Under the hypnotic spell of Dante read in Johanna's lovely, husky voice, all had lost track of the time.

Lord Clifton rose from his chair to bestow a gentle kiss upon his wife's waiting lips. "Whatever visions passed before you in slumber, my lady, you look even more beautiful than you did before."

"And you, my lord, are as striking as ever."

They didn't take one another for granted, and they never had. And Lord Clifton had obviously retained his keen eyesight. For his wife of almost 19 years was, as he said, a lovely creature possessed of a frail, delicate beauty. Her dark-brown hair warmed by red overtones set off the perfection of her clear, white skin. It was a full face she claimed, with softly rounded cheeks and full lips. Her dark eyes were snappy and always looking for something to find humorous or sad, but not much in between. All the Durwins nourished a well-developed sense of humor. Her stature, before the accident which paralyzed her, was much like Johanna's, maybe an inch taller, but she was tiny as well.

How Lord and Lady Clifton came to be together was a love story in and of itself. After the bloody Battle of Poitiers on Monday, September 18, 1356, Sir Gordon Durwin, as Lord Clifton then was known, a valued knight of Prince Edward, was resting, sitting on the blood-spilt ground, seeking to gather his wits. The 40-year-old bachelor was sipping quietly on the wine the Black Prince had ordered distributed, waiting for the victory celebration to begin, when he heard a soft weeping in the brush nearby. It was a girl, only 15 or so. She hadn't been able to make it back into the walled city of Poitiers before it was shut up tight. The doors to the town still held fast, keeping the French townspeople safe from the English, although their king had already surrendered to his cousin, the Prince of Wales, the Black Prince—called thus not because of a sullied heart or soiled deeds, but because he always chose to wear black armor.

"Why do you weep so?" Durwin asked softly in French, a comforting hand upon the girl's head. When she turned her face up to his, he gasped at her beauty, and the fear in her eyes twisted his heart painfully. He took her to his tent and there learned that her father was killed in the battle. She had no mother. Durwin cared for her on the march to Bordeaux, an English stronghold.

It took over two and a half years for a treaty to be brought about, and during that time Durwin brought the girl, whom he fondly called Rosamunde due to her complexion, into his household. When Prince Edward sailed back to England at Easter of 1359, Durwin did as well, only he returned with his bride Rosamunde and their infant daughter—returning a much richer man both monetarily and emotionally. For years he had deemed the state of marital bliss one which he would never attain. The military had been his life. He was a soldier and happy to be one. But because of his brave service for the king, Sir Gordon Durwin was granted lands in Oxfordshire and given the title Lord Clifton.

His love for Rosamunde had never faded. Indeed, Lord Clifton was still protective in nature toward his wife. Rosamunde, much changed from the girl he found on the battlefield 20 years before, humored his need to watch over her. She still adored him, even though the great difference in their ages seemed to be widening now that Lord Clifton was in his sixties and beginning to ail more frequently.

Lady Rosamunde made a shooing motion with her bejeweled hand. "Get along, everyone!" she cried, especially to Johanna. "I'm too hungry to wait much longer."

Obediently, Johanna laid the book aside to wait until after supper. After all, she was hungry as well. "I shall go change now," she announced as though it were her idea. "Come along then, Margery!"

Margery efficiently gathered the embroidery supplies and followed her lady out of the room.

The parents looked at one another and shook their heads, unable to imagine life without strong-natured Johanna about. They knew they spoiled her shamelessly with all the expensive tutors and books they provided. They also knew she was blessed with an insatiable thirst to broaden her mind and deepen it. And yet, Johanna was always so much fun, the frivolous side to her nature all too willing to exhibit itself. It was easy to lavish her with delicacies of the mind and other delights. Fine clothes, trips, and trinkets. Lord Clifton would have given her a fine horse as well, but Johanna hated the creatures.

It wasn't the normal way of raising a child in those days, but because of a riding accident, Lady Rosamunde had become paralyzed from the waist down when Johanna was only two. Gordon became too lenient on both of them, and they relied on his easygoing ways to take the sting out of what could have been an unbearable situation. Not long after his wife's recovery, he bought a beautiful pleasure carriage. Johanna had practically grown up in that vehicle, the long train of horses driving them across the countryside for visits with the gentry of the area and especially the Countess of Witney. Rosamunde saw the excursions as a way she and her daughter could be active together and spend a great deal of time in one another's company, even though she couldn't walk.

Such days were great fun. When the Durwins' carriage pulled up to a manor, the inhabitants knew they were in for a good time, for Rosamunde was an accomplished conversationalist and could remember with a startling accuracy names, dates, and events in the life of each person whom she had ever come across.

Consequently, Johanna's childhood was filled with the mirth of her mother, who was independent in mind if not in body. The small amount of discipline Johanna was forced to endure came from the initiative of Lady Clifton. Johanna developed a cynical sense of humor from Ned, the irascible servant, and from her father she realized it was possible to be utterly strong and utterly gentle at one and the same time. He had been dependable on the battlefield in the prime of youth, an excellent horseman who could wield any manner of weapon, and he took that commitment to duty and transferred it to his family once his battle days were done.

He became angered only when it was absolutely necessary. And then, it wasn't a pretty display at all. As much as he allowed his wife and daughter a long lead, he was also very protective of their safety and jealous of their reputation. Perhaps Johanna had never experienced the fullest extent of his ire because she knew instinctively where the boundaries were laid down.

Just now he was most mellow, the exertion of traveling through the storm having tired him a bit. The couple chatted amiably, like old friends, as Johanna and Margery climbed the steps to the loft above her parents' solar where she and Margery slept. Margery drew a gown out of the chest and laid it on the bed, but before helping Johanna into the garment, she took up a brush and began to dress her lady's hair. She divided the thick blond hair down the middle and braided each side just above the ears. The braids were wound into two thick coils, one on either side of her head, and Margery attached a small silk veil at the back of her lady's head which fluttered down to Johanna's shoulders.

The gown itself was very simple, made of royal-blue brocade. The bodice, buttons parading down the front in single file, fit snugly to her body, and from the low waistline a full skirt fell, trailing slightly at the back, its hem decorated with white fur. She donned a heavy jeweled chain which boasted five large topaz stones.

Lord Clifton begged his lady's pardon and repaired to the solar, hastily changing from his riding clothes into a fancy doublet the color of wine. Rosamunde demanded a formal table at Durwin Manor, and neither her husband nor her daughter would dare approach the dais wearing anything that wasn't their finest.

The call to supper was heard, and the occupants of the solar and its loft quickly exited the room and made their way to the table on the dais. But before the food could be served, an unexpected guest was announced. It was none other than Lord Geoffrey Alden of Castle Chauliac, the most notorious libertine in the shire, and the most charmingly handsome rogue that Johanna had ever known.

Earlier that chilly day, as the storm clouds thronged the western sky, a proclamation was read from the southern porch of the parish church. The church had prevailed in that very spot for centuries. Once a humble Saxon parish, the only telltale signs of that civilization's involvement in the ancient building was the long-and-short work on the doorjamb. Since the days when William the Conqueror took the isle of Britain, when this church was a long-term sanctuary for the Saxon rebel Lord of Oxneford, much about the building had changed. It had grown, and a central Norman bell tower was added, looming over the graveyard which steadily rose in altitude as bodies turned to dust and more were placed on top. The tower was imposing, with arched windows and interesting brickwork around the crenelated, square top.

But no one was looking up at the tower as the message was read in a loud voice by the royal courier bearing the royal crest. Lord Clifton stood by the courier's side, as did the parish priest, Father Theodore—a dour German whom the local bishop installed as a favor to the man's father. No one cared much for the impersonal fellow who cared nothing for them, but he had the monopoly on religion in their village, and they felt it was better to have him than no shepherd at all. But no one was looking at him, either, as the loud voice of the messenger rang out the news which would affect them all.

The Black Prince was dead.

His life had been waning for five years. Dropsy. Pain had become a resolute companion, and almost every month he experienced a hemorrhage. Many times before his attendants had been sure their lord was approaching his final skirmish with death, and now, weary after years of illness, he had faced the last foe without fear, for that was his way. The final battle was over, and he had fought a good fight. But even a warrior such as he could not play the victor to Death. After being displayed in the Westminster Abbey, his body was to be taken to the city of Canterbury and there buried in the grand priory church which saw the murder of Thomas à Becket two centuries before on the orders of King Henry II.

What the messenger did not read in his undetailed account was that the Prince of Wales bore his infirmities patiently, accepted his weakened state in a most manly manner, never breathing a word of complaint against God. An active man, a soldier unparalleled, to be confined to bed for so long—it would have been almost understandable for an anger at the Divine to surface. But not so Edward. On June 7, the day before his death, he distributed gifts to his household servants and retainers, whether their rank was high or low, and he begged his father the king to continue kindly with his friends and servants. A will was drawn up—his brother John, the Duke of Lancaster, made the executor along with his friend William of Wykeham—and with these words he made arrangements for his funeral: "And it is my will that at the time when my body shall be conducted through the city of Canterbury up to the priory, two war-horses covered with my arms, and two men armed in my arms and in my crests proceed before my body. That is to say, one for war with my arms in full quartered, and the other for peace with my badge of ostrich feathers. And that he that shall be armed for war shall have a man armed carrying after him a black pennon with ostrich feathers."

After Edward made his will, his son Richard, nine years old, was brought in to take away the gifts he had given, and it was then that his faith shone forth from the frail body, once manly and bold, strong and brave, now emaciated and ravaged by the lengthy disease. The room was hushed and close as his faithful advisers and knights leaned forward to hear his whispered words, spoken in French, the language of the English court. "Dear gentlemen, consider, for God's sake, that we are not masters in this life. All must pass by this path; no man can turn aside from it. So, very humbly, I beg you please to pray for me."

The next day was Trinity Sunday, and the Black Prince prayed yet again as the nation prepared to celebrate the holy feast. Perhaps he felt the chill of death enter his room for the last time, never to leave again. Perhaps he heard the timbre of heaven and tasted the balmy, sweet air of Gilead.

> Blessed Trinity, whose name I have always honored on earth, whose glory I have sought to magnify, in whose faith, although in other respects a miserable sinner, I have always lived, I beseech Thee, as I have always celebrated Your festival on earth and have called upon the people to be joyful and celebrate Thy feast with me, to free me from the body of this death and deign to call me to that most sweet feast, which is celebrated in heaven today.

He bade the doors of his chamber to be opened wide, and all the men who had served him well entered the grand room. Once so virile and grand himself, the great warrior seemed almost childlike in the middle of the bed, but even then his vibrant spirit could not be quenched. For in heart, if not in form, he was as vital as he had ever been, and that fact was readily observed. They stood round his bed, words impossible, devastation piercing their hearts. For many years they had served this gracious hero faithfully and well and had come to rely on his constancy and to feast upon his kindness.

"Gentlemen," he said, with a look of warm fondness in his eyes, "forgive me. By the faith that is due to you from me, you have served me faithfully. I cannot of myself give to each his fitting reward, but God by His most holy name will rend it to you in the holy heaven."

As he spoke, the once-stalwart faces of those who had accompanied him onto the field of battle, whether in victory or defeat, those who had never left him, crumbled. The room became so full of the sound of sobbing, weeping, and grief that he could barely be heard. But even on his deathbed, the Black Prince rallied to the occasion, his voice clear and loud enough to be heard over the unashamed weeping of the valiant men who loved him so deeply, who had followed him courageously into battle, deeming their lives of little account next to the prince's good pleasure. "I commend my son to you. He is very young and little. I pray you to serve him loyally, as you have served me."

After that King Edward and the prince's brother John arrived. They placed their hands on the Holy Scriptures and swore to care for Prince Edward's wife and son, and to comfort young Richard, to help him, and to ensure that his right to the throne would not be taken from him. The concern that his son would one day become king was foremost on his mind. All the princes and barons assembled swore to that end, and Prince Edward thanked them for their loyalty. He had been a faithful, loyal leader in his lifetime. Kind to his men. Merciful and always gracious. And now he was rewarded by their presence as they lent him their hearts and hands to ease the transition from life to death to life anew.

And the grief continued. His wife, a beautiful princess always much loved by her husband, stood with a handkerchief pressed to her lips with one hand, the other held the hand of her husband. Her heart was breaking, and she wondered if she would ever leave this chamber alive, for surely, as Edward died, wouldn't she also? She almost prayed it would be thus, for she could never love another the way she had loved him.

Herald Chandos watched in sadness, and recorded later on for all the world to know, "Of lamentation and sighing, of crying aloud and sorrowing, there was so great a noise, that not a man in all the world, if he had seen the grief, but would have had pity at heart."

One man, clothed entirely in black, stood with the rest, his bearing noble, his grief too deep for tears. He looked on, feeling each second wane with the final beats of the prince's heart. *I've served him all my life*, the warrior thought, wondering what he would do now, but knowing that his life would not cease to be of purpose because the Prince of Wales would die. Sir John Alden thought of all the campaigns they had fought together in France, of his own willingness to lay down his life for Prince Edward, even more so than for England. The military was his life, but at 40 perhaps it was time to choose a different direction. Many such thoughts were abounding as the vigil continued. His eyes met the prince's, who nodded so slightly that only the knight saw. It was a personal thanks for a devotion that had lasted many years—a devotion his royal majesty had never taken for granted.

Finally the prince breathed a prayer as a monk of Saint Albans, standing nearby, hastily scrawled the last words of this most worthy of men. "I thank Thee, oh Lord, for all Thy benefits. With all my power I ask for Thy mercy that Thou wilt forgive me for all the sins that I, in my wrongdoing, have committed against Thee. And I ask with my whole heart the grace of pardon from all men whom I have knowingly or unwittingly offended."

"With his death died the hope of Englishmen," it was written.

And it seemed to be so as those who had gathered at the parish church in Oxfordshire on that next afternoon of June 9 turned to go, some with heads bowed reverently, lips moving in prayer. Others staring in shock. Some weeping for their dead hero. The mourning of the Black Prince had begun. Even as the storm began and the first raindrops fell.

Lord Clifton watched them go, and as they shuffled away—a mass of drably clad humanity whose lives held little hope for the most part, and even less adventure and glory—his heart was downcast. All Englishmen and women had taken a great deal of personal pride in their valiant prince, and now he was gone. But Gordon Durwin's predominant thought was just how he was going to break the news to Johanna.

He was still pondering on the as-yet-future event while they seated themselves upon the dais for supper that evening. Unfortunately, another visitor came in on the heels of roguish Geoffrey Alden and his aunt and uncle, the Earl and Countess of Witney. It was the neighborhood thorn-in-the-flesh, Lord Godfrey de Mer.

Lady Johanna tried unsuccessfully to hide the distaste which she felt upon his entrance, all those blond curls flopping around large, myopic blue eyes. The dainty, bow-shaped mouth which sat below the arched nose didn't do much to come to the aid of his utter uncomeliness. He had no chin, either. And from the side he distinctly resembled a trout. Johanna had been calling the 25-year-old baron "Lord Codfish" for years. And his surname, de Mer, meaning "of the sea," was almost too fitting to actually be true.

Godfrey was one of those people who was much too smart for his own happiness. His great intellect was counterbalanced by a complete lack of social skills. His propensity to spit on the rushes of the floor at least once a minute disgusted Johanna utterly, causing her never to look at him as they spoke for fear she would have to actually *see* the revolting action. She and Margery always joked about it afterward, wondering how one person could expectorate in one hour what seemed to be the daily allotment of saliva of at least three people. *Roman rhetoric* were two words no one dared utter when Godfrey inhabited the room, for doing so would guarantee two hours' worth of boring mental expectoration from the mind of Godfrey de Mer.

From his seat next to her, Lord Geoffrey spied her stifled expression and chuckled warmly, laying a warm hand over hers as he leaned close. "I would wager now that you're glad to see me."

"Of course I would rather sit next to even you, Lord Geoffrey, than that pasty-faced mackerel who comes to call far too often."

"I don't know whether to take that as a compliment or not, my lady."

"Do what you wish with it."

"If I did as I wished, I would simply sit here and stare into your eyes, Lady Johanna."

Johanna's hand flew to her mouth to stifle a loud cry of laughter. "Oh, Geoffrey, stop being so whimsical. We've known each other too long for such talk. News of your reputation reached Durwin Manor years ago."

"Yes. Yes, I confess I'm known as a libertine, but I assure you, that is not an accurate report."

"Not on my account, anyway."

"No. You're every inch a lady, Johanna. I would rather drink poison than defile you."

"Rather extreme to say so, don't you think, Geoffrey? So I take it that you have no designs upon me?"

"None. Unseemly or otherwise. I would not even feign to sully your reputation by making any advances of that nature."

She sipped her wine and looked about her at the activity of the room. "And yet you just made an advance."

He grinned. "I'm caught." He shrugged. "You are right. I cannot help myself when I am near you. Your beauty has finally captured me after all these years of friendship."

Johanna leaned forward and looked down at Margery, who sat with the steward and other high-ranking servants at a table just below the dais. "You'd better keep your voice down, Lord Geoffrey, if you don't wish to displease Margery. She can be most formidable when it comes to her duty regarding me. Hear me well. You certainly do not wish to experience her displeasure."

"So you displease her that much at times?"

Johanna shrugged. " 'Tis none of your affair."

"She's a rough one to have about, eh?"

"Not really. She's quite devoted, actually. And because her feelings are so true, I tend to allow her liberties which many maidservants would never be afforded. But enough of this."

"Nay, I'm not through yet. So is there another man who holds your heart that it should be locked so formidably against my onslaught?"

"That's not for you to know. And calling your feeble advance an onslaught is being much too gracious about the matter."

His smile was wide and beautiful and, unfortunately, not in the least daunted. "Feeble, eh? We'll see about that, Lady Johanna. One day you'll need me. My reputation may be that of a bedchamber charmer, but I assure you there's more to me than rumors."

Lady Johanna yawned. "Please, Sir Geoffrey, this whole topic of conversation is beginning to bore me exceedingly."

"Which is exactly why you should consider my offer. I can be most amusing."

"Yes, you are amusing, to be sure, but I had no offer other than to sit gazing into your eyes. And as comely as they may be, Lord Geoffrey, they cannot compare to the sight of the meal which now arrives. I'm very hungry, good sir, and not for you."

She pointed gracefully to the procession which began from the kitchen. The matter was closed as far as she was concerned. Nevertheless, she allowed a sideward glance at her dinner partner. It was easy to see why so many ladies had fallen for his charm. Lord Geoffrey Alden was a handsome fellow with large brown eyes and black curls which tumbled onto his forehead and skimmed the top of his ears. He was tall and well-dressed in a dark-blue doublet, and was actually quite a charitable fellow when it came to the poor and sick. But with women it was another matter altogether. Despite what he claimed to the contrary, there was the truth of it. He and Johanna had been friends for three years now, with Geoffrey coming to dine at least once a week. That being the case, many felt it their duty to report to her of his misconduct.

Lord Godfrey de Mer's obstreperous voice resonated nasally just as the food was being served. Johanna sought to ignore the grating tone, but it was impossible. Godfrey always seemed to speak to the entire hall, not just to the person seated next to him. Just another of his multifarious annoying qualities. "Terrible news, eh? To think that the Prince of Wales, after all these years of sickness, is finally dead!"

❧ THREE ❧

Paralyzed by the blurted news, Johanna didn't move. She couldn't. There wasn't any danger of fainting, for that was not her constitution. The conversation persisted all about her, like a mass of buzzing flies, alight with the news. And though she heard their words, all her fantasies and dreams about this man, the Black Prince, became even more lustrous, larger, and more precious now that he was gone. Her hero. Magnified yet more by his eternal passing. She had seen him once as a child when he had graced their home for a meal on his way to York. He had smiled down at her, gently rubbed his hand over her hair, and proclaimed her as lovely a fairy princess that ever there was. He admonished her to do well at her studies and to love her parents, and she had done all she could to adhere to his counsel. She remembered the way his coppery-brown hair shone in the candlelight, memorized each one of his handsome features, and vowed at eight years old to love him forever.

Now it was all so difficult to comprehend.

She cast a reproving glance in her father's direction. His eyes were upon her, worry holding them steady upon the face of the child he adored so. He felt old and tired of never making the right decision when it came to Johanna's emotions. Being a father was many times more difficult than being a soldier, he had come to firmly believe over the past 18 years.

Why didn't you tell me? The words were unspoken, but the expression on her face gave them voice. Turning to the rest of the party, he said in a loud voice, "Today is my daughter's birthday. We have tomorrow to mourn our prince. Let us rejoice this night."

She understood and immediately forgave.

But after the meal, as the darkness thoroughly shouldered the twilight from the sky, she slipped outside to sit in the courtyard. The bench sat near the dovecote, and the beautiful white pigeons soothed her with their gentle cooing, their noises not having to compete with the rain which had stopped a while before.

The Black Prince. Even now his body was probably already lying in state in Westminster Abbey. With his death died her most tenacious fancy and another vestige of childishness.

She had to see him one last time.

❧ ❧ ❧

"I've always thought of approaching darkness as the earth shuddering," Johanna said softly to Lord Geoffrey when he joined her in the courtyard. He made no reply, could tell she was upset, and, never missing an opportunity, decided his shoulder was better than most to be cried upon.

"How soon can you be ready?" Her surprising question caused him to turn quickly toward her.

"Ready?"

"To take me to London."

Geoffrey kept his face serious whilst inside him a smile of satisfaction erupted. Lonely roads, a dark night. "My horse need only be readied here in your father's stable."

"That won't do. I detest horses. Can you bring a carriage or a litter?"

"Of course. Whatever you wish."

"Meet me by the church in two hours. I'll feign sickness and retire. My parents won't be long in following. It shouldn't be hard to sneak out after everyone is settled. I don't want to be gone from home for long, Lord Geoffrey. But if I told my parents I wished to go to London to see the prince's body, 'tis something I don't believe they would understand."

"Understand what, Lady Johanna? They are most attentive parents, are they not? I know an indulged woman when I meet one. And you *are* indulged."

"Supremely so. But although they know how much I've admired Prince Edward all of these years, they never knew that I was in—" She stopped, knowing how foolish it sounded.

"—in love with him?" Lord Geoffrey finished incredulously. "Johanna, I've known for years you found him fascinating, but in *love* with him? You seem too headstrong for girlish infatuations."

Johanna continued to stare into the darkness, far from tears, but feeling a deep sadness at the passing of many things. "Silly of me, I know. Considering how much older he is than I am."

Geoffrey's tone was dry. "Not to mention the fact that he was destined to be king."

"Or that he was happily married."

"Oh *that*," Geoffrey waved a breezy hand. "A happily married man is most attractive to many women. The ultimate challenge, I suppose."

"That's part of it, I suppose. And knowing he could never be mine was another part, so he was safe to love. But I don't know why I'm telling this to *you* of all people. If I don't place my heart back under cover, you'll eat it for supper. I trust a healthy respect for our friendship all of these years will prevail."

"Naturally it will. Worry not, Lady Johanna. Despite my reputation, I do not enjoy the taste of blood."

Johanna believed him, but only because she wanted to get to London, and he was the quickest, easiest way. And so they met minutes prior to midnight and settled into the two-wheeled carriage. It was an older vehicle bought years before by Geoffrey's uncle, the Earl of Witney, who had adopted Geoffrey and his older brother and sister many years before, when Geoffrey was only a baby. The carriage was neither comfortable nor lavish, but Johanna didn't expect Geoffrey to bring the countess's pleasure carriage, which was always drawn by five horses in tandem.

"Wasn't your uncle curious about where you were going?" she asked as the carriage wheels began to turn.

"No. He is used to my late-night excursions."

Her eyebrows raised. "And you call *me* indulged?"

"Hmm, you've spoken truly. Perhaps that's why I like you so much . . . other than your beauty, of course."

Johanna shook her head. "I'm not at all beautiful. Not really. It's just the hair."

"Pardon?"

She pulled off her veil to reveal the white-blond braids. "My hair. Most men love me for my hair. That's all."

He laughed. "Surely you jest! You have a lovely face as well."

"Hmm. So you say. Trust me, it's the hair. All that blondness cascading down my back. But I don't allow any of them to get to know me beyond that. I've always thought hair color was a rather silly basis for infatuation, as silly as a woman's looks. So . . . go ahead . . . undo the braids and run your hands all through it, and then look at me afterward, Lord Geoffrey, really look at me, and tell me if you think I am as beautiful as I was before. I'm really not that comely at all. And you'll know your infatuation with me is completely unfounded."

"You're not serious, are you?"

Her blue eyes didn't change at all in their expression. "I assure you, I'm perfectly serious. Go ahead."

Lord Geoffrey leaned back in his chair, rubbed his clean-shaven chin, and examined her. "I don't think I'll accept your offer, as pleasant as it sounds. You're grieving the prince, and I would be taking advantage of such."

Johanna laughed. "So you're playing the noble suitor? Offers like this only come once from me, Lord Geoffrey, most certainly. And you'll never hear me utter such an invitation again."

"I still decline."

"As you wish." She pinned the veil back in place, a bit relieved. Geoffrey was disarmingly handsome, but he was so frivolous . . . compared to the prince. And not nearly so safe. She preferred to keep men like him off guard, and so far this night she had been succeeding. "It seems you like a challenge."

"Yes, I do that. Can't abide an effortless conquest."

"Oh, pah! You don't fool me. I'm sure there are many servant girls at Castle Chauliac who want only to please you, Lord Geoffrey."

"If the rumors be true, yes. But you shouldn't listen to such talk. I like more of a challenge than that. You, for instance."

She shook her head at him. "I'm more of a challenge than you'll ever know. You'd be advised to forget about this sudden infatuation for me you've conjured up from only who knows where. For some reason I feel suddenly ill." She decided it was definitely time to close this conversation. "I believe I shall nap for part of the journey."

He handed her a cushion, and she lay back and closed her eyes. She didn't want any more of such talk, and didn't know why she had begun the line of conversation in the first place. *I'm just not myself tonight*, she thought as sleep quickly descended upon her, the ruts in the road doing little to prevent her from succumbing to repose. Her last thought was of the Black Prince, his pleasant smile, and the way his eyes had looked into her childish ones and made her feel as if she were the only little girl in the world right then. Of course she had fallen in love with the man! So had an entire nation.

Lord Geoffrey cursed himself as an idiot while watching her peaceful, sweet face in the moonbeam which fell upon her creamy skin. He should have taken her offer, but something held him back, despite his completely ignoble intentions toward Johanna. It was as if she were going to her bridegroom on this journey, and she must not be defiled in any way. *Curse you, but if you aren't turning into a man of sentiment!* he blasted himself and decided that sleep was the best thing right then. Besides, there was always the journey home, and he knew his charm would be multiplied tenfold when her thankfulness to him for bringing her to say her last good-byes to the Black Prince was added into the equation.

❧ ❧ ❧

Johanna woke well before Lord Geoffrey. She looked at him briefly as he slept. It was hard to believe the cherubic face not far from her own could actually belong to such a notorious fellow. It was easy to imagine him as a child, his dark lashes forming shadowy crescents against his cheeks. The black lashes curled endearingly upward. His breathing was soft and even, and his hands curled slightly where they rested on his slender stomach.

And yet she felt nothing.

Men like him, while not common, were fast becoming so. She had heard tales of abduction due to the lust of a man toward a woman, but so far she had never experienced an adventure of such a magnitude. Nor did she want to. She knew what Geoffrey was after, as far as she was concerned. But what did *she* have to gain from his company?

Margery had asked the same thing only the day before. "I don't understand why you let him keep coming around, my lady. He's not nearly as intelligent as you are, and you have no interest in him for marriage."

"Of course I don't! I just enjoy his company. The only people I ever talk to are you and Maman and Papa, and my tutors, who aren't exactly men I would call the friendly sort. And then there's Lord Codfish, whom I don't think even you would count."

"No. That's true. But he's so . . . so . . . *unseemly!* The things I've heard—"

"Enough, Margery, I've heard them all as well. More times than is quite necessary. But that doesn't keep him from filling me in on all the local gossip, and some of the tidings of court as well. He *does* go there every so often and is my only source of news."

"Not to mention the effusive compliments he pays you," Margery said wryly.

"There are those. I like hearing them."

"You honestly think he means them?"

Johanna crossed her arms. "Well, why wouldn't he?"

At that point Margery had walked out of the room muttering something about youthful pride and empty vanity, but Johanna paid her no mind. It all came down to the same thing: The company of Sir Geoffrey was better than nothing at all, whatever *his* reasons were for consistently seeking her out.

He was destined to be sorely disappointed in that regard.

Johanna was neither stupid nor naïve. She had read far too much in her lifetime not to know what happened in the bedchamber between husband and wife, and she knew as well that the participants in such activities were not always married. But she wanted to be married when love descended upon her in the form of a man.

Faith didn't render such a resolve in her, for Lady Johanna Durwin had little of that. She had always been too busy in her books and fancies to care for the deeper things of God.

Church was just a necessary evil, as far as she was concerned. Father Theodore had seen to that. But she *had* been raised by two parents who knew the value of life without regret.

She knew Lord Geoffrey's intents were not noble, despite his protestations to the contrary, but there was enough feminine vanity inside her to think that just perhaps she was the only woman whom he deemed worthy of a little self-reform. She wouldn't discount everything he said as a lie. To do such would be to demean her own charm and loveliness, and no woman ever did that in her innermost thoughts.

The carriage rolled on toward Westminster Abbey.

So . . . the Prince of Wales was dead.

Who now? She hadn't exactly been searching for the perfect man. As long as Prince Edward was alive, her ideal stood before her. But now that he was gone, it seemed rather more severe—her dream of a pure love, a pure man. Someone noble and kind, a fighter, a lover, a poet. She wanted it all. A sort of god like those of ancient Greece, a modern Hercules. And she would have it. That much was certain, because Johanna had made up her mind it should be so. And Johanna always got her way.

That man certainly isn't you, dear Geoffrey, she thought. Nevertheless, she was thankful to him for bringing her to London. He was a wild man, no doubt, and she had to be doubly wary of him on the way home.

The sun was rising.

Geoffrey was right, she decided when she thought about the prince. *He was much too old to be so lovelorn over.* Old enough to be her father, certainly. But then, her father was old enough to be her grandfather, so men's ages in relationship to her were already a bit skewed. Older men intrigued her, piqued her interest with their intelligence and experience, their ability to properly gauge what was truly important and what was not. Poor Geoffrey could never compete with that.

She began to paint a picture in her mind of the man who would give her his love. All of his love. But all she could picture was the smiling face of the one who had lived his life for his royal father and his country—the man who now lay cold and dead in the nave of Westminster Abbey.

❖ FOUR ❖

A *prince who married for love.*

Lady Johanna Durwin now stood in the hushed church of the Abbey of St. Peter's at Westminster, looking at the still face of Prince Edward . . . the Prince of Wales . . . the valiant Black Prince. She couldn't imagine what Princess Joan was feeling now, if her own heart felt so blasted and dried by the blistering winds of grief. But she recalled the tale of his courtship and marriage—the tale she had begged her mother to recount to her over and over again. How many times when she was crying from some girlish hurt did she imagine him kissing away *her* tears? Or imagine him aflame with love for her once she got a little older.

"You're so beautiful," she whispered, so softly that none of the other mourners could hear her, and she began to cry shamelessly. And why not? No one was there to kiss away her tears or tell her that everything would be all right. No one was there to take care of her, lead her away from the bier and hold her tightly. No one was there except many strangers. She had made it thus. And yet she was glad.

And curse it all if I haven't forgotten my handkerchief, she thought, fumbling in the pocket of her gown. But she soon forgot about being ladylike and dainty. Not one to cry very often, Johanna was finding the experience very cathartic. She remembered Prince Edward as he had been when he was young, not this white specter which lay still and in decay before her eyes. This was not the Black Prince. He was gone now. Never to be forgotten by Johanna or by the nation he had served so faithfully and loved so well.

"Thank you," she whispered again, and reached out to touch the wooden platform. The mere thought of him had been a source of joy for many years, and she would never cease to be grateful to him for the whimsical delight his life had provided during the awkward, sometimes painful years of maturation.

It was the final good-bye to a dream.

She turned and left, walking slowly around to the north transept and out into the noontime sunlight of Westminster where Lord Geoffrey awaited her. As was her way, Johanna never looked back.

🙖 🙖 🙖

Back at Durwin Manor, Johanna's departure had been discovered. Lord and Lady Clifton were saving their anger for later when Johanna would return. But until then, the gloom of the prince's death weighed down the heavy air of the manor house yet further.

Alone, Lady Rosamunde sat in her solar. As most of the other noblewomen of England, she had followed the exploits of the Black Prince for many years. Even now, as the summer breeze whispered across her veiled headpiece, she remembered a conversation she had 16 years before. She had been only 19 at the time, still young and whole, and was visiting in the great hall of Castle Chauliac with two-year-old Johanna bouncing on her knee. The woman she spoke to was none other than the Countess of Witney, Lord Geoffrey's aunt. The subject was none other than the Black Prince's soon-coming marriage to Joan, the fair maid of Kent.

"Have you ever heard anything more romantic in your life?" the countess said, aglow with the news. For despite the fact that she was almost 50 years of age, she was just as in love with the Black Prince as every other woman in the kingdom. She twisted the large emerald ring which festooned her left forefinger. "It's fast becoming the talk of all England. And rightly so! I've never heard of anything more romantic on his part and more calculated on hers."

Rosamunde leaned forward. "Tell me all you know."

"With pleasure, my dear. Apparently he was appealing to her on behalf of Lord Brocas. In fact, he's been intervening on behalf of many hopeful suitors—friends of his—ever since her husband died last year."

"I can see why. She's a beautiful woman."

"Oh yes," the countess said dryly. "Beautiful *and* cunning."

"But isn't she the prince's cousin?"

The older woman waved a hand. "Do you suppose the pope will withhold the dispensation? I think not!"

"No, you're right about that. So what happened when he implored her for Lord Brocas? Can't abide the man myself, mind you."

"Really? I've always liked him. She became quite downcast and said, 'I shall never marry again.' And during the course of their conversation, she repeated the statement several times."

"I guess she kept hoping he would ask, 'Why?' "

"Precisely. Well, he sought to cheer her, saying such beauty would be wasted in widowhood and that if they weren't cousins, there would be no lady under heaven whom he should hold so dear as her."

"He fell in love with her right then!" Rosamunde surmised dreamily.

"Yes, if he wasn't in love with her already. Which I happen to think he was. And then she sprang like a feral cat with fangs dripping honey and claws coated with sugar—she began to cry."

"And it worked?"

"Apparently so. Because after that he took her in his arms and rained tender kisses over her tears. I know," the countess nodded as Rosamunde closed her eyes in ecstasy, "it's what we've all dreamed of at one time or another, isn't it?"

"What girl doesn't have such fancies at the age of 13? How do you know all this anyway?"

"Do you think they would have been left alone together?"

"Of course not!"

"Well, there are members of court with hearing as sharp as a fox's, make no mistake about that."

"They certainly weren't being very discreet, were they?"

"He was the Prince of Wales and had just found love. I doubt if being discreet was foremost in his mind. But let me finish! I've been dying to tell someone ever since I heard it this morning! He gave her the message from Lord Brocas, telling her he was a gallant gentleman of England and a very charming man. She was still crying when she said—and I'll try to remember the words my friend told me, because she swears it's practically verbatim and certainly bears repeating—'Sire, for God's sake forbear to speak of such things. I have made up my mind not to marry again, for my heart belongs to the most gallant gentleman under the heavens, and for love of him I shall have no husband but God, so long as I live. It is impossible that I should marry him. So, for love of him, I wish to forsake the company of men. I am resolved never to marry.'"

Rosamunde's brows raised in surprise. "And he didn't see through that speech? Sweet heavens, talk about overdoing it!"

"I know. 'Tis why everyone thinks he was already in love with her even then. After that he begged her to tell him who it was, but the more eager he became to know, the more she beseeched him to desist his questioning. Eventually, she even fell on her knees and begged him for God's sake and for His mother's, the sweet virgin, to forbear."

Rosamunde giggled and held up a hand to her mouth. "It's too wonderful, and so very dramatic."

"Yes, well, the prince is not a fool or one to be put off so easily, so he told her that if she did not reveal to him the name of this most gallant gentleman in the world, he would consider himself her deadly enemy."

"He doesn't care to dally about, does he?"

"Our prince? Naturally not. So then she said to him, and I quote again, 'Very dear and redoubtable lord, it is you, and for love of you no gentleman shall lie beside me.'"

"Very nicely done! Mentioning the marriage bed in such couched terms was pure genius. She could teach us all a thing or two."

"You can imagine after that the prince was aflame with love for her, and he swore to God that as long as he lived no other woman would be his wife!"

Rosamunde clasped her hands. "What a lovely tale! And to think the Black Prince is finally settling down after all of these years! He's got to be at least 30 by now."

"Not all that old. Consider your Gordon."

"Oh that! Gordon's ageless."

"So despite the king's disapproval, it seems they are deeply in love and looking forward to a happy marriage."

"Imagine, a prince who's actually marrying for love."

"It's the stuff of which bards' ballads are made," the countess said appreciatively, and pushed a tray of sweetmeats over to Rosamunde who, with a sparkle in her eye, partook of a pear tart.

So many years ago, Rosamunde thought now, understanding why Johanna had gone, but not understanding why her daughter hadn't been able to confide in her. Still, there was a bit of adventure in Johanna's soul, Rosamunde knew that well. The crippled lady who had been confined to the care of others for so long yearned for a similar escapade, but knew it was impossible.

❧ ❧ ❧

"Who was that man you were speaking with?" Johanna inquired as she stepped up into the carriage. She had noticed the man in the abbey, but it was dim, and she couldn't really see his face. His black brocade doublet was extremely plain, cut very simply without the elaborate oversleeves so many members of court had been taking to lately. His leather hip belt, while costly and well-fashioned, was also quite plain, and the black hosen and short boots only added to the austerity of his garb. He had watched her for a while at the tomb, but she had grown used to the admiring glances of men long ago, and so pushed him from her thoughts quite easily until she spied him talking with Lord Geoffrey. And then, she had seen only his back. But beneath the small cap, warm brown hair waved down to the nape of his neck. The legs beneath the hosen were powerful and strong, the shoulders broad. She couldn't see his hands.

He was gone now. But she was still somewhat curious.

"Who was that?" she asked again.

"It was my brother."

"Your brother? Sir John?"

"None other. Naturally, he had a host of questions to ask me, seeing me here with uncle's carriage in the middle of Westminster."

"What was he doing here?"

"The same thing as you, I suppose. He's a knight of the Order of the Garter and was one of the prince's most trusted friends. Been on all of the French campaigns since he was 16. I imagine he came to mourn."

"How old is he? I thought he was a great deal older than you."

Geoffrey rubbed his chin as the carriage began the drive back to Oxfordshire. "Well, let's see . . . if I'm 29 . . . and John was 11 when I was born, that makes him just 40."

"Oh . . . he's old then. He didn't look that old from behind."

"We don't go gray early in the Alden family. He's most youthful despite his age. Probably because he's never had time for women."

"No?"

"Not really. He was married long ago—an arranged marriage, as you might well guess. But she died in childbirth . . . the child, too."

"How awful!"

Lord Geoffrey shrugged. "I don't think he ever was all that fond of her, but he did feel terrible when she died. He left Castle Chauliac for good after that and proceeded to give his entire life to the military. Despite all the prince's and princess's attempts at matchmaking, he's managed to remain unattached. I don't know what he'll do now that Prince Edward is dead."

"Seems to me that fighting half one's lifetime is fighting long enough."

"'Tis true. But I can hardly imagine him leading the country life. Too tame for a man like him. He's a tameless sort. Yet, who can tell. At his age he might truly be getting tired of such a transient life."

"I, for one, am tired of all this trouble with France."

"War is what a nobleman lives for."

"Maybe you should all try putting in an honest day's work," Johanna said dryly.

Lord Geoffrey looked shocked and decided not to dignify her barb with an answer.

"Still," Johanna pulled out the needlework she had brought with her, "I would liked to have met him."

LISA SAMSON

"I don't think so, Lady Johanna. His heart is not nearly so warm as his hair color. You've seen him—all dressed in black, so somber and serious. He's terrible to have as an older brother. Always so quiet and disapproving. 'Tis good he is a man of few words, for he seems to make his thoughts known without them! I would hate to have to listen to everything twice."

"Maybe he feels more responsible than is normal, considering your parents died when you were so young."

"He's never been around enough to justify such a statement. Still, as I said, he's quite formidable. Quite ferocious on the battlefield. And I've seen him fight, too. He's a whirlwind." Johanna couldn't help but hear the pride in Geoffrey's voice, though he would have denied it was there. "No," he continued, "there are much more pleasant fellows for you to become acquainted with, Lady Johanna, if it is indeed acquaintances you are seeking."

Her cheeks became red. "I seek nothing of the sort, Lord Geoffrey! If I want some manly attention, I have only to snap my fingers and the swains come running."

"And you're so humble about it, too," Lord Geoffrey smirked. "You had best start lowering your standards, Lady Johanna. Despite your beauty, you're not getting any younger. Most women your age are married and well into the state of motherhood by now."

"Well, I'm not most women," she stated flatly. "I would rather be by myself than marry someone I can outthink and outspeak."

"There is no other man like Prince Edward out there for you, Lady Johanna."

"No . . . you're right. I'm not going to even bother looking for one. And if I'm not going to bother looking for a gallant man such as that, I'm certainly not going to go looking for the acquaintance of bores, buffoons, and village idiots either . . .

48

or ferocious old soldiers for that matter! I'll let him come to me instead."

"My, my, you're very hard on those of the masculine gender, aren't you? I assume I haven't a chance, do I?"

Johanna softened with a smile. "No. You don't, Lord Geoffrey. It's not that I don't like you well enough, in a friendly manner of speaking. It's just that I don't trust you one whit more than I could trust Lucifer himself."

"You misunderstand me then, my lady."

"Do I really? A man reaps a reputation from the deeds he has sown. A bad reputation doesn't appear from nowhere."

"People don't always correctly interpret the things they see. However, even though my intentions have always been pure toward you, Lady Johanna, I know when a pasture is green and when it is brown, and this is the brownest pasture I've ever been in."

Johanna laughed at his dry tone of voice. "You've remarkable vision for one supposedly so arrogant. I thought you liked a challenge."

"A challenge, yes. An impossibility, no. And yet, I must confess to a small amount of chagrin, for I so enjoy your company."

"I didn't imagine you as one to give up so easily. But I don't see why we need to cut off all form of discourse, my lord. Because I've rebuffed your advances, there's no reason for you to cease your visits with your aunt and uncle to Durwin Manor. I've not ceased to enjoy your company, so we'll just leave it at that. Agreed?"

His brown eyes twinkled. "Agreed . . . for now."

"And you promise to never try and seduce me or spirit me away in the night to some faraway place to deprive me of my maidenhood?"

"As I keep saying, I'm not that sort of fellow. But if I was, do you think it would work even if I did try?"

"No."

"Then I don't believe such a vow is necessary. You know what the Gospels say: ''Tis better not to vow at all, than to—'"

"Oh please, Lord Geoffrey, Scripture coming from your mouth is too much for even me to bear. Stay within your own boundaries, for heaven's sake, and we'll both be much the happier for it!"

The rest of the journey was spent in pleasant conversation. Geoffrey told her all the news he had garnered while waiting for Johanna at the abbey. After a while they stopped for a meal, took a stroll to stretch their legs, and were off again. It was after bedtime when Johanna walked quietly into the hall of Durwin Manor with every intention of sneaking up to her loft. The fire had burned low in the grate, but it was well near to blazing in the furious eyes of her mother.

❧ ❧ ❧

Meanwhile, at an abbey estate several miles from Westminster sat noble Nicholas de Litlyngton, abbot of the Monastery of St. Peter's, looking over the books. The abbey was in a fine financial state due to the administrative genius of his predecessor, Abbot Simon de Langham, who was now the Archbishop of Canterbury.

It was almost time to begin the project he had been dreaming of since he had assumed his position 14 years previous. For more than a hundred years the new church building, begun by King Henry III, had remained uncompleted. Half of the nave was still made up of the old Norman structure completed in 1065—a year before William the Conqueror invaded England. In its day it was the grandest of structures, but when the Gothic form of architecture eclipsed the Norman, King Henry wished to rebuild the abbey in that most graceful of styles. The ceiling of the new portion soared 90 feet above ground, whereas the Norman abbey boasted of only a 60-foot drop. Flying buttresses, graceful arcs which supported the outer walls and the heavy lead roof, enabled more windows to be placed in the stone walls. The pointed arch of the Gothic window was graceful and fine, and the tracery was delicate and infinitely more artistic.

The old portion, standing so incongruously along with the new portion, seemed like a squat little man when compared to the statuesque height and artistry of the Gothic section. How beautiful it would look when the transition was complete! It was Abbot Litlyngton's dream to carry out the project. Already he had done much to improve the abbey. Stained glass now graced the windows of the cloister, allowing the monks to work in comfort during the winter, for Litlyngton was not a young man, and he knew the importance of warmth for productivity. Around the cloister walls were paintings. One was of the crucifixion with John and Mary present, another was of the history of the monastic house. More paintings adorned the nave, and the chapter house boasted a stunning work depicting the apocalypse. The Westminster Abbey was rivaling even the beautiful St. Stephen's Chapel in the Palace of Westminster as far as the grandeur of the paintings to be found within.

Artistry was at its peak under Abbot Litlyngton, for even as the patronage of artists begun under Henry III remained, it had reached its zenith now that Nicholas de Litlyngton was abbot. Under such an influence of the arts, the monastery itself was turning out fine painters from the ranks of its monks.

"Soon," he said to his clerk with a smile, "it will all begin again. I cannot wait to hear a multitude of masons working."

The clerk, a gentle monk, smiled in return and began to gather up the books to bestow them back in their rightful place in a large wooden treasury chest.

"Before you go," Abbot Litlyngton said, "tell me what happened at chapter today."

And so Brother Tobias proceeded to rehearse what was covered at the daily chapter meeting—a time when all the monks gathered in the Chapter House to hear a chapter of Scripture read and go over the business of the day. For these days the monastic life was becoming lax, with "separated abbots" taking little interest in the daily lives of the monks, and the monks torn between pangs of conscience that their life had become less rigid and the realization that with all human institutions change was inevitable, and not all change was a bad thing.

Litlyngton didn't like feeling so separated from his men. Hidden on his estate beyond the gates of the abbey was no way to run a monastery, and he decided to start another project as well. He would build himself a house within the walls of St. Peter's. Perhaps such a move would render him no longer a stranger in the place he loved so dearly.

ohanna sat upon her bed, reading. "I'm too old for this."

Margery shook her head with disapproval. "Well, my lady, for you to go gallivanting off to London like that with only a note left behind, can you blame her for being so upset?"

"I thought surely Papa would come to my aid. But he said nothing when she confined me to the manor for the next two weeks. She even said I was to have no visitors. At my age!"

"Mothers take their responsibilities seriously no matter how old their children are. And you *are* still living under their roof." Margery repositioned the gown she was mending for Rosamunde. "At least you're not confined to the house," she shrugged. "We can still go out for our walks."

"There's something to be thankful for. I haven't been punished like this for years."

The lady's maid laid her sewing in her lap. "Do you really blame them for being so harsh? It was one thing to go off in the middle of the night to London to mourn Prince Edward, my lady. Even your mother said that was understandable. But to choose that libertine, Lord Geoffrey, to transport you... You're fortunate to be getting off so lightly!"

Lady Johanna's eyes snapped at Margery. "I don't need you to punish me with your tongue as well, Margery."

"No, you don't, my lady. It's just that I care. And I don't think you realize how dangerous a man Lord Geoffrey is. He appears to be nothing more than honey and milk, but I assure you, servants *do* talk, and there's many a young maid at Castle Chauliac who is no longer fit for a decent man's bed after Lord Geoffrey got hold of her."

Lady Johanna impatiently waved the argument away. "I wish to speak of something else. Lord Geoffrey is amusing, that is all. I'm not as stupid as you and Maman and Papa might think. I don't understand all this fuss. I'm home safely, and after bearing this humiliating treatment, I certainly won't be doing something like *that* again."

"And 'tis a good thing. Now then, why don't you continue with your tapestry before it gets too dark? Here, I'll even thread the needle for you." She rose from her stool. "You've been spoiled for far too long, my lady."

Johanna felt too dreary to argue, and let Margery take out her bag of needlework. Even after the length of linen was in her hand, she still didn't feel much like embroidering. She felt too much like a prisoner. So she gazed out the window onto the green meadows where the crofters worked their farms and thought how easy life must be for such people.

At supper her father gave her the good news that her punishment was to be decreased by a week. She only had three days to go.

"Oh, Papa! I knew you would talk her out of it!" She threw her arms around his neck.

"I'm much too soft when it comes to you, Johanna. But you mind this now. For if you ever do something like that to us again, you'll bring my gray head down to the grave in worry. A punishment infinitely too drastic for the both of us, I would say!"

"Yes, Papa. I promise never to do that again. I guess I never realized the true extent of Lord Geoffrey's reputation."

She made sure the right amount of contrition was found in her tone.

"As your father, I exhort you to stay away from him at all costs, Johanna. Especially now."

"Does that mean he is banned from Durwin Manor? Oh please, Papa, Geoffrey is my only source of company other than the Cod—I mean Lord Godfrey. I promise not to go off with him again, Papa, I do."

Gordon's blue eyes softened as he sighed. "You may allow him to visit you here, but only with your mother or Margery present." He looked at her warily. "It isn't you that I don't trust, Daughter. You haven't a greater interest in him than I am aware of, do you, Johanna?"

She laughed. "Oh, Papa, have a little more confidence in yourself. You've raised me not to admire men the likes of Lord Geoffrey Alden in that manner. And I assure you, I have no romantic notions toward Geoffrey, or anyone else for that matter. He's just infinitely more amusing than Godfrey de Mer."

"I don't perceive that as much of a compliment, Johanna. In my humble opinion, the dogs which eat the scraps downstairs are more amusing than Godfrey de Mer."

❧ ❧ ❧

"She actually had you take her to London? Alone?"

Geoffrey laughed and quaffed his ale. "Yes. It must be a first for her."

His compatriot smirked. "Oh, she has many firsts left her, no doubt."

"Intriguing, really. She's not naïve by anyone's thinking, Gilbert, but there is a way about her that is so removed, skirting about the edges of men's awareness—tantalizing, yet promising absolutely nothing."

"Exactly. Leave her alone, Geoffrey. There are much fairer ones in the region, for bed or for betrothal. Lady Johanna leaves me cold, if you want the truth. All that white skin and white hair."

"How can you say such? She's comely—in a most unusual way, to be sure, but very comely for all of that."

Gilbert arched his brows and baited his friend yet more. "Too much brain and not enough girlish simplicity. That's Lady Johanna Durwin. You'll find too much knowledge dulls a woman for her mate's enjoyment. Forget about her. She's too much like a man."

"I think you're being too harsh on her, my friend. She's every inch a woman."

"Well, she should be. Eighteen years old and still unmarried."

"By her own choosing."

"That's what they all say."

"It's true with her, Gilbert."

Gilbert laughed aloud. "So it's true, is it? You've gone and fallen in love with her, haven't you? I told you when you set out to make her closer acquaintance that it was an exercise in futility, Geoffrey. But you didn't listen. 'She's interesting to be with, Gilbert,' you said, 'a witty way to pass the evening,' and now your heart will be worse for the wear."

Geoffrey flushed in the dimness of the public house. "You don't know what you're talking about, Gilbert. Johanna has always been great fun, and that's all. I've never been in love with a wench, Lady Johanna included, and I never shall be."

"That's not what you said about Lady Olivia last year or Evelyn before that."

"I wasn't thinking clearly."

"You never are, Geoffrey. For once you win them, it's off to the hunt once again. But I have a feeling that Lady Johanna is different."

"Then your feeling is wrong."

"Well, then," Gilbert said jovially, "enough said on the matter. Here's to being a free man with money to spare."

Geoffrey lifted his goblet like a man and hit it against Gilbert's. They continued their friendly conversation on other matters, but deep inside Geoffrey felt like the biggest fool in Oxfordshire. He had gone and fallen for the most unapproachable lady there was, and the situation could be seen as nothing more than hopeless. He had gone and fallen in love with Lady Johanna Durwin. Surely he was a bit more creative about his love life than that? It seemed as if every man in the area had fallen in love with the woman, even for just a little while. And that was true. Many Oxford students came through the doors of Durwin Manor at the invitation of Lord Clifton. They were initially fascinated by his educated, lovely daughter, but were soon put off by her disdainful manner. Geoffrey knew he was one of the few men Johanna could bear. And now that he was enlightened as to her infatuation with the Black Prince, he knew why most men retained her favor for so small a span.

Either I'm closer to her ideal than most, or so far from it that a comparison is the farthest thing from her mind. He was honest enough with himself to know it was the latter.

"Curse the wench," he muttered as he galloped by Durwin Manor the next afternoon. He knew it was useless to call upon the Durwins. After his hand in helping her to London, he probably was far from a favorite of theirs right now. However, Lord Geoffrey wasn't a man to be put off quite so easily when a woman was involved.

He turned around and headed for the courtyard. A groom quickly took his horse, and he walked up the stairs and into the great hall. All was quiet. The only person who inhabited the great room was Lord Clifton himself, who sat sharpening the blade of his sword—a ritual he had never given up over the years. It returned him to his youth, when he was stronger and angrier. He liked remembering what it was like. Taking care of his sword did that for him.

Lord Geoffrey cleared his throat. "Lord Clifton."

The older man turned toward Geoffrey. "About time you came around, Geoffrey. I'm afraid I'm the only source of company here this afternoon. Johanna has gone for a ride with her mother in the coach over to Castle Chauliac to see your aunt. I'm surprised your paths failed to cross."

Geoffrey felt a bit uncomfortable, and he didn't want to ask why she wasn't somewhere about the manor. Yet he felt compelled to comment anyway. "I'm glad her confinement is over so soon."

"Yes, I suppose you would be. It was actually over almost a week ago. We fathers have a way of feeling sorry for our daughters. Even when they do certain things."

"A week ago? I would have been here sooner if I had known."

Lord Clifton's eyebrows raised. "So you only came to see Johanna. Not to offer your apologies?"

Geoffrey bristled a bit inside. He always did at any form of reprimand. "The lady asked for my help. I would have been a cad not to have agreed, considering how much she's admired the prince all of these years."

"Your reputation did not render the situation seemly, Geoffrey. My daughter took a great risk in trusting you."

"Sir, my reputation does not truly reflect the—"

"Enough, Geoffrey. Don't take me for a fool. If your uncle wasn't such a close friend of mine, Geoffrey, I would run you through right now for the damage you may have caused."

"But, my lord, I only decided to do her bidding when she became quite overcome."

"It was not your decision to make, Geoffrey."

"But her distress was quite acute, sir. How could I have refused?"

"You *should* have refused her, knowing that to be seen alone with you could mar her reputation forever. However, she has been made aware of the fullest extent of your notorious ways. So I trust you will keep your tongue in this matter. If it is found out that she was with you alone on a trip to London, her reputation would be sullied beyond all possible cleansing."

"I'm sorry, Lord Clifton."

The older man's voice was not angry, just firm. "And you should be, son. Not that I really believe you other than I choose to for Johanna's sake and the friendship between our families. My daughter is my most precious prize. I know we've indulged her in the past with her refusal to marry. But she will marry one day, and to a man of good report. Men can rise above their reputation by good deeds or a valiant heart, but once a woman is so branded, she will forever be regarded in such a way. Only a man of purest intent shall have my Johanna."

"That will be hard to find in this day and age, sir."

"That may be true of your friends, Geoffrey. But there *are* men of good repute left to be found in the kingdom. For this reason I've forbidden Johanna to see you except inside Durwin Manor and with a chaperon in attendance. She assures me there is nothing happening between the two of you of which her mother and I would disapprove, and I believe her. But her reputation must be protected at all costs. We have not a long lineage such as you Aldens to fall back on, so we must keep ourselves noble because we act in such a manner."

"I understand you perfectly, sir."

"Good. Johanna will not be home for several hours. I'm sure you have other places to go."

"As you wish, sir."

"Then we understand one another?"

"Yes, sir. But you must indulge me a moment to tell you that my intentions toward your daughter are of the purest kind. I'm well aware of my reputation, but I would never want to transfer it to Lady Johanna. I've no intention of asking for her hand in marriage, or of offering any kind of hand except that of friendship."

"I don't believe a word of it. But Johanna seems to like your company, so I won't stand in the way of a simple friendship. But only if you keep the boundaries I've set."

"As you wish, sir. I shall not meet her anywhere but here at Durwin Manor."

⚜ ⚜ ⚜

"My father would be most upset if he knew I was talking to you right now," Johanna whispered, scared yet excited.

Lord Geoffrey's voice was reassuring. "It's all right. No one knows I'm here. I snuck in through one of the passages down near the river."

They were in the minstrel gallery, looking down on where the Countess of Witney and Lady Clifton sat chatting together most contentedly. Each Tuesday afternoon Rosamunde made the trip to Castle Chauliac, and had been doing so for years. Today was no exception.

"Where did you tell them you were going?" he asked.

"Just for a walk in the bailey. But when I heard your call from the gallery as I passed, I had to see who was up here."

Lord Geoffrey smiled, and it lit up his face most beautifully. "You're curious, just like I am. I saw your father today. He told me I wasn't to see you but at Durwin Manor."

"Yes, he gave me the same restrictions last week."

He took her hand. "Then why are you here with me?"

"I should ask the same of you. I'm here because I've always been rather naughty about restrictions." She pointedly pulled her hand away. "I don't like them much."

Lord Geoffrey immediately understood her message. "And I thought it was because of me alone that you deigned to go against his wishes."

She laughed, much to his chagrin. "Your thoughts are ill-founded, Lord Geoffrey, and filled with conceit. I'm going outside now, before Mother sends Ned after me."

"When may I come and call on you, Lady Johanna?"

She shrugged, looking at the door, feeling rather caged and ready to be out in the fresh air. "Anytime you wish, Lord Geoffrey."

"I'll see you tomorrow then," he promised.

"If that's what you want."

She hurried out of the gallery, down the steps of the keep, and out into the bailey, where she soon became an engrossed observer of all the activity, particularly the new addition that was rising across the way. Half an hour later, Ned came to fetch her. It was time to go home. Father was glad to see her when she arrived and invited her to read some more of Dante to him. But she pleaded sickness, retired to her loft, and fell asleep well before her supper was brought to her by Margery.

Six

Lady Norma Alden was a spinster in every sense of the word. Men held little interest for her other than their hunting capabilities and their penchant to fight wars and so bring exciting news from afar for her to wave away. Given this, she should have been a nun. But she was utterly claustrophobic, and the thought of staying within a priory for the rest of her days was horrifying for she had no interest in her own gender either, and what she referred to as "their petty peculiarities." Norma Alden knew devotion however to two things: family and God.

She was also John Alden's twin sister, and his self-proclaimed mother, wife, nanny, and nursemaid. Self-proclaimed, for Sir John wanted none of these roles to be played out by her. Or any other woman. And he never had. But Norma was 20 minutes older than John, and she never let him forget it.

Warm-brown, wavy hair and light-brown eyes which missed nothing connected them visually. Norma was a female version of John. Their skin was neither fair nor swarthy, but had a certain ruddy cast—a permanently healthy glow which made both of them look as if time would use its hand lightly against them. Neither could remember bearing much sickness along the way. Except for Norma, and that was only once, and it had almost cost her her life. But John had been there when no one else was. John had sacrificed his own safety to nurse her back from the grave, and it was this which quite possibly tied them more closely together than the fact that they had grown to viability in the same womb.

Norma was in a dither. The keep of Castle Chauliac was scrubbed from top to bottom. The rushes scattered on the floor, though changed only two weeks before, were swept out the door and hauled away. Fresh ones replaced them, the smell of sweet grass and clover imbuing the cool interior of the castle with a fresh snippet of the July wind.

She pulled one of the maidservants aside. "Now, Helen," she said seriously, her voice low and calm, always well-modulated and gentle, but perfectly capable of conveying her various moods to the servants, "Sir John's room is ready?"

The 17-year-old bobbed a curtsy. "Yes, my lady. Everything is just as you said."

"The new carpets laid?"

"Yes, my lady, this morning."

"Good, I'll go inspect it then. Have a last look. I was simply waiting until it was done before I went up all those stairs."

She slightly lifted the skirts of her gray gown and ascended the stairway, the great ring of keys bouncing musically against her left leg. *Why my brother likes that tower room so much is a mystery to me*, she clucked. *It's farther away from the family than any other room in the keep.*

If she hadn't known better, she would have suspected John preferred the circular chamber due to its history. Several years after the Battle of Hastings, a Saxon weaver woman was imprisoned for many months at the hand of one of the de Shelleys' more nefarious ancestors: a cruel knight named Odo de Chauliac. She bore her imprisonment with grace and dignity, creating yards and yards of beautiful woven braid on her tablet loom for the de Chauliac family while she waited for her husband, a young Saxon rebel, to rescue her. Sir John admired those with a brave, quiet dignity. After hearing the tale at the age of 16, he was granted permission to transfer his belongings there, and he had never talked of moving since. The fact that its two windows afforded a view of the bailey and the river, respectively, probably facilitated Sir John's decision as well.

Norma examined the chamber with slow eyes.

All was in order. She knew he would be furious about the carpets, rich in a burgundy hue, which sprawled on the floor at the foot of the bed and on the side of the room nearest the door. Sir John disdained luxury of any nature. He was a hardened soldier, used to cold nights before battle in a small tent with only his cloak for a covering.

Maybe now that he's home for good he'll let himself get a bit soft.

Norma almost laughed at the thought, which was about as close to laughter as she ever got. The only soft spot her brother possessed was his love of music. *I must make sure Old Duncan has John's lyre polished and tuned*, she remembered suddenly.

But for now her eyes inspected the room once more. The bed, covered not with a downy, silken coverlet, but with sheepskins and fox pelts, was aired out and fresh. The blanket chest near the door stood polished and glowing with the reflection of the window. And a small table sat beneath the glass window, a small assortment of books, clean parchment, ink, and new quills on its oaken surface, awaiting his pleasure. Sir John Alden was a faithful correspondent with many throughout England and even Europe, writing letters at least two hours every morning. Norma had no idea what he wrote about, and the thought of asking him never entered her mind. Candles were everywhere for his nighttime reading. Light was his only personal luxury.

"Yes," she breathed in through her nose, smelling the remaining scent of the flowers she had set in here yesterday but that had been taken away by Helen earlier, "all is just as it should be."

She paused at the door, turned around, and looked one last time. A rose lay on the floor, sticking out from under the end of the bed. Quickly she ran back in, grabbed the rose, and shut the door behind her.

"Duncan!" she cried as she hurried down the stairs and into the hall to find the bard, "does the lyre need to be restrung?"

But the bard was not to be found in the large room whose walls, which supported a 30-foot-high ceiling, were lined with swords, shields, and pieces of armor. However, the lyre sat upon the hearth, shining with three coats of fresh wax and waiting eagerly for the expert hands of its owner to bring it to life once again. Tonight, probably. But most definitely tomorrow.

Norma nodded in satisfaction. She had done all she could to let her brother know she was glad he had returned to her safely.

❧ ❧ ❧

It had been too long since he had been in battle. Over four years ago the English forces, led by the Prince of Wales and King Edward, had regained Thouars. It was the end of the Black Prince's military career, for he had to rouse himself from illness to do such.

When he had returned to England, Sir John stayed in London, hoping for some manner of war to erupt. But nothing more than internal bickering captured the country's attention. Still, his lord was sick, and he would not forsake him for the good life at Castle Chauliac. Not that it was as good there as it had once been. The Black Death almost 30 years ago had wiped out many peasants. Roughly a third of the population had been extinguished, and the wealth which the lords had enjoyed from the lands their churls farmed was severely diminished. It was the great plague which had killed Sir John's parents and three of the six Alden children. Sheep grazed where prosperous farms once stood. Many of the great manor houses had gone to ruin. Even now, the country was nowhere near to complete recovery.

Still, life at Castle Chauliac was nothing to complain about. Listening to Norma cluck over him like some overprotective hen couldn't be any worse than listening to the men argue over the pope's power in England. As for himself, he rather agreed that the church should have no say in the secular concerns of the kingdom, that the ever-increasing wealth and worldliness of the church seemed to overshadow its spiritual role, and that the government was becoming increasingly corrupt and incompetent. But he was not a man to voice his opinions. No statesman he.

If it couldn't be said with a sword, Sir John Alden simply wouldn't say it.

He could see what would happen anyway, now that the prince was dead. The prince had favored reform, agreeing with the people who were tired of the double taxation they had been paying for many years. The prince's brother John, the Duke of Lancaster, would now voice his traditional opinions more openly. Sir John had to give him a small measure of grudging credit in that he was always loyal to his brother while he lived. But Lancaster, married to Constance, the daughter of Don Pedro, had designs on the throne of Castile. Ties to the papacy must be kept strong at all costs if he was to achieve his goal.

In some ways Sir John had to admit that such ambitions showed a loyalty to the vow Lancaster had made to his brother on his deathbed—the vow to ensure Edward's son, Richard, would inherit the throne upon the death of his grandfather, the king.

Sir John waved an impatient hand, as if to shoo the thoughts away. There were other things to think about. Perhaps Norma, never failing to voice her opinions in her letters to him, was right. Perhaps it was time he went soft. Lived a country life.

"I might even get myself a dog," he muttered.

"Pardon me, my lord?" His most trusted man-at-arms leaned toward him from his horse.

"Nothing, Niel. Continue on. I want to make it home before nightfall."

❧ ❧ ❧

Castle Chauliac had originally been built by Lord Stephen de Chauliac, a baron of William the Conqueror who came over from Normandy and fought valiantly with his two sons at the Battle of Hastings. Beam Dune Maur was the fortress's original name, and it had been in existence for more than a millennium—first as a Briton hill fort, then as a Roman outpost. When the Saxons invaded, great wooden halls were built upon the mound, within the Roman curtain wall.

Odo de Chauliac, Stephen's eldest son, had begun the stone keep—in which the Earls of Witney had lived for centuries now—in the year 1068. The de Chauliac family, whose name had evolved to de Shelley over the three centuries since they had landed on the island, was proud of their home, which now included not only the keep which snuggled up to the Roman wall of the inner bailey, but more buildings which surrounded the inner court as well. Outer curtain walls were erected in the 1200s, and this large outer bailey was used most frequently as a training ground for the earl's soldiers. A large kitchen next to the keep and several of the Roman towers were expanded into buildings of their own right. A chapel, built by the mason who built the Westminster Abbey for King Edward, sat across from the keep. The present

67

earl, whose garrison had grown considerably under the auspices of his nephew Sir John, was in the process of building a great hall and several large, modern chambers for himself and his family, separate from the keep. But until these buildings were finished, the old keep would continue to house his family. Now that Sir John would someday assume the earldom, the surname of the Earls of Witney would no longer be de Shelley, but Alden.

The old earl was eagerly awaiting his nephew's homecoming. He was a tall man, very fat, with a very occasional but severe temper. But his heart was soft, and when his temper got the better of him, he spent the next month making up for it. The countess always joked about it, saying whenever she wanted some new dresses or a necklace, all she had to do was provoke her Stephen in some way to anger, and the desired item would invariably be hers. All in all, Lord Stephen de Shelley, the Earl of Witney, was a good man. Severely imperfect, but able to feel and give affection freely, and thus was well-loved by most who knew him.

And as the earl sat before the massive square of the wall fireplace, a new installment to the keep 50 years before, he remembered his sister—the mother of John, Norma, and Geoffrey. Elaine had been a lovely girl, quietly headstrong, upright, and kind, if not always exuberantly so. She had married Lord Alden and gone to live in the north, near the border of Scotland. Alden was as rugged as the land which bred him. Stern but fair. Not given to displays of the affection which ran deep inside him.

John was a clear combination of the two, Lord Stephen thought. His austerity was natural, having grown up until the age of 12 in a cold castle with few luxuries and only hard work to warm him. Not that he ever complained about it. He was good to his siblings, caring for them when he was needed, for Elaine had become quite fragile after the birth of her fifth child. The doctors warned her that to have another would be dangerous, but she bore Geoffrey anyway, and it nearly killed her. Her stubbornness alone kept her alive. Unfortunately, the plague hit their village less than a year later, and no willpower or strength of mind could overcome the Black Death.

Lord Stephen shuddered to think of it, almost 30 years later. Two children they had lost, he and his countess, despite the fact that they had sealed off the castle to anyone incoming. Somehow it had broken through anyway and had been quick to do its damage within the walls of Castle Chauliac. By God's grace alone, the countess was one of the few to survive the sickness, and Lord Stephen hadn't succumbed to the respiratory strain of plague which had ravaged his earldom that winter. His trusted steward had died only eight hours after the initial signs had shown themselves. The plague could take a man of perfect health and transform him into a corpse quickly and with little effort.

Several months later, news came from the north of his sister's family, and he had ridden out right away. A heart-breaking scene awaited him. Young John caring for Norma, who was writhing on her bed, and also tending to Geoffrey, only ten months old. John was a stalwart lad of 12, and he was one of the lucky ones upon whom the fatal illness never fell.

"Uncle," he had stood to his feet and bowed formally, "you came. Thank you."

His face was neither tear-stained nor pale, but his eyes fully contained the ordeal he had been living through, and seemed older than the hills which surrounded the austere castle.

Norma miraculously survived, and Geoffrey, due to John's watchful care, never succumbed. A week later they were on their way back to Castle Chauliac, accompanied by the Alden family's bard—a man known only as Duncan. The eldest Alden never spoke of the Black Death again, nor told his uncle that he alone had buried his father, his mother, the twins Bertram and Caspar, and his favorite sister Bridget—two years his junior—in the midnight of winter when Norma was asleep in her bed and baby Geoffrey tucked warmly in his cradle by the fire. The death toll on the Alden household was higher than average. John was thankful that he merely survived.

"He never was one to question God," Lord Stephen said softly, thinking of the strength his nephew was born with. "He will do well as the next earl."

"I agree."

Stephen looked up, startled at the realization that he had spoken the words aloud. His wife was now beside him.

"Come sit with me, Margaret, my love." He patted the seat next to him.

"Enough with the chair, Dear. Let me perch on your lap. What's left of it!"

Stephen laughed and patted his legs. "As you wish, Wife. I was just thinking about John," he said as she settled comfortably on the great thighs. She was as skinny as Stephen was corpulent. They were opposite in every way except three: They both had a deep faith in God, saw the humor in being human, and loved their niece and nephews like they would their own children had they been given the opportunity of raising them to adulthood.

"I'm so glad he's coming home. Poor Norma."

"I know. I sent her into town to fetch me some more parchment," he laughed. "Not that I needed any. I just couldn't bear to look at her, all jumpy and nervous inside, any longer."

"She loves John more than any of us, I would say."

"Yes. She's never forgotten the fact that she owes him her life."

"Not to mention the fact that they shared a womb."

"That, too." The earl looked intently into the fire. "I know it's almost too much to wish for, but I do hope he'll stay this time. Don't you?"

The countess nodded. "Yes. But John is the type that has always needed to keep moving. I don't believe he's running from anything. He's just never really felt at home anywhere since the plague."

"But we've loved him like a son."

"Yes. And I think he knows that. It isn't us, Dear. It's him. He's a quiet adventurer, our John. What I think he needs is to settle down with a good woman. Have children of his own."

"Try telling *him* that," the earl said dryly. Lifting up the hand which rested on the arm of his chair behind his wife, he began to scratch her back lightly.

"Not I. I learned long ago not to meddle in John's personal affairs."

"As did I, my love."

A shadow fell across the doorway. "If it had been up to you," the voice of the intruder said, "I would have been married to that crone, the Lady Desmond, for ages now."

"John!" the Countess of Witney jumped agilely to her feet and ran toward her nephew, grasping him in an iron hug. "You're back early! Oh dear, Norma will be so disappointed. Stephen just sent her to Oxford not an hour ago to fetch him some paper. Look, dear!" she turned to the earl, who was rising much more slowly to his feet than had his wife, "John's back early!"

"I see, Margaret, I see." He held out his hand for John to shake.

John's lack of emotion was not an accurate reflection of the love he bore for these two in his heart. Yes, he was a firm man, plain in his emotions. But when he loved, he loved well. He just didn't truly love all that often.

"Uncle, you look the same as ever," he said as he pumped hard on his uncle's hand and eyed the earl's stomach, "and are still feeding well for the worn-out old predator you are."

"You know me and a good joint of beef," the earl chuckled, winking at his wife.

John set down his saddlebag. "Still grotesquely in love with each other, no doubt," he said, his mouth twisted wryly, his brown eyes amused. He pulled up a chair and set it near the fire as his aunt and uncle seated themselves in their own chairs. "It's good to see you both."

"Oh, John," the countess's eyes glazed mistily, "we've missed you so."

"Thank you, Aunt Margaret."

"I only wish it were happier circumstances which brought you to us," the earl said, acknowledging the death of Prince Edward.

"Every man must die, Uncle. He was well surrounded by comrades and family as he passed on. 'Tis more than most could ask for."

"Yes," Lord Stephen nodded. "There was none other such as the prince."

John pulled his saddlebag closer to him. "Let us talk of something else. I brought gifts for you."

"Oh, John, you didn't have—"

"You always say that, Aunt Margaret. If I had to, I probably wouldn't have." He undid the buckle on the flap. "I thought you might need to start protecting yourself from this lustful man you call your husband." He held forth a small stiletto in a leather case toward the countess. "Actually, it's more for decoration than anything. And the workmanship was so fine, I thought immediately of you, my lady."

She was clearly pleased as she slid the small knife from its case. "Thank you, Nephew. I've always wanted one of these! It looks Spanish."

"You are correct."

"Then I'm not going to even ask where you got it!"

"And for you, Uncle," he continued, "is a present along the same lines. Here." It was a knife as well, a dirk.

"Did you get this from Scotland?"

"A friend of mine did. They're quite handy after the hunt."

"I haven't hunted in ten years, John!"

"Oh," John looked startled, purposefully so. "Forgive me. That present is for me, not you! Here. This one is for you." He pulled out a wrapped parcel of peculiar shape.

The earl opened it with a laugh and was delighted to find a new hat. "How interesting."

"Everyone in London is wearing them," John explained, as the earl turned the fancy felt hat, which sported a large feather held by a golden brooch. "Quite wonderful," the old man said, putting it on his head. "I can't quite picture you going into a shop for this, John."

"I didn't. Jonathan did." Jonathan was John's faithful personal servant of many years. The countess gave a laugh at the jaunty angle it naturally slid to over Stephen's bald head. "I know you like to keep yourself up-to-date, Uncle."

Stephen laughed. "I don't know, John. Giving your aunt a weapon and myself a hat. I must wonder if things aren't a bit skewed!"

John stood to his feet, the visiting done. "Up to my room—just as I left it, I hope."

The countess shrugged, not about to say a word regarding the rugs.

"Norma again? When is she going to learn? The last time I was here and she put that cursed bouquet of flowers on my desk, I couldn't get rid of the smell for a week!"

"I suppose horses and blood suit you better, Dear?" The countess raised her eyebrows.

"I think you knew the answer to that question before you even asked it." He softly kissed her cheek and left the room. Five minutes later he was back down in the hall, a rolled-up carpet balanced on each shoulder. "Where would you like these?" he asked his aunt politely, trying not to act out the chagrin he felt at the moment.

"Unroll that one there in front of the hearth." She pointed down to the floor, trying not to laugh.

He did so. "And the other?"

"Do whatever you like with it."

As he turned to throw it into the blaze, she stopped him with a cry. "John! Not there!"

His eyes sparkled. "I'll just lean it up against the mantel."

"Thank you, Dear."

"Where's Duncan?" he asked, but the countess only shrugged in reply.

He went back up to his room, threw open the window, and let the summer air of Oxfordshire settle his soul as his servant began to unpack his things. Hopefully it would take away the smell of those cursed roses as well.

❦ SEVEN ❦

Norma, despite Sir John's opinion of her, didn't always do things in a manner ill-befitting her brother. Knowing he was now used to grand palace feasts with elaborate dishes and many courses, a simple bill of fare was what she arranged for his first night home. The first course, a clear broth, was refreshing to the palate and just enough to whet the appetite. The next two courses consisted of fresh vegetables: carrots, turnips, cabbages, and beans, prepared simply, and meats: pheasant, boar, and ox, roasted over the open fire. Crispy grilled trout rounded out the meats. Dessert was comprised of some tarts and a custard.

Norma also was excruciatingly familiar with the heavy-handedness of the castle cook with spices. The simpler the dish, the more likely it was to be edible.

The entire time the meal was being served, Sir John was quiet, but he ate more than she had ever seen him consume at one sitting before. Trying a bit of everything and not stubbornly refusing anything except the roasted boar and the beans. It was his way of expressing appreciation, and it was enough for her. Once again, it proved that she knew her brother better than anyone else, and that was cause for a bit of self-congratulations.

The earl lifted up his goblet several times, bidding the others drink with him in gladness of his nephew's return to Castle Chauliac. And the servants, soldiers, and guests who filled the hall were only too happy to comply with his wishes. For the wine which flowed that night was the finest Burgundy had to offer and was lifted only on the most happy of occasions.

After the meal was done, Geoffrey, bolstered by two brimming goblets of wine, finally welcomed his brother home. "Glad you made it home safely, John."

"Thank you."

"Is everything to your liking?"

"It is now."

"Norma's rugs didn't take your fancy, I see."

"No. They weren't your idea, were they?"

"Of course not. Rugs aren't something that normally capture my attention, Brother. You know that."

Sir John agreed. "So who is capturing your fancy these days?" He took a sip of wine and looked Geoffrey in the eye. It was always somewhat disconcerting when Sir John Alden looked one in the eye.

"You don't do well with a bit of pleasant conversation before pushing up your sleeves, do you, John?"

"Not if I don't see the need for it. Just answer the question. And please, at least tell me she isn't married this time."

"No . . . she isn't married. In fact, she refuses to get married. And not because she's destined for the church. She's looking for the perfect man."

"And you came along at the right time, I suppose," Sir John commented dryly before taking another sip.

"Ha, ha, Brother. No. She already told me I don't begin to match up to her qualifications. But I think I'm breaking her. I really do."

"How so?"

"Well, her father has forbidden us to meet together outside of her home, but just the other day she spoke with me alone here at Castle Chauliac."

"Ah well, take heart then, Little Brother. 'Tis only a matter of time before you have her as your own. Is this one destined to attend your bed as bride or mistress?"

Geoffrey shrugged. "What's the difference?"

"One day you'll know the difference, Geoffrey. And I pray that it's because you truly find love, not because an irate husband steals your head from your neck." Sir John got up from the dais and went to join the bard, Duncan, down by the fire. But Sir John's lyre sat silent that evening, and the noble knight leaned back in his chair, listening to the delicate strumming of the harp and remembering the days when Duncan had been his only friend. The silenced but well-remembered days of a youth that had died before its time.

Norma joined them several minutes later, sitting at her brother's feet. He laid his large hand upon her shoulder. And it meant the world to her as they sat together, both saying nothing, for they rarely spoke to each other.

☙ ☙ ☙

Just after his brother retired to the fire, Sir Geoffrey mounted his horse and rode in all haste for Durwin Manor. *Johanna,* he thought. *Just to watch her for a while.* The way her small body moved so gracefully, and the way the firelight ignited her tresses made him yearn for her. She was wrong to give her hair the credit for her beauty. For there was something else about her—a subtle sensuality which seemed to invite men to come, even as her words and smirking mouth pushed them away. She was one to be desired, but never forced. *Slowly . . . carefully*—those words were the two keys to pursuing the elusive Lady Johanna. Perhaps his brother was right. Perhaps he didn't know yet what love really was. But if anyone could teach him, he was sure Lady Johanna could. It was those eyes! So pale and icy-blue, yet somehow burning and effervescent, teeming with more life than the ocean itself dared to hold. Even the pale lashes failed to dilute their potency.

Supper would most certainly be over, but perhaps some lively entertainment was being afforded those gathered in the hall of Lord and Lady Clifton. Traveling minstrels and wandering bands always knew that a welcome would be theirs at Durwin Manor. It wasn't at all strange to hear bards from the most remote corners of the British Isles or view the entertainment of troupes from across the Channel. No expense was spared, for both Gordon and Rosamunde knew such diversion pleased Johanna greatly and helped to ease her loneliness.

Geoffrey began to reconsider the conversation with his brother. It was always the same with John. Geoffrey could never seem to say the right thing to his older brother. His heart blistered afresh as he watched Norma and John sit there so closely together, so calmly, without words, their affection so deep and comfortably taken for granted that it went beyond any real outward display. And whom did he have to be quiet with? Certainly not his siblings. Being so much younger than they, he was the archetypal little brother, always in the way, never quite the same as the others, an afterthought, younger than his years. He pushed the whole cursed family out of his mind. Except for Aunt Margaret—she had always made an extra effort to be kind to him, to love him as her own.

Durwin Manor looked warm and inviting in the distance with its windows, shining golden, beckoning him come. After assigning his horse to a groom, he trod up the stone stair steps and into the hall. All the servants were gathered, Lord and Lady Clifton, Margery, of course—all listening to Johanna read *The Divine Comedy*. She acknowledged his presence with a serene, very regal nod of her head, and Margery immediately gave him her stool and sat on one of the long hewn benches with the rest of the servants. The steward politely handed him a cup of wine, and he listened as Johanna read of paradise. Her voice was low and smooth, and its tones washed pleasingly over Geoffrey as he raised his cup to his lips. Her long neck, the deep voice, the proud bearing were utterly queenlike, and he recognized that right away.

> Looking upon his son with the love
> Which both of them eternally breathe out,
> The primal and ineffable power
>
> Made whatever spins round in mind or place
> In such order that he who contemplates it
> Cannot but have some taste of God himself.
>
> So, reader, raise your eyes with me
> To the high spheres, and straight to the part
> Where one motion strikes upon the other;
>
> And there begin to brood upon the skill
> Of that performer who, in his own mind,
> So loves it that he never takes his eyes off it.

After a while Geoffrey looked self-consciously around him. Johanna's dulcet voice now felt more like a drone—the poem seemed to go on and on. Beatrice this and Beatrice that, and admonishments to the reader to stay put (a necessary precaution on the part of Dante as far as Geoffrey was concerned), and didn't anybody else find their skull pounding with the boredom of it all? Why didn't she stop and join him for a quiet cup of wine? Smile at him with those pearly teeth and glittering eyes?

Finally, he could take no more and was smart enough to see that any time talking to her alone would be much too long in coming, if it ever did. Whispering his thanks to Lord Clifton and sighing inwardly on the way out the door, he breathed in the cool evening air and headed toward Oxford.

Johanna had never once looked up from the poem. Perhaps his friend Gilbert was right about her after all. Perhaps she was too much like a man.

That night Geoffrey found solace in the arms of a certain widow on Banbury Road. And when he returned home as the sun rose over the Thames, he passed by the castle chapel, its yawning door welcoming the morning air. Sir John was on his knees by the altar, and he didn't notice Geoffrey as he walked by. But Geoffrey saw his brother, who was always in prayer at morning's first light. Yet he pretended he didn't notice him, because he didn't want to think about the fact that above all others who claimed to love him, John prayed for him the most.

"He has a funny way of showing he cares," Geoffrey muttered as he changed clothing up in his room. And in a way, Geoffrey was right. John's love for him, though distant upon the surface, was an iron one. He knew if he didn't seek to mend his moral garments and assume the robes of manhood, his brother would somehow make sure he did it anyway, even if it meant picking up the tailor's needle himself. John wouldn't be nearly as kind about where he placed his stitches either.

❧ ❧ ❧

The previous evening, well before Geoffrey returned, before Sir John even thought to retire to bed, the polished lyre was quietly lifted from its perch on the hearth as the servants settled down for the night's sleep. Its owner went walking into the summer evening with Duncan by his side. The two remained utterly silent as they migrated from the warmth of the hall to the cooler air of the outer bailey.

A more poignant picture could not have been created by an artist's brush. Duncan was hunched and shriveled, but there was a certain spring to his step, as if the skinny legs contained in the tight hosen and the long, narrow feet swimming in the long, pointy shoes were trying to burst from their confinement. Constructed much like a child's toy, his arms were impossibly skinny but his hands were large and able. God had been kind, for this man suffered not from arthritis or any aching of the joints, and his playing was as fast and clear as it had ever been. His white hair, yellowed by the years, grew past his shoulders and separated on either side of his pointy ears. Together with a beard grown down to his chest, his hair seemed to accentuate the ebony blackness of his eyes. Duncan was dressed in a doublet of green wool, black hosen, and shoes. Sir John had no idea how old was the ancient Scottish man who hailed from the Hebrides, but that Duncan had been the bard to his grandfather, who had died 50 years before, was a fact.

They sat down on the banks of the river, saying nothing at first, merely enjoying the music of nature. The thrusting scrape of the crickets' legs, the breeze catching in the leaves of the beech trees, the creaking of the great oaks as their branches swayed in harmony with the rest. And the river lapping gently against the banks as it flowed toward London and out to sea. The music of creation, answering the chorus of the angels in its own earthbound melodies.

"Welcome home, my lord." Old Duncan's Scottish accent was warmed by his gladness. He was grinning like a monkey just to be beside Sir John—his trusted charge and faithful companion—once again. "I'm glad you're back. Ye were sorely missed."

"You were missed as well, Duncan."

"And what kept ye in London so long?"

"The hope that France would do something to anger King Edward. I didn't stay in London all the time, though, Duncan. I spent some of my time up north, seeing to the Alden holdings."

"Your da would be proud of ye, Johnnie. If I could tell him of the man you've become, I would. What's the castle like now?"

"It's almost a ruin. It's become a useful quarry to the locals."

"Weel, someday you'll be able to build it back up again. If it's worth it to ye."

Sir John shook his head. "It isn't. I enjoy it because the living is rough and provides a badly needed change from London. I'll never wish to bring it back to its former glory."

The bard's dark eyes shone. "Ah, my lord, in the days of your grandfather, it was a grand place. It was a shame he was such a . . . never mind. Your da did the best he could with what was left to him."

"I've no reason to bring it back." His words were sure and needed no explanation. Sir John's fingers found the strings of the lyre and began to pluck a lilting melody, almost haunting, but more lovely than the breeze on which the notes were borne away.

"Ah, one of the songs from Wales," Duncan nodded appreciatively. "I still remember it, lad." And he joined in. "Ye still remember all that I've taught ye. Will ye be singin' for your old friend tonight, my lord?"

"Not tonight, Duncan. The sighing of the treetops is more worthy of accompaniment than my feeble attempt at song."

"Weel, tomorrow then."

"Aye, old man. Tomorrow."

"Will old Duncan have many tomorrows with ye, laddie?"

Sir John breathed in the fresh air around him and realized he felt better than he had in years. London was so foul in the summertime, so grimy in the wintertime, and fall and spring were made for the countryside. "There will be many tomorrows, my friend," he declared.

The bard grinned. "Those are the words I wanted to hear. I'm getting too old to count my days as sure, Johnnie."

"Beneath all that stringy muscle and grizzle, you're stronger than I am, Duncan. You'll outlive me by 20 years."

Their music continued well into the small hours of the morning, until Duncan's gray head bobbed lightly toward his chest. Under the sighing stars a calm repose was claimed by both, and hours later they were wakened by the first song of the lark.

❧ EIGHT ❧

The old carriage rounded the corner of the wall into the courtyard, its gaily painted wheels bestowing shallow furrows upon the dry dirt of the courtyard. The vehicle was almost worthy of being dubbed rickety, almost worthy of the name "contraption." But not quite. That state was still two or three years down the dusty or muddy roads which crisscrossed England. The carriage was like many pleasure carriages of the day: 17 feet long, roofed by arched wood tilts covered with tightly stretched, gaily painted leather.

A bit of comfort for the occupants was achieved by a shock-absorption system of sorts. The main wicker body in which they sat was suspended from the four corner posts of the undercarriage. No well-to-do female could imagine what it must have been like to travel on wheel before this invention—and indeed, centuries before, the cart was mostly a farm vehicle.

"'Tis no surprise women's gowns became more elaborate and costly once the pleasure carriage became popular," Johanna's tutor had once told her, "now that they are protected from the dust and the mud."

Lady Johanna ran down the steps of the manor house and jumped up to help out the occupants before the driver or one of the servants could alight from their lofty perch. "You're here!" she cried to her uncle, who rode alongside on his mount. Leaning inside to make sure that her aunt and cousins were truly the occupants of the vehicle, she let forth a cry of excitement as her only relatives began to issue forth—all four of them—quickly and loudly. Almost all talking at once.

"... seemingly the *longest* trip I've yet to endure."

"... of course I got the flat pillow to lean on..."

"Aren't the flowers just beautiful in Oxford this time of..."

"If I had to hear once more about the sorry state of someone's hair," her uncle said, as he helped out the final occupant, his wife, "I was about to gallop away!"

"Uncle Reynard!" Johanna threw herself into his arms. He was her father's youngest brother. "You're finally here!"

He glowed at the sight of his only niece. "You're as lovely as ever, Johanna."

Aunt Matilda rushed to embrace her as well. And her cousins—Mary, 16, and Iris, 15. Douglas, 13, the youngest of their brood, having not yet uttered a word, leaned in pubescent arrogance against the carriage, head tilted slightly back and to the side. Johanna paid him no mind.

"Inside, everyone! We're serving dinner an hour early. I'm sure you must be famished after driving all morning."

Matilda gathered her skirts and started up the stairs. "You know your uncle, up with the birds!"

Sir Reynard Durwin laughed. "Actually, Mattie, I think we were victorious even over our feathered fellows this morning."

Inside the hall the reception was much the same. Gordon embraced his brother fondly, happy to see the man who was so much his junior. They looked very different from one another, as actually they were half brothers, Reynard being the son of Gordon's father's second wife, and the son of his old age. But despite the age difference, the devotion between the two brothers was as easy to see as if it had been displayed at market with ribbons and pennants. And Matilda and Rosamunde, both from Normandy, had much in common. Already they were sitting together, chatting furiously, using their hands as much as their animated voices to make their point.

With much fanfare and ceremony and general good humor, dinner was announced and the family proceeded to the dais, Lady Rosamunde carried by the faithful Ned.

"Is that strapping man still good for a laugh or two?" Matilda asked as Ned set Rosamunde down gently on a chair.

Rosamunde glanced up at him. "Ned? Oh, he's good for much more than that, Matilda...to any woman who will have him! And believe me, he's a favorite down in the village...or so he says."

"Funny, you don't look the lecherous type, Ned," Matilda commented as the servants began their procession with the food.

Ned shrugged, eager to take his place down at his own table. "I'm not, madam. Plainly, my lady wishes to see me as such. You see, it makes it seem much more romantic to have a sporting fellow carrying you around all day like a princess, rather than a simple man such as myself hauling a sack of barley!"

Rosamunde's eyes glittered. "A sack of barley! Is that what I am to you? A sack of barley?"

Ned smiled at Matilda and whispered just loud enough so Rosamunde would hear. "At least a sack of barley knows how to keep quiet!"

Rosamunde slapped his hand loudly and sent him on his way. When he was seated among some of the other servants at one of the long tables which lined the hall, she leaned toward her sister-in-law, speaking in their native language. "Actually, I believe Ned is quite enamoured of me after all these years."

"Why do you let him say the things he does?" Matilda successfully hid her shock at the familiarity she saw between lady and servant. Her household wasn't nearly as large as the Lord

Clifton's since Reynard was merely a knight, but she ruled the servants she did employ with a rather firm hand. It was that Norman blood of hers, always after some conquest or another, demanding obedience and loyalty above all else.

"*Let* him get away with it? Oh my dear Matilda, 'tis why I've kept him around for so many years! Can you imagine how boring my day would be without Ned along to liven things up?"

Matilda had to admit the truth of that, but chose not to give voice to it. A trencher of bread was set before her, and she reached to the platter in front of her and sliced off the leg of a grouse with the sharp little knife she wore tucked in her belt. When the succulent meat fell right off the bone and onto her tongue, Matilda sighed. "As ever, Rosamunde, your cook is working miracles downstairs."

"He's quite wonderful," Rosamunde said as a bowl of soup was laid before her. Not able to get much exercise, Rosamunde ate sparingly. "I'm complimented time and again because of that man. One day I fear he's going to leave me for Castle Chauliac. The countess has been hinting at such for years."

"How *are* the de Shelleys?"

"Splendid. Last week Johanna and I were visiting the countess. Their oldest nephew, John Alden, arrived yesterday from London. You remember Sir John, don't you? Now that the prince is dead, he feels it's time to retire to the country."

"Or perhaps that is wishful thinking on behalf of the countess."

"That could be. Even with Norma still around and Geoffrey refusing to leave the fold, she longs for John."

Matilda listened intently. "I can't imagine a man like that ever settling down." Sir John's fame as a warrior knight was known all over England. She had always been fascinated with the man—in a far-off way, of course. "Have you seen him yet?"

"Heavens, no! I doubt I shall. You know how reclusive he is on a personal basis. Especially toward women."

"Must have been his wife's death which drove him to feel that way. I can hardly imagine watching her waste away like that with their unborn child in her belly. Certainly I remember not being able to keep anything down, but it only lasted for several weeks. She never stopped. And him by her side each day, watching her die."

Rosamunde waved that thought away with her hand. "He was away in France when she died, fighting with the Black Prince. If I were you, I wouldn't ever romanticize Sir John Alden. He's a soldier through and through. He was married to the military and never wanted a wife to begin with. I'm sure he thanked God the day his bachelorhood was reinstated."

"Rosamunde! What an awful thing to say!"

Rosamunde shrugged. "Perhaps. But all I can say is, I feel truly sorry for the woman who ends up married to *that* man!"

"Why? He's steady and dependable. And you know he would be a faithful husband. If he ever does decide to settle down, I mean."

"That's true. Married or unmarried, if there's anyone destined for a celibate life, it's John Alden!"

Matilda didn't say so then, but she didn't agree. She found Sir John an amazingly attractive man. The way he moved. It was so athletic, so fluid, with a manly grace. Like a wolf running over the frozen moors. And a certain wildness emitted from him as if he wasn't altogether tamed, not completely civilized. Yet outwardly he was always chivalrous. It would take a strong woman to subdue a man such as Sir John. Matilda would like to see it happen, just to prove that every man needs a good woman, whether he realizes it or not.

The meal continued. Course after course. Johanna was getting restless, and so were the cousins. She rose from her seat and, leaning in from behind her father, she placed a hand on his shoulder. "Papa, may we be excused? I think my cousins would like to walk a bit after being cramped up in the carriage all morning."

He placed his bony, wrinkled hand, still strong, on top of hers. "Of course, my dear. Thoughtful of you to notice their discomfort." And he went back to his discussion with his brother as to whether or not the Duke of Lancaster's traditionalist views were really what the country needed right now.

"Come hither! Papa says we may leave now."

The three cousins sprang to their feet and ran ahead of Johanna through the hall to the solar to the other end and up the steep flight of steps to Johanna's loft. Johanna watched them go, marveling at the changes that had taken place in them over the last year since she had seen them. Mary, the eldest, had inherited all of the family's looks, it seemed, with chestnut hair which fell past her waist and that she wore loose and liquid. She was a vain girl, though not maliciously so, and had a tendency to complain—her red, full lips naturally pouting. Her breasts were no longer those of a pubescent girl, but of a woman, and she was beginning to assume that womanly grace about her that seems to blossom in the summertime for most girls. Her walk was definitely good, Johanna decided, but the hand movements were still a bit immature to be labeled "ladylike." *I'll have to work with her on that.*

Iris, a bit buck-toothed and always squinting from her shortness of vision, was a plain little soul with hair the color of coal, shiny and slick, eyes a nondescript color of dark with short lashes, and a body that hadn't yet lost its baby fat, and most probably never would. But her heart-shaped face was sweet and open, and her charming optimism would land her a good marriage. Johanna overheard her mother telling her father, "That Iris looks like a girl built for breeding," which didn't sound like a good thing to Johanna, as it reminded her of horses. Nevertheless, she had always had a fondness for Iris, who was easy to be with, always cheerful, and completely unprepossessed. She loved flowers and dogs and hearing the bard sing in the evening, and would often lay her head in her mother's lap to have her hair stroked. Causing other people to smile was a source of great joy to her . . . so Iris did it often.

Douglas . . . well, Johanna didn't know what to make of the poor lad. His voice—what she heard of it—was somewhere between boy and man, and the once-clear skin of childhood was now inflamed with small pustules, even on his back, she noticed as they changed into older clothes for walking. The curse of adolescence had landed. He hid a basketful of insecurities beneath an arrogant exterior and a puerile smirk. But Johanna thought there was hope for him yet because of the thick, sandy hair which waved above his eyebrows and the bright-blue eyes which were framed by darker lashes. The fact that Mary teased him mercilessly about the light layer of hair which was growing above his lip, calling him "Sir Fuzzimouth," wasn't helping him adjust any more quickly to puberty. But Johanna knew she would be able to bring him out by either making him feel like a man or making him feel like a boy again. She had only to find out with which manner of Douglas he still identified himself.

"Hurry now!" she chimed, clapping her hands three times as Margery quickly hung her more formal gown on a peg behind the door and showing the visiting Durwins' servant where to bestow their clothes. " 'Twill soon be noon, and it's not a particularly quick walk!"

"Where are we going?" Iris asked, eyes alight with the thought of a new adventure.

Johanna smiled. "You'll see."

"I trust I won't get too mussed up," Mary complained. "Your excursions invariably cause me to look like a street urchin, Johanna."

With arched brows, Johanna turned to Douglas. "Does she always complain this much?"

He raised his eyes. "This has been a good day for her. She probably hated everything she ate at dinner, but knew Mother would reprimand her severely if she complained aloud."

"Shut you up, Sir Fuzzimouth!" Mary ordered.

"Make me!" Douglas countered, and they were a noisy bunch as they descended the steps, called good-bye to the parents who still graced the dais, and burst out the door into the early July sunlight.

༂ ༂ ༂

Sir John stared at the massive chandelier which hung from the high ceiling of the castle hall. Suspended by six chains, the great brass circle held almost too many candles to count, but Sir John knew there were exactly 60 of them. He was probably the only person at Castle Chauliac, besides the man in charge of the candles, who knew exactly how many were there. The number of stones that made up the wall fireplace, how many nails held together the giant studded door which led outside, even the amount of steps it took for the marshal of the hall, his great white staff in hand, to travel from the door which led down into the kitchen to the dais—Sir John knew the exact count of each of them.

The pompous old peacock was all John could think when the dignified man, clothed in a doublet of scarlet, entered the room to the sound of clarions and announced dinner. The seasoned knight winced and declared that when he became earl he would eat in his solar—a calm, solitary meal, a simple meal—and leave the hall to the devices of the servants, the soldiers, and Norma. Which made him put another item on his mental agenda for the next year: *Find Norma a husband.*

He stared out the window near the dais at the patch of sky framed by the rounded stone arch. It was a fine day for roaming, he decided, and he would do just that. *If this interminable meal ever ends,* he thought as he spooned a cabbage and quail pottage, heavily spiced with cardamom and cubeb, into his mouth. He thought about the castle garrison which Lord Stephen had given him responsibility for.

"The men didn't seem to be doing all that badly this morning," his manservant, Jonathan, had said a little while before when Sir John had gone up to his room to wash and change for dinner.

" 'Tis plain to see you're not a fighting man, Jonathan," Sir John grumbled as he put on the customary black doublet and hosen. " 'Tis plain to see we've had no decent campaigns to fight these last five years. They've all gone soft. And the new recruits . . . " he would have shuddered if he had been the type, "practically hopeless."

"Then you've got your work cut out for you here. And you were worried you would be bored with only hunting and reading."

"Hmm. No. It seems relaxation is out of the question. One never knows what France will do, Jonathan. The king may call for us at any time, and I've no wish to show up with this bunch of knaves. Many of them had no idea how to even hold a lance, much less properly employ one. I've set the knights to work as well. They're going to be taking the men through the most rudimentary training exercises this afternoon."

"Some of them won't like it, my lord."

"No. They won't. And that suits me just as well. I like them better when they're angry."

Which was true. There was less small talk when people were angered, and Sir John hated small talk more than anything else. War wasn't something to prattle on about—it was a man's duty. Simply that. And if he happened to be good at it . . . well, so much the better for him. He looked back at the chandelier and began to count the candles again as he waited for the next course. God bless his aunt, but whenever she planned the meal it went on for hours. Inferior food . . . and so much of it! That patch of sky kept stealing his gaze from the others, and he knew he had to get out of there soon. Reaching to the trencher in front of him, he pulled a hunk of bread off a larger loaf.

Lord Stephen did likewise. "A bit behind on the second course again, they are," he sighed, knowing Margaret wouldn't be pleased. "So what are your plans for the afternoon? I think I'm going into Oxford to see the bishop. He always offers a fine cup of wine in exchange for some genial conversation."

"I should be training the garrison myself this afternoon; however, I'm leaving it to the knights. I'm off to hunt. It's been far too long."

"I recently acquired another hound, John. You might be interested in trying the dog out. Of a very fine bloodline. Or so says the previous owner. Geoffrey doesn't hunt often, and I don't at all anymore, so I'm afraid the poor thing hasn't had a chance to show off."

Sir John was interested. He had always had a fondness for dogs. Especially ones that made themselves useful. Sheepdogs and hounds delighted him. "Fine. I'll take him with me and see how he does."

"She," the earl corrected, almost pointedly. "*Her* name is Annie. Long legs, beautiful auburn hair, big eyes."

Sir John was relieved to see the trencher holding the second course laid down in front of them. "Well, Uncle, sounds charming, but I've never been fond of redheads."

Lord Stephen laughed and cut a piece of meat from the roast. "Dried-out again," he declared in disgust. Sir John took that as his cue to excuse himself, and he quickly negotiated the stairs to his room in the tower.

It took him no time to change into an old, dark-green doublet and hosen. Ordering his servant to fetch him a skin of wine, some bread, and some cheese, he went out to the stables to have his horse saddled and to find Annie.

❧ NINE ❧

It had been a summer where the rain was kind and the sun was particularly nourishing to all the foliage of forest and field. Sir John, bow in hand, Annie at his side, trod through the meadow surrounding the castle. It was bright with daisies and forget-me-nots, as well as the white ellipses of the sheep's coats as they grazed in contented languorousness on the clover. Next he carefully crossed some crop fields which were being worked by the villeins—the wealthiest class of peasant who worked anywhere from 20 to 40 acres. Sir John knew that he should spend the next few months getting to know somewhat the cottagers, villeins, and small holders who farmed the land of his uncle's fief. But he would rather wait to do that until after the garrison was whipped into some semblance of order. He couldn't imagine leading that band of rascals into battle.

He remembered what the de Shelley holdings were like when he was a small child, and the decline saddened him a bit. So much had changed since the plague. The de Shelleys' demesne, the earl's personal lands which weren't rented out to peasants, grew mostly sheep now. It wasn't very much like the old days anymore when the serfs had to work the lord's demesne two out of six days a week. With one-third of the

94

people destroyed by the relentless epidemic, even some of the peasant fields had been left to lie for years now.

The forest floor was moist and smelled of the earth from which the trees grew. Sir John had no idea what manner of animal he was after today. The hunt was just an excuse to get away from the stony confines of Castle Chauliac, walk in the cool of the woods, think about the future, and come up with a more definite battle plan. But if a mature buck crossed his path, he wouldn't dream of letting it get away.

The hunt was more of a game to Sir John than to most men. He brought only one arrow with him. If he missed, so be it—the game was over. Anyone could pummel a beast with arrows, pursue him relentlessly, wearing down the creature. Sir John preferred a more skillful approach, a more even sport. One man. One beast. One chance to face the soulful eyes of the deer and be the victor. Any other way, and the exhilaration was stolen from him. And Sir John would never have that, for he was as serious in sport as he was in battle. It made him a careful hunter, silent and deadly. For when John shot, he almost always made his mark. Which was why he liked to hunt alone.

He made his way to a creek which eventually fed into the Thames. It was one of his favorite places. Especially the waterfall which fell with frothy decline into a swimming hole. It wasn't a deep hole—merely chest-high. But the cool of the stream was always welcome against his body—his many wounds, most of them old now, almost sighing when the water rose to cover them.

Truth was, the heavy training he had been undergoing with his men had made him somewhat stiff, although only he knew of the discomfort his weathered joints were experiencing. The only times he ever wished for a wife were when his sword arm ached up at the shoulder on rainy nights, or his knees throbbed after walking several miles too far. Not that he would ever care to admit that his body was in anything other than perfect condition. He knew that outwardly, with the many scars which crosshatched his forearms and thighs and the puncture wounds left by several arrows, he was far from perfect. But his agility, speed, and fighting ability were very important to him. And they were all affected by his state of mind.

The pool would soon be near, and then a swim. He had seen no sign of a deer yet, and he was on the protected hunting grounds of his uncle, so there should have been several in sight by now. But nothing.

Annie trotted along beside him, obediently, but far from content. Her nose sniffed at the summer air brimming with more scent than one poor hound should be forced to ignore. Sir John felt a bit responsible for the old girl's happiness. Perhaps he would at least try and get a squirrel or a hare before they returned. Hopefully the small animal would give Annie a nice run, the scent of its blood dripping during its flight sending her mad with want and pleasure. Yes, Sir John loved dogs like Annie. Their makeup was so simple as to be utterly charming. He wouldn't know what to do with a complex creature like a woman.

A laugh sounded loudly from up ahead, coming from the direction of the pool. Sir John silently went to investigate, inwardly irritated that someone had gotten there first.

꙰ ꙰ ꙰

"It's too cold!" Mary harped.

"Your parents will be appalled!" Margery stomped one foot for emphasis as Iris giggled loudly when her feet touched the water.

The Durwin clan looked up at her as if she were nothing more than an irritating small fly or gnat. And that's just what Margery felt like: a buzzing, insignificant insect of the smallest variety, barely seen, hardly heard. Buzzing about their heads. Always buzzing.

"I dare them to even try it!" Douglas spoke from where he stood near the waterfall.

"You would!" Johanna retorted from where she stood on the bank, splashing water up at him with a well-pointed toe. "You daren't even soak your feet. You can just go soak your head for all your dare means to me, Cousin!" Johanna began to remove her round cap and veil. She unpinned her coiled braids, her long blond hair catching the dappled sunlight which peeked through the leaves as she worked her fingers through the plaits. Arching back her head, she shook the tresses free.

Margery gasped, then buzzed anew. "Lady Johanna, this is most unseemly! I forbid you to go swimming. It would be one thing if it was just you girls, but in front of Douglas! 'Tis unseemly!" She bent down, picked up the cap, and handed it back to Johanna. Her lady grabbed it and quickly threw it into the middle of the pool.

"See there, Margery. *Someone* has to go get the hat, and it might as well be myself! Besides, Douglas is just a boy. Why should I mind if he sees me in my undergown? 'Tis as modest as can be!"

Margery looked at Douglas, then at Johanna, then back to Douglas. He hadn't moved. "She's not exactly correct," he drawled, belying the fact that he wasn't *just* a boy at all. "But since I'm not overly fond of such small, skinny specimens as you, Johanna, by all means, throw yourself in the water. Don't hold yourself back for my sake."

"Oh, listen to the big words of little Sir Fuzzimouth!" Mary taunted.

"Shut up, Fairy Mary!"

"You shut up, little man!"

"Please!" Iris begged. "Both of you be quiet. It's too lovely a day to have it marred by your bickering!"

Johanna had her answer as far as Douglas's state of mind. He was still stuck somewhere in the middle, but perhaps thinking in a more manly way than she had previously given him credit for. Now she *did* feel a bit self-conscious as she unhooked her gown, but she wasn't going to back out. After all, he was only a 13-year-old! And her cousin at that.

The gown fell in a heap at her feet, and she stepped out of it, Margery quickly whisking it off the ground. "All right, in I go!" Drawing a full breath into her lungs, she executed a shallow dive into the pool, disappearing below the surface before going deeper to search for the now-submerged head-piece.

"She's taking her time about it," Mary complained 15 seconds later, picking at a small piece of bark which had fallen onto her lap.

"I can't see her in there," Iris's brows were knit. "Do you think she's all right?"

More seconds went by, and still no Johanna.

"She's just playing a joke on us," Douglas declared. "I'm sure she'll come up pretending she's floating to the surface like a dead—"

Johanna shot out of the water, an upward projectile, springing with the strength of her legs from the bottom of the pool. She grabbed ahold of Douglas's doublet and, before he could finish his sentence, he was in the pool with her, sputtering and coughing as he surfaced.

The atmosphere became tense as his face reddened, and all wondered what his reaction would be. Suddenly, he reached out a hand, quickly dunked Johanna under the water, and laughed loudly. His puberty-racked voice broke in the middle of it, and everyone joined in, suddenly feeling very jolly indeed.

Even Margery smiled broadly, despite herself.

Iris soon had her gown off, and so did Mary. Douglas threw his sopping doublet onto the bank, his smooth young chest glistening with water droplets. And the cousins spent most of the afternoon playing games in the cool waters of the stream. But much too soon the heavens darkened prematurely as thunderheads were driven across the eastern sky by the dark winds of a storm. Margery hastily gathered their things and shooed them along, praying with sweaty palms that they would make it back to Durwin Manor before the rain started and the thunder shook the ground. She had never remembered so stormy a summer in all her days.

Sir John clicked to Annie, and they made their way back to Castle Chauliac, oblivious to the drops of heavy rain which fell from the opaque sky.

❧ ❧ ❧

"I'm beginning to come to the conclusion that this storm will never end," the countess declared at supper. It was a small affair—only she and the earl and Sir John sat at the table in their solar. Geoffrey was in Oxford, and Norma had pleaded a sick headache before retiring early in the afternoon to her room.

The countess lifted a piece of cheese to her mouth and took a bite. "I must get a new cook, Stephen, I really must. When we are reduced to eating cheese and fruit for supper because she can't put a decent meal on the table, well, something's gone awry!"

He warmly patted her hand. "I know, my dear, I know."

"I keep trying to convince Rosamunde Durwin to lend me her man, but she refuses."

"Do you blame her?"

"Not for one minute! If she wasn't my friend, I would try to lure him here anyway. But I couldn't do that to her, poor dear. In her condition she has few physical joys to speak of. Hopefully, she'll have us over soon for dinner. I haven't had a decent meal in over a week. Not since we were at the bishop's!"

Lord Stephen decided a change of topic was in order, but to placate his wife he said, "All right, darling. Do what you must."

"Thank you, Stephen. I'll begin writing letters tomorrow!"

He turned to his nephew. "And how went the hunt? I noticed there was no venison cooking tonight."

"No, Uncle. 'Twas an unfortunate bit of hunting that befell me. I thought to go for a swim, but the pool which lies before the waterfall was already heavily occupied."

"Sorry about that," he said, eyeing a burgeoning tart. At least the castle's pastry chef knew her job.

"No matter. Only some young people having fun. I actually enjoyed watching them for a while. Not a care in the world have they."

"Tell *them* that!" Lady Margaret quipped.

"Who were they?"

John shook his head. "I barely know the staff here at the castle, let alone the neighbors. But they weren't peasants, that much was certain. One was almost into womanhood. Her lady's maid kept referring to her as Lady Johanna. A slip of a girl."

The countess perked up. "Johanna? Did she have long blond hair?"

"Oh yes, very long, very blond. Johanna who?"

"Why, Lady Johanna Durwin, of course. My dear friend Rosamunde's daughter. You remember Lord and Lady Clifton, don't you? If anyone would be swimming in broad daylight, it would be Johanna. She's a brazen thing! Doesn't pay much mind to her old father's reprimands although never in large ways. I believe she's quite devoted to Lord Gordon, actually."

"Her maid did say her parents wouldn't like it."

"Oh, that's Margery for you. But Johanna knows her parents better than that. All they did, I'm sure, was tell her to dry off, put on clean clothes, and stay by the fire for the evening. I've never seen more lax parents when it comes to discipline."

"She certainly looked like she was having fun," Sir John added, cutting a pear in half.

"Naturally. The girl lives for fun and her books. Which I imagine she finds fun or she would never study so faithfully."

"Sounds like a frivolous thing."

Stephen nodded. "She seems that way to me. Besides, she's Geoffrey's friend, which can only tell you one thing!"

"Geoffrey's friend? Are they . . . ?"

"Heavens, no! Not that he would ever turn her down. She's been sought after by most of the young men in these parts at one time or another. A girl with brains and beauty. Hard to come by," the countess loyally defended Johanna's character.

"And a good thing," John bit into the fruit. "Women who think too much cause a great deal of trouble."

"Precisely!" agreed the earl. "Besides, she's much too young for you, John."

Sir John bristled. "Who said anything about me?"

"Well, she *is* beautiful, Nephew. You must admit that."

"I would be blind not to see that. Much too beautiful for an old soldier like me."

The countess smiled knowingly. "So you like neither brains nor beauty? I wonder what quality a woman must have to capture you, John?"

Sir John took another bite of pear, not about to attempt an answer to the question—an answer he didn't know himself.

TEN

The visit of the cousins, and subsequently all their escapades, ended two weeks later, and Lady Johanna sighed with relief as she watched the coach rolling back in the direction it had come. It had been a nice diversion from her solitude, but enough was enough, and two weeks of tramping through the woods, singing round the fire, and playing jokes on everything and everybody, especially poor Margery, made her yearn for the incredible comfort of silence.

Margery pushed a wayward piece of black hair behind her ear. "Tired, my lady?"

"Exhaustion is more like it, and now I can rest for a few days, catch up on my reading. And my poor Black Prince is still waving a half-finished sword in the air. I must get back to my tapestry."

"I'm sure you'll enjoy that. 'Tis a beautiful day. Why don't we walk down to the meadow with a blanket and soak up the sunshine?"

"No thank you, Margery. I want nothing more than the quietness of my room."

Just then the sound of a galloping horse entering the courtyard stole their attention. Johanna stood in dismay. "Just what I need: a visit from Lord Codfish de Mer!"

Margery stifled a laugh.

"Johanna!" he bubbled as he dismounted. "You look ravishing! I was hoping to find you at home."

"Hello, Lord Godfrey. This is a surprise."

He took off his cap, his blond curls springing to freedom as he bowed from the waist, almost losing his balance. "I just happened to be riding by on my way home from Oxford, and I thought I would stop in. Perhaps we can discuss these books I have here." He pointed over to a bulging saddlebag, much to Johanna's horror.

"What would the topic of these books be, Lord Godfrey?"

"Roman rhetoric, of course!"

"Of course. What other topic is there?"

Another horse entered the courtyard. Johanna was never so glad to see Geoffrey Alden come riding in as she was at that moment.

She ran over to him. "Geoffrey! I thought you would never get here!" She elbowed him unobtrusively and whispered, "Play along—"

"Well, here I am, Lady Johanna! Just as we planned yesterday," Geoffrey said loudly.

Sir Godfrey's bow-like lips pouted. "Oh . . . I see I've disturbed your plans. If I had known you had plans, well, naturally I wouldn't have . . . You couldn't possibly care for Roman rhetoric, could you, Sir Geoffrey?" The question was an indictment on two counts.

Geoffrey laughed loudly and very masculinely, considering the present company. "I won't even deign to answer that! Perhaps another time, Lord Godfrey—maybe 80 years from now? Come now, Johanna, let us go inside. I've brought the item I told you about yesterday."

They turned to go, leaving Godfrey standing there, looking as if he wished he could find a stream to return to and quickly, or that not being possible, at least another fish to swim with. Johanna took pity on him, and none on Margery. "Lord Godfrey, Margery here loves Roman rhetoric. She really is quite well-educated for a woman of her station. Why don't you show *her* your books?"

Margery's black eyes glared at Johanna, but she knew she was trapped.

"Do you?" Lord Godfrey's interest was immediate and transparent. After all, he had nothing better planned for the entire rest of the day.

Margery smiled politely and vowed a subtle future revenge upon her lady, recalling an itching powder which might find its way into her lady's undergown one of these days. "We might as well see what you've got, my lord. Come over to the bench then and show me your books. I'll fetch my needlework and return shortly."

Johanna and Geoffrey were already seated in the hall when she hurried back through with her embroidery. "Beware, my lady!" she cried with a laugh. "Beware of the vengeful maid! And if I were you, I would beware of that rogue you're with as well."

"Margery!" Johanna yelled. "That's quite enough!" But Margery was already down the stairs and on her way to Lord Codfish and all his Roman delights.

"You Durwins certainly take a lot of cheek from your servants," Geoffrey commented after Johanna ordered some wine be brought.

She shrugged. "It's our way. In case you didn't notice, our social circle is neither wide nor varied, and they provide us much amusement. We only surround ourselves with the most intelligent, witty of servants."

"I can see it now: When they come looking for a job, you three Durwins sit there on the dais like some tribunal of the church saying, 'We realize you've been a laundress for ten years and come highly recommended, not to mention the fantastic arm muscles you developed from your toil, but can you tell a joke? and if so, give us your best one now, please.'"

Johanna poured the wine which had just been brought out and set on the table between them. "Enough criticism of the Durwins. Tell me of yourself. I've seen little of you these days, with my cousins here taking up all my time and energy. What has been keeping you occupied?"

"Oh, the usual," he waved the question away. His supposedly undying affection for Johanna had waned within a week of its advent, and he had no intention of telling her of his newest love which, he believed, might actually be the real thing this time.

But Johanna would have nothing of it. "Do you truly believe I'll let such a cagey answer sneak by me unnoticed? You'll have to do much, much better, Sir Geoffrey. I'm sure it has to do with a woman, so you might just consider getting it over with and tell me everything."

He smirked. "Lady Johanna, I would hardly expect you to understand."

"Of course you wouldn't, Geoffrey. If your behavior is unseemly, well then, 'tis only what I expected, and the same old news I would rather not be bothered with. But if you've found someone exceptional, then 'tis my joy. Either way you come out without disappointing me one way or another, for I expect absolutely nothing from you, Lord Geoffrey."

"Fair enough. All right, I shall tell you about her."

"I was right. It *is* a woman! Tell me everything."

"That's what I was planning on doing before I was so rudely interrupted."

"Sorry. Go on. Who is she?"

"Her name is Helen, and she's a . . . maid . . . at Castle Chauliac."

"That certainly must be something new for you, Geoffrey," Johanna said sarcastically, knowing his taste in women was usually quite pedestrian.

Geoffrey said nothing and merely looked at the contents of his cup. He was not laughing, nor even smiling. Johanna stared at him for several seconds, dumbfounded. "No witty comebacks comparing women to horses? Come now, Geoffrey, you disappoint me."

Geoffrey still remained silent, and his lack of retort caused Johanna to feel like a most heartless soul. She placed a hand on his arm. "Is this more than just one of your infatuations? Do you love her?"

The look in his eyes was all she needed to see. "I can hardly believe it." She breathed in heavily and sat back in her chair. "What are you going to do? Have you defiled her?"

He brought his fist down heavily on the table. "No! And I won't hear you speak of her in such terms. She's a lovely thing. A pure thing. Accepting and affectionate, but not merely a trifle for me to do with what I will!"

"What makes her so different from all the other women you've used?" Johanna snapped. She hated it when men raised their voices to her.

Sir Geoffrey immediately softened. "I don't know. It's just her nature, I suppose. She's a happy person, Johanna. Truly happy, way down inside her, and it seeps up to the very surface of her skin. She never gets angry or irritated, but only seeks to please me and the others whom she serves."

"Sounds like a milksop."

"No. Nothing like that. It stems from the fact that she's content with her life. I've never seen such true strength in anyone before. It's not that she's merely accepted her life and is trying to make the best of it. She's simply content with who she is. And she's kind and soft, and she has these brown eyes..."

Johanna sat silent for a moment, being completely female and comparing herself to Geoffrey's description of Helen. She was the opposite of Johanna, to the extreme. Yet, she was relieved to hear the news. Knowing her parents didn't fully approve of Sir Geoffrey, it wasn't easy to have him around quite so often. "So what are you going to do about your feelings for this Helen girl?"

"I don't know. I've caught her glancing my way many times, and I've tried to make myself available for conversation with her when she comes to tidy my room in the mornings."

"Does she know how you feel about her?"

"No. Why would she even guess such a thing?"

Johanna raised her brows, mouth twisting with sarcasm. "With your impeccable behavior in the past, it must be the farthest thing from her mind! Will you pursue her?"

"I don't know. If I do, it will be in secret. At least for now."

"It will have to be, or your uncle and aunt will put an immediate stop to it, perhaps even relieve her of her position."

"I couldn't do that to her. She is the sole support of her parents."

Johanna suddenly softened. "Geoffrey, is there anything I can do to help you?"

He looked miserable—in love, mind you, but utterly miserable. "No. If you were the praying type, I would ask you to do that. But since you're not, and I'm not either, I suppose we'll just have to leave it up to fate and hope my relatives don't find out."

"Will your brother be upset?"

"Ha! He's the one I fear the most! Most likely he would end up showing *me* the door of the castle, not Helen!"

"Does he really hate you that much?"

"Hate me? No . . . he just despises me. And between those two emotions there is a huge difference. Sometimes I almost wish he did hate me. At least then I would know exactly where I stood."

❦ ❦ ❦

Johanna finally lay down on her bed. No reading to the servants this afternoon, or chatting with Papa, or traipsing about the countryside with Maman in her carriage. She deserved to rest, and that was just what she planned on doing.

Poor Margery. She was still down in the courtyard with Lord Codfish. By this time he had begun his life story, and Margery, too mannerly to do otherwise, sat there and patiently listened while she plied her needle. Much to her delight, a messenger appeared, and she made her excuses to a disappointed Godfrey, and rose to go inside. "I'd better give this to my lady. You must have something better to do than entertain a lady's maid all morning, my lord."

Lord Godfrey cleared his throat, saying, "Yes, that is probably true. Nevertheless," his voice became a little too high and a little too loud, "I enjoyed talking with you, Margery."

"Good-bye then. I'm sure you'll be over to dinner soon."

"One can always hope." His eyes looked heavenward, remembering the last meal he had had with the Durwins, and how delicious everything had been. As annoying as the Codfish was, Margery couldn't help but feel sorry for him. He was lost in his studies most of the time, and while well-respected at the university, he had no one who cared much about him personally. He lived all alone at Meadowbrook, his estate, with only his servants and an aunt so ancient as to be incoherent on good days and raving on bad ones.

"I'm sure you'll be receiving an invitation soon," Margery smiled encouragingly, gathering her skirts in one hand and holding onto her embroidery in the other. She hurried inside with the message.

Lady Rosamunde was sitting in her solar sketching. She despised needlework, although she always had a piece she worked on when other ladies came to call. The sunlight coming in through the window gave her a youthful glow, a pink splendor, which pleasingly complemented her ivory gown.

She sighed as Margery entered. "I think it's going to rain either today or tomorrow."

"Is your back bothering you, my lady?"

Lady Rosamunde nodded and held out her hand to receive the message. "Who would have thought that having a horse throw you could so affect the rest of your life? Well, never mind, 'tis the past."

"And if anyone has done their best to live a good life despite their infirmities, it is you, my lady."

"Thank you, Margery. You are a kind soul." Her eyes scanned the parchment as she quickly read the lovely handwriting before her. "Is the messenger awaiting my answer?"

"Yes, my lady. I'll fetch your paper." She walked over to the table where the writing supplies were kept.

"No, Margery. Just write it for me yourself. Tell Sir John Alden that we would be pleased to accept his invitation to dinner next week, and that we shall be most looking forward to the occasion."

"Yes, madam. And will you?"

"Will I what?"

"Will you really be looking forward to the occasion?"

Rosamunde's eyes sparkled. "Oh yes, most certainly. 'Tis not every day one gets to meet a hero such as John Alden."

Margery began to write. "I've heard myself he's a hard man, my lady."

"Oh yes. But it makes him that much more intriguing, don't you think?"

"I think you've been listening to your sister-in-law too much, madam!"

Rosamunde laughed. "Perhaps you're right, Margery. In any case, the fact that such a man is inviting anyone to dine with him is most unusual. Perhaps he's softened up over the past few years."

" 'Tis not an area in which I'm qualified to judge. Will it just be you and Lord Clifton attending, or Johanna as well?"

"The three of us to be sure. He invited Johanna specifically."

✥ ✥ ✥

Sir John Alden broke away from the training session and stormed across the courtyard as Geoffrey dismounted from his horse in front of the stables. His face belied the rage he was trying desperately to control.

here have you been all morning?"

"What are you talking about?" Geoffrey retorted. "I know nothing about it!"

"I gave orders for everyone to be present for training at sunup this morning. You were no exception."

"What do you mean? Do you honestly expect me to play war with you?"

Utilizing his well-developed self-control, Sir John kept his voice calm. "We have a responsibility to our uncle as well as the king."

"The king, the king, the king," Geoffrey drawled and rudely tried to push his way past. "You have enough loyalty for the both of us, Brother. Carry on without me." He turned an insolent back on his brother and hurried up the steps and into the keep, but the ired knight would have none of it. Sir John quickly instructed one of the older knights, and the training began afresh. He followed his brother up to his solar.

Geoffrey became angry as John walked into his room. "For the love of all that's decent, John, leave it be! Let me alone! It's what you've always been good at. Why change now?"

Sir John ignored the intent of the last remark. "What paltry fighting skills you possessed have all but rusted away these past five years, Geoffrey, and you are not fit to do anything else."

Geoffrey studied his brother with bitter eyes. "Oh no. Of course not. You've always assumed I would happily follow along the path you chose for yourself. Thank you, but no. I would rather not give my life to a king who doesn't know my name or to a country that ravages the people of France as if they were chattel."

"Don't try and play the righteous one, Geoffrey. Your false justifications for unmanly behavior mean nothing to me. You've taken hold of a life of ease, and you'll be cursed if you let it go now."

"That's right, John. You're so perceptive, once again. So what is it to you?"

"Grow up, man! You're 28 years old, and you have no purpose."

"I enjoy my life just as it is, Brother. That is my purpose."

"Life isn't about enjoyment, Geoffrey. It's about duty, honor, responsibility."

Geoffrey yawned. "This is really beginning to bore me. As usual. Why must you keep talking like an old woman, the same things over and over?"

"I'm trying to make a man out of you, little brother, because it's plain to see you aren't up to the job on your own."

"Well, don't bother. I'm man enough when I want to be. Far more than you've ever been."

John's eyes glittered dangerously, and Geoffrey realized he might have gone too far this time. "You leave my personal affairs alone."

"Why not? *You* certainly have. Not that it's any business of mine."

"No. It isn't. You're following a dangerous path, Geoffrey. It was one thing when you deflowered chambermaids and laundresses, but now that you're going after a finer mettle of female, you may find yourself in trouble."

"Are you referring to Lady Johanna Durwin? Well, if you are, you don't have to worry on that account. She is old news. She succumbed quite easily to my advances, and now she's become rather a bore. Still, I hate to simply drop her, so I'm letting her down easily," he lied.

"Even if I believed you, what is that to me as long as you kept your affair a secret?"

"I always keep them a secret."

"Someday you will sully the Alden name beyond repair, Geoffrey. Not to mention the damage you're doing to your mortal soul."

Geoffrey laughed harshly. "Don't bother me with religion. Not now. I simply don't think I could bear it. Leave me alone, John, and if it is to my own demise, then know that it is damnation upon my own head, not yours."

The anger left John suddenly. "That's where you're wrong, Geoffrey. You've been my responsibility since the day our parents died."

"Then I alleviate you of your duties right now."

Sir John shook his head. "That isn't possible. I swore to both Father and Mother I would see you someday make a fine man. And that is exactly what I intend to do."

"A little late arriving to do the job, I would say."

"Perhaps, but that doesn't make my purpose any less sure, my cause any less valid."

"So I had better grow up quickly if I want you off my back?" Geoffrey surmised.

"Exactly. There's no other way to be rid of me now, my brother."

❧ ❧ ❧

After supper that night a quiet comfort eased itself down hearthside as darkness, still two hours distant, groped further around the globe. Sir John and Norma sat by the fire with

Lord Stephen and Lady Margaret. Duncan played a ballad taught to him by the de Shelleys' old bard before he passed away. Set in the days of the Norman invasion, it told of a stonemason's son who became an outlaw—a man named Griffin and his true love, Lilla.

"How did Griffin come to be named such?" Norma asked her uncle after the song was finished, knowing it was a de Shelley name and not an Alden one.

"I don't really know, Norma. That was 300 years ago, and he was a Saxon. Unfortunately, our family doesn't perform too well in this song. The antagonist is Odo, a de Chauliac. He loved Lilla as well and headed a plot to kill William the Conqueror."

"What happened to him?"

"He failed to do it, but he escaped and marauded gold and other fine cargo off the coast of France and Spain for years, taking the loot back to a secret location in Scotland. He supposedly pined for Lilla for the rest of his life, and when she died many years after he had last seen her, he heard the news and took his own life."

"A tragic man. So different from the inhabitants of Castle Chauliac today. It's hard to believe we weren't always English," Norma said softly. She had a love of England instilled into her by her father and mother before they died.

"It's obvious you aren't often at court, Norma," Sir John said, playing softly along on his lyre with the old bard. "They speak French there as a matter of course."

Norma could be as bullheaded as her brother. "I get tired of hearing the French go on and on about their language. I love our language. It suits us well—a bit rugged, even ornery."

The countess smiled. "Speaking of ornery, I received word back from Durwin Manor today, John, in regard to your invitation. They accepted gladly."

"Maybe they could bring their cook with them," the earl said, not altogether joking.

"Good." John began to shift his playing style from plucking to block and strum, and the countess, a jaunty sparkle in her eye, rose from her chair, took Norma's hands, and pulled her onto her feet as well. They danced in circles around the men, much to Norma's utter chagrin. But she wasn't one to douse her aunt's merriment with her own lack of enthusiasm. And so her heavy feet plodded along with Lady Margaret's nimble ones in a dance that somehow recalled a meeting between a fairy and a very tall troll.

"It's about time you took an interest in the neighborhood," Lord Stephen said loudly above the din. "It makes me most happy, John."

But John wasn't listening then. He wasn't listening to anybody or anything other than the music. The music . . . it had been the one constant in his busy life where nothing ever seemed to stay the same.

ళ్మ ళ్మ ళ్మ

Rosamunde's expression fell in disappointment. "Oh, darling, are you sure you're not well enough to come? The countess will be sorely disappointed."

Johanna let out a couple of good coughs from beneath the covers and croaked, "I'll be fine after a good day's rest, Maman. Please, express my apologies to the de Shelleys."

"Oh, I will. You can be sure of that! I still think you're playing me false, Johanna. You've no fever," she pulled the covers off her daughter's face, "and your coloring is fine. You're neither pale nor flush."

Johanna coughed again and pulled the covers back over her head.

"And your cough sounds dry. If you won't go, at least tell me why. You're much too old to be playing these kinds of tricks on me, my daughter."

Johanna pushed the covers back down with a sigh. "The truth is, Maman, I do not wish to meet Sir John."

Rosamunde's eyes opened in surprise. "Truly? Why, Johanna, I've never known you to run away from anything."

"I'm not running from anything. He just sounds so . . . so awful to be near. Geoffrey says—"

"Geoffrey's opinion of anything or anybody should never be taken seriously. He's a spoiled, selfish child."

"Be that as it may, Maman, it can't all be false. Have you heard about the way he walked out on his wife while she was on her deathbed, having reprimanded her for not taking care of their child even while it was in her belly? He sounds absolutely horrid."

"Johanna, you're just listening to stories. He was away on a campaign when she was pregnant. He had to do his duty by the king."

"What about his wife?" Johanna cried. "Here she was, wasting away a little more each day and he's—"

"Enough, Johanna. Personally, I've never liked the man either, but none of us has ever heard *his* side of the story."

"Besides that, he despises Geoffrey. His own brother!"

"Geoffrey deserves to be despised, Johanna. He's a rather likable, conversational fellow, I'll grant you, but at 28 years of age he should be much farther along in life than he is. The earl and the countess are much too lenient with the lad."

Johanna frowned. "I still don't want to go."

"All right," her mother sighed as Ned stood by the stairway, shaking his head at the fact that, once again, Rosamunde had given in. "If that is what you wish. I don't like it, and I'll tell you plainly. 'Tis a bad decision you're making."

"I'm sorry, Maman. But I cannot help the way I feel."

Rosamunde signaled to Ned, who came and picked her up off the bed. "Yes, you can. We all can help the way we feel. And please, for heaven's sake, get up and get dressed. At least have the fortitude to make your decisions without hiding them beneath the bedclothes! Let us hasten, Ned. I do believe the carriage should be waiting."

They started down the stairs. "We leave behind us the most spoiled child in the kingdom of England," Ned said.

Rosamunde sighed, drumming her fingers along his shoulder. Ned had become more and more like a piece of furniture over the years. "You're absolutely right. How can I fault the countess for her treatment of Geoffrey when I'm doing exactly the same thing?"

"It's time Lady Johanna was married off. Time she settled down and got on with being an adult."

"I know, Ned. It's just that once she's gone . . ."

Ned said nothing for a moment, and then laughed. "Once she's gone, we won't have to listen to that boring Dante anymore!"

They chuckled together as Ned deposited his lady inside the carriage, seeing to her comfort and then his own before they rolled north toward Castle Chauliac, with Lord Clifton riding his favorite stallion in the lead.

৵৵ ৵৵ ৵৵

I must have been insane to have issued this invitation, Sir John thought as he counted the candles on the chandelier yet again. There were still 60 of them, although one of them had gone out prematurely. He hated that, but he couldn't expect the heavy iron-and-brass aperture to be lowered for only one wayward candle.

They had been chattering for what seemed like hours but which was only ten minutes. *Where is the food?* he thought, looking at the slant of the noonday sunlight as it came through the door.

"If I weren't such a scrupulous woman," the countess was saying to Rosamunde, "I would spirit your cook away. I'm

117

afraid you might be rather glad the food took its time in coming once you see it." She shuddered.

"Why don't you find someone else?"

"Oh, I am trying to do just that! These things take time, you know."

The earl nodded. "I've gone through a year's worth of paper in only a week, she's written to so many people about the problem."

"Why don't you try the de la Marches?" Lord Clifton suggested.

"Who?" asked Rosamunde.

"The Earl of Lambeth. Near London." Lord Clifton rarely had any domestic suggestions within him, but this time he surprised them all. "Yes. I remember the earl quite well, from years ago in France. He told me that his kitchen has been putting out great cooks for over 150 years. Perhaps there's someone there, an undercook, who will be able to come to Castle Chauliac."

The countess clasped her hands with delight. "I shall write him tomorrow. Do you know him, Stephen?"

"Not well. John probably does, more than myself."

Sir John shook his head. "Not really. Although his soldiers are always extremely well-trained and well-equipped."

The earl laughed. "Soldiering. 'Tis all John thinks about."

I've got to get out of here. John looked around desperately, wondering if there was any way he could leave without being rude. All this talk of cooks and earls. "I'm sorry your daughter couldn't be here, my lord," he said to Lord Clifton, remembering her unique, ethereal beauty.

Gordon sighed. "Yes. Poor Johanna. She doesn't get sick very often. I cannot imagine what's come over her."

But Sir John knew. It didn't surprise him at all that she had refused to come. If it was true that she was Geoffrey's lover, then... But it couldn't be true. Even Geoffrey seemed incapable of defiling such loveliness to satisfy his own superfluous needs.

Rosamunde spoke up. "I'll make sure she comes next time, Sir John. When she hears what a sparkling time she missed, I'm sure she'll be most regretful of her illness."

Was a bit of sarcasm found in Lady Clifton's words? Sir John was sure he heard it, and he leaned forward, looking her in the eyes. They locked gazes for several seconds, and he smiled. Finally he had met an honest woman!

༻✿ ༻✿ ༻✿

Lady Johanna braided her hair with quick and nimble fingers, just one braid down her back. She then changed into an old gown. Margery sat on a stool, disapproval stuck to her face like a barnacle on the bottom of a barge.

"It's not your place to refuse to help me," Johanna said with irritation. "You've no right to question my actions."

"Your mother would be furious, you going off swimming now when you should be having dinner with the de Shelleys. Besides, you've been there twice already this week. How am I ever going to explain this?"

"You won't have to. I'll return well before they do. In fact, you don't even have to come with me. Perhaps Lord Codfish will come calling when I'm gone."

"I wouldn't jest so heartily about the matter. You haven't heard the last of your prank the other day. I'm just waiting for the right time to strike. Besides, you're trying to get me off the topic. I'm of a mind to tell your mother anyway."

"You'll do no such thing!"

"Oh I won't? You could get hurt out there all by yourself. I would be doing much less than my duty if I let you go unattended."

"I don't want you there. I'm just going for a quick swim, and then I'll come home. Why don't you have the cook prepare us a knapsack, and when I get back we'll go down to the meadow, take our needlework, and soak up the sun." Johanna took her maid's hand and gave it a warm, placating squeeze. "Please, Margery. I'm rarely completely alone. Just this once."

Margery looked at her skeptically. She could feel herself beginning to soften, and she hated when she did that. "All right," she said, throwing out her good sense along with her disapproval. "You have two hours. And if you're not back by then, I'm going to come find you."

Johanna hugged her quickly. "Thank you, Margery. I knew I could count on you. I always can." She ran from the room.

Margery began tidying up the room, muttering. "She can count on me, all right. Count on me to give in like a ninny. I'm as bad as her parents. Oh, Lord," she looked heavenward, "You gave me such a job to do here! Such an utterly impossible job! Give me strength, mercy, and a lion's share of sanity!"

Johanna burst through the door and ran down the steps, through the courtyard, and out into the fields. Her braid bounced between her shoulder blades, her fair skin was flushed to a delicate pink, shaming all the flowers of the meadow she carelessly trampled underfoot on the way.

❧ ❧ ❧

The length of the meal was exceeded only by its lack of distinction. No one had the stomach for many of the dishes, though they continued to stream from the kitchen at an alarming rate, one after another, in a parade that held aloft platters which were the ideal of mediocrity. Even the dogs lost their appetites, choosing rather to fall asleep with half-empty bellies. The countess consoled herself that the poor folk of the area would have a fair amount of food distributed to them come morning, but she wondered if such charity was truly worthy of the label.

Dessert was a much more enjoyable affair.

"Come, let us repair to the fire," the countess invited with a graceful gesture. "At least Duncan will not disappoint us."

"We'll be there presently, my dear," said the earl. "I've a new horse I would like to show Gordon."

"As you wish, my love."

Sir John begged the ladies' pardon as well and left with the men. But soon he saw that he was not needed as the conversation, in the space of ten minutes, had gone from horses to religion to Malmsey wine. Seeing that everyone was occupied, he knew the time to escape would never be better. The garrison was beginning afternoon training, but Sir John had made prior arrangements with several of the knights to proceed with the regimen while he entertained his guests. Not that he had believed for one moment he was the one who would really be doing the entertaining. Known by many as strong and silent, only he knew his lack of enthusiasm in verbal play was not due to indifference; rather, he had little confidence in that area. There were few men with whom he could really talk: Duncan, and two other knights in the Order of the Garter that he had been fighting alongside for years. For the most part, John was quite content to listen.

And just then he was listening to the call of the delicate breeze which shuffled the hair of all who worked in the courtyard: the armorers, bowyers, laundresses, fullers, smiths, and stable hands. The kitchen boys tended the household garden while the cook mused over its fresh offerings with a sadistic sparkle in her eye, making the murder of a vegetable seem like a reasonable charge. It was warm and the sun shone strong, defying any type of cloud, big or small, to darken its blue satin backdrop.

Thinking how exhilarating it would feel right now to work up a hardy sweat fighting in the courtyard, Sir John also knew that as their commander it was important for him to show his trust in his knights' leadership. It would be best to stay away, let them be in command for the day. His lyre-playing had become a bit rough, and the contemplation of a cool, quiet spot in which to practice was a pleasant one. Decisively his feet turned, and he walked back into the keep to procure his much-loved instrument, relieved he had left it in his room the night before and not in its usual place by the hearth where the ladies were now gathered.

The waterfall was his chosen place of respite.

Once through the gate house, he rode hastily for the swimming hole, hoping that another rambunctious group of young people wouldn't beat him to the spot this time. Not that he was planning on swimming. Music was what he needed, not water. Although at other times a dip by the waterfall would have been just what he was looking for. Sir John was a good swimmer, a strong swimmer. The castle he grew up in, Seforth Castle, was settled on the shores of the sea. He remembered well the cool, northern waters and swimming under the majestic, cloud-filled sky. Norma never liked the sea, but his sister Bridget had, and they had spent hours together in the chilly waters, splashing one another, dunking, racing along the shore, always moving at a frantic pace to keep warm. His mother never stopped them, the pair being the healthiest of the lot of them.

He still missed Bridget, 30 years later. She had been much like Geoffrey—carefree, fun, laughing at everything—and he had loved her for it. Why couldn't he love his brother like that?

John didn't know. It was something which had occupied his prayers for years, but every time he saw his brother, those same feelings roiled inside him: impatience, disgust, and sometimes even indifference. He fought violently against the indifference, knowing that Geoffrey still needed him, even if Geoffrey himself did not realize this. And he had to admit that being over in France as much as he had did little to aid

Geoffrey's quest for manhood—the quest each boy made whether he realized it or not.

Geoffrey's training was proving to be disastrous. It simply wasn't possible for Sir John to train his brother fairly. He expected too much too soon and was powerless to do otherwise. It seemed impossible that while John could take a country bumpkin who had never held a sword and make him a first-rate swordsman, Geoffrey made no progress under his elder brother's harsh tutelage. A sore predicament for both of them. The solution wasn't an easy one to accept, but he knew, for his brother's sake, he must follow his instincts. The question was, when and what would Geoffrey's reaction be when he found out he was to be leaving Castle Chauliac?

The pleasing sound of the waterfall caressed his ears. Serenity awaited him.

To his dismay, as he crested the rill which bordered the stream, he saw someone dive into the water. Her hair was almost white, and he recognized her as much by that as by the tiny form of her body.

eeling ill, eh? He couldn't help but warm to the girl's audacity. She hadn't come running merely because he called.

He thought of Geoffrey's claims, and he wanted desperately not to believe them. But even he had to admit that his brother's charm with the ladies was a fact not to be disputed. Besides, at 18, Lady Johanna Durwin was probably most desperate to win someone's hand in marriage. Her gown lay in an unkempt ball upon the bank. The sight of it embarrassed him, wondering if it had been like that many times before due to his brother. Geoffrey *might* be telling the truth, but he knew better than to take him at his word about anything.

Turning his horse to go, he hesitated. She hadn't come up out of the water yet. He remembered that last time she was here she had held her breath for quite some time before she pulled the boy into the water. Still . . .

He rode the horse to the water's edge, dismounted, and peered in curiously. It hadn't rained or stormed in well over a week, and the water was clear.

"She's not there!" he said incredulously. Then he became alarmed. Without further thought, he pulled off his boots, breathed in deeply, and dove smoothly and shallowly into the water. He could feel the water whoosh past him upon entry, feel it next to his scalp, its sudden coolness on his fingernails. And when the first rush of speed was over, he opened his eyes in the watery gloom. Above him he could see the flicker of sunlight through the leaves, below him the stony bed. There was no sign of Johanna. Surfacing for breath, he stood there in great puzzlement for just a moment, and then dove back under, toward the waterfall. It fell in lacy whiteness no more than six feet from the ledge of rock where it originated.

To his great surprise he saw a large, dark spot in the rock. Swimming forward, hearing the rush of the descending water ever louder as he drew closer, he was amazed to find it was an opening. *When had that happened?* he wondered as he swam through the hole, hoping it wouldn't be long before he could surface and take in some air. *It must have been exposed from one of these storms.* Almost as soon as he was through, he swam up and broke through the skin of the water.

A gasp echoed around the small cave. Not his own. It was dark, only a dim light emitting from the submerged opening. Not nearly enough to distinguish anything other than bodily shape or form.

"Do not fear, my lady. I bid you no harm." Was that really his voice? It sounded so different here where rock and water encountered one another in such a confined space. He liked the sound of it. Deep, warm, and slightly heroic, even if he felt foolish admitting it.

There was no answer, and he felt the need to explain. "I was riding my horse when I saw you dive into the pool. When you failed to surface, I feared something was wrong. Once I dove in, I saw the opening to this cave. Are you still here?" He could see nothing, and her breathing had stilled.

"Yes. I come here often lately. To be alone."

The sound of her voice, accusing as it was, enchanted him. It was husky, yet smooth. A quality of mellow gold and summer rain, with a hint of the roughness of autumn leaves. "Then I'm sorry I disturbed you. I shall take my leave."

He hesitated for a moment, waited for her reply—surprisingly, refreshingly disappointed. Sir John turned toward the entrance.

"No, wait," she said. "I like your voice. Stay awhile. Talk to me. 'Tis not often I find myself alone with a man."

Sir John arched his brows at what might well be considered a falsehood, but of course she could not see. He felt like someone else here in this dark, warm, enchanted place. The sound of the waterfall could still be heard, the smell of moist rock mingled with her scent added to the illusion that perhaps he had found himself in a different world altogether. A world where he understood people, and they weren't afraid of him. " 'Tis not often I find myself alone with a woman in a submerged cave."

She chuckled. He loved it. "There's a ledge over here. Come sit down."

"Thank you." Soon he was sitting next to her on an outcropping of rock, their lower halves submerged yet in the depths.

"Who are you?" she asked reaching out. Her hand made contact with his arm.

Sir John panicked for a brief moment, checked himself, then decided he wouldn't give his identity away so easily. It would spoil everything if she found out he was her lover's brother. "I don't find that extremely relevant, my lady. Not here."

"Why do you call me 'my lady'?"

"For no other reason than that your voice is lovely and your scent that of a lily."

"You are most poetic, sir. Surely, you're not a soldier then, for one with a heart of poetry cannot mete out violence on the field of battle. At least, that is what I've found to be true."

"Then you've met many soldiers?"

"No. But I've met many poets!"

"I see," he chuckled. The darkness was still thick and heavy, the close air they shared was humid. It changed him— the anonymity provided him with a shelter of confidence. "What if I told you I am a soldier?"

"I would not believe you."

"'Tis easy enough to prove. But I would hate to shatter your misconceptions, your fondness for placing men onto tidy little stacks that fit your description."

She sighed heavily. "'Tis not offensive I wish to be, sir. But to understand my adamancy, you would have to understand me. And since we are being anonymous, I don't think I should reveal anything to excess."

"As you wish," John conceded, but pulled up the sleeve on his doublet. "Still, just to give you something to think about, my lady," he reached out and took her arm, placing her arm upon his forearm, "convince me if you can that these scars came from a pen."

She ran her hand over the muscled forearm, feeling the raised network of battle scars, and she breathed in quickly at the feel of the soft hairs beneath her fingertips, the marked flesh underneath. All at once, the gesture became intimate, as if by feeling the nicks of pain, he was allowing her to become privy to what had shaped him as a man. A shock of awareness ran through her when she realized the strength of the soldier who held her captive.

Captive?

Nay, she was free to leave anytime she wanted. That much was clear. But she wouldn't. She wouldn't relieve herself of this man's company yet. She wanted to know more about him, whatever he would tell her, which she was doubtful would be much.

"So . . . you *are* a soldier then. *And* a poet . . . of sorts."

He laughed. It felt good to him. "You try not to hand out your compliments too effusively, do you, my lady?"

"No. Not when all I've got to judge it by is one well-worded compliment. Besides, I've found with men that they compliment themselves enough without me adding more verbiage."

"You certainly seem to know a lot about us."

"I guess you could call me an avid observer of all things male," she laughed.

"So we intrigue you?"

"I suppose that men have always fascinated me. Not that I've ever admitted that to anyone before, but here in this cave it seems safe enough to talk about almost anything, doesn't it?"

"It does. I've always found us to be rather dull and predictable. We fight the wars, till the land, hunt, enjoy a good cup of mead, love our children, cherish our wives."

"And all that without revealing nary a snippet of who you are inside."

His voice belied his surprise. "Truly? I find that funny that you should think so. We are driven by two things: love and power. If you find out which of the two is more important to the man, you can know the man completely."

"Can a man be ruled by both desires?"

"Yes. And that is a man most miserable. Unless he is able to completely separate himself from his home when he is at war or doing his work."

"I've always thought a man should be able to forget about power and ambition when he walks across the threshold of his own home."

"That is a hard thing to do, indeed—"

"Especially when the women they return home to have a secret wish to be the king!" she interrupted.

"But blessed is the man who finds the balance. Perhaps you will find such a one someday. Have you many suitors?"

"Heavens, no! Not anymore."

"It sounds as if you don't wish to."

"I don't now and I never have. I've been fighting them off for four years now. I'm 18, you know, and still unmarried." She said the words proudly, which puzzled him. According to Geoffrey, she was desperate to find a man. Then again, that was according to Geoffrey.

"And that's a good thing?"

"Well, yes. Of course it is." She stopped, as though he would naturally know the reason why.

"And this is because—?"

"I don't find that extremely relevant," she mimicked his earlier words. "Not here!"

If he had held a cup, he would have toasted her. "Then you must have your own unique reasons. Most women would be heartbroken if they weren't married by the time they were your age."

"Most woman would accept any sort of man as long as he put fuel on her fire and could give her lots of children to eat up the food she cooks."

"That kind of life is repugnant to you?"

"Yes," she said honestly. "There must be more to a relationship between husband and wife. My parents love each other greatly. But while there's harmony between them, I don't feel a real—" She couldn't find the word.

"Unity?" he replied.

"Yes. That's it exactly. When I marry, I want this man to be so much a part of me that I don't know where I end and he begins. I want us not to be merely playing the same song, he taking the low note, me taking the high note. I want us to be the same note, the same melody, playing only one tune in a seamless, unbroken song. Does that make any sense to you?"

John was quiet for several seconds. The fact was, it made perfect sense—such perfect sense that he realized that it was what he, too, was always looking for. "Yes. I understand."

"You do? Truly?"

"I'm not married now, nor have I ever wanted to be. I've never found a woman who knew who I was before we even met. That's it, isn't it? An instinctual knowledge, one of the other?"

"It's almost as if it is an unattainable goal. An impossible vision."

"It is."

"I can't believe that, good sir. There must be a man who knows me, inherently knows me. Somewhere out there."

"Perhaps your standards are simply too high, my lady."

"Oh, they are! I know that I'm looking for the perfect man! I know my parents often wonder if they will have me around forever. And if my life keeps up the way it has been going, they do well to wonder just that. I set the Black Prince up as my hero for years. As long as he was alive, I had hope that there was another just like him. Strong, courageous, able to love a woman wholeheartedly."

"He was a good man."

"You knew him?"

Sir John hesitated, wondering if it would give his identity away, then decided it would be all right. "Yes. I was one of his knights for years."

"You must tell me about him!" she said excitedly.

"I would hardly say we have the time now. I must be getting back soon."

"So should I, but I'm so enjoying myself. I love the unexpected."

"I always hated it," he confessed. "Until now. Why are you here?" he asked suddenly.

"What do you mean?"

"Here in the cave? Is it, as you said, to be alone?"

She hesitated. "I don't really know the answer to that."

"Has someone hurt you recently?"

Johanna laughed. "Oh, no! My heart is my own. It always has been. And yet I am a woman, with a woman's needs. Sometimes the loneliness is great."

John experienced a slight disheartening. Maybe Geoffrey was telling the truth. She spoke of "a woman's needs" so casually. But, too, it was obvious she had no lasting affection for his brother, any more than Geoffrey did for her. "I do know what you mean. I never let women close to my heart either."

"So, we are both closed up tight then?"

"For now. Who knows what the future may hold?"

"That is true, sir. One cannot see down the road ahead. Perhaps fortunately so. But I'm feeling a bit morbid all of a sudden. I'm afraid if we don't change the topic, I shall have no other choice but to swim away!"

"We can't have that, can we?"

"No. I have to admit that I'm enjoying being here, tucked away unbeknownst to anyone. It's like being a child again. Did you have any secret places in your home that you never told anyone about? A place you would escape to for hours with a book and a candle?"

"Something like that. Although my places weren't the small, private places of which you speak. I would sneak outside after everyone was asleep and claim the starry sky as my own, thinking that no one for miles around could possibly be sharing the atmosphere with me, that no one else was looking upon the configuration of the heavens that my eyes were devouring."

"That's all very grand! I must be much easier to please. I found an old springhouse near our home. It was a wonderful place. I would read there for hours."

"You like to read?"

"I love it. I try to imagine what the people who wrote whatever it is I'm reading were like. I make up lives for them—the lives I wish for them to lead. And usually I'm most disappointed when I learn the truth."

"We're all disappointed by the ordinariness of people, I guess. 'Tis probably why neither you nor I are married," he guessed.

"If you look anything like you sound, good sir, I'm surprised the ladies aren't fawning all over you!"

John blushed in the darkness. "I suppose I have the advantage over you then, for I saw what you looked like before you dove into the water."

"Then you know me?"

"I'm new to the region. I've been helping with the training over at Castle Chauliac."

"Oh." Johanna's voice became cold. "I was supposed to be there today to sup with the de Shelleys and their nephew."

"That would be Sir John, I suppose? Or was it Sir Geoffrey?"

"Sir John! If it was Geoffrey, I wouldn't be sitting here now. I'd be dining at the castle."

"And why is that?"

She leaned closer to him, as if a minion of Sir John was lurking nearby to catch any hearsay and relay the message to his evil master. "Because he despises women. Sir John is a cold man who cares only for fighting. Surely you are aware of that?"

John tried his best to pretend he was someone else, but the warmth of her through the water was quite distracting. Her breath upon his neck as she whispered in his ear was warm and sweet. "Well, yes. But that quality makes a fine soldier, don't you think? I would want to fight beside a soldier like him during any battle."

"Perhaps. But I wasn't going there to see him fight."

"I think you are unfair to form an opinion of the man without having met him. Perhaps he is charming!"

Johanna let out a great laugh. "Charming? Sir John Alden? Oh please, noble sir, I don't think even he would label himself as charming."

He laughed. "No, you're right about that, my lady. Not for a minute of his life has Sir John ever thought of himself as charming."

"I must go. My parents will probably be making their way back from Castle Chauliac soon. I promised my maid, Margery, that I would not let them find me gone. She always feels so responsible for me. Why don't you swim out first?" she suggested. "Then I'll come out a minute later after you've gone, and I'll be none the wiser as to who you are."

"Thank you for indulging me, my lady. I'm sure you must find this all a bit mysterious."

"Which is exactly why I'm enjoying it! If you were someone I knew, I would just be having a typical conversation in the dark."

He didn't like the way *that* sounded. Nevertheless he bade her good-bye and turned toward the light. Then he looked back over his shoulder. "I'll be training here with the garrison for a while. May we meet again?"

"Here?"

"Yes. Here."

"When?"

"Two days from now, but later in the day, after training is over and before supper begins."

"I'll be waiting."

"Why?" he asked, not really understanding himself what he could be embarking on.

"I don't know."

"I don't either." He took a deep breath and was gone.

THIRTEEN

S ir John waited.
For his clothes to dry. For his skin to stop tingling. For his mind to stop racing. For his heart to stop pounding. For his head to stop spinning. He had ridden away quickly, knowing Johanna wasn't exactly a woman of her word, if her obedience to her parents, or lack thereof, was any indication. But he had returned a little while later to sit on the bank, take down his lyre, and strum softly, pensively. His music had always echoed the state of his mind. It was why he enjoyed playing so much.

It made easy the recalling of the long-ago days on the field. The days when music fulfilled a need to all the men who gathered about the warmth of the camp fire. When the hunger of the belly had been banished by bread and meat. When all came to listen, hoping to appease the emptiness to which a lonely man fell prey. Lonely for home and all that home means: four walls and a roof stuffed full to the rafters with a cozy joy and crowned by the love of a woman dearer than all the treasure the world could ever hold.

On nights when the moon was awful and clear—a laughing specter sucking up their loneliness as a feast—Sir John knew his music quite possibly meant more to his men than all the soldierly advice he had given by daylight.

Although he had no loving home of his own back in England, he could understand the needs of his soldiers to remember fondly those they had left waiting behind. And while he remembered no wife, no love so deep the cords of which left him battered and bruised when alone, the plaintive melodies and haunting words caused him to recall Bridget and all those he had left behind in the north to decay in their graves. Even their memories were a comfort during the lonely night.

And now, sitting by the stream, remembering the maid with the white-blond hair, he felt fully refreshed.

And somewhat alarmed at the state of his well-being, which wasn't well at all. Sitting there, he looked down at his hands as they plucked the lyre. It was an ancient instrument he held—relic of the bygone Saxon days of Beowulf and great gatherings of tribal people who learned their history from the bard. He didn't know how old the seven-stringed instrument was, with its delicate carvings gracing the wood, for Duncan had given it to him when he was a child, and it was of unknown origin then. But he had always revered the lyre and loved learning to play it just as much as he now loved playing it. He couldn't remember a time when it didn't feel comfortable in his hands, and one of the few early memories of conversation he had was Mother telling his father she didn't realize such small hands could actually play such an instrument. But Sir John had mastered the lyre much like anything else he sought to do, with discipline and purpose. And yet, the lyre wasn't something he attacked into submission like in jousting or swordplay. It was something he wooed. It was something he stroked lovingly and with tenderness, for only then would the ancient harp respond just as he loved her to.

He thought of Johanna.

And he decided that pursuing her, even as the mysterious knight in the cave, was probably a futile undertaking. She wasn't a harp. He couldn't play her and expect her to sing merely because he strummed. He hardly knew where to begin.

Then he heard Duncan's voice so long ago he could hardly believe he remembered the words. It was the first day the instrument was placed in his hands.

"Teach me a song, Duncan!" he cried.

"Not yet, laddie," the bard said as he curled the boy's fingers around the frame. "Ye must get to know her first, Johnnie, carry her with ye everywhere, feel the smoothness of the wood, the sharpness of the strings, the roughness of the pegs. Feast upon the beauty of the carvin', the luster of the wood, and remember the beautiful music you've heard from other lyres and know that this, too, is capable of givin' such a pleasure to your ears."

And so that is what John had done. For two weeks when he wasn't helping his mother or father, the harp was in his hand. And the more familiar it became, the more he grew to love it. Thirty-five years later, his passionate affair with his harp had not waned, but had grown as each gave to the other exactly what was needed.

❧ ❧ ❧

Lord Clifton lifted his spoon to his mouth, tasted the savory pottage, and sighed with pleasure. "Bless the cook. I've been hungry all day."

"Mmmmmm," Rosamunde agreed. "I feel so sorry for the countess, and yet not sorry enough to send Henry over there!"

"Heavens, no!"

Lady Rosamunde turned to her daughter. "Oh, Johanna, the food was abysmal, but I do wish you could have come. Sir John was most disappointed that you weren't there."

Johanna didn't respond. Her mind was on someone else.

"And he is quite a handsome fellow! His hair is absolutely beautiful!"

Gordon laughed. "I'm sure he would love to hear you say that about him, my dear."

136

"But it's true! It's this lovely brown, Johanna, and it has a gloss to it that reminds me of your embroidery silk."

"How old is he, Maman?" Johanna asked pointedly.

"Oh, darling, what does that matter?" Rosamunde really meant the question.

Her daughter shrugged. "I don't know, Maman. I hardly think I would have a good time in the presence of a man old enough to be my father."

"But he has a most youthful demeanor," Lord Clifton said, not taking offense at all.

"Probably because he wasn't married for very long," Rosamunde said dryly. "I've always said marriage ages people."

"Thank you, my dear."

"No, I don't mean that in a bad way. It's just another area where one feels extra strain. And strain ages one. You know it's true, Gordon."

"Well, you look as young and lovely as ever, dear Rosamunde."

"That's because I *am* young." She turned back to Johanna. "As I was saying, Sir John may be older than I am, but not by many years, and he certainly has a youthful quality about him. You've spurned suitors your own age . . . I thought perhaps—"

"He seems cold to me."

"Oh, darling, you've never met the man."

Her father looked at her with a rare disapproval. "That's true, Johanna. You surprise me. I thought I had taught you never to judge something or someone unless you've seen it with your own eyes or have weighed the evidence."

Johanna looked down at her meal and picked delicately at the meat with the tip of her knife, consuming little. She had much to think about. And she couldn't even put a face to the object of her thoughts. Then, having Maman persistently interrupt her thoughts with talk of that ogre Sir John, it was simply all she could do to keep from begging to be excused.

Lord and Lady Clifton continued to chatter about the afternoon, but Johanna was remembering another conversation. Never had she been able to talk to anyone like that. Perhaps it was the anonymity of the situation, but she didn't think so. This man was different, special. She didn't know why, but he struck a chord within her which no one had been able to do, no matter how hard they tried. And her body and mind still sang from his gentle words and calm presence.

She could hardly picture him on a field of battle.

I will go to Castle Chauliac, she decided, *and watch the garrison train. Perhaps I will find him.*

From down at her table, Margery watched. Her lady was acting most strangely. Johanna was *never* subdued. She determined to find out why.

❧ ❧ ❧

"Do you want to talk about it, my lady?" Margery's voice was hushed in the darkness. She could tell by her lady's breathing that Johanna was not asleep.

"About what, Margery?"

"Whatever it is that's bothering you. You've been different since you came back from the stream."

"I don't know what you mean."

"Yes, you do. You're preoccupied and quiet. You've never been quiet since I've come to serve you."

"Thank you for the compliment, Margery. And I'll thank you also to remember your place."

Margery sighed. "You always say that when you want to change the subject. Which leads me back to my question. I know that something happened out there. Why don't you tell me about it? Does it have to do with Lord Geoffrey?"

Johanna's voice became a little tender. "Margery, if something of import ever happens to me, you'll be the first to know. I promise."

"All right, my lady." That had to be enough, Margery supposed, and turned over and tried to find sleep. And she succeeded long before Johanna.

I can't tell Margery or anyone else about him. He's just for me. A sacred being somehow. Sacred to me. And secret. He must remain a secret.

The darkness became a luscious thing, a screen upon which she could relive the moments in the dark cave, remembering his voice, his intelligence, his strength, and what she perceived to be the passion that drove him: a fearless heart that sought to love.

꧑ꕥ ꧑ꕥ ꧑ꕥ

She couldn't sleep much at all. Her dreams were filled with him. He was blond one moment, dark the next, strong-featured, then classically handsome. Different faces weaving through one deep, lovely voice, one true heart. A beating heart, in very time with her own, was heard above all else. *I've always known you,* she thought, as she dreamed. *Can you not see? We've known each other forever.*

The next morning Johanna slipped away early from the manor. She rode in the carriage almost all the way to Castle Chauliac, then bid the driver stop.

"I'll walk from here," she said, spying that the portcullis was already raised, and tradesmen were busily coming and going. "Wait until I return. I should not be too long." The driver nodded as he dismounted, spread himself on the bank, settled his cap over his eyes, and crossed his arms in front of his chest for an early-morning nap.

Johanna gathered her skirts, turned on her heel, and walked up the dusty road which led through the gate house, determined to figure out just which of the knights whom she could already hear beginning the day's training was the man

139

who had stolen her heart, whose very remembrance caused her to thrill most delightfully.

❦ ❦ ❦

Sir John found himself in the chapel on his knees even earlier that same morning. Sleep had eluded him as much as it had Johanna, and his thoughts, normally purposeful and directed, were scattered by memories of her. Never had he met a woman like her, and yet, she wasn't perfect or truly of noble actions. His feelings for her intensified his feelings for his brother. How could a woman like that fall willing prey to a man like Geoffrey? Twenty-eight years old and still a boy! No. Geoffrey had to be lying. This woman had given her heart to no one, and he could hardly believe she had allowed anyone access to her body either. The dislike he felt toward his brother intensified. Had the man no honor that he would defame Lady Johanna's reputation?

All manner of criticism against his brother erupted in his breast, and that despising feeling emerged again. It was sin to feel such blackness against his own kin, he knew. And Sir John bowed his head again in repentance for his feelings. But after several minutes, he found himself just as angry at Geoffrey.

I'll be here all day if I do not get hold of this! he thought with annoyance, and repented yet again. Geoffrey was the only person in the world who maddened him thus. He bowed his head, and with the iron will that had helped to make the Black Prince a victorious military man, he forced such thoughts out of his mind and focused again on prayer.

When the sounds of training began in the outer bailey of the castle, he rose to his feet, feeling a bit better. For Sir John truly believed that God loved him, that Jesus died for his sins, and that one day, somehow, despite the fact that he could never aspire to the sinlessness of the Son of God, he would inherit the kingdom of God. He remembered that upon his knees that morning, and it was enough. Inner peace was renewed. His soul was refreshed.

❧ ❧ ❧

By the time Lady Johanna walked through the gate house, the training was fully in progress. Swords clashed, horses thundered upon the turf at the lists, and shouts and grunts were heard above the din. Wishing to remain anonymous, she stayed close to the walls.

And she listened.

It was useless to look. It had been so dark in the cave. And she chided herself for the romantic notion she couldn't help but feel that her heart would whisper to her, "That is the man."

She soon realized it was useless to listen as well. The noise was much too loud, too indistinguishable. Even if her knight had been shouting, she wouldn't have been able to recognize the voice. Still, she stood there until the sun was well into the sky, finding a bit of satisfaction in knowing that she was looking upon him whether she realized who he was or not.

"Clyde! Hugh!" the angry command caught her attention as a man strode toward several men who were practicing with their swords. The strength he commanded and the way he walked as if he were the sole ruler of the ground over which he trod mightily fascinated her. "Go about it like that and a Frenchman will drain your blood with his first draw!"

Johanna chuckled at the dismay on the men's faces as they ceased to fight, leaned on their swords, and wiped their sweaty faces with their forearms. Now that the knight was speaking in lower tones, she couldn't hear the reprimands they were receiving, but she watched in continued fascination as the magnificent knight—for she could only suppose he was a knight—pulled his sword out of its sheath and began to instruct his men. The change in him was instantaneous as he became a teacher. He explained carefully, or so it looked, and showed each man individually what he was doing wrong.

They stood in rapt attention, his every word made of gold.

And then he challenged one of the men. Johanna watched as he moved so fluidly, with an easy, athletic grace, his sword arced in the air. His body circled and spun, his feet moving with precision, taking him exactly where he wished to go.

Perhaps that is my knight! The thought held great excitement for her and caused her heart to quicken. Hardly daring to even breathe at the thought of being alone with that man, of having his arms around her, of feeling his lips upon her palm—for yes, surely her knight would be one that would not only kiss the back of her hand, but her palm as well—Johanna continued to watch him. Her palms began to tingle with anticipation. She would give him her hand when she saw him next, and see if she had been right about him.

The excitement welling up in her was intense, amazing her with new emotions. This man was handsome, mighty, and obviously intelligent. At least she told herself that, for never had she been struck so completely by a man's appearance and rugged demeanor. He was not "charming" or what she would consider "personable," but it was obvious his subordinates respected him, even liked him for who he was and the knowledge and experience he wished to impart to each one of them. *Surely that is my knight. It must be.* And yet this was a man made for men, not for the ladies. No softness there, no lovely words such as those spoken in the cave. She liked that immensely—his ability to be one person with his men and another with her. Just being near him made her feel safe.

Oh, Johanna, you buffoon!

This man probably wasn't him at all. Perhaps he was one of the knights upon horseback at the other end of the bailey. And being in full armor as they were, it was hopeless to even try and get a glimpse of anyone in that group.

Reality struck even more strongly when, the instruction suddenly over with, one of the soldiers bowed and said above the din, "Thank you, Sir John. That will change everything!" (Johanna was horrified. Sir John! Why hadn't she recognized him from the abbey?)

"It's always worked for me," he replied.

"Johanna!"

Her attention was stolen as Geoffrey broke free from his group and ran toward her. Sir John's head turned toward her as she greeted his brother warmly. His eyes narrowed.

"Carry on, men!" he shouted and returned to another group of foot soldiers with a hardy shout, stepping up their exercises to an even more vigorous pace. "Back with your men, Geoffrey!" he shouted over his shoulder.

"In a moment!" Geoffrey called back. Johanna had an animated smile upon her face. Geoffrey held one of her hands as he excitedly conversed.

Sir John cursed himself and the sudden jealousy he felt. The new emotion surprised him utterly, and he tried to push down the feeling. But no matter how harshly he attempted to do just that, it was impossible. Had the time in the cave meant so much more to him than it had to her? Obviously so.

All eyes were upon him. Would he allow his brother to break rank, even defy him like that? None of the others would dare such insolence unless . . .

"Geoffrey! Now!" he barked, storming toward them.

Geoffrey looked sweaty and exasperated. "Please, Brother, I'm only trying to make our guest welcome!"

The bailey became even more still, everyone looking on in curiosity.

"I didn't realize you were training to become the housekeeper, Geoffrey, although I must say an apron would become you. Get back to your group."

Everyone laughed as Geoffrey grew red, then returned to the others.

Sir John faced Johanna. "And as for you, my tiny lady, a small thing like yourself should think twice before coming here and exposing your ladylikeness to such ruffians as we. Why, the men will be distracted for the rest of the day!"

Johanna's eyes flamed. "You condescending—"

"Ah, ah, ah . . . no rough language among us, please. As soldiers with lily ears, we're all unaccustomed to such talk!"

The men laughed louder. Johanna stomped her foot. "How *dare* you!"

Sir John smiled amid the others' enjoyment, and she pushed past him harshly saying, "I see the battlefield has done little in the way of cultivating your manners, Sir John. Perhaps your aunt will be more amenable to my presence."

He bowed chivalrously. "As you say, my lady. I've never been much of a hostess. Now Geoffrey there . . ."

The men roared, but nevertheless they parted like the Red Sea as the female fireball cut through, determined not to so much as blush.

"Back to work, you spineless curs!" Sir John shouted amiably, and the training resumed. But inside John felt troubled once again. He saw the way Johanna had looked at Geoffrey, and as much as he tried to convince himself that his brother's claims were lies, doubt still cast its shadow, impelled by his growing affection for the tiny maiden with the great temper and strong will.

He vowed not to return to the cave the next day as they had planned. Let her have Geoffrey! Someday she would see what a mistake she was making, and his biggest fear was not that he wouldn't be around to pick up the pieces, but that he would still be all too willing to succor her breaking heart.

'Tis glad I am not to have fallen in love before this, he thought. *I should probably thank my brother for keeping me free from the chains of matrimony! From saving me from this momentary insanity!* For that was all it had been, he decided—a mere slipping of the mind, a dalliance into the unusual.

It was settled. Tomorrow Johanna would come to the cave and he wouldn't be there.

❧ Fourteen ❧

Sir John rode briskly down the road from Oxford to Castle Chauliac. The road was lonely that night. A misty drizzle settled on anything that happened to impede its progress toward the earth. He barely noticed the slight inconvenience, actually glad for the close stillness of the hazy atmosphere.

A little while later the atmosphere began to lose the weight of the mist, the sky drastically thinned, and the moon shone pale behind a milky halo.

Surprisingly, it had been good to get to town. Having spurned dinner with his aunt and uncle, he had ridden to visit the master of Balliol College, where he had studied so many years ago. John Wycliffe had always been a good friend to him, as steady as Sir John, but in a scholarly way. He was good for John's soul, was a man who walked close to God, and was always delighted to see Sir John Alden pass under the lintel of his door and into his chamber.

John didn't go to bare his state of unrest with Wycliffe; rather, they shared a cup of wine together and talked of many things. Sir John enjoyed the fact that Wycliffe didn't believe like everyone else did simply because everyone else did. He mined Scripture for the priceless gems of truth, and he did it because he was the type who rarely trusted in the word of other men. Like John, he had to find things out for himself.

The two men admired one another greatly. And the day flew by, Sir John a bit shocked when Wycliffe told him he had been "rethinking the doctrine of transubstantiation." But he was always willing to hear the reasoning behind the shocking statements Wycliffe threw in his direction, and usually the reasoning was sound, whether or not Sir John agreed with him. Wycliffe was a vocal opponent of the papacy, his influence widespread. His support when Parliament refused to continue the payment of tribute to Rome was duly noted and appreciated by John of Gaunt and many Londoners who were tired of emptying their pockets year after year to both church and crown. So controversial was he in his rejection of the priestly hierarchy—including pardons, indulgences, pilgrimages, the uses of images, and the veneration of the saints—that these same Londoners had to rescue him on two occasions from the inquisition of the ecclesiastical authorities. They called him a "slippery" fellow.

"God's grace," he had said many times to Sir John, "and not our own merit is what salvation is dependent upon."

And Sir John believed him.

It had been good to get away from the castle for a little while. The intellectual stimulation of a man like Wycliffe had been exactly what Sir John needed to take his mind off Geoffrey and Johanna. He was pondering whether or not the communion host really did become the actual body of the Lord when he rode by the village church in Witney.

A movement by the door stole him from any heavenly thoughts whatsoever as he saw the only woman in the region who had hair that could dispel the very darkness of night. A few seconds later he rode past his brother's horse, tethered by the wall of the graveyard. She disappeared into the stone church.

He wanted nothing more than to dismount, storm inside, and knock both their heads together. But it wouldn't accomplish anything and would only serve to alienate him further from his brother and give Lady Johanna another reason to dislike him. And he already had enough to repent about come morning.

⤲ ⤲ ⤲

Sir John sat in the darkness of the cave, cursing himself for his weakness. But he had said good-bye to Geoffrey shortly before, and surely with his brother soon out of the region, it would be much easier to win Lady Johanna's heart. He had never seen Geoffrey so angry as he was when he heard he was leaving Castle Chauliac. It actually did Sir John good to see his brother behaving so forthrightly . . . for once in his life. Perhaps he truly would find the man inside him under the lively training of Nicholas de la Marche, the Earl of Lambeth. And if he did, well, Sir John knew he must win Johanna's heart before a much-improved Geoffrey returned to steal it out from under him.

Sir John wasn't used to following his heart. It felt weak, though not unmanly. For certainly the pursuit of a woman was hardly a feminine activity, yet he certainly didn't feel very soldierly sitting there dripping-wet in his shirt and hosen in the middle of a dark cave. Hidden beneath a waterfall yet.

Absurd. Ridiculous. Bewildering . . . if she hadn't been so attractive to behold. He recognized, if others failed to, that Lady Johanna's beauty wasn't perfect. But she was stunning, and something about her pulled him to her—some combination of comeliness, a full heart, and a merry soul. To him she was the most beautiful woman he had ever seen, and though even she herself would have argued with him on that point, he knew her looks were important to her.

The more he thought about the situation, the more absurd it became. He had given up ideas of marriage, love, a woman to hold, many years before. In fact, the idea of settling down and starting a family had become almost repugnant to him over the past few years when he realized that he wasn't as young as he used to be and, even more, how unwilling and unable he would be to suddenly bend himself to the whims of someone else! A picture of a nagging woman, hands on hips and mouth running in a forever critical manner was the picture his brain chose to place upon him when he heard the word *wife*.

Johanna was nothing like that image. Young, luscious . . . a sweet song, a ripened pear, the first warm breeze of spring. She was all of those things. Someone to grow old with.

He pondered the youth of the maiden who captivated him. True, she was old for a maiden, but he was still old enough to easily be her father. The remembrance of Lord Clifton, so much older than his wife, pleased him as he sat there. Still, the whole thing seemed increasingly ridiculous. What would a blossoming young maid want with an old, weathered soldier like himself—an old soldier who had no idea what to do with a woman!

I am of all men most foolhardy!

And still he sat, promising himself that if she wasn't there soon he would leave and never return.

Meanwhile, on the bank, Johanna excitedly removed her outer gown and stared down into the pool. She felt nervous, her body heat heightened and her cheeks flushed in anticipation. It had been an ordeal to get out of the house without anyone noticing, but somehow she had convinced Rosamunde that she needed Margery's help with her drawing. When the two were busy together, chatting like chicks at the same time, Johanna slipped away.

She licked her lips in anticipation, dove into the pool, and swam beneath the waterfall and through the opening.

When she surfaced in the darkness, a pair of strong arms went around her, and the deep voice saying simply, "You came," thrilled her with a tingling song of future anticipation.

"Of course I did."

He lifted her easily up onto their ledge, hating the broad smile of relief which he could feel his mouth assume, glad that she couldn't see it. She clung to the broad forearms as he settled her on the ledge, and she again felt the many scars which attested to his bravery and his ability to survive.

"Do you always win?" she questioned him.

"What?"

She ran a hand over the surface of his right arm, making his veins feel as though they were on fire. "Your battles. You've many scars. This one here," her finger trailed with the lightness of a butterfly along a particularly thick, raised scar which began on the back of his hand, trailed in a long, slim, snakelike "s" up his arm to disappear beneath his sleeve, "this one here, this serpentine one, feels as if it gave you trouble for many days afterward."

"I'd be liar if I said it was only a scratch. It became infected, and I would have lost my arm if it hadn't been for the prayers of my men."

"So . . . a miracle of sorts?"

"They *are* possible, my lady."

"You believe that?" She withdrew her hand, and he pulled himself up onto the ledge beside her.

"You're here with me now."

"Hardly a miracle. How could any maid with red blood flowing in her body refuse the invitation of a man such as you?"

"You hardly know me, my lady. And you've yet to see my face. Perhaps I am a beast in disguise, like one found in a tale of old. Perhaps this cave is enchanted, and only here I can assume the form of a man."

"The form of a warrior," she corrected.

He laughed. "Warriors lived hundreds of years ago, wore pelts, and wielded heavy axes. I'm simply a soldier. But maybe before I assumed this form I was a warrior beast, some sort of ancient thing." He couldn't help but see the truth behind those words. "One can never quite tell just who it is one is meeting, my lady."

"Then this meeting is, as you say, indeed a miracle. And what keeps you from turning back into a beast and devouring me whole?"

" 'Tis a sad tale, my lady. For, you see, the same sorceress that put the spell upon me which made me a beast forbade me to ever speak to or love a woman, so . . . I always assumed that eating one whole would be out of the question as well."

"And have you listened to her commands?"

"Until now."

"So does that mean I am in danger?"

Sir John knew he had allowed her to trap him. But he quickly evaded. "I'm speaking to you now, aren't I?"

Johanna felt disappointed. "I thought perhaps to get a profession of love from the beast."

"Oh no, my lady! 'Tis much too soon for that. For you see, although I may be a beast, I am not a rash, irrational creature. I would never break the second of her commands without being entirely certain that love was returned."

"Then we shall have to just wait and see, won't we? But we shouldn't dally overlong, my mysterious knight. In less than a month, these waters will be much too cold for man . . . or beast!"

Their laughs echoed in the darkness.

"I'm so glad you were here, sir. I haven't been able to stop thinking about you since we met two days ago."

Sir John liked the sound of that. "That makes me happy, my lady. A humble soldier such as myself could hardly hope to be favored by the honor of your thoughts."

"What have you been doing since we last met?"

"Oh, ranting about the countryside, killing small game and tearing them apart with my horrible fangs and two-inch claws."

"Come now, tell me the truth."

"We're still quite busy up at the castle."

"A motley bundle of men?"

He nodded. "Sometimes. Most are eager to learn, and when a man is eager to learn, that is all the encouragement I need to go in and make a soldier out of him."

"You sound quite experienced. What area is Sir John using you for training? Swords, lances, horsemanship?" Perhaps she would be able to find out more about him.

"Yes."

"You're evading me, sir knight!"

"I saw you at the castle yesterday . . . talking with that rogue Geoffrey Alden, by the way." He pretended to know nothing about their supposed affair. "I don't wish, therefore, to give any of my secrets away."

"All right, I'll change the subject." She skirted the issue of Geoffrey as well. "You promised to tell me about the Black Prince. And you must tell me about the Battle of Poitiers. It was where my father met my mother. I feel a bit responsible to it for my very existence! But perhaps you are too young to have fought there."

"I'm sure you've heard all about it from your father. Why do you want me to relate the details of the battle to you when you already know them?"

"I actually just wanted to find out how old you are," she laughed.

"Why don't you simply ask?"

"All right. How old are you?"

"Old enough to be your father, by the sounds of it!"

"Not *my* father! Yet you seem so young."

He shrugged. "'Twas always a complaint of mine. When I fought at Poitiers at the age of 20, everyone looked at me as though I were only a lad. A youthful appearance can be most afflictive when you are a man."

"I'm sure it makes no difference how old you are. Young men can be so foolish. And I've always felt rather old for my age. I know I can be silly and girlish at times, at least that's what Papa says, but deep inside it seems as though I was born old."

"You are a lovely creature, mon amour," he spoke to her in French, "no matter how old you are."

She felt flushed as his words, mere words, caressed her. "Tell me the story of Poitiers. I wish to hear it again as only you can tell it, my knight."

"Maybe someday, my lady. But for now, I hate to ruin the beauty of this cave with tales of bloody battles and royal ambition. As you say, the autumn will soon be upon us, and the enchantment of our cave will cease to be."

"But I want to know all about you, how you fight, what you—"

"Shh, mon amour." He put his fingers against her lips and held them there gently, moving them across the softness to glide across her cheek and bury themselves in her hair. "There's always time."

His hand left a trail of loving fire, of passionate innocence, across her face, and she held her palm to its surface. He gently took her hand in his, lifting it to kiss the back. Slowly he turned it over, his lips resting, lingering upon her palm.

"I knew you would kiss my hand like that," she said softly, with satisfaction.

He kept her hand tucked in his. "Of course you did, mon amour. We've always known each other, haven't we?"

·⚜· FIFTEEN ·⚜·

Johanna's lips were still tingling with the remembrance of the knight's fingertips upon them. They had been calloused, yes, but so warm and real...searching for her somehow.

Mon amour.

"Yes," she whispered to herself, still thrilling at his endearing words, "I am your love." She didn't think once or even twice that her heart was traveling more swiftly than her head would have dared allow it to go before. All she wanted was to be with him. Again and again.

Lady Rosamunde and Margery were waiting in the great hall, both looking quite frustrated with her when they took in her soggy appearance.

"Is that why you wanted to be rid of us," Rosamunde said, "so that you could go swimming again?"

Johanna nodded as Margery looked at Lady Rosamunde and quipped, "We've been deserted again for mere sport. I don't know what it is that attracts you so to that place, but I've a mind to find out!"

"You'll do no such thing! Either of you!" Johanna cried, her blue eyes lit by the fire of indignation. "I'm 18 years old, and if I want to go swimming...I'll do just that!"

"Well then, Daughter, that's fine, but don't expect us to entertain your admirers for you while you are gone." Rosamunde was piqued. "We'll simply send them along to your stream for you to deal with them there."

"What do you mean? Who was here?"

Margery puckered her lips, sucked in her cheeks, and began to move her lips up and down.

Johanna was immediately remorseful. "Lord Codfish again? Oh, Maman, Margery, I'm so sorry! How long has he been gone?"

"You just missed him!" Rosamunde snapped. "And he came here not but a few moments after you crept down from your supposed nap. Don't think I didn't spy you out the window, running across the meadow either, Johanna."

Johanna stood up as tall as she could, which wasn't very. "Am I to be punished?" she asked proudly.

"Tomorrow. I invited him to come for dinner, and I told him that not only could he sit next to you, but he might also stay for a while afterward, bring his rhetoric books, and discuss them with you. I told him you had taken a sudden keen interest in Roman rhetoric."

"You didn't!"

"I assure you I did," her mother said. "Now go change. You've another visitor awaiting you in the garden. Most anxious to see you. Wasn't he, Margery?"

Due to the Lord Godfrey matter, the two had plainly become coconspirators—an outcome Johanna could have hardly foreseen taking place from her mid-afternoon jaunt. And she didn't like that one bit.

"Who is it?" Johanna asked.

"Lord Geoffrey."

Johanna hurried up to her room, followed by a triumphant Margery, to change clothes.

She stepped out of her gown. "Don't think you will get away with this, Margery."

Margery helped her out of the undergown. "With what, my lady?"

"Transferring your allegiance from me to Maman."

Margery handed her a fresh undergown. "I don't know what you can possibly mean by that."

"Yes. You do." She jerked the creamy ivory wool garment down over her head. "I tell you I won't stand for it."

"Do you want to wear the light-blue or the dark-blue gown?"

"The light-blue. As I was saying, I won't stand for it."

"Yes, you did say that, didn't you? Twice, I believe." She calmly pulled the gown over Johanna's damp head. "But that's not for you to command, my lady. Ultimately, I work for your parents. Furthermore, when you started sneaking off behind my back, being secretive about your emotions, you began the process yourself. Have I ever proven untrustworthy of your inner confidences?"

Neither Margery's expression nor her voice belied the fact that she had been hurt by Johanna's secrets of late, but her eyes did. The eyes that Johanna had always loved so. Johanna softened as Margery laced her gown. When she finished, Johanna turned around and embraced her fondly. "I'm sorry, Margery."

"Will you tell me what's going on?" the tall maid was quick to respond, extricating herself from Johanna's somewhat embarrassing embrace.

"Of course I will. As soon as I'm finished with Lord Geoffrey. Wait for me here."

Margery blessed her lady with one of her rare smiles. "So we're back on course now?"

"Yes, Margery, and sailing for a long-becalmed harbor. Do you forgive me?"

"Yes, my lady. 'Twould be a sin not to."

❧ ❧ ❧

Geoffrey paced about the garden, not really seeing the flowers or the climbing ivy which softened the stone walls, its waxy leaves gleaming in the late-afternoon light. He was angrier than he had ever been at John. And the fact that he wasn't doing anything to stop his brother's plans made him angrier than he had ever been at himself as well.

"How are you, Geoffrey?" Johanna cried as she ran down the steps.

"I'm foolish, that's how I am," he replied much too loudly for her comfort. Johanna hated scenes. Thank goodness, hardly anyone else was about.

"That's old news. Tell me something else!" she replied, trying to cheer him up. "It isn't every day a man of your stature is fool enough to fall in love with a servant girl."

"If only that was all that plagues me, then my life shouldn't be tumbling down around me like the walls of Jericho."

"My, my, that is bad, Geoffrey. You had better come to the bench, sit here, and tell me what has happened."

"All right."

They were sitting side by side, the scent of roses floating over from the arbor behind them yet noticed by neither of them. "It's John."

Johanna bristled at his name, remembering the scene in the castle bailey. "More trouble?"

"I'm afraid so. He's sending me away to Marchemont Castle. It's because he says he cannot train me militarily, so someone else must do it."

"But you don't want to be a soldier. Heavens, you've managed to escape the life all these years."

"I know. But the fact is, I haven't made much of any kind of real life to substitute for it either. My brother is concerned for my well-being, that much is true, but he leaves me no choice in choosing a destiny."

"Do you think that is really the reason you're leaving?"

"That's the only reason he gave. He told me he wrote to the Earl of Lambeth a little while ago and told him to expect me shortly."

"He just *told* the Earl of Lambeth you were coming? Doesn't he have even the common courtesy to *ask?*"

"John never asks for anything. He does what he sees fit, and nothing less than that will do. Curse the man!"

"I agree." Johanna rested her chin on the heel of her hand. "There must be something you can do. Why all of a sudden? Why now? It isn't as if you've been living any other type of life for the past ten years."

"John hasn't really been home for an extended stay until now. Perhaps he didn't realize what a waste of a man I've become."

"You're not a waste of a man!" Johanna defended him. "You're witty, intelligent, and charming. I'm never bored when you are around."

"Thank you for your confidence in me, Johanna, but I don't want to fool even myself in the matter. I'm not doing anything of purpose with my life, and even you can't disagree with that. I just wish I had been given the opportunity to make the decision for myself."

She chewed on a fingernail. "It could be worse. He could be sending you off to a monastery. What about Helen? Have you revealed your feelings for her at all?"

"Yes. In a very small way."

"Did she respond in kind?"

"Yes, much to my delight. She was so shy and sweet, but she allowed me to hold her hand while I handed her a flower I had picked out in the meadow."

Johanna wanted to retch, it sounded so drippingly romantic, but she hid her disgust at such blatant sentimentalism. "Could your brother be aware of it? Servants do love to talk, you know."

Geoffrey's brows raised. "Do you really think...? It certainly is a thought. And naturally, he would rather have me gone than to defame the great Shelley-Alden family by actually falling in love with a servant."

"Think about it. Could he have seen you with her?"

"No. I usually only talk with her when she's tidying my chamber. But if he went into my room at all, he could have seen the parchment on my writing table. It's filled with her name. I even drew her picture."

"That was foolish if you wished to go undetected. Certainly another servant saw the papers and started wagging his tongue down in the kitchens about the matter. Sir John could have found out a number of ways."

"We are never really alone, are we?" Geoffrey sighed.

"No. Not really. I'm sure this is really all about Helen."

"It wouldn't surprise me if I found out that was so. John failed so miserably in his marriage, it seems he wishes for no one to be happy in love."

"Do you remember the marriage?" Johanna was highly interested in the topic.

"Yes, I was 11 when she died. And she lived here at Castle Chauliac. I remember seeing her waste away, and he never once came to comfort her. Stayed in London receiving reports from my aunt every day. The day after she died he returned, buried her without a tear. I suppose it was then he decided that having a wife wasn't worth the inconvenience."

"What a horrible story! No wonder she died, without him there to help her feel better. Was she in love with him?"

"I was too young to discern such things. All I know now is, he would be most displeased to find out that I was enamored with a chambermaid. If he does know."

"It seems your brother has a way of being places, finding out things that are entirely none of his business. I think you should go right back to the castle, face him, and tell him that you and only you will decide what your future is going to be!"

Johanna's cheeks were flushed with passion, thinking that no man had a right to rule another man's—or woman's, for that matter—life.

Geoffrey's smile was genuine this time as he took in her ire. His brown eyes sparkled beneath the endearing black curls. "Oh, Johanna, you are so adorable when you're angry, and especially on my behalf!"

"Then you'll go back?"

"I know I should, but what can I tell him? I don't *know* what I wish to do with my life. If I'm to spurn his plans, I must have some reasonable alternative."

"Well, *that* I cannot help you with. Only you can decide."

Geoffrey really did feel foolish, sitting with such a strong-minded woman, feeling suddenly very inept and not liking the sensation. Perhaps John had been right all along. "No. I do believe I'll go. I'll submit myself to the humility of training at my age, and while doing so I may find a direction. There will be many nobles and dignitaries passing through the gate house of the Earl of Lambeth. Surely an avenue I never knew existed will open up for me there."

Johanna had to agree. "You certainly have nothing to keep you here."

"And as the nephew of the Earl of Witney, I will be treated as a fellow noble and with respect. Two things John has never given me."

"That's true, Geoffrey. I hate to admit it, but a change of scenery could be just what you need. Even if it was your dour brother's idea in the first place. I just wish he didn't have to go around forcing his way upon everyone without even asking them about it first."

Geoffrey seemed surprised at her antagonistic ardor concerning his brother. "Why do you dislike him so, Johanna? You've never really met him, other than the confrontation in the courtyard, and I don't believe he meant anything he said to be taken personally."

She lifted her chin slightly. "He said enough, believe me. And what you and everyone else have told me is enough as well. Clearly, he despises women, and that is enough for me to thoroughly dislike him. I saw him in the courtyard yesterday, all martial and tough." She conveniently forgot her initial reaction to him.

"His men respect him; you've got to admit that."

"They fear him," she said unfairly. "Men that rule others through fear are men for whom I have no time."

"Among others," Geoffrey said dryly. "But I believe you've misjudged the man."

"I'll be the judge of that."

"Naturally, Johanna."

"I can't understand why you're so willing to defend him. You must be a greater man than I thought. But let's hope for his sake the day I meet him isn't soon, for I'll tell him exactly what I think of him. And until then, I'll simply do my best to stay away from him."

"That should be easy enough. John isn't a sociable fellow. And now, I mustn't be either. I'm afraid I had best be off."

"But it's getting late. Why don't you bide here at Durwin Manor for the night?"

He shook his head with a grimace. "There are yet a couple hours of daylight at my dispense. And I wouldn't want John to think I had run right into the arms of my—" He stopped abruptly.

"Your what?"

He shrugged, standing to his feet. "My friend," he finished, taking her outstretched hand. "Right into the arms of my friend."

Johanna allowed him to pull her gently to her feet. "I thought that's what you were going to say."

And so, to do the behest of his brother, Geoffrey left several minutes later. Johanna repaired to her loft, where Margery was waiting patiently as she worked on a soft length of linen.

She told her maid all about the mysterious knight of the cave, of the feelings he invoked in her, and that possibly—just possibly, mind you—she might be in love for the first time in her life.

This time, Margery pulled Johanna into an embrace lasting only long enough to prove that Margery was truly happy for her lady. She poured them both a cup of cider, and they sat cross-legged on the bed as Margery plied Johanna with as many questions as she could think to ask.

The call to supper sounded. They all ate the delightful meal, and that evening, once again, the small community which abided at Durwin Manor congregated before the fire to hear Johanna read and the bard strum softly by way of accompaniment.

Geoffrey was gone, and soon the summer would pass on, proving that life never stayed the same. It simply kept changing in the same old way.

❧ SIXTEEN ❧

The next two weeks skittered quickly by for Johanna. She had been back to the cave, Margery now on guard nearby, four more times, and each time she grew more and more enamored of the knight who awaited her inside. He still had not revealed his identity to her, although he told her it was easy enough to find out who she was after her visit to the castle. Johanna had let the matter lie. She wasn't ready for things to change just yet. Hearing about his childhood had been wonderful: roaming the wild moors and bringing armfuls of heather back to his mother, fishing in the sea by his home, hunting with his father. He seemed to know much about the Alden family, whom his father served, so he said, as a knight. Many nights he spent before their fire in the old castle, listening to the bard, Duncan.

"I feel as if I've always known you," she said earnestly one afternoon at the beginning of August. "And yet, I don't even know who you are."

John's voice, its warm tones, made her shiver as he spoke. "I've every intention of revealing myself to you . . . someday."

"I know. But for now, this is enough."

"Is it, Johanna? When will it cease to be?"

"I'm in no hurry to go anywhere, sir knight. I'm enjoying my life as it is right now. Just feeling this way, being so excited, anticipating our visits . . . 'Tis all so new. I want to savor it, not move on to something else until I've tasted all the possibilities here."

"Yesterday we received word of Lord Geoffrey from the Earl of Lambeth," he said suddenly, listening for any subtle changes in her breathing.

"How fares he?"

"You haven't heard from him yourself?"

"Not yet," she sighed. "I suppose our friendship was a passing thing in his mind. But you must tell me how he is doing."

"Horribly. He's even more miserable there than he was here. The training is most rigorous at Marchemont Castle."

"Isn't it at Castle Chauliac as well?"

"Yes, of course. But Sir John had trouble being hard on his brother."

"As far as training goes anyway." Johanna's tone was sarcastic.

"I see Geoffrey confided in you about his brother."

"Yes, he did. A great deal. But I won't bore you with the details. And I certainly wouldn't want to taint your feelings for your friend."

John was disappointed. He desperately wanted to hear all that Johanna had heard about him. He knew the rumors that had been circulating for years in regard to his first wife. Had Johanna heard any of them? "Thank you, Lady Johanna. Sir John and I have always been extremely close. You are a rare woman, indeed, if you can hold your tongue, my lady."

"Oh, I can hold my tongue all right. About many things."

"So I take it our meetings are still a well-kept secret."

"Only my maid knows about us."

"Is that safe?"

"Of course. Margery is the most trustworthy person alive."

"She must be, if you would entrust her with so great a secret. I'm sure your parents would be appalled to know of your whereabouts just now."

Johanna chuckled. "Wouldn't they? Especially Maman. She keeps dropping hints that we should really have Sir John over for dinner at the manor. My father agrees, says he would love to do some hunting with the man. For some reason, I think they have designs upon him for my future."

"Sir John, eh? As the future Earl of Witney, he'll be quite a worthy mate for you, don't you think?"

"Oh, as far as that goes, I would be marrying well above what even my optimistic mother could have hoped for. It is simply puzzling to me, that's all. Maman has never been overly keen on finding me a mate. Yet, I suppose she thinks the time is coming, for I haven't exactly pursued the matter on my own. She married for love, and I suppose she thinks I should have the same privilege."

"Do you believe that is possible?"

"Marrying for love? I do now."

John felt a great strength infuse him, and he reached for her hand. "Do you love me, Johanna?"

"What I know of you, I love extremely well, sir knight."

"Have you ever loved a man before?" His voice deepened, and his other hand began to stroke her arm.

"No."

"Do you know what it really means to love a man?"

"I think I do. I know how *I* would love a man."

"You use the future tense. Do you really love me as you think?"

"I love a man in a darkened cave. But I believe I would love you even more strongly in the light of day."

"And how would you do that?" He put his arm around her and drew her close to his side. Her head rested against his chest, and he could smell the scent of flowers in her hair, and the overall scent that was hers alone. "Tell me, mon amour. Tell your knight how you would love him."

Johanna thought for several seconds, her head whirling at being so close to him. The feel of his hard chest behind her head, the strong arm pulling her ever nearer, his hand resting possessively on her arm. "I would waken you each morning with kisses and summon the angel of sleep much the same way. I would pillow your head with my breasts each evening as we would lie together before the fire, and I would run my fingers through your hair, whatever color hair that may be. Each day, when you were gone, I would never stop thinking of you, and each evening when you came home I would wish there was some way to be closer to you. But no matter how close we became, it would never be close enough."

As she spoke, John's eyes closed, and he pictured the life the two of them could lead together. It was so beautiful and so painful. For he knew that if she really knew to whom she was speaking the words, she would never even think to say such things.

"Lady Johanna," he whispered hoarsely, "you know that can never be, do you not?"

"I know only what I want to be the case, sir knight. Anything is possible. Are you trying to tell me you really are an enchanted beast?"

"The truth isn't so far from that, my lady. For once you see me in the light of the outside world, you will run from me in anger, feeling betrayed and foolish."

She reached up and held the hand that rested on her arm. "I don't know how that is possible. These times have been so wonderful. It wouldn't matter who you are. Unless, of course, you're Sir John Alden, which you're *not!*" She accompanied the words with a laugh.

But John didn't even smile. He had been foolish to begin this charade. "Why would an esteemed man like Sir John come to a cave day after day?" He returned the joke. "I would warrant he has better things to do."

"Most certainly. But we seem to talk about him much too much. I was enjoying the previous conversation immensely."

He tightened his arm around her, trying to forget for the present time that he was indeed John Alden, and trying to assume the role of the knight of the cave completely. Even if Lady Johanna loved him as such, and only for a little while, it was worth it.

"Do you love *me?*" she asked suddenly.

"Yes. Much to my own demise, perhaps. But love you I do. And I, too, love you well."

She turned in his arms. "Would you kiss me then, before I leave?"

"Must you go already, my lady?"

"Yes. The water grows cold."

Sir John shook his head. If he kissed her now, she would always pine for the knight of the cave. It somehow seemed too much of an assurance that things would go on like this always. And he knew that could never be the case. He realized that this whole charade was utterly futile and could lead nowhere as long as he bore the name John Alden. "I cannot, mon amour. I want to most desperately, but I cannot."

Instead, he took her hand in both of his and raised it to his lips. Johanna warmed to his touch, turning her hand over so that he might kiss her palm. He gladly obliged and then slid off the ledge, reaching forward to help her down.

"Good-bye, my lady."

"Good-bye, my knight." She put her arms around him and held him to her for several seconds, trying to feel every inch of him, wanting him ever nearer. "In two days' time I'll be here waiting for you."

Sir John said nothing, merely extricated himself from her most pleasing embrace, drew in his breath, and swam out of the cave and back to his real identity.

❧ ❧ ❧

The lyre lay silent beside him as he stared into the camp fire. Breaking twigs in half and throwing them into the blaze was all that Sir John could do in his present state of mind. Even old Duncan didn't care to play. It was late, and he knew his young master was most troubled when he suggested they sleep out in the woods that night.

"Why dinna ye go on an' tell me about it, Johnnie? Save yourself all the sweatin' you're doin' as to how to start. Just make a beginnin' and go from there."

Sir John gave Duncan a tight smile and shook his head. "It's a disaster."

"Ah, weel, then it mustna be bad, lad. Ye've lived through many o' them."

" 'Tis a woman."

Duncan was surprised. "A new *kind* of disaster, then? Ye'd best start right at the beginning then, my lord. I'm not much experienced with women myself, but I'll lend me kindly old ear in your favor."

"I knew you would, Duncan. Do you know of Lady Johanna Durwin?"

"Aye. A right fine one she is. A real beauty, there's—"

"—something about her," Sir John interrupted. "I know. That's what everyone says." And he proceeded to tell Duncan all that had taken place, the old bard growing more surprised with each word. This sounded nothing like his John, and yet, love did crazy things to even the most tightly laced humans.

"So my quandary is this," John finished up the tale. "She loves me as the knight of the cave, and hates me as Sir John—"

"—though she's never really met ye."

"Yes. Which, is highly unfair on her part, to listen to hearsay and so judge a man. But nevertheless, despite her unreasonable prejudices, and they *are* unreasonable, I am still despised. And once I reveal myself to her as John, it will make everything we shared together in the cave a lie."

"Well, it already is a lie, lad!"

"Not really. I never told her I *wasn't* John."

"Did ye talk about John like ye knew him and like you werena him?"

"Well, yes . . . but I—"

"And did you mislead her durin' those conversations?"

"Yes. I did."

"So . . . everything you shared together *was* a lie, wasna it?"

"Yes, Duncan. You're right. It was. How did I let myself get into this?"

The bard raised and lowered his shoulders. "As ye said, there's something about that lady. Dinna be too hard on yourself. Recompense can always be made, lad. That's what is so wonderful about our God."

"I know I was wrong to mislead her like that—"

"Yes, you were. But 'tis nothin' our Lord willna forgive if ye ask. But from now on it's simply up to you. Ye must never go back there."

"But I'm drawn. I feel so helpless. And it is a feeling I most despise. I haven't felt this helpless since—"

"Don't say it, Johnnie. I know. Ye dinna have to talk about that ever again."

"So if I stop visiting her in the cave, what do you suggest I do? Having tasted her love, Duncan, I cannot abstain forever. I want her more than I've ever wanted anything in my life."

"Then ye must woo her as yourself, my lord. 'Tis your only course of action. As ye said, what's goin' on there in the cave, 'tis nothin' more than a labor in vain. In the end, it will lead you nowhere."

"But when I'm with her there, I feel strong and assured. Like no way I've ever felt before with a woman. My voice is smooth and low, I say all the right things and am the man she wants. When I'm not there I'm surly old John, the wicked older brother of Geoffrey, who, according to him, was her lover before he left for Marchemont."

"And you can look beyond that?"

"I have to. I love her. The future possibilities are worth far more to me than her past failures."

"But—"

"Don't say it, Duncan. I know what you're going to say."

Duncan remained silent, knowing he was going to bring up a very touchy subject with his master, and thinking it might be better just to listen to Sir John and keep quiet.

"Besides, I don't think Geoffrey was being truthful. I can't bear to think of never showing up again, her there waiting for me and leaving without ever seeing me again."

"Ye must, lad."

"What if I went back to her once more? Told her I was finished at Castle Chauliac. That I was leaving for home and would not be returning."

"No. Ye mustna leave room for hope. Ye must break her heart, lad. For if ye dinna do just that, ye will never be able to come as yourself and mend it with your love."

Sir John knew Duncan was right. And the thought of Johanna, wounded by the callousness of his own doing, made his heart break for her. It was an impossible situation. All the inadequacies he ever felt as far as women were concerned returned, and he wondered how in the world he would ever win the lady's heart.

Aye, an impossible situation, indeed.

The men reached for their lyres simultaneously, each exhaling deeply as his hands made contact with the wood, each lost in thoughts of his own making. Yet somehow the music which rose from the instruments to float above them was haunting in its harmony and subtle in its passion.

SEVENTEEN

Darling, do go down to the kitchen and check on dinner. Ned had to go into Oxford for the morning, and I cannot do it myself."

"Yes, Maman," Johanna dutifully replied, setting down her needlework and standing up. She stretched a bit. The morning had seemed intensely long, and this small errand was most well-received on her part. Besides, the world of the kitchen was one into which she loved to descend. It made her think of the Inferno, getting more and more heated with each spiral down, but at the bottom awaited some of her favorite servants and smells which would in and of themselves put meat on the bones of a starving man.

It was evident as soon as she entered the large room that they were quickly working themselves to a frenzy. Guests came quite often to dine, but this guest was from Castle Chauliac, and whenever anyone came down from the castle, it was a reason for the kitchen staff to hoist all the sails and proceed at full speed.

"Good day, my lady!" Henry, the chief cook cried. Literally. His knife was chopping onions at what looked like a dangerous pace. He sat at a great trestle table near the large pit which held the main fire, the heat of the coals warming his handsome face. Henry was only 30 years old and the delight of all the castle wenches. He was tall and smart, and his passion for food was evident to all who knew him, making him even more desirable. What was true of all dedicated men was true of Henry: His passion for his work, his dedication, made all the other aspects of him even more attractive. The kitchen help couldn't do enough to help their overseer. Indeed, he was nicknamed by the women as "the kitchen god."

Three lambs roasted on spits, the handles turned by half-naked scullions, and inside the two wall fireplaces at least four iron pots were bubbling up a medley of aromas that brought hunger to Johanna's belly with a vengeance.

She shook her right hand rapidly down near her side—not from agitation, but because it seemed to be feeling tingly lately, uncomfortably so. "Maman sent me down to check on dinner. The men should be returning from the hunt soon. At least, I hope so. It all smells so wonderful. I don't know if I can hold off that long!"

Henry smiled his saucy grin and hoisted himself off the bench, scooping up the onions, regarding their sight and scent with adoring eyes, and then throwing them into one of the pots. "You sit down there, my lady, and I'll fetch you a small bowl of pottage to stay your hunger. We can't have you wasting away, can we?"

"Of course not! Whatever you've got there, I'll eat. You know that!"

"I certainly do! Many a picky household I've served, but not the Durwins. It's a pleasure cooking for you all. Why, I think I would even turn down working at the castle itself, I enjoy it so much here. Ida!" he called to a lady who was kneading a large pillow of dough at another table. "Have you got a loaf ready to come out of the oven?"

"Yes, I do! Help yourself. I would get it for you, but . . ." She held up her sticky, floury hands and shrugged with a smile. Henry grabbed the wooden paddle and proceeded to extricate a golden loaf from the oven against the wall. In no time he had sliced off a piece and spooned up a bowl of pottage which consisted of turnips, parsley, linnets, sparrows, and quail, all bound together by a vast amount of spices and a little broth. He set the bowl down in front of Johanna. "There you are, my lady! Tell me what you think. 'Tis a new recipe. My own concoction."

Johanna's eyes sparkled as she took the first bite. Then she took another bite, and another and another. And Henry was satisfied.

"The proof is in the eating," he said proudly and hurried off to tend to the roasting lambs.

Johanna ate every drop of the delicious pottage and decided that just a little bit more wouldn't do her any harm. She rose from the bench and took her bowl over to the caldron. Just then a scullion came running by with a bucket of water from the well. He didn't see the onion which had rolled onto the floor, stepped on it, lost his footing, and tumbled into Johanna.

Realizing she was about to fall into the fireplace if she didn't do something, Johanna threw down the bowl, grabbed onto the blistering side of the caldron with her right hand, and pushed herself off in the opposite direction, taking the boy with her.

Several of the staff gave a cry and rushed to her aid. The reddened palm of her hand was already starting to blister angrily. After applying a healing plaster, they bound her hand and sent her upstairs. Johanna really didn't know what all the fuss was about, for although the burn looked painful and sore, it didn't really hurt at all.

Funny, she thought with a shrug, and proceeded to report to her mother that everything in the kitchen was going just as it should.

❧ ❧ ❧

All too soon the men returned from hunting. At least that was how Johanna felt about it when she remembered afresh who made up the party. She was finally going to come face-to-face with Sir John—a man she had come to dislike so intensely. Poor Geoffrey, off at Marchemont Castle without a friend in the world. He really was a cruel man to afflict his brother with such high expectations.

Spirits were high as the men rode into the courtyard with their prizes. A doe hung suspended between two of the horses, the arrow still protruding from its left eye. Johanna recoiled at the sight.

"She's a beauty, eh, Johanna?" Lord Clifton put his arm around his daughter's shoulders as they walked together at an easy pace into the great hall. "You should have seen the kill. Sir John only takes one arrow with him and only takes a shot if he knows he will put the animal down right away. It was sheer poetry."

"A merciful killer?" she asked pointedly.

Gordon sighed. " 'Tis better than a cruel one. If you had ever been in a battle, Johanna, you would know what a great difference there is. Anyway, I've never seen such a shot. Come celebrate with us, Daughter. Pour me a cup of wine, sit by my side, and tell me you'll always love me as much as you did when you were eight years old!"

Johanna smiled at that. "Of course I will. There's only one man in my life who will never change, and that is you, Papa. Come to the dais, and I will pour you that wine. You must be thirsty."

"We all are. If you would extend the same courtesy to our guests, I would be most grateful, Johanna."

"Of course." As the only daughter, it was Johanna's place to serve as hostess, especially considering her mother's infirmities.

The men clambered up the short flight of steps. At least some of them did. Those lower in status sat at the table directly below the dais and were happy to be there, considering the luscious aroma which was wafting up from the kitchen. But all were talking loudly, the day already a legend, the celebration eagerly anticipated.

Johanna grabbed a large flagon of wine from one of the servants and began to pour the red liquid into the silver goblets which sat at each man's place. She felt distinctly feminine and suddenly very mature, aware of her small, graceful body, and the luxurious hair which flowed down her back.

There were eight men altogether seated there. Several knights from Castle Chauliac, her father, Sir John, Lord Stephen, who had arrived after the hunt, and Lord Godfrey who, surprisingly enough, loved to hunt when the weather was just right. Lady Rosamunde, the countess, and Johanna added a bit of feminine flair and brighter color to the otherwise darkly clad gathering. As she expected, Johanna was to be seated in between her father and Sir John. Was her knight among the group? Her eyes examined each man.

Sir John sat quietly as she poured his wine, saying nothing when she finished and moved on. But he was aware of each movement she made, his own body strung more tightly than a Welsh longbow with the tension of being so close to her. The brush of her sleeve upon his shoulder, the soft whisper of her breath on his hair as she reached forward to grab the goblet. It was infinitely more intoxicating than the wine which she poured.

Johanna finished her duty amid the admiring glances of the knights and, of course, Lord Godfrey. *It could be worse*, she thought. *I could be sitting next to Sir Codfish.*

"Congratulations on your kill, my lord," Johanna said formally and through obligation as she was seated with the help of both Sir John and her father.

"Thank you." He sat down. "If I don't get to kill something every couple of days, I become a beast."

Johanna shrugged, failing to see the humor of the statement. Prayers were said, and the food began to arrive in plenty. She didn't eat much, but listened to the conversations all around her. She loved to hear her father and Lord Stephen talk to one another. They had that easy gait to their conversation that old friends do, moving easily from one topic to another. Sir John, on the other side of her, said nothing, and ate nothing either, except for some bread. He took sparingly of his wine as well, sipping not in a brooding fashion, but merely content to observe.

A man's man, she decided after trying to engage him several times in conversation, despite her wishes to the contrary. A soldier with few sociable qualities. She decided to have some fun with him. After all, she already didn't like him, and she never had been one to refrain from speaking her mind.

"I perceive you don't care for my conversation, my lord."

He turned toward her sharply. "I'm a man of few words." He looked away.

"And you like it that way, so I should mind my womanly place. Is that it?"

He refrained from showing his discomfort. "Something like that."

"Still reveling in the compliments of your fellow hunters? Your tongue seems to be more loose in the company of your comrades in arms. I know that right well!"

Sir John said nothing.

So Johanna filled in the silence. "I don't know how you can feel like such a hero. People kill things all the time."

"Did I say I was a hero?"

"No . . . but—"

"Don't put words into my mouth."

She decided to concentrate on her food. All her presuppositions about the man had been correct. He was surly and thoroughly disagreeable. Cold.

"Have you heard from your brother recently, my lord?"

"Yes."

"He was a friend of mine."

"So I understand."

"You sent him away from his home," she accused.

Sir John immediately bristled at the topic of his brother—an automatic reaction. "Pardon me for not being as chivalrous as some, my lady. But I'll thank you to mind your own business. My decisions with Geoffrey have nothing to do with you. Unless, of course, there was more to your relationship than mere friendship."

Johanna shrugged and decided to ignore him for the rest of the afternoon. And that's exactly what Sir John preferred, fuming at himself for behaving exactly as she had expected. He was already furiously planning an alternate attack. Nevertheless, Johanna remembered him with a sword, and stole a sideways glance at him, looking down at his roughened hands and finding them strangely beautiful, as if she knew them instinctively.

Her father captured her attention when he and Lord Stephen began to speak of Dante, and several minutes later when she looked up, Sir John's seat was empty. He thanked Lady Rosamunde for the lovely meal, made his apologies for leaving so soon, and walked out the door with a stride even Alexander the Great would have admired.

Johanna did, too. Albeit most grudgingly.

❖ ❖ ❖

"He's exactly what I thought he would be!" Lady Johanna reported to Margery not much later as she changed from her formal gown and into something more practical.

"I'm sure you're being too hard on him, my lady. After all, you only just met him, and no one makes any claims that he has a flair for conversation."

"I found him rude and sulking."

177

"Sulking? A man like him? Never. Men like him don't sulk. They brood."

"Well, brooding then."

"He shoulders a great responsibility, my lady. And you must remember, 'tis not overlong since the prince has died. Men grieve differently than we do."

Johanna's eyes lit up. "Was he close to the prince?"

"From what I hear, they were very close. He was a knight of the Order of the Garter. Surely that means he wasn't merely a passing acquaintance."

"Maman says he's coming for supper tomorrow evening as well. I'm supposed to read from Dante afterward. She's going about this all wrong. Men like him don't want a woman who can translate from Italian to English. They want a woman who will sit by the fire and darn their doublets saying, 'Yes, my darling. No, my darling. How are you feeling, my darling?' Actually, upon further reflection, men like him don't want a woman at all."

"Maybe he merely has trouble relating to them. Not all men are the likes of Lord Geoffrey. Or even Lord Godfrey."

"Lord Godfrey? I would hardly call him a man who fares well with the ladies."

"No. But he likes their company well enough, and doesn't mind talking to them, even if the topic of his choice isn't necessarily interesting."

Margery began to brush Johanna's long hair. "The fact is this, my lady, Sir John will be around for a long time. You might try and make the best of it. Give him a chance."

"How? He won't even talk!"

"Maybe he will, if you find something of common interest. I can think of a topic right away that interests both of you extremely."

"What is that?"

"The Black Prince!"

Lady Johanna shrugged but conceded nothing. Instead, she sat there thinking about John's hands. There was something about them which told a different tale, sang a different song than what was initially evident. But she didn't know what.

"Are you almost finished, Margery? I'm most eager to be outside."

"Yes, my lady." She made one last stroke from Johanna's brow all the way back to where her hair ended eight inches below her waist. "Do you want me to put it back for you?"

"Not today. All I want to do is sit outside and ply my needle. So much has been going on lately, I fear I've neglected my poor dead prince."

"You mustn't let your memorial to him go unfinished," Margery agreed, gathering their embroidery supplies, "if only because you've worked on it for so many years. It would be a shame to stop now. But do you think you can accomplish anything with your hand in such a condition?"

"Oddly enough, it doesn't really hurt. It is a bit stiff."

" 'Tis strange it isn't bothering you more. But I'm glad you're not feeling any real discomfort."

They were out the door and on their way a minute later, both enjoying the August warmth, knowing cold days would be upon them all too soon. Johanna had no idea just then of how cold her winter was really going to be. And it was a good thing, for summer was still favoring her kindly, and she was happy and young, and maybe she was truly in love.

Walking along, she smiled to herself, recalling the voice of her beloved, the way his hands had caressed her face, arms, and hands. "Let's go to the stream," Johanna suggested.

"Are you meeting Sir Mysterious today? I thought that was tomorrow."

"It is. I just want to remember him and the way he makes me feel."

Margery shook her head but did her lady's bidding. "I don't know about all this, my lady. It's been several weeks since you met him. You would think that surely by now he would—"

"Enough, Margery. I can trust this man. Though I've never seen him, I know he would never harm me."

"How do you know? You're usually such a reasonable young woman."

"Love wouldn't be love if it was always reasonable, Margery."

They continued walking. But several minutes later, nearing their destination, both stopped.

"Do you hear music?" Johanna whispered.

"Yes. It sounds like it's coming from the stream."

"I thought so, too. Let's go quietly. Perhaps whoever is playing doesn't wish to be disturbed."

Margery nodded. "It sounds quite lovely."

Their footsteps became much lighter as they followed the path of the stream. They came upon the musician from a distance. A dog sat by his side, and he seemed lost in his music.

"Who is it?" Johanna whispered.

"I'm not sure exactly. But if I'm not mistaken, it looks like it could be Sir John!"

EIGHTEEN

Surely not!" Johanna whispered. She could hardly believe the words. "Sir John playing a lyre? I don't believe it."

"You're probably right. I doubt if it is he. Probably just a wandering minstrel. Why don't we sit here where we'll remain undetected? 'Tis a lovely tune the fellow plays."

Johanna agreed with the compliment her maid payed to the minstrel, but her natural curiosity would never let it go at that. "Stay here. I want to get a bit closer to see who it is. I'll be right back."

Johanna circled around a bit so she could see the man's face. She almost gasped aloud, but pressed her hand to her mouth to stifle the reaction. His eyes were closed, and the breeze ruffled the brown, wavy hair. *I can hardly believe it!* The way he sat so peacefully, at one with the ground beneath him, at harmony with the sounds of nature. His face, serene and beautiful, resting in gentleness, was heavenly in form, sweet, at peace. The contrast to the man she had dined beside only an hour before would be unbelievable if she hadn't seen it with her own eyes. And his voice . . . now that she was closer she could hear that he was singing along with the harmonious notes his sensitive fingers plucked on the strings. It was a full voice, neither high nor low, not highly powerful like many of the bards and singers whose voices had filled the hall of Durwin Manor, but it was utterly pleasing, softly plaintive, and highly emotive.

"It *is* Sir John!" she whispered to Margery a minute later as they deposited themselves upon a soft, mossy patch of ground, close enough to hear him singing, and began to embroider.

"I told you not to judge the man so quickly, my lady."

"But how could a man like that make such beautiful music? And his voice . . . surely someone who sings so beautifully—"

"Do stop prattling on, my lady. How can I hear him with you whispering in my ear so!"

All seemed lost in the spell of the man playing. His dog lay comfortably beside him, head cocked to the side, eyes almost glazed. And Johanna and Margery were seized two-handed by the spell as well, lost in the world of this new Sir John. Most confusing it was to both of them.

Undetected, they sat there for quite some time until Johanna motioned to Margery that it was time to go. Quietly they gathered their things, Johanna extremely puzzled at the finding of the day. Sir John continued to play, oblivious to the fact that he had entertained a most captive audience.

◈ ◈ ◈

"Well, the least you could have done, Brother, is to send word that you wouldn't be home for supper!"

Sir John looked at Norma as if she were some curiosity and nothing more.

She crossed her arms. "I suppose you've dispensed with all manner of courtesy?"

"Norma, I was alone. If Annie could have given you the message, I would have gladly sent her. Now I'm retiring, and I do not wish to be disturbed."

"Always as you wish, John." She was delighted that she had sent Helen up with a bouquet of flowers for his table only minutes earlier.

But John barely noticed the cheerful collection of blooms. All he could think about was tomorrow afternoon when Lady Johanna would come to the cave, only to meet with heart-break. He bade his servant good-night, stripped himself of his clothing, and lay down wide-eyed on the bed, haunted by what he had yet to inflict upon Johanna.

Sir John Alden was of a rare breed of man who soldiered with a clear conscience. Many men killed others in battle and heard their cries long after the conflict had ceased, when the blood which had collected on the field had become cold. Not John. His eyes were shuttered against the men which fell beneath his lance and blade. What he did, he did for his king and for his friend, the prince. What he did he did for England, and he never questioned whether or not it was right or wrong. As a vassal to his sovereign lord, the king, he had sworn to fight for him. It was about keeping a vow, about honor. And that kept him from questioning the motives behind his lord's command to war with the French.

But now, lying in the darkness, he understood a bit more the horror of meting out pain and suffering. He made a decision. Even if it made it harder to win her in the end.

❧ ❧ ❧

Dearest Johanna,

Good fortune has befallen me here at Marchemont Castle. I am to be married in a month to a lovely lady who is a friend of the earl's daughter. Her name is Lady Ellen Compton. Who would have thought I would find myself thanking my brother for sending me away?

I wanted you to be the first to know.

Geoffrey

Johanna could hardly believe the words. That Geoffrey wasn't in love with Helen after all wasn't a bit surprising! After all, he had once professed such love for Johanna as well and had as quickly lost interest. But that he had found the woman of his dreams . . . it was astounding. Sir John had actually done the right thing by his brother. And the man could sing and play the lyre so beautifully . . . and the way he had fought with his sword. Everything about him was poetry.

Was there anything left to dislike him for? Other than the scene in the courtyard, of course.

Not really. But it seemed too easy to admit that. After all, their conversations together hadn't exactly been amiable up to that point.

"He *is* rather rude," she said aloud.

"Who?" Margery asked.

"Sir John."

"What made you bring that up?"

"I just received a letter from his brother."

"Oh, that explains it then. And how is the rogue faring? Charming all the maids at Marchemont Castle?"

"Apparently not all of them. He's getting married next month."

Even Margery was shocked. "Apparently miracles happen all around us."

Johanna laughed. "Yes," she thought of her knight, "apparently they do."

❧ ❧ ❧

Johanna surfaced into the cave. "Are you here?" she asked.

But there was no answer.

184

She waited, wondering where he could be, filled with anticipatory excitement, thrilled that any minute now he would be swimming through the opening to meet her. He plagued her mind with thoughts of him. All the memories consisted of were a dark form and a mellow voice. The memory of his arms, scarred and manly, and how safe she felt inside their sweet circle of strength. The gentleness of his fingers, so roughened on their fingertips. His musical voice.

Hurry, my love. Come to me! her heart cried out.

But there was no answer.

After a while she began to think he wasn't coming, but she refused to let hope die yet. Perhaps something happened, an emergency of some sort detained him. She knew that he would do whatever he could to be here as he promised. After all, he loved her, didn't he? Surely he was a man who meant what he said.

❧ ❧ ❧

Sir John sat upon the bank, watching the waterfall, seemingly mesmerized by its lacy descent. Many times his fingers reached for the buttons of his black doublet, but he remembered that going to her now would be for nothing.

How long will she wait for me?

The minutes turned into an hour, then two, every moment she lingered another arrow in his heart.

❧ ❧ ❧

Johanna could stand the cool waters no longer. It was time to go. Tears prickled the backs of her eyes, but she refused to cry until she knew if she had truly been deserted by him. Dread clotted in her stomach, and she feared the worst. She remembered the words he had spoken—that if she ever found out who he truly was, she would feel angry and foolish.

It made no sense.

Neither does staying in here a moment longer.

She slid off the ledge and swam through the opening, surfacing into the late-afternoon sunshine, surprised to hear the dulcet musings of Sir John's lyre.

"My lady," he quickly kneeled and offered his hand. She accepted his help and soon stood on the bank beside him. She reached down and dried off her face with her gown. "What are you doing here, Sir John?"

"Here." He held out an ancient brooch of Saxon origin, the kind used to hold a mantle about the neck of a man. It was silver—a smooth topaz stone gracing its carven surface.

"Is it from . . . ?"

He nodded.

She took the pin, her fingers pruned and pale, the hard metal looking as if it would tear the waterlogged skin. "Did he tell you everything?"

"He told me to give this to you. He left two nights ago."

"Where?"

"Home."

"Where is that? Up north?"

"I cannot tell you that, my lady. I'm sorry. He told me you mustn't know where he is going. He said you would understand."

"He was wrong then. Will he be coming back?"

"I don't think so. In fact, I know that he will never return."

Sir John could see her struggling to contain her emotions. "Did he say anything else?"

He knew she was searching for anything to hold onto when she fell asleep, alone in her bed that night, and he willingly gave it to her. "He said he would always love you."

"Why did he leave then?"

"He thought the cave was just a fairy-tale happening, my lady. That you could never really love him once you had seen him."

"Was he disfigured in face? If that was it, I could surely overlook—"

"No. He wasn't disfigured in any way but on the inside, my lady."

"I don't understand what you are saying."

"He told me to tell you that the beast in him was the victor, whatever that means, and that it always would be."

"But that seems impossible. He was such a wonderful man."

"Yes, a most noble, chivalrous knight of the highest form. If you loved him, then you chose well."

"I must go." She turned, clutching the pin to her breast. Then she returned her gaze to Sir John and held out the pin. "Here. Send it back to him. Tell him it will never replace what we had. Tell him I'll never love anyone but him."

"I will, my lady." He reached forward and took the brooch. "I'm sorry to bear such ill tidings."

She smiled sadly. "You did it most kindly, sir. Thank you." And then she walked away.

"Lady Johanna!"

She turned. "Yes?"

"If you need anything . . ."

"Thank you."

Sir John followed her from a distance to the edge of the wood. Once in the meadow, Johanna broke into a run, her hair flying free, the tears escaping bitterly. But he couldn't see them as they fell onto her bosom, blending with the water of the stream.

❦ ❦ ❦

John went directly back to the castle and penned a message to Lord and Lady Clifton that he would, much to his disappointment, be unable to join them for dinner that evening. Then he called for Annie and once more escaped the castle.

Johanna ran up to her loft upon arriving at the manor, intending not to come down ever again.

❧ ❧ ❧

"My lady, you must eat something!" Margery pleaded.

"I will. But not today."

"But in the past three days you've only taken water. I fear for your health."

Johanna took Margery's hand in both of hers. "I've never done something halfheartedly in my life, Margery. I promise you I will eat when I am ready to live again."

"When will that be, my lady?"

"When I realize that my knight wasn't as important to me as the food which fuels my body."

"And you will realize this?"

"You answer the question for me, Margery. You know me better than anyone. Will my lust for living prevail?"

Margery knew the answer immediately. "Do you wish to be alone?"

"Yes. For now."

"As you wish, my lady."

❧ ❧ ❧

"How is she?" Sir John asked Lady Rosamunde that evening.

"Not well. I do not know what ailment has taken her down so, but she refuses to eat, taking only water."

"May I go and see her?"

"I'll see if she wishes it. Margery!" she called to the maid, and Margery appeared shortly thereafter. "Yes, my lady?"

"Ask Johanna if Sir John may come and see her."

"She sleeps, my lady. For the first time since the illness struck."

Sir John couldn't believe it. "She hasn't slept for three days either?"

"No. But she does so now. And it is my guess that when she awakes she will finally have her appetite return to her."

Sir John turned to Lady Rosamunde. "It is a good portent that she sleeps, my lady."

"Yes, it is, Sir John. Thank you for caring enough to come by. Shall I send you a message if she awakens and takes a bit of food?"

"Yes, please do."

"Shall I tell her you were here to see her?"

"No, thank you, madam. I must be getting back now."

"Give my regards to the countess," said Rosamunde. "Thank her for her concern."

"I will."

NINETEEN

The words issued from his mouth softly, gently, with the awe of creation suspended in the phrasing, the love of the Creator rounding out each inflection. The inhabitants of the hall sat, hanging in a rapt medium of time, somewhere between heaven and earth, man and God.

> The Glory of him who moves everything
> Penetrates the universe and shines
> In one part more and, in another, less.
>
> I have been in the heaven which takes most
>   of his light,
> And I have seen things which cannot be told,
> Possibly, by anyone who comes down from
>   up there;
>
> Because, approaching the object of its desires,
> Our intellect is so deeply absorbed
> That memory cannot follow it all the way.

Johanna stepped softly from her parents' solar and into the great hall. The reader's voice, gentle as it was, had carried up to her loft. It drew her, not like flotsam to a maelstrom, although the feeling was slightly spiraling and almost as intense, but like a cherry blossom is pulled off by the spring gust, gently whirling in the long-sought-after current which melted the ice and snows farther north.

It was getting late. But no one seemed to notice. They were being transported from Dante's purgatory into paradise— that place where the light of the Almighty shines most brightly. Johanna lingered in the doorway of the solar, listening as Sir John continued reading, obviously given the task by Lady Rosamunde, whose chair was beside his.

He looked up suddenly, as if he felt her presence, the memory of being near her a more tangible thing than a thought, able to announce her presence when she herself made no sound and little movement.

When he ceased reading, all eyes turned to see what he was looking at.

Lord and Lady Clifton smiled in delight. Rosamunde beckoned her forward. "Johanna! My darling."

She walked forward. "Maman."

Lord Clifton put an arm around her. "How are you feeling?"

"Hungry."

That was all Henry the cook needed to hear. He scrambled to his feet and was on his way down to the kitchen to prepare her a platter.

"And what has brought this change of appetite?" Gordon smiled.

"I heard the reading of Dante, Papa. And it was different than it has been the last three nights when you were reading it."

" 'Tis true enough. I've never been good at reading poetry. I'm afraid the servants have had to endure much in your absence."

"Well, Papa, I'm glad you found so worthy a replacement. Sir John takes a trip through purgatory and makes it poetry. You take poetry and make it a trip through purgatory." Her words were dry, but so very Johanna that everyone let out a collective sigh of relief. And while John didn't smile outwardly, he felt a release victoriously invade his tension and fill him with a quiet joy.

Sir John stood to his feet and offered Johanna his chair. "Perhaps you do your father an injustice. After all, I was given the privilege of reading about paradise."

"A privilege indeed, sir knight," she conceded. "But please do not let me interrupt you or steal your privilege away from you. I would so like to hear more."

"As you wish, my lady."

He looked back down at the manuscript and once again began to translate the words of Dante for the benefit of them all.

> When I notice that Beatrice had turned round
> To her left hand, and was looking at the sun:
> An eagle never looked at it so steadily.
>
> And as a reflected ray will always issue
> From the point at which the direct ray struck...

John looked at Johanna at this point, now eating her meal, and he was encouraged by the words. He could never be the knight of the cave, but a reflective ray always issued from the direct one. And in that way, he might win her love. Perhaps she would someday realize that the knight had only been the reflective ray of love, and he, Sir John, had always been the true ray, the direct ray, the ray which would someday illumine her with the light of womanhood, of passion, and of wifely love.

> Just like a pilgrim anxious to get home.
>
> So from her action, received through my eyes
> Into my mind, my own action was made,
> And I gazed at the sun, in a way we don't.

The words seemed revealing to John, a prophecy, and he thought surely all those around him realized the state of his affections. She was here, eating, determined to arise from her bed of grief and continue. His course was now determined, and together they would see the sun in a way most humans aren't allowed. He was certain of this.

"I shall stop now for the evening," he announced abruptly half an hour later, much to their disappointment.

"But please, Sir John, it was just getting interesting!" Rosamunde pleaded.

Johanna almost choked on her wine. "Oh, Maman, you didn't grasp a word of what he said, did you?"

"No. But it was so beautifully put, Johanna darling!"

John set the volume on the table. "The credit for that should go to Dante, not myself, my lady."

"Correct," Johanna agreed. "But I agree with what Maman meant to say. It was interpreted most beautifully. Will you come back tomorrow evening for supper and grace us with your talents once again, Sir John? That is, if you wouldn't rather be drinking and carousing with your knights."

If John had been a jovial man, he would have laughed aloud. Instead, he merely bowed with a chivalrous air, most solemn and knightly. "As you wish, my lady."

Johanna finished up her meal after he left, looking forward to tomorrow evening. Hearing Sir John read would be a nice, quiet way to go about her return to the world. She had sense enough to know that the enchantment of the cave would never be revisited, that it was truly a one-time occurrence, an adventure more than most women were afforded.

The question now was this: Did she purpose for a lonely life because her high expectations would never be met, or did she marry for the sake of marriage and to make her parents happy?

She had no answer.

❧ ❧ ❧

The next evening was just as she expected. Sir John, in a quiet yet confident manner, read of paradise, and Johanna and Margery worked on their needlework. The burned hand, though not painful, tingled quite regularly. Despite the mesmerizing words of Dante, Johanna couldn't help but notice that the same hand was feeling quite stiff. More so than ever before. She commented about it quietly to Margery, who suggested it might be from the burn.

They continued to listen. But sooner than anyone expected, Sir John laid down the book and declared that the time had passed them by once again and the ride to Castle Chauliac was a dark one.

The servants dispersed to set to their final chores before bedding down for the night by the fire in the hall. When the farewell greetings were given, Ned carried Rosamunde into the solar, Lord Clifton following behind him, and Johanna declared she would walk with Sir John out to the stables.

"Thank you for coming," she said as his horse was brought around by one of the stable hands. It took all the lad's strength to keep the spirited dappled stallion from breaking free from his grasp. Johanna immediately recoiled from the beast.

Sir John noticed. "You don't like horses?"

"No."

He pulled the horse's head down and whispered something in its ear as he stroked its face softly. The horse calmed immediately, although Johanna thought he didn't look happy about it.

"Have you ever ridden one?"

"No. And I trust I never will."

"One day you shall," he declared.

"No. Such beasts are not to be trusted."

"You're right. And when you understand that, you might start to understand him."

"Then why bother?"

Sir John gave her one of his rare smiles, and the light from a nearby torch illuminated his face. It caught Johanna completely off guard. The dim light showed him for his age, but she thought the lines around his eyes and mouth were beautiful, the gray hair above both ears bespeaking a life filled with physical hardship. "I bother because I have to have some mode of transportation, and this is the simplest form."

"I suppose sword-fighting in the midst of battle from a carriage window could prove to be a bit impractical," she joked.

"A bit." He turned to mount. "Thank you for inviting me, Lady Johanna."

"Thank you for coming to read. Will you come again sometime, Sir John?"

"You have only to ask, my lady."

"Thank you . . . for . . . for knowing. I don't know why, but that made me feel better, as if I wasn't alone. After all, he left you, too."

"Yes. His help will be missed."

"Has he always been like that?"

"Like what?"

"I don't know . . . unreliable, quick to abandon his post . . . something like that."

"Perhaps. It was the first time that knight, although I had known him from many years, actually came to my aid. It was never meant to be an extended stay, I suppose."

"No. But still, I thank you. You could have been most severe with me for meeting him like I did and in your forest."

"No, my lady. For somehow, I knew his heart."

"I know I don't need to ask you this, but for my own peace of mind I will. You'll keep this matter most secret?"

"Have no fear of that. I promise you no one else will find out the cause of your sudden, and thankfully, short-lived illness."

The horse started stomping. "I had best be off. Gale gets impatient if I keep him standing still for too long. But first, Lady Johanna, I must inquire about your hand. Is it paining you? Your mother told me about the burn."

"That's the strange part of it, Sir John. It looks sore and painful, but it doesn't hurt me at all. And yet it tingles greatly. I suppose I should be thankful I didn't fall into the fire completely!"

"May I see it?"

She nodded and placed her right hand in his hand. He undid the bandage and inspected it, noting her fingers curling upward in a clawlike fashion. "Can you straighten out your fingers?"

"Not really."

"Let me see your other hand."

She complied. "This one feels fine. I will be glad when this heals, for I'm not able to work my needle with the same ease as before."

He nodded, retied the bandage on the right hand, and released her hand. "I trust it heals soon, Lady Johanna. Take proper care of it, even if you can't feel the pain, lest it begins to fester."

"I will, Sir John. Thank you for your concern."

He put his foot in the stirrup and bounded up on Gale's broad back, landing lightly. Before he could say a proper goodbye, the dappled stallion was running out of the courtyard. Johanna hurried up to her loft and watched him as he disappeared down the road, Sir John and Gale becoming one form as speed freely enveloped them in her breeze.

Johanna smiled and shook her head, wondering how she had ever thought that man was an ogre. He was such a gentleman and truly chivalrous. That his concern for her was genuine she could not doubt, even if it was spurred by his pity for her. There could be no finer knight in the kingdom, she was certain. He would be a good friend now that Geoffrey was gone.

Margery helped her out of her gown, handed her a soft linen nightgown to don, and proceeded to care for her hand. The maid was all aglow over Sir John.

"A wonderful man! Simply wonderful!"

"Did Maman give you a few extra denarii to say such?"

"Of course not! I merely don't want to let an opportunity like this pass you by."

"Matchmaking, are we?"

"Yes, and don't make any mistake about that. Sir John is the finest available man in these parts, my lady. You would do well to—"

"*You* would do well to remember that my marital state is only my business, Margery."

"But my lady—"

"Enough. I agree, Sir John is indeed a wonderful man. Comely, chivalrous, talented, and strong."

"He's your warrior poet, my lady. Think about it!"

"He's old, Margery. Why would a man like him be interested in a girl like me? Our status cannot compare to his. Besides—" The rumors of his wife's death resurfaced in her mind.

"Besides what?"

"Never mind. It's really none of my business, and not my place to say anything about. The fact is, he's too old, too experienced, and too esteemed to be interested in me, Margery. I'm the daughter of a lord who only just received his title. Hardly a long lineage to attach himself to."

Margery's black eyes sparkled. "I've worked for people with long lineages. They're just like everyone else, only they haven't the sense to realize it. Sir John doesn't seem the type to fool himself with grandiose delusions. I'm sure if you invited him to call here again, he would come."

"I don't think I'll have to do that."

"And why is that?"

"Because Maman is already conjuring many ways for the two of us to find ourselves alone together. And to be honest, I'm still fairly sore in both heart and body from this recent ordeal. I would rather she did all the work. Even if it is, in the end, for naught."

"You underestimate yourself, my lady. But then, as I've always seen it, the best of women always do."

TWENTY

The beautiful creature came up to us,
   Clothed in white, and in his face,
Something of the trembling of a morning star.

He spread his arms, and then he spread his wings;
He said: "Come: the steps are close by here,
And now you will find that they are easy to climb."

For this invitation few are chosen:
O human race, born to fly upwards,
Why do you fall at such a little breeze?

—from Purgatorio XII

The sweat froze on John's brow as his fervent prayers became even more intense. He knew the signs. Had seen them before on his travels and even here in England.

"Please, gracious Lord, don't let this be happening."

Was this merely a little breeze meant to test his faith in the One who had opened his heart to another of His creations? He prayed desperately that this was what it was. And he knew faith was rewarded, that miracles were possible. That her symptoms were from something else was his hope. And hope was something he surely understood. Sometimes it was all that was left to a man on the field of battle, and he had learned to cling to it years ago—not as a man relying on it because he was weak, but as a strong man who knows that he could never be his own source of strength.

He had come directly to the chapel upon his arrival from Durwin Manor. And, unbeknownst to him, a vigil began, for now the sun was beginning to rise across the land. How had the night passed so quickly? He remembered many such nights, including the long night in the abbey, spent on his knees and holding his sword, before he was knighted by King Edward himself. Prayer was not a foreign thing to Sir John. It kept him from being as lonely as everyone thought he was.

God was there.

He arose, promising to return that night for Johanna's sake and, he had to admit, his own. He couldn't lose her now. They belonged together: the fair young maiden and the grizzled, scarred old beast. Looking back at the small altar one more time, he prayed again quickly that it would be so.

~ ~ ~

The countess reached forward and picked up a plum. "He's been to dinner there twice now, Rosamunde. Do you think she's softening toward him?"

"I don't know. He's so much older than she is, and although that has never bothered me with Gordon, I think it does with her."

"Why? John is so fit and a fine specimen of manliness."

"*I* know that! What woman with a little experience wouldn't? However, she's never let herself get at all close to a man before and has always turned them away before she could really get to know them. She isn't capable of recognizing such a jewel."

"Well, he is that."

"Perhaps," Rosamunde hesitated, "perhaps she feels Sir John would never be interested in *her*. After all, he is of a higher social standing and is experienced in all manner of life."

"That's ridiculous! Johanna is a lovely girl. Anyone can see that!"

"*I* think so. But we both know her well. And you must admit, it isn't as if the Durwins go back to the Conqueror. I'm actually surprised you're encouraging him to marry so far beneath him."

The countess waved a hand. "Why is it so surprising? I only want John's happiness. He was never the same after his parents died. It matters not if the woman isn't the daughter of a duke or an earl. If I wait for such, he'll die without knowing real love."

"And you believe my Johanna is capable of giving that to him?"

"I do. She's waiting for someone, Rosamunde. She always has been. And it is John. He would be kind to her . . . a good husband."

Rosamunde swallowed hard and asked the next question. She had a right to, as Johanna's mother. "But what of his first marriage?"

"It was many years ago, Rosamunde. He was only 20 at the time. I never really knew what went on there."

"So most of what I hear is rumor?"

"Some of it. All I know is that when John was with Elaine, she never so much as touched him, looked at him, or gave him a smile. She was a cold girl—given to petulance when she didn't have her way. Most times it was as if he didn't exist."

"He would never talk about it?"

"Not John."

Rosamunde sighed, assigning the topic a far corner of her mind to be brought out later on that day. "I suppose not."

The countess perked up and reached forward to pat Rosamunde's hand. "As I said, my dear, that was many years ago. I've seen his eyes when Johanna's name is brought up. Something is definitely there. Now," she most decisively changed the subject, "let me tell you about the letter I received from Marchemont Castle the other day."

"News about Geoffrey?"

"Heavens, no! They've graciously agreed to send up someone from their staff who has been training under their cook for years! Isn't that wonderful news?"

"I should say so, my lady!"

"He's costing me a pretty fortune so I'm going to plan a proper feast and invite everyone I can think of!"

"Then I'll be there ready to experience a true delight of the palate."

The countess chattered on, and Rosamunde nodded at all the right places, but now that her hopes of making a marriage were finally taking shape, she couldn't help wondering if John was really right for her daughter. She would have given anything to know what had actually happened all those years ago between him and Elaine.

❧ ❧ ❧

The fire was a mass of glowing coals on the hearth. Sir John sat with Duncan, talking quietly. It was raining too hard to be outside. Their words were hushed, neither wishing to disturb the servants sleeping all around them on the floor of the great hall.

"Do you think I'm overreacting, old man?"

"Nay. But it sounds as if even she doesna know what is happenin' to her. Ye need to check her arms."

"How? I can't very well meet her and say, 'Would you mind pulling up your sleeve so that I can look at your arm?' Can I?"

"Ye may have to."

"I was hoping there would be another way."

"I'm sorry, lad."

"So am I, Duncan." Sir John stared sightlessly into the fire. "I'll send her a message in the morning, ask her to meet me in complete privacy at the stream."

"Meet it head-on, lad."

"That's always been the way, old man. A grievous thing to be a man."

"I'm sorry, my lord. You of all people deserve to love."

"But it seems as if it will elude me forever."

"Don't forget about your faith, my lord. These are the times when we must cling to it for comfort."

Sir John stood to his feet, tired and weary, but he walked through the rain anyway and into the chapel to keep the appointment he had made that morning with the only One who could do anything to help him now.

❧ ❧ ❧

Margery shook Johanna gently. "My lady!" she whispered loudly. "Wake up. I've a message for you."

Johanna sat up slowly, leaning upon her hands which were both feeling very numb. "Who is it from?"

"It came from Castle Chauliac."

She reached forward and broke the seal, her eyes quickly scanning the parchment as Margery sat next to her, awaiting the report of the contents. "It's from Sir John. He wants me to meet him down at the stream, at the waterfall, right after I receive this. Did the messenger stay for an answer?"

"No. He handed it to me and left."

"Well, up quickly then. I'll hurry. Men like him don't like to be kept waiting, and as he's been nothing but kind lately, I believe I'll favor him with a speedy arrival."

"Do you wish for me to accompany you, my lady?"

"No. The message said for me to come by myself."

"You don't think it has anything to do with . . ."

"The knight? Perhaps. It is my hope, much to my own dismay."

A quarter of an hour later Johanna was walking across the meadow. When she entered the woods and arrived at the stream, Sir John was waiting for her. She looked upon him from afar as he sat staring out beyond the stream, a brooding expression sitting heavy upon his brow, deep in thought. The woods were still dripping moisture from the rains the night before.

It had been quite a storm that ravaged the land after John took his departure from Duncan. He had felt the stone walls of the chapel shiver under its impact as he spent the night in prayer. And down beneath the waterfall, the opening to the cave was once more concealed.

"Sir John!" she called cheerfully, trying right away to set a more jovial tone. He stood immediately to his feet and bowed slightly from the waist.

When she arrived at his side, he took her hand and bowed again. "Thank you for coming, my lady."

"Certainly, Sir John. I must say that your note made me most curious. What is it that is so urgent you wish to tell me so early in the morning?"

He took a blanket down from Gale and spread it by the banks of the stream. "Here, sit upon this. The ground is still wet."

"Thank you. It's getting cooler now, isn't it? I suppose my knight and I wouldn't have been meeting much longer."

"No. 'Tis true enough. But I didn't summon you to talk about the knight."

Her heart sank.

Sir John drew in a massive breath, gathering fortitude for what he was about to do next. "Lady Johanna, may I see your hand again?"

Johanna chuckled and put it into his grasp. "Is that why you brought me here, to hold my hand? Or are you still concerned about the wound?"

"Indirectly." He undid the bandages. "You say it's healing fine?"

"Yes. Every night and in the mornings Margery tends to it for me."

"Good. Is it still stiff today?"

She nodded. "Even more so, and my fingers keep wanting to curl upward. I've never experienced anything quite like this. I fear I shall have to lay aside my tapestry for a while for all the good I'm doing it. The going is extremely slow."

"Johanna, would you lift up your sleeve so that I might see your arm?"

"What? Sir John, this is all becoming a bit unusual, even for me. I don't understand what you are doing."

"I have a good reason. Please, Johanna, do as I ask. I want to look above your elbow."

"Only if you lift up your sleeve as well," she said in a joking manner, but meant it completely.

"If that is your wish."

Together they tugged on their sleeves, each pulling the fabric up over their arms. Both gasped as the forearms were revealed: one thin and feminine, one muscular and masculine. One bearing pale patches, slightly raised and well-defined, illumined by the morning sun and Sir John's examining eye. The other bearing a thick, ropy scar that looked like a snake.

❧ TWENTY-ONE ❧

ords failed her as she stared down at his arm. Her hand went forward of its own volition as if it remembered what the hideous scar felt like under her fingertips. *Serpentine.* Wasn't that what she had called it? Several seconds passed, Sir John not realizing the reason for her quandary until he looked up and saw how her eyes were imprisoned in their own line of sight.

Beneath the gentle touch of her fingers his corded muscles tensed, then relaxed as the exploring hand traced upward and her eyes stared in fascination at what she had felt but never seen.

"It's you."

"What do you mean?"

"The scar. The snake scar. I've felt it many times, you know." Her words were lighter than the atmosphere, breathless. She didn't know whether to love him or hate him just then.

"I wanted to tell you, Johanna. But I knew you already hated me . . . who I really am."

Then her blue eyes looked up into his. They locked together in a gaze so full of deep intent and instinctual knowledge it was as if she had always known he was her heart's only

206

love, that only him was she capable of loving. She couldn't understand why she didn't realize it before.

"I *know* who you really are, Sir John. You *are* the knight of the cave."

"I'm also Sir John, a beast of a man."

"To others, perhaps. Not to me."

"Never to you, my lady. Never again. Walking away from the cave that last time was the hardest thing I've ever done."

"But you came back. Dressed as Sir John, admittedly, but *you* came back. It was always *you* from then on, wasn't it?"

"Yes."

"How could I have not known? You made sure I was going to be all right. So caring. So kind. Worried about my hand..."

Her arm. She remembered and looked down.

It bore a large patch of pale on her forearm and one above her elbow which worked its way around to the back of the arm. The affected skin was dry as the sweat glands were destroyed, and there was no hair on her arm where the condition had taken over, literally squeezing the life out of the follicles. She bore the peculiar marks of someone infected with leprosy.

But she didn't realize this.

"I'm still not sure I understand why you wanted to see my arm, Sir John. Did you know about my skin condition? Margery and I only discovered it a few weeks ago, and I can't imagine she said anything to you about it."

"No, my lady. Margery said nothing. Is there anything on your other arm like it?"

She pulled up her other sleeve right away. Nothing.

"You have me most intrigued now, Sir John. I've had many men make advances toward me, but this is surely the most unusual!" Her words were bright, but his expression was not, and she noticed right away. "What is it? You've something to tell me, don't you?"

"Have you ever come into contact with a leper?" John asked abruptly, knowing no other way to ask, hoping the answer was no.

Johanna's eyes widened. *Leprosy?* But the memory was still firmly embedded in her mind, and she nodded slowly. "Yes, when I was 12." She remembered that day in the hut as clearly as if it had happened only moments before. She told him of the bloodshot eyes of the leper as he screamed in her face, his saliva spattering onto her ... the water bucket and how she had drunk from its contents with his dipper.

His eyes became transparent in their expression, wide corridors to his heart lined with pain. "When you told me you couldn't feel any pain from that horrid burn, I suspected it. Your fingers stiffening and curling up was more evidence that it might be so."

"You must be wrong, Sir John. It cannot be leprosy. Perhaps it is just a malady of the skin ... some sort of growth. See? 'Tis just an acute drying. Margery has been telling me that if I don't tell Maman about it soon, she'll do it herself. Surely I'll have to see a doctor right away! I simply refuse to believe it's leprosy. He'll know what remedy will clear it up."

Sir John suddenly clung to a bit of hope as well. Perhaps Johanna was right. If she was, it would make all the difference. "Come then, my lady. We'll go to Castle Chauliac right now and have our physician examine you. Will you do that for me?"

She remembered well their talks in the cave, the love she had felt emanating from him through the darkness, the love she felt coming from him now. "Yes, Sir John. I will. For you. Take me there right away."

❧ ❧ ❧

"How could I have missed such a thing? I don't know what to say ... what to think ... oh, my Lord ... oh no." The words tumbled from her mouth as she sought to grasp the situation but couldn't, and really didn't want to for that would make it real. The doctor had gone from the chapel where she was examined, head bowed in sadness that he had been the one to diagnose the bright young woman's condition. It was as Sir John had said.

The knight stood before her now, holding her healthy hand in his. "Johanna, I'm sorry. I wish I knew what to say, what to do."

The world imploded. It suddenly occupied a smaller space than Johanna ever would have thought possible. Everything she knew and loved was slipping away. And all that was left to her was a man she barely knew, and yet the man with whom she had fallen in love.

Just then even that wasn't enough. And all the strength she had exhibited throughout her life fled from her. The fiery gleam which warmed the icy blue of her eyes died, and she crumbled to her knees on the dusty stone floor.

Death, hovering like a great winged bat, her only comfort now.

A sighing groan escaped from her lips as inside of her the tears began to collect behind the dam of her self-control. Seconds later they burst through, and silent sobs convulsed her body as her hands reached up to cover her face. They were shaky and clumsy, yet guided her closed eyes to a firmer darkness. Colors and patterns whirled and danced a macabre composition the harder she pressed down.

Sir John, having seen such collapses many times before, knew, as he did when he told mothers of their sons' death, that it was best to wait. That it was futile to try and pull them from their sudden, newfound world which overwhelmed and disturbed every fiber of body and soul. A world where reason and light and possessions and people were abandoned and all that remained were pulsations of feeling, waves of emotion crashing ceaselessly, relentlessly, terrifyingly.

And so he waited. Not helplessly, but lifting his soul in prayer to the only One who could help Johanna now. After what seemed a long time, he noticed a change in her weeping as reason mingled with the helplessness. The silent sobs began to dissipate to a slow rise and fall of the shoulders, and her voice returned with soft cries. It was then that he moved forward, crouching down beside her, tenderness outlining every movement of his body, every feature of his face labeled with concern.

She accepted his embrace, her body yet stiff, but as the morning waned, her muscles slowly began to relax. And her body yielded, curving into his, her head burrowed into his chest. The crying ceased finally, as he knew it would, and he continued to wait, patiently and in love.

She raised her head. "I thought I had escaped it because I hadn't contracted it before now."

"Sometimes it takes many years for the disease to manifest itself."

"You're in danger, Sir John."

"I don't think so, my lady. I've been exposed many times before, and it came to nothing. That matters not. I wouldn't trade these times with you. What will be will be, for we are in God's hands. And God may yet give us that miracle we talked about."

But Johanna did not believe him on any count. "I must leave Durwin Manor. My parents will be in danger now that the disease is manifest. Poor Margery—she's been taking care of my hand. Do you suppose she's . . . ?"

"I don't know. You must warn her."

Johanna shook her head almost violently. "I cannot go back! You understand that, don't you? I will not put my family in any more danger. Papa is an old man . . . and Maman . . . Oh, Sir John. Where am I to go? I must show myself to the priest, then what? Where do women lepers go? Must I wander the countryside alone?" And Johanna wept again, bitter tears, despite the fact that she tried to control her emotions. John reached for her and once again tried to wrap her in his scarred arms.

But she pushed him away.

"No! Stay away from me!" She wanted to scream as the leper had done to her so many years ago, " 'Leprosy! Leprosy! Get out!' "

John would have none of it. Despite her protests, he pulled her into the large circle of his arms, holding her against him, her cheek against his chest. "I'll protect you, Johanna. As long as I'm around, you'll not be alone."

She pulled back. "It cannot be that way, Sir John. The spell of the cave is broken. The enchantment is gone. You're just old Sir John, and I'm a leprous young woman. I must go somewhere. Can you not tell me where I can go? Surely there is a lazar house somewhere nearby, isn't there?"

Sir John looked upon her compassionately. "I know of a leper hospital near London, Johanna. St. James the Less. It's for young women."

"You must take me there, Sir John."

"I can take just as good care of you myself, if not better, my lady. And what of your parents? Surely they don't wish to be cut off from your life completely. They've the wherewithal to build you your own little house on a secluded part of the manor. You will be well provided for that way."

"Thank you, Sir John. But I will not make myself a danger to you or them. Will you take me there? To St. James? Today?"

"I will do as you ask only because I know you won't be talked out of it. It is a terrible life you are asking for, Johanna. With winter coming—"

"I care not! I must protect my family. And I must protect myself, for I do not think I could bear to be so near to those I love and never again touch them or feel their arms about me. I do not wish to be remembered as decayed and worn, but as young and . . ." her voice caught as she projected herself into the future, "beautiful. Please, Sir John, you must do as I ask. And if you do not, I'll find a way to get there myself."

"I said I would take you. But only on the condition that you tell your family before you go. We'll take a carriage around to Durwin Manor. You'll want to pack an extra gown and some warmer clothes for the coming winter. The conditions will be most rudimentary, Johanna. If you want, I can always return later with your books."

She nodded. "All right, I'll tell them. They'll need that."

"I'll order the carriage."

"I want to make this as easy on them as possible. I want it to be done as quickly as possible."

Their eyes locked, and he again understood her completely and she him, as they always had. "I couldn't bear a long, tearful good-bye either, my lady. I will never leave you, Lady Johanna. I will be with you at every step."

❧ ❧ ❧

> Crushed and amazed I turned to my guide,
> Just like a little child who runs to find
> The person in whom he has most trust.
>
> —Paradiso Canto XXII

Margery stood as a stoic, her emotions too great to flow out of the small opening of her great humanity. Ned held a sobbing Lady Rosamunde in his arms, and Lord Clifton, pale and misplaced, looked as if time was choking him, clutching at his throat with taloned fingers, aging him drastically with each minute that passed. Johanna looked out of the carriage at the four of them.

No one waved or smiled.

Her eyes smarted and burned as she turned away, hot tears scarring her cheeks. Her heart still beat forcefully as the fear which had thrown its grappling hooks into it when she looked upon her arm continued to pull her down in the bowels of its own peculiar darkness.

"No more crying." Alone in the carriage, she said the words aloud.

Sir John rode alongside on Gale, looking in the window every several minutes, making sure she was all right. It was all happening so fast. She understood his need to be outside, not cooped up in the vehicle where he must engage in sympathetic conversation, yet knowing not what to say.

In a way she was glad to be alone.

Strapped to the top of the carriage was her wooden trunk. It held several changes of clothing, her winter cloak, warm boots, hosen, and Dante's *Divine Comedy*. Fresh rags and healing ointments were cradled among the softer items. Margery neatly folded her warmest blankets and laid them on top of the contents. She didn't know in what conditions her lady might find herself, and she prayed she was sending her off well-prepared. Even as she did so, she wondered how soon it would be until she followed the path, for surely she had caught the disease sometime over the past three years. Perhaps Margery would escape it as John had.

The needlework was left behind. No use. She would never ply her needle with any kind of skill again, and Johanna decided firmly she would not fumble along pathetically at what once gave her so much satisfaction. It was best to remember the beauty, not prolong the decline. The Black Prince himself meant little anymore, and yet, he signified so much.

She closely examined her hand.

It looked the same for the most part—the thin fingers with the short nails that always seemed to collect a small bit of grime from somewhere, much to her chagrin. She had made a habit of picking at her fingernails ever since she was a child and began to do so now, holding her hand out flat every so often to stare. The tendons flared, spokelike, from her wrist to her fingers, poking up through the thin, yet pliant skin which covered the back of her hands. One ring, an oval sapphire, circled her left forefinger, the gold and blue standing out against her white skin. Blue veins made a bumpy path over the tendons, up toward the gently protruding knuckles.

She had never seen a leper's hands, but she had heard descriptions of them. The way the fingers literally disintegrated from the infection, as the leprosy eroded the soft tissue and bones, the remains of the fingernail ending up somewhere near the knuckle. Ulcerated, sore, stinking. It forced a shudder to radiate out from her inner chest and down her appendages. Johanna had never really thought much about hands, had taken for granted that they would continue to serve her without complaint until some other, innermost portion of her body gave up on the prospect of living another day.

Yet she stared on at her hands imagining, wanting nothing in the future to come as a surprise, wanting never to have to say, "I never thought it would be like this." She tried to imagine the horrors, the debilitation, the slow decline. Johanna hardened her head, if not her heart, and determined that she wouldn't take this as a weakling who gave up right away. Her life was worth much, whether anyone else thought so or not. And where she was going, her very life was all to which she could lay claim, and only that.

"Charm is deceitful, beauty is vain . . ."

From his mount, Sir John watched her staring at her hands. He didn't know her thoughts, but his own trailed down much the same path as hers had. The fingers would become more clawed with time, practically unusable. More patches would most likely appear on her legs and her other arm, perhaps her face, causing paralysis. *Oh, Johanna.* He was blind to the scenery before him and saddened that what would ultimately keep them apart was even now bringing them together.

The hours passed slowly. Johanna was able to doze, exhausted by her emotions. John wanted desperately to be

214

beside her, to cradle her head upon his chest, to have her feel his warmth, to assure her that she would in no wise be deserted.

There was still time to reverse the direction of the carriage. To take her up north with him to Seforth Castle and care for her there. It was a much more pleasing prospect than the course of action Johanna had chosen to take. Life in a leprosarium was far from pleasant, he knew that much. And if the disease didn't kill Johanna, the physical hardships and rigorous routine might do the job on their own.

He recalled hearing about a lazar house at Kingston where, near the beginning of the century, they rioted against the strictness of their regimen, actually destroying their own hospital. Sir John couldn't imagine such desperation. It took all of his self-control not to command the carriage driver to turn the vehicle around. But he knew Johanna's dignity must be preserved. The only decision now left to her must be hers alone.

Prayer was her only redress for the misery Johanna was about to face. If he could have, Sir John would have risked his very life to have taken the disease from her. Those beautiful hands that he had held so often in the darkness of the cave should not, before death, go the way of all flesh. How long before the rest of her would follow and decay in the grave?

Johanna had that precise notion as well, wondering when it would all be over. The beginning of the end had come upon her, at the age of 18.

ক্ষত ক্ষত ক্ষত

The sun was beginning its descent when Johanna was awakened by the cessation of the carriage. Sir John's face appeared at the front opening of the vehicle. "We must rest the horses. Will you come out?"

"Yes."

He reached forward with his hand to help her, but she ignored it, grabbing onto the foremost tilt and pulling herself out in one motion.

"I have a little food."

"No. I don't want to eat."

"I assumed as much." Sir John wasn't hungry either, but he took out some bread and broke off a piece, knowing that hunger made him irritable, and he couldn't afford that on a mission like this. "Would you like to walk a bit? I see an orchard at the edge of that meadow there."

"Yes, let us go there. The horses have to drink anyway, do they not?"

He nodded, and they began to walk forward. Sir John knew he needed to speak to her now. She needed to be assured that he still cared for her even now, and always would. "Did you bring your quill and ink? Some parchment?"

"I believe Margery packed some writing supplies."

"Good. You must write to me."

"As long as I can, I will."

The hands.

"I'll be a faithful correspondent. I'm not usually good at that sort of thing, but this is different. It's you."

"You have a poetic soul, I believe. I'll enjoy reading them."

Her sad attempt at looking for a bright spot wrenched his heart.

The meadow grasses smelled sweet, the tall clover brushing against them as they trod toward the orchard. Silence reigned once again, but neither was uncomfortable, for a future between them, however undetermined regarding duration, had been secured.

"You won't be alone, my lady," he promised.

"Do you speak of God?"

"God and myself. For no matter what happens, my heart lies in your hands."

"Dying hands, Sir John."

"All hands are dying, Lady Johanna. But the soul is another matter. It is only the soul which divides a man from his Creator, only a soul which brings him to God's heart. For that reason a dying soul is most grievous to bear."

"Then I am twice cursed."

He stopped. "A dying soul can be easily healed, Johanna. Never forget that, no matter how your body weakens. You have only to trust in God."

"I wish I had a faith such as you, Sir John. But I'm afraid I do not."

But John wasn't daunted. He just purposed to pray for her yet more. And he had every confidence that God in His mercy would reveal Himself to her.

TWENTY-TWO

Sir John!" Johanna called out of the carriage window. "Are we nearing Westminster?"

"Yes, my lady. Very shortly."

"Might we stop at the abbey?"

"As you wish. May I ask why?"

"To say good-bye to the prince." *And many other things*, she thought.

"All right. His body will be taken to the abbey at Canterbury shortly to be entombed."

"Then our timing is perfect."

Both thought the statement absurd but didn't say so.

❧ ❧ ❧

Once again Johanna alighted from the carriage, realizing that it had been less than two months since her feet had touched down on this portion of earth which surrounded the abbey. She never expected to be back so soon, and not under the present circumstances.

Sir John was at her elbow. "Shall we go in?"

"Thank you."

Through the north entrance they walked, beneath the giant rose window whose small panes of blue, red, yellow, and green shed dappled light of many hues upon the stone floor of the transept during the day. But darkness had fallen several hours before. What was a noisy place, the bustling activity of all manner improving the abbey literally before the eye, now lay still. Painters, busy creating masterworks on the walls and on the other side of the wooden partition which stayed off the dust of new construction from the now older section, had cleaned their tools. Great poundings and orders being called were silenced, just the memory of an echo now. The masons' yard, tucked outside in the corner where the north transept and the nave met, was quiet, the dust settled on the blocks and carvings in a grainy, deadened film. The workers had gone home for dinner and were probably fast asleep in their beds.

John escorted her up to the bier which lay in front of the high altar. The body of the prince was now held in its coffin.

"Why must he lie in state for so long?" she whispered to Sir John.

"All must know he is truly dead. No imposters must come along later, claiming to be Edward and so seek to take the throne."

"Which was why they paraded the body in the streets of London soon after his death."

"Yes."

"Seems a pity that one who lived such a noble life must be on public display in death. Hardly fitting for bones and dust to be leered at by the masses."

" 'Tis the way of it, Johanna. And his soul lives on."

"Will you be at the funeral when the time arrives?"

"I will be with the procession from Westminster to Canterbury. 'Twill be next week."

"He would have wanted you there, for you were his friend, were you not?"

"I would like to think that. There were many others who bore more weight in counsel with the prince."

"But none more dependable to loyally carry out his orders."

"Perhaps not. Although you make me sound like some sort of pet."

"No, no. Never that. Just responsible."

" 'Tis my nature."

"Then it's a good one, Sir John."

"Not always. I tend to have the same expectations for others as I do for myself."

"Geoffrey?"

"Especially Geoffrey."

"I remember when I was here with him. It was the first time I saw you, Sir John. You looked imposing and brooding and broad."

"Forgive me if I unwittingly put you off, my lady."

She quickly shook her head. "No. No. You still look all three of those at times, but I feel as if I know the inside of you now."

"You do, Johanna."

"Will you come and visit me at the hospital?"

"I couldn't force myself to stay away."

"I know. That makes me happy, Sir John. And yet I grieve for you almost as much as for myself."

"Why is that, my lady?"

"It would be better if I died quickly. Then you would not live your life in hopes that I will become better."

"Never say that, my lady. If there is a reason to hope, there is a reason to live. It is hope alone that has kept me alive. Hope borne by faith."

"You love well the church then?"

"Not merely the church. I just try and be faithful to God."

"A living soul?"

He smiled and nodded once. " 'Tis my prayer."

"Do you come here often?"

"When I'm in London, yes. It calms me for some reason. It is the embodiment of the cross and the hope of the resurrection."

"Do you pray much, Sir John?"

"It is my prayers which give me the hope through which I live, my lady."

"Then pray for me, my knight."

He took her hand and turned to look at the high altar and the tomb of Edward the Confessor behind the screen. Miracles had supposedly taken place there. For a long time the recessed portions in the base of the raised tomb, cubbyholes for prayer, were always filled with pilgrims seeking a cure for their infirmities. But now the cult had lost its fervor. Still, if miracles had happened once, perhaps they could happen again. Somehow, the thought of a tomb holding a dead saint healing a woman of leprosy seemed too much to take seriously. He would have to go straight to the Source of all miracles.

The thought made him feel as if he bordered on blasphemy.

But his friend John Wycliffe would have greatly approved. And that made his normally dour mouth turn up at the corners just a tiny bit.

"What makes you smile?" Johanna asked.

"I was thinking of my friend John Wycliffe. A man of great prayer."

"Have him pray for me, too."

"I will. But will you not pray for yourself, my lady?"

She shook her head. "Nay. A woman of prayer I've never been."

" 'Tis a shame then. You must feel an awful weight upon yourself in regard to your destiny."

"I don't know what will happen when I die."

"I was talking about your destiny day by day."

"Well, if it's up to me, then I have no one but myself to blame or praise. I've always liked it that way."

John knew Johanna was heading down a long road now that she was so very ill. She would end up loving God or hating Him. But as her health deteriorated, she certainly could not remain indifferent. She was beginning to ask questions. Always the beginning of any change.

Her eyes were once again resting on the coffin. "Do you remember when we were in the cave and I asked you to tell me about the prince and the battles you fought with him?"

"Yes."

"When you come visit me, will you tell me about such things? Not because he fought there, but because you did. It will give me something to think about, and whilst I'll never be able to set the tales down upon my tapestry, I can still lay out the colors and the details in my mind."

"I'll gladly do it, my lady."

"I suppose I must go and show myself to a priest."

It was Sir John's last chance to try and change her mind. He turned her to face him, keeping his hands around her upper arms. "Johanna, it's still not too late for you to consider my alternative. I could take care of you myself. I have a castle up north, far away, secluded by the sea. We could go there. I'm sure Margery would accompany us."

"No, Sir John. I cannot. I will not do that to you."

"But I want you to, my lady."

"You do now. But how long will it last? As I progressively decline, it will not be so easy. I don't fully know what this disease entails, and I don't think you do either. Not really. My beauty will fade, and I cannot tell what will be left behind. No, I will go to a priest now, here, and take my vows."

She walked away. A lone figure down the vast, empty nave.

❧ ❧ ❧

Johanna was examined by a panel of clergy and declared an outcast.

By the time midnight arrived, she was taken before the altar of a side chapel and told to kneel down before the altar on a large swath of black cloth which was draped over two trestles.

Mass was said.

And she took communion through habit. It was part of being recognized as a leper as far as she was concerned—part of removing herself from the world, from harming others, from prematurely reminding them of the horrors of the grave.

Mass was over.

She stood up directly afterward and fresh earth was cast upon her feet, the priest's words sounding in her ears like the gong of a death knell: "Be thou dead to the world, but alive unto God."

And then the oath.

"Do you swear never to enter churches or go into a market, or a mill, or a bake house, or unto any assemblies of people?"

Johanna nodded solemnly, each shallow dip of her chin cutting her off further from society.

The priest continued, his voice monotone, hiding his revulsion at being so close to a leper, but trusting that God would aid his charity by keeping him free from the disease. "Also, I forbid you ever to wash your hands or even your belongings in a spring or stream of water of any kind, and if you are thirsty, you must drink water from your own cup or from some other vessel. From henceforth you are forbidden to go out without your leper's dress, that you may be recognized by others. And you must never go outside your house unshod. Also, I forbid you, wherever you may be, to touch anything you may wish to buy."

Johanna continued nodding, the back of her neck aching as the muscles tensed more and more with each word that shoveled yet another spadeful of dirt upon her grave.

"You must never eat or drink with clean persons, nor even talk to them unless standing to the leeward side. Never touch a child! You must always stand clear of strangers when begging for the scraps of food which must be thrown at you and not handed to you."

The priest handed her a warning device—a bell of wooden clappers—as well as the peculiar, distinctive hood and cloak a leper wore in public. "These are for the well-being of society," he said, "so they might know not to venture near you when you are among them. Do you take these vows, Lady Johanna Durwin, and promise to abide by the particularities therein?"

"Yes."

It was done. She was officially an outcast from society.

"Then we will find lodging for you," said the priest.

Sir John stepped forward. "I will be taking her to St. James the Less, Father."

"I do not know if there are any beds available in the hospital itself, but there are huts scattered about the woods nearby, and she will receive treatment."

Johanna shuddered, not daring to ask what the treatment would entail.

"You may go. Put on your hood and cloak as soon as you leave the church, Lady Johanna, and I charge you never to enter these doors again. Sir John, I shall pray God's mercy upon you."

Just then, the abbot himself, Nicholas de Litlyngton, stepped forward from the gloom beyond. He laid a kind hand upon her shoulder and looked with true caring upon her face. He said only these words: "Look unto God, sweet child." And Johanna was enveloped by a kind of love she had never experienced. A Christian love that loves beyond all boundaries and tears through walls, though he had never met her before. The love of Christ Himself—though she failed to recognize it for what it was.

So Johanna left the beautiful abbey behind. The abbot stood on the doorstep as she climbed into the carriage, and the priest joined him—a drab sentinel making sure she never returned to the land of the living.

When the carriage pulled up around one o'clock in the morning, the gates to the leprosarium were closed for the night. True exhaustion found Johanna, and a blissful sleep, dark and oblivious, came to rest upon her there inside the carriage.

A watchful Sir John spent the night outside, where he was most comfortable, yet sleep failing to bless him with its presence as he gazed at the gibbous moon, cracked and broken by the silhouette of the branches overhead.

❧ TWENTY-THREE ❧

"Unfortunately, we've no empty beds here in the main building," a pale young woman, seemingly healthy and clad in the gray robes of a nun, explained to Johanna, substantiating the words of the priest. Only three nuns were left at the hospital, and they nursed the 25 patients. "So many lazar houses have closed down since the plague, and the famine before that killed off a major portion of the lepers here in England. Many hospitals are being used for other purposes, so the few that are left are a little crowded."

"But you have room for her otherwise, Sister Magdalena?" Sir John asked.

"Yes. I'm afraid the only place available is in one of the huts. Unfortunately, you'll have to walk a bit to get to the refectory for meals, and," she shrugged apologetically, "they're not much to look forward to."

"May she have food brought in from other places?"

"No! Absolutely not! We have the women here on a strict diet. Anything of a rich consistency is strictly forbidden. And foods with anything other than a soft texture are also forbidden, as it makes sore mouths sorer."

Johanna was content to let him ask all the questions. It seemed to her that she had just landed herself inside a convent. And truthfully, the hospital was run very much like one.

"You'll arise for prayers when the bell tolls at 5 A.M. After that, the animals must be tended. We do have able-bodied hands for the bigger jobs—the harvesting and tending the pigs—but the patients take care of the smaller animals, the garden, and of course the fish ponds.

"We break our fast at 10, and then hear Mass at 11 in the chapel. After Mass we tend to the housekeeping here. You will be assigned several tasks which must be done daily. At 4 we have dinner, such as it is. We have one serving of meat or fish each day, and each patient is afforded one loaf of bread a day. Then the cleaning up must be done. After which, prayers are said, and you are then allowed two hours of free time until it is time to retire at 8 o'clock. You must have enough sleep. It lightens the sweat of any day, refreshes the patients for their labors, and keeps whole and sound the nature of both man and beast."

All during this time Sister Magdalena, hands folded crisply in front of her as she walked, a long chain with a cross on the end hanging around her waist, was showing Johanna the different rooms of the T-shaped complex. The refectory, and the dormitory where rows of beds would later be filled up for the night, made up the crossbar of the T, and the chapel the downstroke. Several beds were occupied by those who could no longer rise. The high-ceilinged church led directly into the dormitory so that the patients who were incapacitated could still benefit from the solace of the Mass, which was said each morning.

"I'll show you your hut," the young nun declared after they viewed the kitchen and stepped out into the garden, which was mainly a vegetable garden. "As you can see," her arm swept around, "we are one of the more heavily endowed houses in England. Fresh vegetables and meat are something that is uncommon in the poorer leprosaria. The prioress here, a leper herself, is most conscientious regarding the care of her charges. She is a noblewoman like yourself."

Sir John felt a little relieved at that. "There, Lady Johanna. Perhaps you will become friends."

Johanna said nothing, but observed closely her new surroundings.

"I'll go to the carriage and fetch your box," Sir John declared.

"And what is inside the box?" Sister Magdalena inquired.

"Blankets, clothes for the winter. A book."

The officious nun nodded her assent, and they waited for Sir John to return, the sister pointing out the boundaries of the land which the leprosarium owned. Sir John returned with the box on his right shoulder, and they began to walk toward a bit of woods. Quite sparse. "Anyway," the nun continued talking at full speed, as if her vow of poverty had until recently included silence as well, "the abbess has connections all over England with wealthy families, and she's done much to improve life here for all of the patients. I shudder to think what will happen when she dies." She spoke of death so easily that it temporarily jolted Johanna. But this woman was surrounded by death on a daily basis—of course it had lost its mystique.

They passed several huts, each with wooden sides and a thatched roof, a glassless window, and a door. "I'm afraid it gets cold in these in the winter, even more than it does in the hospital. It's a good thing you brought some extra blankets."

"May she light a fire?" Sir John asked.

"Yes, but she must collect the firewood on her own time. In the winter, with the darkness arriving so early, that is extremely difficult."

"I'll find the time." Johanna hated to be cold.

"May she have a lamp and a table? Is there a bed?"

"There is a small pallet. No lamps, no tables. I realize Lady Johanna is a lady of quality, but we cannot have an extra measure of discontent among the other inmates. All she'll be using this hut for is to sleep. Any other activities in which she might wish to indulge—writing, reading, and the like—may be done during her free time in the refectory. There are tables and lamps available there."

"Is there something to put over the window?" he asked, glad that winter wasn't upon them yet. It was actually a beautiful evening, though it felt like nothing of the sort.

"Yes, inside there are wooden shutters." They walked through the low door. "See?" she pointed to the plain wooden pieces.

"It won't do much to keep out the cold."

"Glass windows are too expensive," the nun replied. "And unless you wish to purchase them for all of the huts, the shutters must do."

"How many huts are there, sister?"

"Five."

"It shall be done."

"Thank you, Sir John, but I do not know who you will persuade to come and put them in," she shrugged.

"I'll find a way."

"You would be surprised what people will do for an extra denarius or two," she surmised.

"I'm counting on it."

"Well, St. James appreciates any sort of improvement, and glass windows in the huts will be most welcomed, if not a little fancy for our likes. But see here, I must show Lady Johanna where she will sleep."

Johanna looked around her dispassionately. In the past 14 hours, everything had become a means to an end. And yet deep inside, her strong will was at work, bidding her not to go quietly into that long good night.

The hut was even cruder than the one in which she had come upon the hermit six years before. The door hung sadly askew on its leather hinges. The floor—tamped-down earth covered with moldy straw—was littered with sticks and leaves from the woods, as well as small animal droppings. As predicted, there was no table, only two small beds supporting moldering mattresses. One of the beds had a dirty pillow and a jumbled wool blanket smeared across its soiled surface. The other held nothing but the straw-filled mattress.

"What happens in here when it rains?" John asked.

"I'm afraid it gets a bit damp."

That must be an understatement! Johanna thought wryly.

Sir John could hardly bear to contemplate leaving Johanna here. "Excuse us for one moment, Sister Magdalena," he said and ushered Johanna out of the hut. He turned to her and curled his hands gently around her arms, his eyes strongly imploring her. "You cannot stay here, Johanna. Please let me take you up north. I can't leave you here in conditions not even fit for my dog."

"I must stay."

"Why? You will not be endangering anyone in my castle! Please, see sense here, girl! This is a most foul existence you choose."

"I feel foul."

John felt a deep exasperation, but he didn't show it. "What must I do to persuade you?"

"Nothing. I must do this, John. Please, if you don't understand me, then I have no one."

He pulled her into an embrace, and she let him, despite the vow she had taken the night before. "You'll never be alone, Johanna. I promise you that."

She nodded and pulled away. His welcomed affection was making all this so much more difficult. "You had better go now."

"If that is what you wish."

"And I want you to stay away for two months, John. Let me get used to my new life fully and without ties to what might have been. Then . . . please come back to me."

"I'll return at the onset of October."

"Yes, when the leaves are falling."

He pulled her against him again and kissed the top of her head because he knew she would allow nothing more intimate. Not now. And he relished the feel of her small frame against his large one. There was nothing sensual in the embrace, merely an appreciation that just now she was practically the same Johanna he had fallen in love with. Her body would soon decay, and with that, God help him, he prayed that his love would grow stronger.

"When the leaves are falling," he repeated her words and, because he knew she abhorred long good-byes, left her standing outside the hut as the sun further lightened the horizon into a bluer shade of day.

Sister Magdalena issued from the hut. "Was he your intended?"

Johanna shook her head. "No. A friend. The only true friend I've ever really had."

"He'll come back."

"Yes. He will. He's even more chivalrous and loving than the knight in the cave was."

"My lady?" the sister questioned, but received no clarification from Johanna. "Come in now. While you were talking I made up your bed. It looks a bit more cheerful in here now that your blankets and pillows are brightening up the dreariness."

Johanna was too weary to even think that such an oversimplification of what could be beautiful in such an awful place was clearly suspect. Nevertheless, she followed Sister Magdalena inside. The sight of her own things, while they did little to cheer her, gave her a small sense of comfort, knowing she would never entirely divorce herself from the life she had left behind.

"Might I be alone?"

"There now, my lady," Sister Magdalena said with warm understanding, "lie here on the bed and rest. Your partner will be arriving shortly before bedtime. But I hope you will join us up in the refectory before then."

Lady Johanna Durwin wasn't of a mind to promise anything, but she did as the sister suggested, laying her head down on the pillow, hair going unbrushed for the first time in her life. *Margery, Margery*, her heart cried. *Where are you now?*

She slept.

Awaiting the funeral of the Black Prince, Sir John took up his lodgings at the de Shelley family's home in London. He ate a little food and tried to catch up on the missed night's sleep. An impossible undertaking. Finally, he arose and made a list of things to be done that afternoon. The first two items were to employ glaziers for the windows of the huts and thatchers for the roofs. Indeed, the small dwellings would be vastly improved. Beyond those two things, there was really nothing left he alone could do that wouldn't entail razing the little buildings completely.

After the list was made he fell to his knees and bared his weary soul to the One who made him, the One who understood his hurts and his fears, the One who knew him as no other had or ever would. Even though his only chance for an earthly love now seemed more elusive than ever, he knew that one day he would find fulfillment and the end of an aching heart that had begun to hurt 28 years before when he had buried his mother, father, sister, and brother in the dark, driving rains of plague-ridden England.

TWENTY-FOUR

The world does not remember them at all;
Mercy and justice treat them with contempt:
Let us not talk about them. Look and pass on.

—Inferno, Canto III, 49–51

A wretched day dawned in a spectacular fashion. The sky was painted the pale pink of a baby's lips and illumined from beneath the horizon by an expectant sun. But while it was yet dark the chapel bell had tolled, and Johanna was roughly shaken awake by her as-yet-unknown hut mate.

"Get up, *milady*," a wretched woman named Judith spat out. " 'Tis time to go pray to the One who judges us even now."

Johanna rose from the pungent-smelling cot, held her pillow to her, and breathed in the familiar odor of her loft at home. It seemed to give her strength, even as the 17-hour sleep had done. She shook her head as her eyes opened and her new home was once again revealed.

The woman stood there impatiently in the darkness, her body wired with annoyance. "Hurry now, or you'll make us both late!"

"Just a moment!" Johanna snapped as she would have done had Margery used such a tone. Nevertheless, she arose and followed the woman with whom she assumed she was supposed to become joined in some sort of marriage of the dying.

If the woman's initial greeting was anything to go by, life couldn't go by quickly enough. *But,* Johanna thought, at *least abiding with someone so contrary will keep me from growing complacent.* As if there was any worry there.

The light gray of Judith's gown was Johanna's only beacon through the darkness of the trees, and she stumbled along, fully awake, but feeling bleary inside, fuzzy and uncertain of what the day would hold. A leprosarium. She was actually in a lazar house waiting to die. Two mornings before, Margery had shaken her awake with a mysterious message to be read. She could hardly understand how such a small amount of time could wreak such unalterable change. No going back, and forward was just a downward progression. Johanna had reached the apex of her life unwittingly, without ceremony, without rejoicing in the moment. Like the rest of humanity. But somehow it seemed less fair.

She followed Judith into the chapel where the others gathered. The few candles that cast their pitiful light did little to chase away the gloom, and the hushed scraping of leather shoes across the stone floor sounded eerie, like a collection of furtive exhalations emitted by those inhabitants of the colony who had already passed on.

The abbess presently entered the room leaning heavily upon a crutch. She took up a prayer book, stood by a candle, and commenced with the daily ritual in the absence of the priest.

"In the name of the Father and of the Son and of the Holy Spirit . . ."

"Amen!" The room suddenly became a collection of live human beings.

Lady Johanna responded where she was supposed to. Kneeled when called upon to do so, but she remembered nothing of what really went on. Her mind was elsewhere, far away in a watery cave, or sitting quietly by a hearth fire with those she loved. Anywhere but here.

The next three days progressed much as Sister Magdalena had predicted, one activity flowing smoothly into the next. Disciplined, unbending, and as far as the food went, bland and unappetizing. Johanna flowed with the current, consuming the tasteless fare, quietly going about her chores, falling into bed at night without a thought as to what the next day might be like. Her caustic hut mate, Judith, was always ready with a sarcastic remark or two, perhaps an unfounded accusation. But even as conflict was something Johanna had enjoyed with Margery, Judith's gloomy acidity wasn't at all enjoyable, for her retorts were neither witty nor intelligent.

The fourth morning dawned like the others, but after prayers a younger girl, about 16 years old, approached Johanna.

"Lady Johanna?" she said hesitantly. "You are to come with me."

"Where?"

"To the infirmary. On the first Tuesday of each month, you're to consume a special broth. Your treatment begins this morning. I'm sorry." The apology sounded so dreadful. Nevertheless, Johanna walked beside her to the room situated between the dormitory and the refectory, wondering how the girl could sound so apologetic when she herself would be forced to drink the medicine as well. But medicine was medicine, and if it would help to slow the progress of the disease, she would consent to the process. Those first nights in the hut, remembering the faces of Papa, Maman, and Sir John, brought her to a resolution. She would rage against the dying of the light until her eyes were forever closed, frozen shut by the icy breath of death.

But until then the rage—a subtle, industrious anger—would warm her and keep the fire in her eyes burning mightily. It would keep her alive as long as possible. She would see to it.

As she passed along the way, the girl beside her nodded amiably to the other patients who limped by. All acknowledged her with a smile, distorted or otherwise. She was a transparent little figure actually, due to her unassuming walk, her forgettable coloring. As small as Johanna, yet dark where Johanna was pale, she was as sweet as Johanna had been spicy. Ida's fluid, brown eyes missed nothing, and the mouth which framed the crooked teeth told nothing. Yet deep inside a sense of the absurd was rife, and though most of her secret observations were inappropriate inside a leper colony, they did much to keep her own spirits high. Her black hair was impossibly thin, like most of the residents of the hospital.

Johanna noticed the raised bumps all over Ida's face—the disfiguring mask of the disease which so many of the others wore over what had once been youthful, healthy skin. It was just a matter of time until Johanna, too, donned yet another aspect of the leper: the facial disfigurement.

There were no mirrors at St. James the Less Hospital for Women.

But the reminders were everywhere, impossible to escape.

"Are you in much pain?" Johanna asked.

The question took Ida by surprise. She had already grown accustomed to Johanna being the silent one of the patients. "Sometimes the nodules on my legs pain me. They are red and deep and hard." A pause. "And I don't much care for them at all!" she joked with a decisive nod of her head.

Johanna felt her heart warm just a tad.

Ida continued. "But then, none of us do. Except your hut mate, of course. That Judith, I swear by all that's neither sacred nor holy, enjoys each and every stage of affliction that is brought on. Although I must say, her sickness doesn't seem to manifest any signs other than the white, dry patches of skin. Never have I known anyone to so relish the judgment of the Almighty!" she chuckled.

Judgment, thought Johanna. *Is that what this is really all about? Have all here offended God?*

Ida pushed the door of the infirmary open with so much gusto that it slammed into the wall behind it. The infirmarer jumped in surprise. "Little Ida, for the love of the church, how many times must I tell you not to open the door like that!" she bellowed, and Johanna started involuntarily at the loudness of this woman's voice.

Her dispirited iron-gray hair hung down her back like seaweed, and her nails were overly long and filthy. The body which housed the strident spirit looked like the top half of a skinny person was screwed onto the bottom half of a fat one. But it wasn't a pleasing roundness. Instead it was harsh, as though a pair of invisible hands were pushing up on her bottom from underneath, causing it to defy gravity. Eleanor was harsh in all aspects, and Johanna was soon to learn that she took little pity on those she served. She had been a servant at the hospital since before anyone else living there presently had arrived, and somehow she had managed not to contract the disease.

Ida waved a hand at the infirmarer. "Don't mind Eleanor. She seems as one having no compassion, but she's seen more of us die than anyone else. She likes us to think she doesn't care. But I know—"

"—better? Hah! You know nothing of the sort, Ida. Go ahead and leave Lady Johanna here with me. You've got plenty of things to keep you occupied without me having to remind you what they are! Out!"

"All right! Sometimes I think you enjoy this leprosy business as much as Judith."

"Out!"

" 'Bye, my lady," the girl said quickly and left the room, slamming the door behind her.

Eleanor jumped again at the sound, then turned to her new patient. "Well, well, we start the medicinal regimen today. I would apologize for it, but I'm not the type, and I didn't design the treatment anyway. I just dish it up." She turned to the smaller wall oven, where an earthen pot bubbled up a putrid-smelling concoction. With a wooden ladle she dipped into the thin mixture, pulled up a ladle full, and dropped it into a bowl, the cloudy mixture spilling somewhat over the sides.

"What—"

"—is it? It's ridiculous, is what it is. I've been serving up this slime for years, and I've never seen it do a bit of good to anyone. Here, drink it. Watch it though, it's hot."

Johanna felt herself bristling but forced her temper down. "What—"

"—is it? Oh, sorry. I forgot to answer, and here I thought by the looks of you that you'd be the stupid one between us. It's a special concoction. The flesh of a black snake caught in a dry area among stones is cooked in this pot here with some pepper, galingale, salt, vinegar, water, and oil."

"What!"

"You heard me."

"You can't possibly expect me to eat that!"

"Every drop. And I'll brook no argument, lady or not!" Eleanor's hands went upon her ample hips, and Johanna could see that this woman wasn't forced to endure the soft diet they were made to eat.

Johanna decided that even though it was the most revolting thing she had ever smelled, and would probably be the most revolting thing she would ever eat, she might as well get used to it. She had chosen to come here. They hadn't come knocking on her door begging her to live with them. Maybe it *would* do her some good, despite what crotchety old Eleanor said to the contrary.

She lifted the bowl to her lips and took a sip. The expression on her face told all.

"And it doesn't get any better, no matter how many times you drink it!" Eleanor informed her almost triumphantly. "Here, sit by the window and let it cool for several minutes. That way you can gulp it all down in less than a minute, instead of being forced to take little sips and prolong the agony. Besides, the taste of this mess is the least of it. Give it an hour or two to start to work, and you'll deem the taste a trifling nuisance."

Johanna took a stool by the window. Strangely enough, despite Eleanor's words, the awful taste made her feel alive again.

Another patient entered reluctantly and soon was standing next to Johanna, waiting for her brew to cool. In the midst of the misery of the treatment, those forced to suffer under it, gagging down the contents of their bowls, became more closely knitted by the window. Eventually three of them sat there.

"I'm Claire," a stunning, red-headed woman of about 20 said. "I've only been here two months."

The other girl introduced herself. "And I'm Agnes. I've been here for two years now."

"I'm Johanna Durwin." She purposely dropped the lady.

Agnes corrected her. "Oh, Lady Johanna. This must be quite a struggle to be here. At least we're among our own kind."

"The prioress is noble," Claire reminded her, "and I'm not exactly a milkmaid."

"But you're not noble, either. You're just rich," Agnes accused.

Johanna shook her head. "Does that really matter now? We're all lepers."

Claire shrugged. "I suppose not. But old traditions are not so easy to put away. We'll still call you Lady Johanna."

Agnes nodded.

"Well, that is up to you."

Agnes was always one to take the initiative. "We'll start introducing you 'round to the other girls."

"She might need more time to get adjusted," Claire interrupted the effusive plans. "I needed at least a month."

"No. No, I think I should like to get to know the others. I'm not the type to remain silent forever. Little Ida seems sweet. She brought me here to the infirmary today."

"Yes, yes," Agnes nodded. "A real dear. Anyway, you'll like most of the others. Unfortunately, you have to live with Judith."

"Dreary Judith," Claire agreed. "The judgment is here!" she mocked. "It's as if the New Testament had never been written. She would have been thrilled to have been captive in Egypt or Babylonia, and so be able to flagellate herself and everyone else around her."

"Is she a Jew?" Johanna asked.

"Heavens, no! She's not so jovial as that!"

It was the first time Johanna had laughed in four days.

Eleanor hollered, interrupting their sport. "Drink up, you birds! It's had plenty of time to cool down. I haven't got all day to sit around waiting for you to eat your soup!"

"Soup?" Agnes's heavy brows practically shot up to her hairline. "Is that what you call it? I would call it—"

"—quite enough! Just drink the mess and get out of here!"

⁂ ⁂ ⁂

Soon after drinking the broth, Johanna, Claire, and Agnes were told to go lie down on their pallets. Johanna found out why. She was barely through the door of her tiny dwelling, warmed by the afternoon sun, when a spell of such overwhelming dizziness attacked her brain with swirling colors and lights which seemed to rise from the base of her spinal cord to the frontal lobe of her brain.

She wheeled, grabbing onto the door frame, and lurched forward, hoping her bed was there to break her fall. It did, and Johanna gratefully closed her eyes against the vertigo. One of the nuns came to check on her an hour or so later, and Johanna was sleeping.

When she awoke later on, she felt strange, no longer like herself.

Judith sat in the middle of her bed, looking much like someone who was gloating over the spoils of war. She pointed to Johanna's legs and arms. "Look there, milady. They don't look much like *your* arms anymore, do they?"

Johanna gasped. For inside her body the broth was fulfilling its intended duty, causing tissues to swell, her body to bloat. It was horrible. "What is happening?" she cried, still feeling too weak to get to her feet.

"It's the broth. You're supposed to feel this way."

"That can't be right."

"Oh, it is. We all go through it every month."

"Will the swelling go down?"

"Of course. And then after that your skin will peel and your body hair will fall out. The hair on top of your head will fall out as well, but not completely. See?" She took off her hat, dropped her head and, much to Johanna's dismay, showed off several thin, balding patches.

"Does it grow back?"

"I guess it would if we didn't keep taking the medicine every month. Who knows?"

"Does the peeling hurt?"

"No. Not until they put the plaster on you to remove the dead skin. Now that's something to look forward to."

Johanna looked at her with disdain. "Haven't you got your chores to finish up for the afternoon?"

"Sister Magdalena told me to come check on you, *milady*. That's what I'm doing."

"Then go and tell her I'm as well as can be expected for a balding blowfish. I'm going back to sleep. At least this awful treatment provides one with a bit of a respite from the schedule."

Judith shook her head, her lips curled with distaste. "One day you'll find out that there really isn't a bright side here at St. James, no matter how hard you keep looking for it. And when you do, I'll be the first to congratulate you. You really are a horrible person to live with."

Johanna could hardly believe what she was hearing, but wasn't capable of a response until Judith had already left the room. And though it was the perfect rejoinder, it was simply too late. She went to sleep.

❧ ❧ ❧

Several days later, after going insane with itching, Johanna joined the others in the refectory for recreation time. The prioress had agreed to let Johanna keep her writing materials on a shelf in the refectory. Despite the difficulty she experienced at holding her pen, she began to write a letter to Sir John.

5 August 1376
The Hospital of St. James the Less

Dearest Sir John,
'Tis a wonderment to me that this day finds me with a willingness to pen to you warm words of appreciation and thankfulness, yet indeed it must be so. You have been a true friend to what has become a most wretched person, and I shall never forget the kindness you shewed me.

Whether or not this letter will find you in London or at Castle Chauliac I cannot predict, but my intense hopes are that it does find you healthy and content. You must rest assured that I am where I should be. Even as it took me just a bit of time to break through the heartache of the knight in the cave, so it was with this. What life is left to me must not be wasted. Indeed, when life is left at all in a person, that is a cause to keep on living to the fullest extent possible. But then, complaining about my circumstances has never really been my forte.

Many letters from myself will, hopefully, find their way into your tender hands, for my pen will not lie silent as I wait here at St. James. The prioress has graciously given me shelf space here in the refectory for my supplies so that I might correspond during our free time after supper. I'm finding even now that as I write I am transported back to Oxfordshire, and am actually sitting in the great hall of Castle Chauliac with you, watching your face as you read what is written on this parchment. Do you feel my spirit there beside you? In this there is great comfort, and I pray your indulgence on frequent communication from myself. In no wise do I expect you to return in kind, for I know you are a busy man with many responsibilities of the knightly variety. All I ask is that you remember me in your thoughts occasionally. You talk much about prayer. I ask you to remember me to God as well. Everyone here is always talking about Him. Play a song for me tonight.

Writing will become more difficult with time if my left hand becomes debilitated, but until I am no longer able to wield a pen, I will remain confidently your faithful correspondent and friend,

Johanna Durwin

TWENTY-FIVE

Lord Stephen was inspecting the new addition to Castle Chauliac when Norma found him. "Uncle, it's been two weeks now since he's taken anything other than water. I fear for him. The only time my brother emerges from his room is to go down to the chapel to pray."

"Did you try and take some dinner to him?"

"I brought a meal up to him several minutes ago, trying to coax his appetite, and when I knocked on his door and told him I had a tray of food, he thanked me but told me that such delicacies would only be wasted on him."

"'Tis a shame. He missed a good meal," Lord Stephen sighed. "But John must do what he feels he ought. Your father—quite austere, mind you, but very religious—always fasted when something bigger than himself emerged into his life. It doesn't surprise me that John has taken to doing the same."

"But his health, Uncle—"

"Will be fine. My nephew is strong. And do not forget: The food upon which he is subsisting now is of the heavenly kind. Do not worry, Norma. When the time is right he will begin to eat again."

"I suppose he feels there are more prayers to be said."

"Yes. And he loves her, you know."

Norma brushed aside a tear which had escaped her eye much too quickly. "I know. If only I could do something. To see John happy . . ."

Stephen put his arm around her bony shoulders. "It's what we've all wished would happen for a long time."

"And now it seems that it will never be, for I've always known that once John gives his heart away, it will be for good. If only he would rely on us a little bit. That's what family is for."

They stood in front of the new fireplace, carved pillars supporting the massive stone hood which projected from the wall. Already the walls were plastered, painted, and were now being decorated by an artist with a variety of stencils. "I think that's too much to ask of him, Niece. He's grieving, you know. He doesn't want our help, Norma. And I know that your greatest wish is that someday John would share with you his innermost soul. But he never will. John has always guarded his feelings with the utmost care."

Norma turned away, leaving the earl to admire the beauty around him alone. She couldn't blame her brother. They had never been great talkers, either of them. And it was hardest to bear when he was suffering. 'Twas the reason no one ever really knew what happened to his wife. Sir John had said nothing. No explanations. No words of self-exoneration. How helpless it had made her feel, knowing she could do nothing. But there was something she could do for him now, and she chastised herself for not thinking of it sooner. Exiting the new hall, she crossed the bailey and entered the chapel.

There was no surprise found within her when she saw John kneeling before the altar. He didn't look away from the crucifix when she knelt down next to him. He merely put his arm around her and drew her close to his side. "Pray, Norma," he said.

"I will." She bowed her head, and knew better than to ask what to pray for. The Lord Himself would have to take care of that.

❧ ❧ ❧

"It's no use." Gordon Durwin set down the book. "No matter what I read, it sounds like an imitation of the real thing."

No one argued, and the fire in the grate of the great hall continued to burn as it always had. Margery took control, signaling to the bard to come to her. "Play a soft, yet happy tune," she whispered, and he gladly did her bidding.

It made no difference. The atmosphere was just as desultory, just as grim. Before darkness had even settled down completely, Durwin Manor was closed up for the night—the lord and the lady, as well as most of their servants, seeking solace for their loss in the black oblivion of sleep.

Deep in the kitchen, however, Henry and Margery worked together. She read to him from several manuscripts, works of noted physicians, and they began to experiment. Surely they could come up with something to help Johanna. If not a cure, then a way to make her comfortable. They kept their activity a secret, not wishing for false hopes to flower in the bosom of their master. And as often happens in the midst of toil brought about by adversity, love began to blossom.

❧ ❧ ❧

7 August, 1376
The Hospital of St. James the Less

Dear Papa and Maman,
My fondest desire is that this letter finds you both well and comfortable. Our parting was full of sorrow, and had

I been able to make it happen under happier circumstances, I would have in all my power done so.

The hospital here is not as bad as I expected it to be, insomuch as I expected a hollow house filled with all the miseries of hell. Surely it isn't Durwin Manor, but you must not fear or worry over me and my present accommodations. My hut is quite rudimentary, but my hope is to be up at the main hospital as soon as the cold approaches.

Johanna set down her pen. True, she hoped such, but being the last to arrive, she would be the last to be given a bed in the dormitory. Still, best to let her parents believe that life was always improving.

My day begins at five A.M. with prayer, and it doesn't stop until 8 P.M. when I fall onto my pallet. I'm being given all manner of tasks to do, mostly the more exhausting ones, as I am one of the few whose condition allows such work. Myself and a fellow patient named Claire are the strongest here, and we do a lot of the cleaning. Oh, Maman, she is a beautiful woman, and her mother is French as well. Her hair is as red as flame, and when I think that her beautiful face will someday become disfigured, it makes me want to weep. Her green eyes will always be the same intriguing shade no matter what happens with the leprosy, and it is upon them that I try to concentrate when I'm thinking of her or talking to her. She's only been here a little over two months. We do much of the laundry as well, and the afternoons are spent pleasantly in the garden.

Again Johanna felt as though she were painting a lovelier picture than was the truth. The "afternoons in the garden" consisted of backbreaking work, bent over most of the time and weeding or picking the late-summer vegetables. Three hours of this each day would not have been easy on anyone. But their hands were in the best shape to do such work.

Tell Margery that I appreciate the healing salves and unguents she packed in my trunk. My burn is now completely healed, and I've noticed that it is easy to forget about being careful, and I've cut myself several times without realizing it. The little jars have been most useful. Sir John will be visiting me at the beginning of October, and if you would be so kind, may I have some more? I had to walk the food out to the pigs yesterday, and a stone had worked into my shoe. Little did I realize it until I took off my shoe last night and saw a bleeding sore from where the stone had lodged itself into my foot! I never felt a thing.

But despite my hands and feet, my parents, my heart is doing well. I have decided that I will not let this disease defeat me more quickly than it should. And so I take my medicine when asked, eat what is placed before me, and work as hard and furious as possible to stay the doldrums. I am lonesome for Durwin Manor and those that I love, but I go about my day with your faces in my mind, and it helps me tremendously to forbear.

You always have my love, and even here I'll remain in complete devotion, your loving daughter,

Johanna

◈ ◈ ◈

"Why dinna ye go up north?"

"What?" Sir John looked at his bard, mentally shaking himself back to the situation at hand. He had been remembering the words he read that day, penned by Johanna from the leprosarium. Her first letter.

"Go up north, to your castle there. You've got till October when you'll be going back to London. Ye need a cleansing of the mind, my lord."

"I know. I'm making everyone miserable."

"They're not used to seeing you like this. And I think they would be even more disconcerted if you were the cryin' type!"

John had to agree with the man. "Tears aren't for men like us," his father had said when Bridget had died and he hadn't been able to stop crying. She had been the first one to be taken down.

"There's much to be done with the garrison."

"But you've surrounded yourself with good men, able knights. They can take hold o' the reins for a wee bit."

Duncan was right.

"Perhaps it would be a good idea" was all the commitment Duncan could garner from the knight.

Nevertheless, when the soldiers in the gate house raised the portcullis and let down the drawbridge before the sun had arisen the next morning, only Duncan was present to say good-bye.

"If any news comes from Johanna," Sir John charged, "a messenger must be sent right away. I do wish you could come, old man, but I'm afraid the journey, hard as we'll be making it, would be your undoing."

"Aw, my lord, ye dinna need me. Ye'll just be needin' yourself and the Lord Jesus, and the fresh, crisp air of the moors. Go now. I'll be prayin' for both yourself and her lady-ship."

"Thank you, Duncan."

"Ye've got yer lyre?"

"Aye." Sir John motioned to his servant and his most faithful man at arms, and the three of them started on the long journey north. Sir John's belly was full for the first time in almost three weeks.

❧ ❧ ❧

Judith sat upon her dismal pallet, looking even more forlorn than usual. Johanna hurried into the dim recesses of the hut and proceeded to undress for bed. The evening was chilly and she was exhausted, wanting nothing more than to lie down upon the blanket and cover herself with the rest of the pile. Yet, for some reason, it didn't seem as chilly as it had the night before.

A solitary candle sputtered on top of Johanna's trunk.

"A candle, Judith?" She turned to her hut mate in surprise. "No dark vigil tonight?"

"Look." Judith pointed accusingly at the window, which now sported four panes of glass.

Johanna gave a small cry of delight. "He did as he promised. How wonderful! I thought it seemed a bit warmer in here. Won't you be glad for that window when winter comes fully upon us, Judith?"

Judith remained belligerently sullen. "Next thing you know, we'll be carpeting the floor and sleeping in beds with silken sheets."

Johanna began to get into bed. "This upsets you? How can that possibly be so? You'll be so much more comfortable now."

"We are not here to be comfortable. We are here to suffer."

"For what?"

Judith crossed herself. "For our sins."

"I might remind you that this isn't what I would call real comfort, Judith. The roof still leaks, our pallets are still filled with moldy hay, the rats get in through that hole there, and I've flicked more spiders and other insects off myself in the past fortnight than I would care to recall. A little slab of glass in the window does not exactly make this place in league with the king's palace!"

"Well ... *you* would know, mylady. All I know is I'm atoning here on earth, and you're making it that much harder for me. Always so cheerful when others are dying all about you. God is judging, mylady. And the sooner you realize that and accept the position He's given you here on this earth, the happier you'll be!"

"Like you?"

"Humph."

"Judith, you can believe what you will about God. But if your warped view of some Zeus-like being that throws bolts of suffering down from Mount Olympus is any indication of who God really is, I think I'll just go on 'not realizing my position on earth.' As far as I'm concerned, merely by being here and being afflicted with this horrid disease, I'm suffering far more than most people I ever knew. You may take comfort in additional scourging, but I do not."

Judith lay back on her bed and covered herself with her pitiful blanket, the two soft wool ones Johanna had laid at the bottom of the pallet pointedly ignored. "You shall see one day, mylady. You'll still be working out your sins in the flames, and I'll be in a much better place."

Johanna, now lying down as well, was too tired to argue. "If that makes you happy, Judith, by all means go ahead and believe it. But I'll tell you something: Even among death, one can learn many things, the chief of which is how to be kind and helpful. You despise me for my cheerfulness, but if I can bring a smile to the distorted faces all around me, then I, even though my knowledge of God is limited, think that makes Him happy."

I know it brings joy to me, she thought to herself, remembering that it wasn't that long ago she thought her life was completely over.

❧ ❧ ❧

Sweat poured from Johanna's forehead, and she wiped it away with her forearm after leaning the wooden paddle against the side of the laundry tub. "Go ahead, Claire, put in another sheet. I do believe it will be all right."

"Are you sure you can stir with that many clothes in?"

"Yes. I may be small, but I'm still strong."

Claire threw in a soiled sheet. "I think you're overdoing it. But go on, if you must. It means we'll be done all the sooner." She lifted another pot of water that was heating over the fire and poured it into the vat while Johanna began to stir the clothes again, the agitation mixing the soap well in between all the items. They had been at it all morning now, taking turns stirring or gathering water, or sorting garments and sheets into piles. Every Christmas the local bishop bestowed each patient with a new woolen tunic, and at Easter he did likewise by providing a linen tunic.

Claire leaned against the laundry wall, the cool stone beneath her sweaty back a blessing. "The bishop must be an awfully wonderful man to give out so many garments a year, but it makes the girls so much less careful about soiling their clothes. Thank goodness, we don't have to gather those as well," she breathed heavily.

"I think they're beginning to take advantage of our cheerfulness."

"Me, too."

"But at least we aren't nursing the sicker ones, Claire. I don't know if I could do that job very well."

"Or what Eleanor does." She shuddered. "Are you getting plastered today?"

Johanna nodded. She had been trying not to think about the painful procedure. "Yes."

"Isn't it awful?"

"Yes. So let's talk about something else."

"I agree. Why dwell on it?"

Ida walked into the room, limping more heavily than usual. "Good morning, everyone."

Johanna paused the heavy stirring. "Hello, Ida. What brings you here to see us humble laundresses?"

"I'm here to take your place."

Johanna was seized by a fearful dismay. "But I thought I didn't need to be at the infirmary until this afternoon."

"Oh no! 'Tis not that. The prioress wants to see you in her chamber."

She handed Claire the paddle. "Truly? I wonder what she could possibly want with me."

"Sneaking gentlemen callers in again?" Claire mocked.

"Yes. Dozens of them!"

Ida laughed and gave Johanna a gentle push. "Go on, my lady. She doesn't like to be kept waiting."

"Is she rather forbidding when you're alone with her?"

Ida shook her head. "I don't know. She rarely talks to anyone without Sister Magdalena around. Most likely she'll be there as well."

"Oh."

"Go, my lady!" Claire encouraged. "I'm sure there will be plenty of laundry left to do upon your return."

"That's what I'm afraid of!" Johanna said wryly, took off her apron, and left the room.

"I'll stir, Ida," Johanna heard Claire say. "You go ahead and continue the sorting."

Ida complied with relief. Last night her yearly autumn cold had begun, and she was feeling somewhat feverish and not at all well. Last winter her lungs had become so congested that the sweet child had nearly died. She wondered when spring would arrive and prayed it would not be long.

253

❖ TWENTY-SIX ❖

The prioress, whose back was turned to Johanna when she entered the chamber, looked like a collection of veils and draping material. She stood close to Sister Magdalena, who was pouring a goblet of wine, adding a liberal amount of water to the mixture. It was Sister Magdalena who first noticed Johanna's arrival.

"Lady Johanna! Come right in. Have a seat there by the table."

Johanna found herself in a small room, located just off the prioress's sleeping chamber. Obviously used for interviews and conducting business, it had an official air to it with the writing table set in the middle and several stools to sit upon. The small fireplace was dark and empty and, though Johanna had been warm in the laundry, she suddenly felt a chill.

"Would you like a shawl, my dear?" The prioress had turned around and noticed Johanna shiver. She wore a half veil which covered everything but her eyes.

"No thank you, ma'am. I shall be all right."

"Bring the wine over here, Sister Magdalena. I took the liberty of having one poured for you. It's more watered down than what you're used to, I'm sure," she offered an apology, "but heavy wine isn't good for your condition."

Johanna reached forward and grabbed the cup a little clumsily with both hands. "Thank you. I didn't realize how much I had taken Papa's wines for granted."

"When you are raised delicately, like I was, you find that much of what was everyday life was taken for granted—and, I might add, completely dispensable. You must forgive the quality of the vintage as well, Lady Johanna. We don't receive the finest of choices here. Sometimes my family will send me a bit, but that doesn't happen often. For the most part, we get castoffs from the cellars hereabouts."

"Castoffs are a way of life for the leper, I'm learning quickly."

"Unfortunately, that is so. And yet, here at St. James we have it far better than most others that find themselves in our condition."

Johanna nodded and took a sip of the wine, appreciating the way it caused her jaw to tingle a bit. "And you're not having any, ma'am?"

"No. I do not like to take off my veil in public. You'll understand one day, I'm saddened to say."

"Ma'am, may I be so bold as to ask you how long you have been here, and where did you come from? You must be quite a figure of mystery to most of the girls, for they can tell me almost nothing."

"I've been here for 20 years now. I wasn't a leper when I arrived, but had decided to devote my life to the women here at the hospital."

"Then you are a nun?"

She shook her head. "Yes. My father died without a son, and when my uncle inherited the lands and title, I had no real place there. So I left, took my vows eventually, and came here. I grew up not far away."

"And has this life made you happy?"

"Fulfilled. Happiness is a bit too much for any of us to ask for, don't you think?"

"Not always, Reverend Mother. At least not before I came here."

"Determined to find joy?"

"Yes. By finding the perfect man!" She laughed.

The prioress's eyes wrinkled at the corners—the telltale sign that a smile lay beneath them. "I take it your search was in vain?"

"For a while. I was looking for someone just like the Black Prince."

The prioress crossed herself. "Ah yes, good Prince Edward, may God grant his soul mercy. So you did eventually find this man?"

"Yes. But he's much older than I am, and I don't think he would have been interested in a girl like me for long. Although he did declare his love for me. But it was under such unusual circumstances than I can only wonder if such intense feelings would have lasted. Still, he alone has helped me since I found out about my present state."

"The grand man who brought you here?"

"Yes, Sir John Alden."

"A most imposing figure of a man. Strong."

"Truly. Which makes me wonder how a man such as he could really love a frivolous girl such as myself."

"You don't seem the frivolous sort to me, Lady Johanna."

"Oh yes, I am . . . or I *was*. And now that I'm not so frivolous, there's still no hope for us to ever be together."

The prioress sighed. "That, I am afraid, is true enough. Still, you have his love. In fact, he is the reason I called you here." She put a letter on the table. "This arrived for you this morning from Sir John. I know you'll be corresponding with him, and I wanted to ask you to thank him for his generosity in making the huts more comfortable. The winter has always been the hardest time for those in the huts. And yet, better occupy a hut here at St. James than for the women to be on their own out in the forest somewhere, I suppose."

"Judith was most distressed when she saw the window."

The prioress laughed, the veil puffing forward. "Yes, that would be our Judith. Ever since I've been here, there's always been at least one with such an outlook. You will find that to be the case as well. I'm always glad when a bright soul such as you joins our ranks. We're happy to have you here, Johanna."

"I thought you said happiness was too much to ask for?" Johanna's eyes sparkled.

"Well, my lady, you certainly seem happier than most of the women here; I'll grant you that!"

"Reverend Mother, I've come to the conclusion that a horrible injustice has been done to each one of us. It would be even more of one for me to let it have the victory to the extent that I cannot smile or laugh or be pleased about anything. I won't let it gain control of anything other than my body."

"Maybe your frame of mind will do Judith a bit of good."

"I doubt that. Judith wants to be exactly like she is, and I cannot figure out why. She acts as if it is a spiritual matter, but I don't believe her piousness has anything to do with God."

The prioress agreed. "There are many types of leprosy, Johanna. And one kind can afflict all manner of men, leprous or not, and that is leprosy of the soul. I fear Judith's soul is as disfigured as the rest of her. By blaming God so thoroughly, she continues to shut Him out of her life, making her not much good to herself or anyone else. It takes some people more time than others to understand God's ways, especially when one is afflicted so, but I fear Judith may never fully experience His love."

"I'm afraid as far as that goes, I'm not much different. I was never taught much about the love of God, mostly His judgments."

"That is the way of some priests, I'm afraid. But you will come to realize His love for you, Johanna, if you are only willing to seek Him out."

Uncomfortable with the personal nature the conversation was assuming, Johanna finished up the rest of her wine and stood to her feet. "Thank you, Reverend Mother. I've enjoyed our talk. But I had better relieve Ida of my tasks down in the laundry. She isn't really strong enough for such work."

"Make sure you stop and read your letter first. You're a real asset here, Lady Johanna. Thank you for being so willing to help. And cheerfully so."

"No one asked me to come here."

"No one asked you to contract leprosy either."

Johanna shrugged. "Some things just happen."

"And in the end, it all glorifies God."

"I don't know about that, Reverend Mother. Despite what you said about His love, I don't quite see how it could. All I know is that if I'm angry about it, I'll be the one who mainly suffers."

Later that day, Johanna thought about the prioress's words, wondering if the kind woman really believed that such a horrid disease, such a wasting condition of body and soul, could really be glorifying to God.

"And why would God inflict suffering just to show His own glory?" she asked herself, thinking that such a mind-set was rather sick if analyzed too deeply. Surely, God wasn't like that, was He? If so, He could be likened to the pharaohs of old, building glorious cities to their honor upon the crushed bodies of slaves.

And yet, she thought, *where are the pharaohs today?*

John would talk to her of such things. The first thing she would ask him was who he really thought God was to begin with. She knew nothing of God other than ritual, and it seemed formal and stifling when performed at the hands of Father Theodore. In fact, she wondered whether her view of God had been tainted because of the bitter man who shepherded their local flock with a sharpened staff.

John will know, she decided, and began looking forward even more greatly to his visit in October. She purposed to make a list of the questions she would ask him, for if God was truly judging her, she must know why. And if He wasn't, maybe He could, in His benevolent way, make her life easier to bear. There was an emptiness to her soul that she had never before realized was present. She saw it now, and she compared herself to John and the prioress. Leprosy of the soul. Did that manifest itself in many forms as well? For Johanna, caught firmly in the net of spiritual introspection, had to admit that she certainly wasn't any closer to God than was Judith.

❧ ❧ ❧

21 August 1376
Castle Chauliac

My Lady Johanna,

Your letter arrived today, and my heart was made a bit more merry by its contents. It is indeed good news that you are becoming accustomed to your surroundings, although it grieves me to think you must live under such circumstances.

My prayers for you have increased with each day since my departure. You have only to say the word, and my journey back to London to visit you, or take you away if you will allow, will commence. Respectfully, though, your wish for me to postpone a visit until the beginning of October will be granted. You know what is best for you, and at least your present needs are being met.

Until such time as I am graced with your presence, I will be journeying to my estates in the north to tend to several pressing matters. In no wise should you hesitate to contact me there. In fact, my hope is that you will continue to correspond until such time as we should see one another. While awaiting the future pleasure of your company, I will always remain, in my devotion, your loving friend,

John Alden

Johanna clasped the letter to her chest, then lifted it to breathe in the smell of the parchment, hoping some fragment of Sir John's scent was left behind. Yes, she breathed, it was there—that peculiar scent of man, horse, paper, and a breeze. It stabbed her directly in the heart when she noticed the hand bearing the paper was becoming increasingly disfigured and destined to be that way for the rest of her life.

Bitterness threatened to show itself, but she firmly pushed the debilitating monster away, knowing such feelings would own her utterly if she but allowed them the narrowest of footholds.

☙ ☙ ☙

Johanna gritted her teeth against the pain. In that moment as the plaster of herbs and medicines which had been left to dry on her legs had begun to be scraped off with a wooden scraper, Johanna hated Eleanor.

The smooth wood pressed down hard against the raised areas on her calves which had begun to show up three days before, over and over as more of the hardened plaster was removed. She wanted to cry out as each area exploded a painful message in her brain, as her fingers curled over the edge of the table upon which she sat. But it would do no good, for Eleanor hated any display of discomfort and would bring the scraper down hard upon her knee as punishment. The flip-tongued Eleanor of leek-adder Tuesdays became the abrasive, cruel Eleanor of plastering Thursdays.

Johanna tried to put her mind on other things, but it was impossible. For all she could think was that Tuesdays and Thursdays would never stop coming to her until she stopped coming to them.

✦ ✦ ✦

As much as she wanted to write to John that evening, Johanna forsook her free time in the refectory with the others and went straight to bed. Doing laundry, coupled with the treatment, was too much to bear without falling under the weight of exhaustion.

And fall she did, not even making it onto her pallet. She had no strength to rise, but merely reached up to her bed, grabbed a blanket, and fell asleep on the dirt floor.

Two hours later, Judith stumbled over her, and the sight of Johanna's prostrate body brought a smile to her lips. But she quickly wiped it away, fearing God may have seen her enjoyment.

✦ ✦ ✦

Rosamunde lay gasping and sweating. Lord Clifton paced outside the door to the solar, wondering how long it normally took to birth a babe. Her labor was long, hours and hours crawling by . . . and still no child.

Finally, she pushed one last time and out of her body issued forth the child into the hands of the waiting midwife. The woman screamed and cast the misshapen, decaying thing upon the floor, running from the room, her screams echoing in the great hall.

Lord Clifton lifted the babe off the floor, his hands shaking, a look of horror upon his face, and he tried to hand her to her mother. Rosamunde wouldn't have her. Instead, Lady Durwin leaned over the edge of the bed and retched.

Ned stepped forward, took the child, and nodded to Gordon's order of "Get it out of here. Such a thing cannot possibly be our daughter."

Still on the floor, Johanna awoke from her dream, her heart beating wildly, alone in her plight. Somehow she rose to her feet and climbed onto her bed, thinking she ought to pray about something, wanting to, but not remotely knowing how.

TWENTY-SEVEN

Sir John Alden breathed in deeply, the air lifting itself off the sea, refreshing his soul. It was that tangy, salty air that seemed to enclose one in a shroud of silence. An air that welcomed the mists and the cold and coaxed the low clouds of fog in visible patterns of dips and swirls.

Seforth Castle, John's castle, sat upon its own headland, jutting out into the North Sea. It was built by the Anglo-Saxons, an impregnable stronghold protected seaward by a sheer 150-foot precipice. And it had seen many different peoples come and go. The walls still dripped of the conflict when Northumbria fell to the Danes and no English king was left to guide the Englishmen, save Alfred the Great, whose kingdom lay far to the south. The men of Seforth Castle held on valiantly against the gigantic blond warriors from across the sea, and they held out longer against them than any other fortification, saving Bamburgh Castle slightly to the north. Eventually they, too, succumbed, but not before their Herculean blood ran warm over the ramparts, forever staining the sea-wall.

The Normans, taking over Northumberland 200 years later, became privy to a fantastic natural castle site and a warring tradition virtually like no other. It was from these men that Sir John was descended. The blood of heroes flowed in him, and the stalwart heart of the strong women who had braved the cruel northern winds and raised their sons to be like the castle rock upon which they were birthed.

It came into view long before they were close to it. Once it had been a fortress bustling with the activities of men preparing to serve their king in war. But that was many years ago when Edward Longshanks had hammered the Aldens' nearby Scots neighbors into submission. Until Robert the Bruce took over and things quieted down a bit. And though it had stood strong against foreign invaders, it could not hope to effectively battle time itself and the ruining force of neglect.

John knew that he was to blame, more so than his father who was forced to make do with little money after his grandfather lost most of it in frivolous ventures.

But as tragedy had forced John away as a child, so was tragedy returning him home. Things were going to change. Though he would one day be the Earl of Witney, he was presently Lord Seforth—a title he had inherited from his father and spurned years before. The castle was the telltale sign of his neglect. And yes, change would occur, though he didn't know when. But after Johanna was gone, he knew Castle Chauliac would become his least-favorite place of residence.

His man at arms, Roger Morgan, sought his attention. "Sir, upon our arrival will you wish to set up your tent or take up residence inside?"

"The tent for tonight. It grows late, and I must inspect the damage before allowing anyone to enter."

Jonathan, his manservant, called from behind. "Hard to believe it's been three years since we were here, my lord." Sir John had hesitated to bring someone not hardened by battle, but the man could do wonders with an open fire, a pot, and some game. He didn't want to be bothered thinking about food while he was here. And Roger was a fine hunter. But even with such qualifications, the fact that both men possessed the uncanny ability to know when to be quiet and when to be affable was the only reason they were allowed along at all.

"I imagine the building has deteriorated significantly since then."

"Hard winters these past three," Roger commented.

"Yes."

They continued to ride over the flat expanse of ground which separated them from the castle. It sat upon its rock like a stalwart queen, braving the blows of the waves, even laughing in the face of the sea's onslaught. A defiant alcazar with strong walls and a heavy keep, its evolution was plainly evident to the eye. The walls were Saxon, the keep Norman, and the chapel and kitchen had been added only 150 years ago. Those two buildings were by far in the best repair. The stables, wooden to begin with, were visibly crumbling, but they would not be needed tonight.

Up the steep esplanade and into the bailey, the horses negotiated the rubble-strewn path with careful footing. It was plain to see the locals had been using the castle as a ready quarry for their own use for quite some time.

"Terrible shape it's in," Roger remarked, all three of the men looking around them.

Sir John gripped Gale's reins. "They must have assumed no one was ever coming back. I can't blame them. Let's set up camp."

The chapel had remained untouched, much to his relief.

❧ ❧ ❧

The floor of the hut was a soupy mess. Johanna had gone to bed with her shoes on the night before, knowing as she had hurried back after recreation time in the rain that come morning the place would be dripping. And she was right.

Judith was ecstatic, whistling between shivers as she folded her thin blanket and laid it on her pallet. It was still raining this morning, and Johanna was certain the doleful woman was hoping a flood would carry off all their belongings and that they would end up sleeping on the forest floor that night.

But halfway through the day, the sky cleared, and Johanna rushed back to the hut during her chores to open the door and prop open the window so that the little room might dry out more quickly. Much to her delight, a man stood on a ladder which leaned against the hut. A thatcher. A new roof was going on.

Realizing her presence might frighten him, Johanna silently turned around and went back to the main building.

✢ ✢ ✢

Ida, a hut dweller as well, was ecstatic when she heard the news. "Are you really telling the truth? *All* the huts?"

"Yes. I'm not sure when they'll all be done, but I imagine it will be before winter comes."

Soon a congregation of women were gathered around Johanna and Ida. They were in various stages of their disease. Some bore the nodules on their face in severity, some the larger, raised patches which looked like the map of foreign countries. Johanna noticed one poor woman whose face exhibited a large patch by her eye. The tear duct was blocked, and the lacrimal gland, still glazing the eye with moisture, forced its salty liquid constantly down her cheek. Facial paralysis had stricken others, and the foul odor of the abscesses and ulcerations was intense with so many of them gathered into such a small space. And yet some of the women seemed to exhibit, like Judith, the effects of other skin ailments that seemed foreign to those truly suffering with leprosy. But the church officials couldn't be too careful, and they were put

266

away as well. It was all leprosy as far as their limited knowledge of the disease was concerned.

Seeing their disfigured faces leering twistedly with unabashed joy and excitement that someone truly cared about their plight caused Johanna's heart to soften even further to those among whom she had placed herself.

"And who did this for us?" one of the women asked.

Ida cried excitedly. "Sir John Alden! Lady Johanna's light o' love!"

Johanna's face reddened. "He's just a man that I know."

But it didn't matter to the others. They were happy that this winter, though it would be cold, would at least be dry. It was a luxury beyond their previous imaginings.

From near the hearth, the prioress watched sadly. Lady Johanna and Claire were talking with animation to the others, their unmarred beauty striking against the backdrop of deformity and odoriferous disease. She had never been a beautiful girl or a lovely woman, but that had never really mattered, for she had been a retiring sort who would rather have sat and read to her grandmother than be enjoying the social life of court.

The veil hung heavy on her face just then.

In truth, the prioress knew that almost any one of those women standing there ingesting the small crumb of hope that was thrown to them by Sir John's kindness would far surpass her in beauty, deformities notwithstanding, for her visage was the most hideous of all. Each night she viewed herself in the mirror, and though the light of her candle was dim, the thickened skin, heavy and weighted into a series of many folds, was easily seen. It was lionlike and inhuman, not even acceptable for an animal, let alone a human being whose eyes were kind and green and whose voice was sweeter than the honey which pooled in the hives of the castle in which she grew to maturity.

But she had chosen her fate, and there was no returning to the day when she left in the dead of night—a noble orphan wanting only to find love, even if it was the love she gave to others. Sometimes she wondered whether or not she would have chosen to come to St. James had the mirror in her chamber shown her a prophetic reflection, but she usually cast those thoughts aside, knowing it didn't really matter anymore.

The women dispersed and were chatting or working on their sewing and such. Lady Johanna sat at the table, her parchment, ink pot, and quill spread before her. The prioress watched her as she picked up the quill and tried to hold it in her clawed hand. But it was quite impossible to produce so fine a movement from a hand whose nerves had ceased to function normally. The older woman felt a tinge of grief, until she noticed the set of Johanna's jaw and watched her transfer the pen from her right hand to her left.

1 September 1376
The Hospital of St. James the Less

Dear Maman and Papa,

What great joy your letter brought to my heart when it made its way into my hand this afternoon. Life sounds so lovely there in Oxfordshire as autumn unfurls. How much I'll miss you then, for when I smell the scents of September I always remember the many drives we took through the countryside, Maman, in the carriage, just to watch the colors of the season. May these memories never be a thorn to you, but a source of joy, as they are to me.

A new roof is being erected on my dwelling, thanks to the charity of Sir John. The entire hospital is buzzing like the bees on the trumpet vine in the courtyard about his wonderful gesture of kindness. He must be sorely missed by the Earl and Countess of Witney now that he has journeyed northward. His visit to London sometime at the beginning of next month is something to which I am looking forward greatly.

There have been several evenings when the prioress has asked me to read a bit of *The Divine Comedy*. Naturally, my pleasure to oblige was great. But it shows me what a need there is here for more books and education possibilities. Hopelessness abounds in the hearts of many of the women, and if they could only read or hear good literature read aloud to them, it might give them something to truly look forward to each evening. If it is convenient, might not you send down some reading materials with Sir John? Lord Godfrey as well as the earl would most likely be amenable to loaning of their libraries as well. Sir John would be most happy to convey them, and the patients here would be thrilled to regard them as a suitable form of entertainment in the evenings. Ida, the younger girl I told you about in my last letter, is eager to learn to read for herself. Indeed, she is possessed of a good intellect, for she asks the most intriguing questions in regard to Dante.

My life, though pointed in a hopeless direction, is increasingly filled with more meaning than I ever thought possible. In this you must take comfort. You must come visit me before the snows fall and the winter cold makes the travel uncomfortable. With great anticipation until such time as we see each other again, I remain in truest devotion, your daughter,

Johanna

∞ ∞ ∞

Lord Clifton set down the letter he had been reading to his wife. "Well, it certainly seems, my love, that Johanna has taken her happiness with her."

269

The great hall was quiet.

"It's good to hear she's garnered herself a purpose. She needs that," Rosamunde replied.

"Yes. She needs that most desperately."

"I once heard her say to Margery, 'I'd rather live only an hour if it was full of meaning, than to go through an entire lifetime not knowing what it really means to live.'"

"I wish that made me feel better," Lord Clifton sighed.

"So do I, my darling."

※ ※ ※

The sweet smell of the fresh thatch was a boost to Johanna's soul. Walking into the hut after recreation time each evening, she savored the aroma, knowing it wouldn't last forever. Even Judith, though not in any better spirits by anyone's estimation, would have been guilty of falsehood had she said she would rather the old roof be put back on. She was still bitter and sour, but she was dry and less apt to say the things she did. Johanna had always preferred hostility to silence, but with Judith and her scathing "miladies" and faulty reasoning, Johanna was just as glad to let silence rule the day.

Each time she smelled the fresh scent, she thought of John, and would consequently read his several letters which had arrived since she had begun her stay. Tonight it was no different, and she leaned forward near the candle and read the latest, received less than a week ago.

28 August 1376
Seforth Castle

Dearest Johanna,

Your letter was accompanied by a ferocious windstorm, and both were invigorating to my heart. The courier from Castle Chauliac was very pleased to make it to

Seforth in one piece. At least, that's what I assumed when he got off his horse and dropped to his knees immediately in a prayer of thankfulness.

Johanna smiled.

The wind is buffeting the castle even now, and it makes me realize how much work there is to be done. No amount of work, large or small, however, will keep me from my visit in October. It is the anticipation of seeing you once again that keeps me set to my tasks here. There is still much to be done. But little enough of it warrants true complaining. The roof to the hall is now patched, and we have forsaken our tents for indoor comfort. Actually, on a fair night you'll usually find me under the stars. The stars grow colder and more beautiful each night. The stables is the latest project, and some lads from round about have been hired to help. My purpose for going away was solace, and yet another mission has surfaced. Perhaps it is the mercy of the Divine which has made it thus.

You asked of my harp playing and in answer, yes, the evenings have borne upon their breezes the need to play. Many tunes from my childhood have come back to me here in the place of my birth. This time here in the north has been beneficial, and there are no regrets on my part that I succumbed to old Duncan's suggestion. 'Tis a shame you never met him.

The hospital sounds, by your description, a busy place. It is always better to be busy when one is miserable, and that must hold true there as well. Johanna, your letters are so bright and cheerful, but I know you must be suffering. Tell me of your sufferings as well as your joys. My feelings of affection will not buckle beneath the weight of your sorrows. God did not make me thus. He made me able to stand beneath their weight. Trust me in this way, Johanna.

Always faithful in my affections, I remain in love, your devoted friend,

John Alden

Johanna tucked the letters carefully into her trunk. Even as they encouraged, they bred a feeling of hopelessness. What was the use of proceeding with any sort of relationship? And yet the thought of going through this alone was unbearable. She would never sever her ties with John. As long as he was willing, she would rely on him. There was really nowhere else to turn.

She lay down to sleep.

❧ TWENTY-EIGHT ❧

Ida sat next to Johanna as she began reading from Dante's *Inferno*. The refectory held an audience of eager women, but none more eager than Ida. She rested her elbows on the table and her chin in her hands, her eyes sparkling with interest. Johanna translated simply and in an easy manner as she read: "And then they gathered all of them together, weeping aloud, upon the evil shore which awaits every man who does not fear God."

"Do you believe that?" Ida asked later when most of the others had begun to attend to their other interests.

Johanna, used to her own tutors answering her questions with one of their own, responded in kind. "Do you?"

"Yes, I do."

"Why is that, Ida?"

"I just look around me, my lady. There are two types of people in this world: those who fear God and those who don't. If He created the world, something must happen to the ones who don't love Him after they die."

"Perhaps you think God has prepared a place of torment for people like me?"

Ida was taken aback by her candor. "My lady, I didn't mean to imply—"

"I know, Ida. But if I'm intellectually honest, I must admit that, in light of Dante's qualifications, I am not one who fears

God. I've known that ever since I started reading the work. So...answer the question."

"I don't want to."

"Because you believe it to be so, don't you?"

Ida nodded slowly. "I wish I didn't."

"I'm glad you were honest, Ida. Truth be told, I never needed God before. My life was perfect. But I'm not in the habit of needing Him, so it's not in my nature to turn to Him for help."

"Perhaps He's helping you now, without you realizing it."

"I cannot say that He isn't. Surely I wonder greatly how it is that I'm even surviving here on my own. Maybe I'm really not alone. But does God help those who don't ask, who don't care about Him?"

"Look around you."

As the other patients went off to bed, laughter twinkled above the disease and smiles displaced the misery for a while.

"Do you believe in evil, my lady?" Ida asked.

"Yes. Who couldn't?"

"If God was not reaching down to us here, whether we ask for it or not, this hospital would be a place with only misery and pain and death. But despite what we feel in body and spirit, we are able to laugh. That is from God."

"You're right, Ida. I've never judged a piece of literature without reading it first, so it seems I should not judge God, His dealings, or His motives without finding out more about Him. In a real way, though—not just Mass and communion and the like. I've been thinking more about Him than ever before."

"I'll pray for you, my lady."

"You will? Why?"

"That you mean what you say. That you want to find out who He *really* is, not merely look to affirm what you want Him to be."

"An honest quest? That is the only quest I've ever learned to make, Ida." Johanna picked up the book and would have arisen to go, but was detained again by Ida.

"Father Clement is a good man, Lady Johanna," she said, referring to the priest who came daily to say Mass. "You might talk to him."

"I don't much care for priests."

"There are some that I don't much care for either—after all, they are merely men and not God. Maybe I don't expect much out of them because of that. But Father Clement is a good man. I promise you that. Why would he come here every day if he wasn't?"

Johanna raised her eyebrows in consent. "I have to agree with that line of reasoning. Our parish priest is horrible. He has made me distrust all men of the cloth as men spawned by dogma and superstition and, in the end, the quest for power and riches."

"Some of them truly love God, Lady Johanna. It's easy to tell which are which if you care to examine them closely enough. Trust me with Father Clement. He'll be glad to talk to you if the conversations will bring you closer to God."

"I don't know, Ida. I hate to promise you I'll do something and then disappoint you if I don't follow through. I'm a spoiled, only child, and I've never been much good at keeping my promises."

"I'm not asking you to promise me anything, my lady. I just want you to consider doing as I suggest."

"That I *can* promise, Ida."

⚜ ⚜ ⚜

Across the Tyburn River, the Westminster Abbey flattened itself against a twilight sky into a silhouette of black. The central tower jabbed upward into the purple heavens and the bells tolled, calling the monks for vespers.

They filed in solemnly and took up their positions amid the glories of the present finished portion of the church and the dust from the construction of the newer work in progress, which descended upon their heads and shoulders.

Laying on her pallet, Johanna listened to the melodious soundings and wondered if heaven itself was filled with the sound. Bells sounded so differently, one from another, but they were all harbingers of some sort. Death. Marriage. Baptism. Worship. Prayer. Yet in the darkness, Johanna heard a different call amid the sonorous notes—a call to "taste and see the goodness of the Lord."

The sound was suddenly comforting, and she promised herself that after Mass was said tomorrow morning, she would ask Father Clement a few questions. After all, if she broke that promise to Ida, only she would be ultimately disappointed.

❧ ❧ ❧

The next morning at 11 the inhabitants of the colony, those who could arise from bed, stood or sat in the chapel listening to the prayers uttered by Father Clement. Many whispered along, knowing the portions by heart. Some daydreamed, their attention caught by the blue sky outside the window or the flickering flames of the candles near the altar. But Johanna stood with head high, scrutinizing the much-aged priest without apology.

He spoke with a heavy voice, low yet carrying forth the words to each one in the room. It was a voice much used in his lifetime, and the wear of the vocal chords was apparent in the raspy, mannish tones. His face was pickled with age, the structure of the skin obviously weakened by time and the elements, and his teeth bore witness to his age as well. Though he was horribly myopic, his dark eyes seemed to grasp instinctively what was going on around him. Perhaps his ears really did the job, but the eyes were so very clear and perceptive-looking that it was impossible to tell he could hardly see anything that was more than an arm's distance in front of him.

His youth had been one filled with courage as he had accompanied several noblemen into battle, interceding with heaven on their behalf while the battle raged nearby. Sometimes he was forced to pick up a sword merely to defend himself. But now he was old and was glad to take the position of parish priest to the small community here at the leprosarium, as well as to the surrounding inhabitants. It was a quiet life, and he could finally focus on the one love of which his life could boast, the Son of God. He wasn't afraid of contracting leprosy, for he had been exposed many times and nothing had ever happened. And even if it did, he was old, he reasoned, and surely his body was unworthy of such selfish preservation.

He gave the final blessing, noticing Lady Johanna's gaze as he placed the host back into its sacred resting place, gently closing the doors. He turned to face her where she now stood, only several feet in front of him. His pupils dilated in and out, trying to focus on her face. "You wish to speak with me, my lady?"

"Yes, Father. But only if you have the time."

His smile was genuine. "Would you like to sit down here in the chapel, or perhaps some fresh air would be more to your liking?"

"Please, let's go outside. I must make sure the herdsmen are tending to the pigs today anyway."

"Then I'll accompany you at your task. I made a vow to forsake all meat years ago, but every once in a while I get a hankering for a joint of pork!"

Johanna decided right then that she liked him well enough. And so they began the small journey from the hospital building, through the garden and the woods where the huts were situated, and out into a more sparsely wooded section where the pigs roamed, Johanna making sure he didn't stumble over rocks and roots or scratch his face on low-hanging branches. Sure enough, the herders, able-bodied lads hired by the hospital, were trying to capture several of the pigs.

"What is it you wish to tell me, my lady?"

"Nothing. I wish to ask you something. Many things I suppose. Yet I don't quite know where to begin when talking about the things of God."

"This doesn't come naturally to you, I assume?"

"Heavens, no! In my family we've always believed a man's success and sense of worth depends on what is in his head, not his heart or soul. While I've always believed God exists, I've never really had much to do with Him."

Father Clement shrugged. "At least you're honest about it. I've found in my travels that not many people really do want much to do with Him. They just worship their own idea of God for many purposes, I suppose. Fear has something to do with it for a lot of people. And then there are those who please God only because they think the reward will be great."

"Heavenly or earthly?"

"Both, I assume. Although in the heavenly sense, I believe we all wish to escape eternal damnation. If that motive for serving our Lord is considered highly ignoble, well, then there are not many men who can lay claim to spiritual nobility. What is it you wish to learn?"

"It's a new quest for me, really. I simply wish to know who God is."

The priest laughed. "Does it seem like a simple task to you? Does God seem like a simple God?"

Johanna gave him a wry smile. "I suppose not. When I compare the God who ravaged the land of Canaan to the God who sent His Son to earth, I have to admit it doesn't seem like the same being would be capable of both actions."

"Your observation is not a new one. God is a being we'll never understand completely. Why He does the things He does, I don't always know, and anyone who glibly explains His paradoxes away is not being honest with his own heart. But the one thing I *do* know, Lady Johanna, is that He loved me in that moment that His very own Son was crucified. He put Him there on the cross to take away not only my sins but also the sins of the whole world. You are familiar with the atonement?"

"Yes. By shedding His blood, Jesus took our sins upon Himself and made us clean."

"Only if we believe on His name."

"Yes." Johanna felt she had to agree to such a well-known doctrine, but she had no idea what "believing on His name" really meant. She had opened her mouth to speak when she heard Claire's voice calling from the entryway to the kitchen. "Hurry, Johanna! I can't do all this laundry without you."

"I must go, Father. Thank you. May we talk again sometime?"

"Of course, my child. I love saying Mass and tending to the sick in body, but tending to the sick in soul is the greatest joy of my life. I can never ease the suffering of your body, my lady, but if I can by God's directive ease the suffering of your soul, I count it nothing short of a privilege sent from heaven."

───── ❦ TWENTY-NINE ❦ ─────

They met near the gate. Johanna, always aware of her vows, made sure she stood to the leeward side of her visitors. How good it was to see them. Maman smiled pleasantly, saving her tears for the journey home, and wore her prettiest gown of green silk. She thanked Ned kindly when he set her on a blanket he had spread on the grass by the wall which surrounded the hospital. Papa looked much the same—a bit thinner. Nevertheless, he tried to make the occasion a jolly one.

"And if that wasn't enough," he was saying, "we became bogged down in a puddle the size of a small lake. Your poor mother was being jostled about like one lovely coin in a wooden coffer."

"Oh, darling, you exaggerate." She looked at Johanna with mock exasperation, her expression too exaggerated to be natural, belying the tension she felt inside, mirroring the discomfort of her husband. Even Ned, usually so sarcastic and quick to add his bit, was silent and embarrassed.

A silence ensued until Johanna broke it in a cheerful voice. "I see you have a box there. Did you bring me a present, Papa?"

"I think there's a little something from everyone in there. Do you wish to look at it now, or savor the contents in your room?"

"I would like to open it in my room. Seeing you both is all the joy I believe I can sustain. Even Ned is a welcome sight right now!" She laughed and it sounded exactly the same as it always had, but it wasn't enough to erase from their vision her clawed hand and the homely gown she wore to blend in with the other patients, or the new limp from her recently affected leg.

"Ned, take the box to the doorstep," Rosamunde ordered, and the burly man eagerly complied. Anything to get away.

Johanna filled in the silence which then ensued. "How wonderful you both look, and are you feeling well these days?"

Her parents nodded.

"Good. I'm feeling as well as is expected. I mustn't complain overly, especially when my present condition is far better than most of the girls."

"Do they feed you well?" Rosamunde asked, leaning forward at her waist. "Your hair seems thinner, less full."

Johanna self-consciously rubbed her fingers through her severely depleted hair. "That's a kind way of stating it. It's from the treatment. But not to worry, Maman. I'm eating well enough. Mostly soft, bland food that the others can eat with little pain."

"What about your mouth, my darling? Does it bother you?"

"Oh no! I've been craving some of Henry's food for weeks now! What I wouldn't give for one of his almond tarts or a nice piece of beef. It could be so much worse though, Maman. Our hospital takes good care of the patients."

Rosamunde leaned forward, her eyebrows raised as she whispered. "Just be sure when you open your trunk no one is around who believes that rules were *not* made to be broken."

Johanna caught the meaning right away. "Tell Henry he continues to be the man of my dreams. I miss everyone at Durwin Manor so much. How is Margery doing? Has she exhibited any signs of leprosy, Maman? I worry about her so. We were always together, and she bathed me regularly. Is she all right?"

"So far. And believe me, Daughter, we've had her examined by the finest physician in Oxford. He sees no signs."

Johanna sat back. "That's a relief. Still . . . it can take several years for it to—"

Her father held up a hand. "Don't worry. We'll have her examined regularly. In the meantime, she's doing fine, Johanna. She misses you dreadfully. But we're keeping her busy enough with various tasks. The steward is giving her charge over many of the housekeeping duties. And he's just as glad to get rid of them. She's spending much of her time down in the kitchen these days."

Johanna was relieved. "As long as Margery's busy, she's content. Any news from Castle Chauliac?"

Rosamunde piped up. "Well, Sir John is still up north, and Geoffrey is almost married. The earl and the countess are still gasping for breath over that one, I assure you. But their new cook has brought a singular joy to their lives."

"Stephen's grown even larger!" Gordon quipped.

" 'Tis true, darling. But I have to say that as good as the new man cooks, he's still not to be compared with our Henry!"

Johanna smiled as the banter continued, the three of them dragging up old memories, commonplace matters, anything but the true state in which they found themselves. Soon the bell for afternoon prayer rang, and it was time for her to get back to her fellow inmates.

"I must go. Prayers now."

Rosamunde grimaced. "Oh, I'm so sorry, dear. You never were one for that sort of thing."

" 'Tis all right, Maman. They're starting to become a bit of a solace now." She offered no further explanation, and her parents looked at each other with a very small amount of puzzlement showing.

Lord Clifton stood to his feet. "Well, then. We'll be going. We're going to stay with some friends in London tonight and then make an early start of it in the morning."

"Do be careful not to wear yourselves out," Johanna warned.

"There's not much to get home to now," Rosamunde shrugged, showing her candor for the first time. "We won't make it a race."

Johanna's father shifted uncomfortably from foot to foot, wanting to embrace her but knowing she would have none of it. Ned finally saved them all. "Come now, my lord and my lady. We mustn't make Johanna late for prayers and so bring down the wrath of the prioress."

"A lovely woman," Gordon muttered, "lovely."

He turned to Ned and began to help him with Rosamunde, gathering the blanket, making sure the hem of her gown didn't drag in the dirt of the road, picking up the light-green slipper which fell from her foot. When they turned to say the final good-bye, Johanna was gone. They saw her disappear through the door of the hospital. No one else was about. The air was cool. The rays of the sun were slanting low.

❧ ❧ ❧

"Are you sure Judith won't come spying on us?" Ida whispered, Agnes and Claire nodding. Through the doorway, the evening sun illuminated in a golden hue the back of the hut where they sat on the dry earthen floor, gaping into the straw hamper that contained a variety of dainties.

"No. But even if she does find us, won't it be worth it?"

"I've been dreaming of food like this for two months now!" Claire sighed, reaching for a custard tart.

"Two months! I don't believe I've *ever* tasted such food," Agnes said with wide eyes as she stared into the hamper.

Johanna swept an inviting hand over the dainties. "Go ahead, Agnes, take whatever you wish. Everything Henry sent is my favorite, so I'll be happy with whatever is left over. I must tell you that the cheese pasties are particularly delicious. Nice and salty, if you like that sort of thing."

"I do!" Ida reached forward and took one. "Give me salty over sweet anytime."

Claire licked a drop of syrup from the corner of her mouth. "Not me. I love sweet things."

Agnes was still having trouble choosing. "Oh, my lady, I just don't know which to take! Salty...sweet...it all sounds too wonderful. Maybe I should just enjoy the sight of them!"

Johanna would have none of that. "Nonsense." She reached into the hamper and pulled out an almond tart and a savory pasty filled with pork and chicken. "Take these. And eat the pasty first."

"Thank you, my lady." Agnes, here from the streets through the charity of a wealthy merchant, tried her best to lift the delicate treat to her mouth daintily, but she lowered it, looking at the others and feeling awkward and common, not quite knowing how to eat such food. Claire was accustomed to the like and Ida was so lacking in self-absorption that she didn't think twice about it. But Johanna saw Agnes's dilemma and reached into the hamper, procuring a pasty for herself.

She bit down, letting the juice run down her chin a bit, laughing and wiping it away with the back of her hand. "These can be messy, Agnes. There's just no getting around it."

The girl sighed with relief, bit into the flaky crust, and relished the savory flavor of the meat and the perfect balance of spices that cooks only of Henry's caliber were capable of achieving. "Oh, my lady, it's wonderful," she gasped, her mouth still full.

The others agreed.

"I told you. These are all my favorites. And I've always prided myself on my good taste."

"What's going on here!" a voice thrummed from the doorway.

All four jumped.

Judith.

Johanna took the lead. "A secret party. Care to join us?"

"It's against the rules of the hospital to partake of anything other than what is prepared for us."

"Thank you for the reminder, Judith. But if you cared to notice that we're sitting here in a corner eating these behind our hands, you might have realized that we are well aware we are breaking the rules."

"You could be reprimanded severely for this."

"How? More work?" Johanna laughed, peeking into the hamper again. "Claire and I do more work than anyone else. How will more be placed upon us?"

"That's not my problem. All I'm saying is—"

Johanna pulled out an almond pastry. "—you're very hungry after that watery pottage we had to contend with this afternoon. Here," she held it forward, "you look like the type that loves almonds."

"No. It wouldn't be right."

"Oh, come now! One tart. That is all. And don't say, 'Get thee behind me, Satan,' Judith, for it's only flour and sugar."

She held it closer to the dour woman. "It looks good. You must admit it."

"It's tempting, I'll admit that, but nevertheless, I will abstain."

Ida looked at Judith with disdain. "By the love of heaven, Judith, don't play the martyr over a simple tart! It's the last one. And you may never get the chance to eat an almond tart for the rest of your lifetime, as miserable as it is going to be!"

Judith hesitated, and Johanna dove in for the kill. "You have to admit she's right, Judith. There may never be an opportunity like this again."

Judith looked down at the ground, refusing to meet their expectant gazes. After several moments of silence, her hand shot out like an arrow and she grabbed the tart. She went outside to eat in solitude, but before she exited she turned back around, her face as serious as ever. "This step backward into temptation will do much to keep me humble."

The four girls inside thought that was one of the strangest things they had ever heard, and they laughingly told her so.

⚜ ⚜ ⚜

"Take me up to the loft, Ned." Rosamunde resembled a raccoon, her bloodshot eyes peering out of the darkened circles which grief and a sense of futility had drawn in broad rings around them. And he obeyed his lady's orders, negotiating the steps carefully into Johanna's room.

It looked exactly the same, and somehow expectant as if someday Johanna would return. Margery's little pallet still stood at the foot of Johanna's grand one, for the maid still slept there. Rosamunde wanted nothing changed that wasn't absolutely necessary.

"Do you think she'll ever return, Ned?"

Ned knew she didn't expect an answer, and he gave none as he set her down on the bed.

"Tell Gordon I shall sleep up here tonight. I would like Margery to be here with me."

"Yes, my lady. I shall get her immediately. Will you need me anymore tonight?"

"You may go."

She reached over onto the bedside table and took out Johanna's embroidery from the bag which sat upon the wooden surface. Her fingers traveled lovingly over the surface of the linen, the silk threads slick beneath their tips. So lovely. So finely worked.

The unfinished Black Prince still waved his sword with a gallant hardihood, and the flower of England still worked their battle magic in the face of the French. But now he was gone, buried in the priory at Canterbury. The death of a man. The death of a dream. Johanna's dream.

It was all over now. Life had changed forever.

❖ THIRTY ❖

The night temperatures had begun to sink down below all possibility of comfort—so much so that even Judith agreed to let Johanna give her a few extra blankets. The trees of the forest, their leaves blazing with an inner heat, contrasted against the cool darkness and could not be seen under the moonless night. But Johanna knew they were there and was oddly comforted that nature still kept up her normal pace.

Only two more weeks, she thought, the picture of John coming to her mind. She had written countless letters that seemed like a collection of babbling drivel to herself, but when he wrote to her, he never failed to mention that he relished hearing the details of her life.

She was trying desperately to think of him only in terms of fond friendship.

Her role at the hospital was constantly being redefined. The nightly readings continued, and people had begun to look to her for cheerful solace. Since her almost-daily chats with Father Clement had begun, a noticeable change was occurring. Johanna knew her life was heading toward a greater significance. Perhaps it was because she was finally accountable to someone: to the institution in which she found herself, to the noble prioress, and in some ways to Father Clement.

Gone were the days of being able to do whatever she pleased. Even now she felt ashamed at the times she had blatantly gone against the wishes of her parents, knowing they would never really be angry enough to do anything rash. Everything had been so important to Johanna then. But now she found that there were few things that mattered, and what did matter was precious beyond all imaginings. Love. Friendship. Duty. Kindness. Compassion.

It was that attribute of Christ, His compassion, that kept tugging at her heart and mind. That healing compassion, even when He was weary, His feet covered with the dust of travel by foot. He always had time for the downcast. And who could be more downcast than she and her fellow patients?

She knew He was in their midst. She could feel His presence, comforting and sustaining. But she still could not give herself over to experiencing His love fully and freely, the way Father Clement had talked about. It was hard to say what was keeping her from doing so. Perhaps it all seemed a bit ethereal still, and she didn't quite know how to accomplish such an elusive feat. Faith was a part of it all, she knew that well. And she knew she didn't have enough of it yet, and sometimes doubted that she ever would.

But still she regularly sought out the company of Father Clement, enjoying the man's sweet yet strong spirit, his humble demeanor, and careful explanations when he spoke of his faith and his theology. The way he talked of growth through pain was something that was beginning to make complete sense to her. His talk of a dying soul. She had always thought that if God loved someone, He would make that person's life felicitous, easy. But Father Clement was helping her to realize that those who truly make a difference, those who are strong and committed, have experienced their fair amount of hardship and pain.

"It doesn't seem to make it easier when we're going through the dark times, but when we look back and see the man who entered the dark forest and compare him with the man who emerged, we know that it wasn't for naught."

And Johanna had to admit that was true. "Yes. The most frivolous, gossipy women I know have nothing better to worry about. They are shallow and unable to comprehend others' real miseries, so they focus on the small inconveniences of life and call them tragedy."

"Show me a man who has never suffered, and I'll show you not a man, but a boy. We mature because we hurt."

A simple observation of those she had known all her life bore witness to his words. It somehow made it easier for her to bear her present circumstances. Already she could feel the change from girl to woman taking place within. But still, peace was absent.

"And yet," Father Clement continued to say, "the beauty of suffering, if one loves God and His Son, is that we never have to go through it alone."

Johanna thought much about his words, and each day her heart softened yet more and her mind became a fertile plain in which the seeds of truth would someday flourish and grow into plants destined for eternal beauty.

We never have to go through it alone.

❧ ❧ ❧

"No wine for me today, thank you."

The prioress's eyes showed concern. "Is your mouth becoming sore, Johanna?"

"Just a bit."

"I'm sorry to hear it. This is a terrible cross to bear. But let us not dwell on our infirmities today. I called you in for a reason, and that is to ask you if you would mind visiting our bedridden sisters. You have such a contagious way about you when it comes to high spirits, Johanna. They could use a bit of what Sister Magdalena and I have been calling 'Johanna's medicine.' "

Johanna chuckled. "I've never been one to be gloomy for long. If you think it would help, I would be happy to do so. But who will take over some of my responsibilities, or will I do this during my free time?"

"Oh no! I know what it means to you and the others to have you read aloud. Not to mention the catharsis of letter-writing—something I value myself. You will be relieved of your gardening duties for an hour during the afternoons. By the way, thank your father for the books he brought with him."

"All right. I'm glad to comply with your wishes. In fact, I think it's a splendid idea. Poor Ida, I know she does all she can in trying to cheer those who are confined."

"Yes, and she's a dear little soul, but the abscesses in her feet are becoming much worse, her cough has deepened, and I'm afraid—"

"Will she be all right?"

"She's not as well as she seems, Johanna. Your help would be quite a relief to her. Soon she might be confined to the bed as well."

Johanna felt her heart plummet, and the prioress saw the expression. "I hate to put it like this, Johanna, but it's something you must accept. This is a hospital for the dying, not merely for the sick. No one leaves here with breath left in her body."

"I know," Johanna whispered. "At least my head knows. But my heart daily tries to convince me otherwise."

"But you can do much in making the final stages for some of these women at least bearable. No matter how bad the bodily misery, human kindness is always appreciated. 'Tis a wonderful opportunity for service."

"Thank you." Johanna felt humbled—not by the chance to serve such lowly people, but that life was so much larger than she had ever thought possible, that people mattered to her in a way now that they never mattered before.

"You may go. And your new duty will begin tomorrow during the hour before we sup."

Johanna left quietly, feeling a heaviness in her soul to which she had never before been privy. Poor Ida. Poor everyone.

❧ ❧ ❧

20 September 1376
The Hospital of St. James the Less

Dearest John,
Most probably you will not receive this letter until after your visit, but I do so want to write, for my heart is most heavy. The true nature of my surroundings has finally alighted upon me, and I realize that I am in a house where everyone will die before reaching the age of 40. I realized long ago, on the road down from Oxfordshire, that my death was a surety. But I hadn't taken into account the fact that I would come to care about those I was to find myself in company with. None have died yet, but they will. And we all go along, not pretending it won't happen, but somehow thinking it will never be tomorrow or even the next day, just "someday soon."

When I was a little girl, I remember looking upon dead animals in the forest. Poking the bodies with a stick, rolling them over this way and that, fascinated at the stiff legs and arms. And the eyes, glazed and unseeing. For a reason I don't know, I tried to look hard at them, searching for some form of life, anything that would give me some idea of what this animal had been like, what it was doing when it died. I tried to imagine it running across the forest floor or flying from tree to tree, and no amount of prodding with my stick would make it resume its living path.

I feel the same here, except the eyes haven't died yet. We're all lying on the ground, unable to be what we once were, unable to run into the doors of our real homes, to even so much as kiss our mothers on the cheek. We're all unable to move, our legs and arms are stiff, our hands are clawed, our fingers are missing, and our feet drop when we walk. But the eyes remain the same—well, at least the light is still burning inside them. And I don't know what to do for these poor, dying things, of which I am one.

ฬ ฬ ฬ

John plucked softly the strings of his lyre. Normally the melody he played was a rousing song of national pride, but he had softened the tempo, changing it from male to female, and it was lovelier than it ever had been when it was sung after the Black Prince's victory in Calais. John's smooth voice accompanied the notes struck by the harp, and he remembered life in battle, how in some ways it was so much easier, much more simplified than the life in which he now found himself. The memories of the campaign went through his mind as he sang.

England my England,
Such a breed of mighty men, as come forward one
    to ten,

England my own.

At times they had been outnumbered, but they were tigers, baring claw and fang, fighting against mere men, Frenchmen at that. It was a time in his life when staying alive was the main objective, a clear focus, sharp and unbending to his own whims or the whims of time itself. A blood-red blade. A voice dulled by the cry of battle. A beating heart. They were all he really wanted when war became his job.

> Blessed be the Most High,
> Who has given such power to men,
> Who has delivered great, stately, famous, brave,
>   warlike nobles into the hands of a few.
> O dira hostilitas! Oh woeful bloodshed!
> Presumptuous pride cast Philip down!
> Trust in God has raised Edward up!
> France bewails the day of sorrow,
> England delights in the day of joyful consolation
> Which our Lord Jesus Christ has deigned to
>   grant her.
> Praise and honor be to Him forever and ever.

The words he continued to sing softly, without really thinking of their meaning. It was assumed God would favor England simply because it was England. Yet on the last line, Sir John's words were heartfelt. He never thought much about the theology of war, if the God of the universe really favored one nation over another. He merely served his king. It was what he had been raised to do; it was a calling and the purpose for which he had been trained. There was never any question in his mind when the call was given that he should stand alongside his prince and his king and wield his sword to their greater glory and honor.

As a knight of the Order of the Garter, it was his duty. In the arch of the king's military organization, they were the keystone. His most trusted men, the most able warriors and strategists in the kingdom. King Edward thought himself a soldier before anything else, and his self-assumption was an accurate one. For men of Sir John's ilk—men who became tigers, beasts of prey when the field opened wide and the grass reached expectantly toward the heaven for a soaking of blood—it was a good time to be alive.

But now, in the twilight of the north, as he sat upon the great wall which still bore the stains of his ancestors' blood, his mood was softened, his hands sensitive to the play of the strings. And it was not of France that he thought, though in the next verses he absentmindedly sang the maligning lyrics against the country across the water. It was of Johanna.

He thought he had lived in strife before. But it had never been anything like this. And yet to a greater call came a greater meaning. It had been easy to be a soldier. To ignore those he loved, to dismiss their problems as their own. In meeting the French headlong, he had avoided the needs of those he truly loved and who loved and relied upon him. Norma and Geoffrey came to mind. For the first time he was reaching out to a person, not out of duty or training, but because his heart forced forward his arms, filled his eyes with unshed tears, and caused his head to ache with the tragedy of it all. He couldn't force these feelings aside.

Was that what he had been trying to do when he came north?

He didn't know. But it didn't matter anyway, for that was impossible. She haunted him always, through the lifting of the heaviest stones and the raising of the stable walls, through the long, thundering rides along the coastline and the stillness of the popping fire in the evenings. Johanna was always there, her hair shining white in the dark corners of his mind, her laughter filling his soul, the softness of her hand upon his arm touching the cords of memory which bound his heart to hers.

There could be no running away from Johanna.

"She simply wouldn't have it," he though with a smile, the song long over. He stood to his feet, smelling the aroma of dinner as it spiraled up from the pot over the campfire which his servant Jonathan attended.

Down the steps and into the bailey he descended. He passed by the graves of his parents and his sister Bridget, and he stopped, looking curiously at the sunken plots, as if seeing them for the first time from the outside.

❖ THIRTY-ONE ❖

hat?" Johanna set down the leather-bound book and looked at the woman in the bed beside her stool. "I'm sorry. What did you say?"

The woman, ageless by form now that the disease had severed away all youth from her features, smiled a one-sided grin. She was only 23. The words came out thick and slurred from the sore recesses of her mouth. "St. James was blessed the day you arrived, my lady."

"Thank you, Mildred. Shall I continue on, or would you rather converse a bit? I see you've got a pretty flower there by your hand. Where did it come from?"

Again, the smile. She petted the sweet, blooming Michaelmas daisy with her abscessed hand, whose fingers were too eaten away internally to be used ever again, even to hold a flower. Johanna automatically lifted it up to Mildred's nose so she could smell it. "My daughter brought it to me. She left it at the gate."

"Sweet child."

"Yes. She's only seven, but she must be a good girl to remember her mother each Sunday the way she does."

"What is her name?"

"Joan. Little Joan. My husband almost lost us both when she was born. God spared us. And then we were separated only three years later when I came here. I haven't known a moment's happiness since then . . . until you started coming to see me, my lady."

"I enjoy our little chats, Mildred."

"But you would rather be elsewhere. I know that my little bit of happiness comes at a large expense to you."

"I would have to be here anyway. 'Tis the way of things now."

Mildred nodded, her eyes closing. She was growing tired. Johanna began to get up.

"My lady."

"Yes, Mildred?"

"Would you sit here just a little while longer until I fall asleep?"

"Of course, Mildred."

"Thank you, my lady. Surely, God lives in your heart."

Laying a comforting hand upon the woman's shoulder, Johanna wanted to ask what that could possibly mean, but before the words could escape, Mildred was gone. At first Johanna thought she was only sleeping and went to cheer another patient. When one of the sisters came by to check on Mildred, it was obvious she had passed into the realm of the incorruptible.

❧ ❧ ❧

"Sister Magdalena tells me that your kindness in the dormitory has been most beneficial for the bedridden patients." Father Clement was busy putting away the host and folding the linens used during the Mass he had just said.

"I think it has been more beneficial for me, Father."

"How is that?"

"It makes me thankful that I am not as poorly as they. I still have a while before I will be in such a position. And I realize how much of my life I wasted before, serving no one but myself."

"That is a noble outlook. It is good of you to spend your last years of relative health caring for those who are about to die."

"One of the women died yesterday afternoon."

"Ah yes—Mildred. A melancholy soul. She missed her daughter so much; I do believe she died inside long ago."

"Yes, Father."

"One of the few with children here. Most come even younger than you are, my lady."

"There's much to be done here. Always something needs attending."

"Oh, you can always find a calling no matter where you find yourself."

"I'm just learning that now. You've talked much about growing because of pain, and I can see visible evidence of that here. I personally never gave suffering a thought until experiencing their miseries myself. At least, the little I *do* suffer."

The priest's brows knit. "Don't belittle your suffering, Lady Johanna. I know what you are forced to bear each month with that awful broth and the plasterings. Because you have no abscesses yet or debilitating paralysis doesn't mean you are not suffering. To belittle our sufferings is to belittle God's mercy in helping us to persevere."

"But no one wants to hear me complain all the time about it."

"No. But that wasn't what I meant. I meant that to wear an inner mask and to pretend you feel no pain, no fear, no loneliness would be to shut your heart down to God. For if you are not suffering, you do not recognize your need of Him. We all suffer, and once sin came, I believe were meant to suffer."

"Why? That seems so awful."

"Perhaps it does. But when all seems right, God is cast aside. And, you must admit, there are many kinds of suffering.

Not all bear the scourge of leprosy or dropsy, not all have been in accidents, but inside of us we all suffer under the load of sin, whether we realize it or not. Sin is a scourge, a leprous state, my lady, which has fallen on all of Adam's race. Some see it as such without the physical chastening of God and are recipients of His mercy. With others, the lesson must be harsher, an outer reflection of what has always been inwardly since the day we were born."

"So in the end, we all realize our need for God's mercy."

"Yes. Whether that realization comes before we die or afterward." He had finished his task. "I think I will make my rounds and visit some of the patients this morning."

"I'm sure they'll like that, Father. I had better be off to the garden to prepare it for the winter."

"My lady, I pray for your soul."

"Thank you, Father Clement."

"I just wanted you to know that."

Lady Johanna watched as the older man hobbled down the aisle, his arthritic knees giving him more trouble than he spoke of. His robed form disappeared as he turned the corner into the dormitory.

What a cheerful soul, she thought. So different from Father Theodore and the quiet monks of the abbey. His God was One who delighted in mercy and knew what it was to suffer Himself. His God came to earth to take away all sin and suffering, and if that wasn't so—well, Jesus would have been just another Pharisee, another Father Theodore.

❧ ❧ ❧

The abbey bells tolled again that night, as they always did.
A God of mercy.
"Surely, God lives in your heart."
The dying words of a leper woman.

Johanna had wanted to ask Father Clement about the phrase, but something held her back. "God lives in your heart." It seemed so private. Such an intimate thing, too wonderful to share with anyone. So unorthodox. She had never heard those words muttered by a man of God or anyone else. What did the woman mean? Did she have the key to true love with the Almighty?

What does it mean? Her heart cried out the words into the darkness. And at that moment she would have traded all the books she had ever owned, all the poems she had ever memorized, all the erudite conversations she had ever heard just to know the meaning of that single phrase.

❧ ❧ ❧

With the death of Mildred, Judith was moved out and a new patient was moved into the hut with Johanna. She was only 15, and her name was Roesia. In the first evening they were together, Johanna suddenly yearned for Judith's silence. The girl didn't seem to have any idea she was placed in a hospital for the dying. She just wanted to know who was who, what was what, and why. The common girl with dingy, blond hair and a bosom larger than Johanna had ever seen was more of a thorn than any of the treatments could ever be.

Johanna, getting more used to praying as time passed, lifted her eyes toward the window, caught a star in her gaze between the trees, and uttered silently, "Help me, Lord."

She turned her head toward Roesia's bed. "I'm sorry I can't answer anymore of your questions tonight, especially on your first night here. But we have to get our sleep. You'll thank me tomorrow."

Roesia, as if she had not heard one word Johanna said, sat back on the bed and, instead of asking many questions, began to answer ones as yet unasked by Johanna.

"I hear you're a real lady of quality. They told me that up there, and that I was to treat you as such, milady. Well, I'm as used to that as just about anything, and it comes as second nature to me to be around folk of your station. You see, my mother was a cook for the Fitz-Allens—they live not far from here as you well know—and many a times I served them at table." She inhaled a large amount of air. "You'll find I'm quite well-versed in serving the nobility, you will."

"You're not my servant, Roesia."

"Oh, don't you think a thing of it, milady. I'll make your bed for you in the morning, if you want. I don't know what else I can really do for you, but you just say the word. Why, when some ladies would come and visit us—and there were lots of them milady, I assure you that—sometimes I would have to serve as lady's maid, and that was my most favorite part of being a servant. I noticed your chest there by the bottom of your bed. I can keep that all straight and tidy, if you would like."

"No thank you. It stays locked."

"Oh, all right. Mighty peculiar out here with no one out and about but a bunch of lepers. But I'm not one to question the quirks of my betters, I'll tell you that right now. But you just say the word and I'll do it, milady, I will. Never one to ask questions, I'm not."

"Then if you want to serve me, there's no better way to do it right now than to serve me with your silence tonight, Roesia. I'm really quite tired, and tomorrow is broth day."

"Broth day?"

"You'll find out about it soon enough. Although I would wager to say it won't be tomorrow."

"Oh, I just love broth. All kinds."

Johanna couldn't help but grin at her unwittingly misplaced enthusiasm. Was she in for a surprise! Johanna decided not to spoil it for her. "Good night, Roesia. I mean it."

"Good night, milady."

❧ ❧ ❧

Sir John rode through the gates of London, anticipation making his brow moist with a light sweat, though the autumn day was cool.

It was October the first.

h e stood there, dressed in black as always, the abbey bells tolling in the distance as they called the inhabitants of the monastery to afternoon prayer. Noble and handsome, he filled her heart.

Johanna stood up and wiped her hands as clean as possible of the garden dirt. Her first impulse was to run to him, to embrace him. And so was her second impulse and her third. Pounding the turf between them, her feet began to run as he walked toward her, unsmiling but somehow communicating that the sight of her was what he had been dreaming of for the past two months. Her limp slowed her down a bit, but she was determined.

She stopped five feet short of him. "Wait, Sir John! Do not come much closer."

He stopped because she wanted him to. "I want to see you more clearly than this, my lady."

"Come sit with me in the garden, then," she invited.

He agreed and soon they sat, he on a bench, she on the ground several feet away. Silence could have become uncomfortable, but Johanna would not let it happen. She had been looking forward to this for far too long.

"You came much earlier than I expected."

"It's October."

"Yes, but only the first. I thought surely I would have to wait until at least the third or the fourth of the month."

"If I say the beginning of October, I mean exactly that."

She melted again at the sight of him. He was so noble and honest, no duplicity found within him. It was so nice to be with someone who had no ulterior motives. "Oh, John, it's so good to see you. How was your journey?"

"Good. The leaves changing added to the pleasantness."

"Is Jonathan here in London with you? Your man at arms?"

He shook his head. "They're continuing up at Seforth without me."

"Then you won't be staying long?"

"As long as I can. For a week or two, no doubt."

"I'm so glad. And you'll come visit me every day that you're in London?"

"It's why I'm here, my lady."

"Did you find your house in acceptable condition?"

"Yes, thank you."

"And did your horse fare well?"

"Gale? I'm surprised you ask. I thought you didn't like horses!"

"He's different. I see him more as an extension of you, Sir John. Therefore, I find it in my heart not to dislike him."

"As a horseman, I'll take that as a great compliment. Now, Johanna, are you done asking me about my trip? Or will the questioning continue?"

She laughed, reaching forward to grab his hand and squeeze it, but pulling back just in time. "I know I'm babbling on. It's just that it's so wonderful to see you again. I've lived for your visit for almost two months now. And I must tell you, Sir John, that the northern air is doing you well. If I didn't know better, I would think you were Geoffrey's age."

"Heaven forbid! I wouldn't go back that far for anything!"

She pouted. "Why? 'Tis a good thing to be young, isn't it?"

"When you're young, it is. When you get to be a little older, you value the experiences that have brought you to where you stand."

"Then you don't despise my youth?"

"How could I? It is that which draws me to you."

She was suddenly reminded of her state. "In friendship, of course."

"Yes. I suppose that is what it has to be. Although you're still as beautiful as you were the day I first saw you."

"I feel as if you're the only real friend I have, Sir John."

"Then you're not alone in that feeling, my lady. If friendship is all God will afford us in our lifetime, I will serve you gladly in such a capacity and be thankful for the privilege of being with you in any way at all."

❧ ❧ ❧

"Was that Sir John Alden I saw you with today?" Roesia asked from the darkness of her cot.

"Yes. He is a good friend of mine."

"Oh." Her mouth shut tight. An extraordinary occurrence.

"What do you mean, 'Oh'?"

"Never mind. Mum always said if it isn't nice, just don't say it."

"Come now, Roesia. That's never stopped you before. What do you know about Sir John?"

"Not much. Mum was one of the cooks in the house of the parents of his late wife, is all."

"She knew Sir John's wife? What was her name again?"

"Lady Elaine. Yes, as much as a servant can know a ladyship like Elaine. But we hear what goes on upstairs."

"No doubt. I'm sure your mother was only too happy to tell you all about it."

"It was a terrible thing. Terrible. Married her, got her with a baby—presumably an heir—then left her to bear and raise it without him around."

"That's why he married her, for an heir?"

"Why is that so surprising, my lady?"

"Well, you have a point, Roesia. Still, I would like to think there's more to the story than what your mother found out down in the kitchen."

"I'm sure you would, milady. And if you ever find out just what happened, will you let me know?"

Johanna didn't answer. Instead she thought about what Roesia had told her. It just didn't seem like her John at all. There had to be more to the story. And, looking back over the past few months, she had heard many, each just a little different from the one previously told.

꽃 꽃 꽃

The next day he returned, and their conversation began again. This time they were walking through the woods so Johanna could show him the improvements to all the huts.

"Thank you for writing to me so faithfully. I know sitting still for that long must be difficult for you!"

He laughed. Only the second time Johanna had heard him do so. "You haven't changed, Johanna."

"And I won't. I can promise you that."

"How so?"

" 'Tis all I have left. Just me."

" 'Tis all that you've ever needed. Other than God Himself. Johanna," he reached into his doublet, "I have something for you. I trust you won't think it presumptuous of me to give this to you." He held forth a small book—a prayer book. "I used this as a lad. Before my parents died. I found it at Seforth."

Johanna took the book from his hand. "Thank you, Sir John. This must be most precious to you."

"It will become even more so if held by your hands, my lady."

Johanna blushed—she couldn't help it. His compliments were so much more beautiful than any she had heard because she knew how hard it was for him to bare any part of him. He could only say what was truly inside his heart.

"You've changed, John," she said. "I don't even know what I mean exactly. But something seems different about you."

"Going home again was good for me."

"I could tell by your letters."

"Then they don't bore you?"

"No! I could never convey to you how much they mean to me. Don't ever think that."

"I enjoy yours as well. Especially the descriptions you give of people. You're quite handy with a pen, my lady. I especially like hearing about old Father Clement. Tell me more about him."

"I want you to meet him yourself. You two seem to be of like mind. I'm enjoying my association with him immensely, Sir John."

"Well, then, you do have another friend besides me, I'll warrant."

" 'Tis not the same thing. But I do value him. He's made me see life, pain, suffering, death . . . so differently. He's been quite helpful."

"Then you will value that little book. If I had realized then the treasures of truth it held inside, I would have taken it with me when my uncle took me back to Castle Chauliac."

She asked the question with great compassion. "Your parents died of the plague, is that right?"

"Yes. I've never talked about it much. But restoring their home has made them almost alive for me again. So many good

308

memories have come back, and I've experienced yet again the mercy of God and a cleansing by going north."

"John?" She began gathering the fortitude she needed.

"Yes, Johanna?"

"I know you love God well."

"Yes."

"Will you tell me what it means to have God living in your heart?"

He looked puzzled, and she quickly explained where the words came from. "I've been most perplexed since then, as you must realize, Sir John. Can you tell me what you think they mean?"

"Johanna," he began, "I've never been much good at talking, and telling people how I feel about matters is even more difficult, but I do believe I know what the woman was talking about. There comes a time in a person's life when he realizes that God is more than just the One who created the universe and sustains life. That is a big God, Johanna, who can do all that. But it takes a bigger God to come down to live inside a man, whisper to him of His majesty, His love, and His mercy. And when you realize that God is a being to know and love with all your heart, to trust with your very soul, and to serve with all your being, then He somehow comes to stay within."

"But how do I do that? That is what I want to know."

"Do you feel Him, Johanna? Do you look at the stars and know He's there? Do you think about the sacrifice He made through His Son and stand humbled?"

"Yes."

"Then present yourself as a gift to Him, through His Son."

"But I was baptized when I was a baby, given to Him then."

"You must do it yourself. You open your very heart and soul to receive His love and experience the ultimate mercy of the forgiveness of your sins through the death of Christ."

"How?"

"Just pray, Johanna. It is the only way I know that we can talk to Him. You know He's always listening."

✥ ✥ ✥

Johanna prayed that night, sitting outside the hut, long after Roesia was asleep. She wanted to experience the fullness of God, the redemption provided by His Son, and the mercy and love He showed better than any earthly man ever could.

She closed her eyes in a heartfelt prayer saying, "I don't know how it is that You can come to live in a person's heart. But if this is possible, I give You mine, such as it is, for Your home."

After her prayer a light breeze ruffled the blanket she had wrapped around her, she felt a cleansing which she had never before experienced.

And despite the fact that her body was deteriorating at an alarming rate, she—Johanna—was made whole. The leprous soul, once dying and diseased, was made new. The abbey bells tolled the news to no one but God and Johanna.

✥ ✥ ✥

The prioress was kind, granting Johanna extra free time in the afternoon to spend with Sir John. He helped her in the garden so that she wouldn't have to make up for the missed work later on, and they worked themselves up into a wonderful state of companionship. When John had something upon which his hands and body could concentrate, it freed up his tongue more than Johanna had previously thought was possible.

She learned about his childhood, his family, and one afternoon he even told her about his marriage. It answered many questions. Not that they were important anymore, she had decided after the conversation with Roesia. For it was painfully clear to both of them that although their hearts were forever joined in an unspoken love, they would never be man and wife.

"I've always heard that you and your wife were never really in love with each other."

"That's true."

"I suppose that's the case with most arranged marriages."

"It is. But ours wasn't arranged in that way."

"What do you mean?"

"Elaine was the sister of one of my good friends from Oxford. I owed him a debt of gratitude for a matter I'll not discuss now, but I felt impelled by honor to grant his wish when he asked if I would marry his sister."

"Just like that?"

"If you knew Elbert, you would know how convincing he was. Not only that, I had met the maid before—very pretty in a sweet way, from a good family—and I knew I would never be inclined to seek someone out on my own, so I agreed. She wanted to be married hastily, and I went along with it, having no real objection."

"What happened? From what I've heard, you two ended up practically hating each other."

"She was pregnant when I married her. Barely. Although I didn't know that before our marriage. I saw that I had been used and, being young at the time, I grew to despise her."

"Oh."

"Don't look at me like that, Johanna. Elaine never tried to make the marriage work, either. I never so much as even kissed the woman behind our bedchamber door, because that was clearly the way she wanted it."

"They trapped you."

He nodded. "So I went off to London to immerse myself in the king's business. And soon after, I was on my way to France."

"No wonder you didn't care when she got so sick."

"It wasn't that I didn't care, Johanna. Elaine wouldn't let me. She still harbored a great deal of love for the father of the child, and as much as I despised her, she despised me yet more because I wasn't her true love."

"What an awful situation. Why have you never exonerated yourself? You know what people say about you, don't you? My hut mate, Roesia, says her mother served Elaine's parents for years. Their account of what happened is altogether different. In fact, every story I ever heard about it was just a bit different from its predecessor."

"But you didn't believe them, did you?"

"At first I wondered if it might be true. But when I weighed the hearsay against who I know you to be, I knew it must be false. And even if it was true, I decided it didn't matter. I know the man you really are, Sir John. Still, I'm glad you told me."

"For some reason, Johanna, you've brought more words out of my mouth in the last week than I believe I've spoken in my entire lifetime."

She laughed. "I'm glad I do that for you. It's only a fair exchange."

"And what have I done for you?"

"You've opened my eyes to many things, not the least of which is a loving God. It's evident that He lives in your heart, too."

It was a beautiful smile he bestowed upon her. "Thank you, my lady. I do believe that is the nicest thing anyone has ever said to me."

The next day he was on his way back north, with plans to stop in at Castle Chauliac to visit his family.

⟡ THIRTY-THREE ⟡

The Earl and Countess of Witney sat in their new solar, away from the commotion of the great hall and the meal that was going on. It was finished—their new addition to Castle Chauliac. The building, snuggled up against the walls of the inner palisades, smelled clean and new, and their large solar at the end of the great hall held a roaring fire in the wall fireplace. The countess reached forward to pick a piece of partridge up from her trencher.

"We have to do this more often, Stephen."

"I know. I like sharing a meal with you alone, Margaret. I'm sure you are enjoying being away from all of those sweaty soldiers and their loud talk."

"Yes. After years of such eating, a calm meal is a lovely luxury. It was nice having John here for a couple of weeks, wasn't it?"

Stephen nodded and pushed his trencher—the contents only picked at—away from him, content to look at the blaze whose logs were arranged in a particularly beautiful pattern that afternoon. He hadn't been feeling good lately—he had been feeling too large and a burden to his own legs. His sixty-fifth birthday would soon be upon him, and he was too heavy even to ride a horse. It was time to do something about that, for he felt ridiculous riding around in the carriage like only women, the elderly, or the sick did.

"I always enjoy having John around. But this time it was especially nice, don't you think, Margaret? I wonder what's been happening up north? It doesn't seem the same man who left came back here."

Just then there was a knock on their door. Duncan peeped around, harp in hand, when he heard Lady Margaret cry, "Enter!"

"I just thought you would be likin' a bit o' music, my lord," he offered humbly to Stephen.

"Would you rather be out there playing for the men, Duncan?"

"Nay, nay. I'm likin' the thoughts of a quiet afternoon myself."

Margaret grinned. "We're all getting too old for this life, aren't we, my bard? Please take a stool there by the fire and play to your heart's content and ours. We were just discussing John's disposition."

"So ye noticed it, too, eh?"

"Yes. His eyes seem less tortured as well, as though he's finally found peace," the countess surmised.

The earl laid a hand on her knee. "I think you're imagining that tortured business, my darling. He always seemed fine to me. I just noticed he allowed himself to smile every once in a while."

"Aye. I have to agree with my lady, though, my lord. There's been a change in him. Bein' up there with his parents again."

Lady Margaret's brows went high. "Do you think that could be it? I never thought about that. But he's been up there many times since he's grown to manhood, hasn't he, Duncan?"

"Aye, but never to stay this long. It's as if he's finally agreein' to take their place. He's finally steppin' out o' their graves and breathin' his own air for the first time since they died."

"Bless the dear man." The countess shook her head sadly. "We never could take their place or do for him what they could have done."

" 'Tis a blessin' ye never tried to be his mother, my lady. They were very close from the day she pushed him into the world. Aye, I remember it well! The yell that wee babe let forth rocked the castle as if he couldna' believe that someone would separate him from the one he adored so. Just bein' his aunt was all ye could really do, an' ye did that job well."

She pushed her trencher away from her as well and picked up her embroidery. "I did the best I could considering my own grief."

The earl's great hand patted his wife's knee again. "Yes, you did, my dear. My sister was her own woman, and to have tried to be like her would have been fruitless. And never forget, you really were a mother to Geoffrey."

"Yes, our Geoffrey. I truly hope he will be happy with Lady Ellen. It was a lovely wedding, wasn't it?" Her eyes filled with tears.

"Now, darling, be happy. Geoffrey wouldn't have settled down with Ellen if he wasn't perfectly sure of his love for her."

The countess reached for her wine and took a sip to still her emotions, but even then she didn't believe her husband. Geoffrey would never change.

"Do you know what Sir John was working on up in his chamber, Duncan?" she asked, diverting the subject away from Geoffrey.

"Nay. And now that the main rooms are over here, he seemed more reclusive up there in his tower. Even his manservant hasna' any idea what kept him occupied all those evenings."

Lord Stephen expressed his puzzlement. "Strange indeed, considering John is such an outdoorsman. I cannot begin to imagine what matter was so important that it kept him confined to his chamber."

"Or why he was so secretive about it!" the countess interjected. "When I asked him, he just lifted a sparkling eye to me and said I always did have to know all the goings-on around me! Imagine that!"

Stephen laughed. "He always says what he means and nothing more."

She rethreaded her needle with a thread of gold. "Well, maybe one day we'll know. But if I had to guess, it has something to do with Lady Johanna Durwin. Do you know in the two weeks he was here, he sent out six letters to her?"

"Extraordinary, my dear."

"Leave it to John to choose a love who's incapable of loving him in return."

"There's just no other way to say it than the girl's a leper."

The countess became sad again. "Why can't John ever do anything like anybody else?"

Duncan began to play. And it was a merry tune, for he knew that his lord, Sir John Alden, had never been happier. He had found love. It didn't matter that it wasn't perfect.

※ ※ ※

Johanna realized she had been fooling herself that life at St. James wasn't that bad. For when December came and the nights grew so cold that the little hut itself seemed to shiver, it was all too apparent that this was a place of suffering.

Poor Roesia. Despite the extra insulation she carried around, the cold affected her severely, and Johanna experienced a new feeling of pity for the girl on the pallet next to her own. She wrote home and asked for more blankets, but no matter how many they piled on their beds, it never seemed enough. For each morning she would awaken with a nose that felt like an icicle and a feeling of dread squeezing at the nape of her neck that she would have to actually emerge from the covers to run to the refectory. How thankful she was for Margery's foresight in packing an extra cloak. Roesia was even more grateful for the fur-lined garment which Johanna presented to her when her parents brought it down on their monthly visit.

One night, an early snow blanketed the land, and Roesia, crying from the cold, began to cry even harder. She had drunk her broth only two days before, and she was now enduring the apex of the swelling and the itching. The wool of her garments and the drying tendency of the fires around which they sat most of the day to do their chores made it unbearable, not only for her but also for everyone else. Johanna, who had never known harsh pain, thought it couldn't possibly be worse than this terrible itching all over the body, day and night. It was all too much for Roesia to endure. She missed her mother and her brothers and, she sobbed, "I just wish it would all go away."

Johanna couldn't bear to hear her heart breaking, and so she emerged from her cocoon of blankets, pushed her bed next to Roesia's, and held the young girl in her arms until, cried-out, she finally went to sleep.

Christmas was only nine days away. And though the long, dark days did little to lift Johanna's spirits, and the painful treatments never ceased, and the food never became more tasty, and the cold snuck in through every crevice in the walls of both hut and hospital, Johanna remembered that John was coming. It kept her from falling into an abyss of depression, though she had to admit she had never experienced such doldrums—days of it without ceasing—in her entire life.

Gray. Her life was gray.

"But something sustains me, Father," she said to Father Clement as she went with him on his rounds to visit the bedridden in the dormitory one afternoon. "I know it is the

317

Savior and His mercy which keeps me going even in the darkness and the chill."

"He is always there, my child."

"I realize that now. The hope He has given us of one day being with Him in paradise makes the cold less cold and the dark less dark. It makes all the suffering a temporary thing. Something to be borne now, not endured forever."

"Hope is what separates us from those truly to be pitied, don't you think, Lady Johanna?"

"I do now. After all, what else can be taken from me? And yet I have everything to gain."

"And even here on earth, you have the Savior."

Her light-blue eyes gazed up at the ceiling. "Yes. I do. Do you ever yearn to see Him, Father?"

He nodded. "Shouldn't everyone who puts their trust in Him?"

"No. I mean yes. But that's not what I meant. Sometimes I lie on my pallet at night, and I close my eyes tight, and I wish more than anything else that when I open them He'll be sitting there at the end of my bed."

The old priest wished at that moment he could have seen her face clearly. "I've had thoughts like that many a time myself, my lady. I've even prayed for it to happen, I have to admit. But so far my prayers have remained unanswered, or I should say the answer has been no. Visions don't come to many."

She smiled and sighed. "I guess we shall just have to wait a little while longer."

"I suppose we shall."

The sad thing about it, he thought, was that she had only lived for 18 years, and her time of death would most likely fall around the same time as his—a man who had lived 70 years.

They parted ways then, Father Clement going to one set of beds, Johanna to another. Both reached into their pocket and pulled out a prayer book, and the patients to whom they read found comfort not only from the words they heard, but also from the fact that someone cared enough to read to them.

❧ ❧ ❧

Christmas day dawned behind clouds which dropped large flakes of snow upon London, Westminster, and the hospital of St. James the Less. The cold was quiet, humid, and Sir John, after spending the night at an inn ten miles out of town, pulled himself up onto his great horse and rode quickly toward Johanna.

Tucked inside his bag was the present he had been working so hard to finish—a present for Johanna. He couldn't wait to see her face when she opened the parcel and viewed what had taken him months to create.

THIRTY-FOUR

The parchment was fine and smooth. The ink was blacker than the Thames at night. The gilded artwork was more beautiful than she could have imagined coming from someone who could control the reins of a war horse in one hand and swing a sword with deadly precision in the other.

It was a portion of Scripture.

The words were taken from the Vulgate, and she translated them from the Latin as she silently read the story, written by John's own hand, of Jesus and the ten lepers. She had never heard the story before, and before she reached the end, her skin had gone pale and her eyes glittered with emotion. Herein lay yet more hope.

"I never knew He did this." She said the words after she was finished reading. John watched her silently.

He corrected her. "He *does* this."

"What do you mean?"

The air blew chilly about them where they sat in the dormant garden, wrapped in their warmest cloaks. "His power didn't end when He was taken up to heaven, my lady."

"You mean that He still has the power to heal me?"

"Yes. You believe that, don't you?"

She gazed down at her clawed hand and thought of the spot on her leg which had recently made her other foot begin to go numb. "I guess so. For others maybe."

"But not for you? Why, Johanna?"

"I don't know. I never thought much about it, John. But if He is the Son of God and still lives and reigns with the Most High, then He is able to heal. Do you think it can happen to me?"

"I do. But only through faith."

Her skin became flushed suddenly. "And prayer. Isn't that right?"

"I've found prayer to be a miraculous thing, Lady Johanna."

"And you still pray for me, don't you?"

"With almost every breath I draw. Johanna, this is neither the time nor the place to say what I'm about to say, but it never will be, and I want you to know my heart."

She looked into his eyes with expectation, and he continued. "When we were together in the cave, I felt like I was under a spell of some sort. I fell in love with you then, and my feelings, although I've talked only about devotion and friendship since you've come to St. James, have never changed. I've been thinking a great deal about us . . . and although I know that God *can* heal you, I don't know if He will. And so I made a decision while I was up north. It was surprisingly an easy one to make, but one which will take up a bit of time for the next three or four months."

Johanna sat forward, very curious. "Go on."

"I love you. That you are a leper and I am not makes no difference to me. I don't expect you to ever leave here. But I will not live my life at the other end of the country and hear about your slow death from the callous stroke of a pen. I'm going back up after Christmas, and I will finish the restorations to Seforth, hire a steward, and get the estates running again the way they should have been running for years. After that, in the spring, I will return to London and settle in my house for good."

Johanna could hardly believe the words. "Leave the north? But you love it there, John. You've come back from there at peace, and a new quiet exists within you. How can you want to leave it so soon?"

"The north isn't responsible for the way I feel. You are, Johanna. We don't know how much time we have left, and I'll not waste any more of it than I have to."

"Someday you shall return there," she said firmly. "Find a wife. Have children of your own."

His dark eyes glittered. His jaw was firm. "Never. 'Tis why I've restored the estates. I shall retire there someday, leave the earldom of Witney to my brother, Geoffrey. He was more of a son to my aunt and uncle than I ever was."

"But he's so irresponsi—"

"Shhh," he nodded. "I know. But I can't be the savior of everything, Johanna. Not anymore. And I've decided to quit trying. I just want to be with you. 'Tis a simple request. Will you allow me to come to you regularly, my lady? It would make me happier than I could ever dare hope."

"But my disease, my despair. 'Tis not the kind of love you deserve, Sir John. The love of a leper? How can it be enough for you?"

" 'Tis enough because it is you, Johanna. You are all I need."

A tear slipped from her eye. "And when I become deformed and ugly?"

"You'll never stop being beautiful to me. I can promise you that."

"How? Have you seen some of the others in there?"

"I've seen lepers in the advanced stages. But, Johanna, as comely as I think you are, you know that what you look like is not why I love you so."

She reached up and grabbed a handful of her much-depleted hair, so forlorn and thin after months of treatment, no longer her glory. "Well," she said wryly, "it certainly isn't for my hair anymore."

He smiled. "It never was. I love you, Johanna. What's inside of you. That's always been true, from the first day in the cave until now. The question is, Do you love me, my darling?"

"Yes, John, you know I do."

He took her hand. "Then say the words, Johanna. For if words be all with which we must express our souls, let them be most sweet. Tell me you love me."

She was crying. "I love you, my darling. Oh, John, I love you with all that I am, such that I am."

He wanted badly to take her into his arms, but he knew he could not. Instead, he took off his cloak and settled the warmth of it around her shoulders. "Pull this tightly to yourself and pretend that it is my arms which bind the warmth of my body to you."

Johanna knew that this moment was indeed the happiest of her life. And she closed her eyes in the full rapture of John's selfless love. He watched her face, filled with emotion and a beauty he could hardly imagine—the beauty which radiated from her soul now belonged to God, from her heart which had learned to give and give again.

"May I keep your cloak?" she asked several minutes later. "You have another, don't you?"

"Yes. Why do you want to keep it?"

"I want the smell of you next to me when I sleep at night."

"That would give me great joy."

"Oh, John, if only—"

"Hush, my love. Our time to love upon this earth is fleeting. Let's not mar it with impossible dreams. Let us love while we can, in the only way we can, and let us be joyful simply because true love has come upon us."

"You're right. It's just impossible for me not to wish."

"I know. And you must realize I would give anything to hold you in my arms right now, to kiss your lips and savor the sweet smell of your skin and hair. But by yearning for the impossible, I fear we shall lose what we have right now."

"I do love you, John. Thank you for loving me."

"No, Johanna, 'tis I who am unworthy of your love."

"I think," she said with a teary laugh, "we are about to begin our first argument, for I heartily disagree!"

The next day John once again began the journey north.

꒜ ꒜ ꒜

The prioress kindly allowed Johanna to keep the precious parchment made by John in her chamber in the main building. Johanna took a piece of her own paper on the night John left and wrote the words, in the scrawled writing of her left hand, "I will, be thou clean."

"I will."

I will.

I will.

It was another impossible dream, wasn't it? Weren't there so many others in the colony more worthy of healing than she? And yet she knew John was a faithful servant of God, a lover of Christ. Perhaps for *his* sake God would heal her, for she knew she certainly didn't deserve it herself.

And so she felt emboldened to ask the Lord to look upon her with His mercy, to view her plight and make her a recipient of His healing power.

I will, be thou clean.

With fingers shaking from the cold, she tacked the small fragment of paper by her cot, willing the words to be meant for her as well, and knowing that she could will and she could run, but in the end it was God who showed mercy.

꒜ ꒜ ꒜

"That's the most presumptuous thing I've ever seen!" Judith shoved her hand in the direction of the parchment. She had just asked Johanna to read it to her.

"I didn't ask you to come here," Johanna said. "I didn't ask you to ask me what it says either."

"Well, it doesn't matter anyway. If you think that Christ will have the same mercy upon you as He did upon the lepers in the Gospels, you are going to be severely disappointed."

"How can I be any more disappointed in the outcome of my life than I am right now, Judith? At least this gives me hope!"

"Hope? Is that what you're looking for? You're foolish, my lady. 'Tis sinful to hope in something presumptuous like that."

"Who says so?"

Judith stood with her mouth open.

"Just because *you* say it, Judith, doesn't make it so. I spent years growing up under a priest who preached your variety of Christ. He turned my feet from the path to God as surely as the devil himself would have done."

Judith gasped. "How can you say that about a man of the cloth! That's blasphemy!"

"It is not! I say it because it is true! I have every right to ask for the Savior to heal me as those lepers did so long ago. The only differences between me and them is time and that I can't *see* Christ before me now."

Judith laughed a mocking laugh. "You're fooling yourself, my lady."

Johanna stuck her chin out. "Are you telling me you're so much happier than I am, so much more content and close to God, that your way is best?"

"I'm leaving. I won't have you talking to me like that."

"Yet it's all right for you to call me foolish?"

Judith shrugged. "It's all right for me to do it, because I'm only being truthful."

Johanna, in complete exasperation, lay back on her bed and pulled the blankets up over her head. Roesia appeared a second later, and as Judith couldn't abide the girl's chatter, she quickly left the hut.

❧ ❧ ❧

Johanna broke the ice on the water bucket with the dipper which hung on the side. Bracing herself for that first shock of the day when she splashed her face, she reached her hands into the water and quickly pushed it up onto her face, rubbing her tired eyes in the process.

Her hands stopped on an area by her nose and inner eye. It was raised. A new patch was developing.

The disfigurement had begun.

❧ ❧ ❧

25 January 1376
Hospital of St. James the Less

Dearest John,

I can picture you now up there at Seforth. Your descriptions of the castle when you visited me at Christmas were so clear. I'm wondering if the stables are finally finished and if the great hall is yet inhabitable by anyone other than hardy gentlemen such as yourself and your faithful compatriots! 'Tis probably a good thing that I never accepted your offer to go north with you, for though I'm a headstrong woman, such surroundings are fit only for the most hale of men!

You will be most saddened to leave it once it is finished and infinitely more habitable than when you arrived. And certainly you must be getting to know the surrounding nobles. I've always heard the northerners have hearts big and warm to ward away the cold of the clime. The landscape must be beautiful as well.

Johanna looked about her, set the pen down, and felt the patch on her face. It was so near her eye that it frightened her. One of the women at the hospital was blinded from a patch that had made her eye unable to close. The eye abscessed after a while, and she lost all sight in it. Not to mention it was one of the most unsightly cases of disfigurement at St. James.

I wouldn't blame you at all if you decided to stay there and forsake your plans of coming to London. You know I would understand completely, and I am aware that your responsibility to your people is great.

Life here at St. James continues on in the same very slow, very cold manner. We were given a large gift of wood for the fireplaces, and though most of the warmth is kept in the dormitory, the prioress has allowed us to congregate around a good-sized blaze in the refectory in the evenings. Even now I'm huddled here on a little stool with this parchment balanced on my lap. It is worth the extra effort just to keep my fingers warm!

Ida continues to worsen. One of her feet has become so infected that the physician believes her time is very limited. They've tried bleedings, more plasterings, various concoctions of which I will not detail the ingredients considering you may be reading this as you sup, but none afford her any help. My heart is sad. She is such a lovely creature, John, and the first to go to whom my heart felt a true kinship.

Claire and Agnes are still with me every step of the way, and for their friendship I am thankful. Father Clement sends his regards. He so enjoyed meeting you when you visited at Christmas.

I miss you greatly, my John. Your cloak is always near me, and I sleep with it every night, pretending the warmth it gives me comes directly from you. I love you.

Johanna

❧ ❧ ❧

"Please, let me see your mirror!" Johanna begged the prioress several weeks later when she could no longer bear the frustration of not seeing what was happening to her.

Behind the veil the prioress's eyes were compassionate, yet stern. "What difference would it make, Lady Johanna? What happens, happens. There's nothing you can do to change it."

"I've never been one to run away from myself. Please, won't you help me?"

Johanna had to know. It had been three months since she had first touched the patch, and the disease must have touched something deep beneath the surface of her skin for she knew by the numbness, the sound of her voice, and the way her face felt when she spoke that she was experiencing some kind of paralysis. John would be coming down from the north in less than a month's time.

The prioress tried to hide her exasperation. "Please trust me, Johanna. 'Tis better not to see."

"It's that bad?"

"No worse than what many of the women are going through."

"That bears little comfort."

The older woman laid a hand on her shoulder. "I know. Believe me, I understand what it's like to bear the outward marks of the disease."

Johanna suddenly felt remorse. "Of course you do. Forgive me."

"There's nothing to forgive. Johanna, most of the others don't ever ask to see themselves, but I understand why you do. There on the chest by the window is a hand mirror. I'll leave you to your privacy."

She left the room so quietly that it was hard to believe she was using a crutch. Trembling, Johanna limped toward the chest, the brass mirror on its surface looking like a living thing, a coiled serpent ready to strike her for daring to disturb its slumber.

❧ ❧ ❧

"I've tried and tried in my letters to talk him out of coming back to London," she was saying to Claire as they prepared the soil of the garden for planting. It was late March, and the balminess which had pushed winter away for another year was in the air. Johanna was in no condition to be doing such hard work, her leg was now completely numb, the foot dropping whenever she lifted it to step. Her limp was acute, and the going was difficult. Yet she was determined not to give in easily. She would fight it with every step she took. And she continued to forsake the use of a crutch.

Her parents had been wonderful, visiting her every month and bringing more of Margery's and Henry's salves with them. So far, none of her wounds had abscessed. Each night she examined her hand for burns and scrapes. Her feet she painstakingly looked over as well, making sure that if a loose stone had worked its way into her shoe that day she liberally applied the salve and dressed it with the clean rags Maman always made sure were in ample supply.

"Not only do I not wish for him to see me looking like this," Johanna continued to Claire, "but every month we bloat and peel and smell most foul. So far his visits haven't coincided with the treatment, but if he's living here, he'll see me then as well."

329

"I don't know, my lady. Perhaps you had best be honest with him."

Roesia leaned on her hoe from across the garden. "I agree, my lady. My mother always told me 'tis best to be honest."

"I don't think it has anything to do with being honest or dishonest," Johanna quipped, slamming her hoe into the earth. "It's all about whether I wish for him to see me like this."

Claire pushed back a wayward red curl, looking so beautiful that Johanna felt her stomach sicken with a dull pain. "Do you think it will make a difference to him?"

"No."

"Well, there you are then!"

"But it will make a difference to me."

The other girls were silent, going at their task with a vigor born of discomfort. But Johanna's mind kept churning. Was it as easy as John said it would be? Could they really love each other within the boundaries set by nature? She didn't see how he could cherish any number of days with the disfigured, foul-smelling thing she was becoming, no matter how noble and selfless his intentions were.

THIRTY-FIVE

John heard a footstep on the path near the garden bench on which he sat. It had been almost four months, and he was about to see her. He breathed in and turned, his face falling in disappointment.

Claire hurried toward him as he stood to his feet. "I'm sorry, my lord. Lady Johanna will not be able to visit with you today."

"Is she all right?"

"The winter has been hard on her."

"But is she all right?"

Claire smiled gently. "She's not dying, if that's what your concern is, my lord."

"Is she sick?"

"Yes. Perhaps if you come by next week, she'll be able to come see you then." Claire knew she wasn't being completely truthful. But "sick at heart" counted, as far as she was concerned.

"As you wish. I assume by your hair that you are Claire."

She self-consciously held a hand up to her red hair. His strong presence made her so much more aware of herself, and for a moment she understood why Johanna felt the way she did.

"Yes, my lord."

He held out a bouquet. "Would you give her these for me? I thought they might cheer up her hut."

"Of course. Come back next week, my lord. She should be able to see you then."

He agreed and left a bit downhearted, but more concerned for Johanna's well-being. At least there was much to get done in regard to his house. He had also received an invitation to see the princess and her children—something he was actually looking forward to. It seemed that her husband, the Black Prince, had been dead for a lifetime.

Claire took a seat on the bench and stared down at the sweet bouquet of wild roses and apple blossoms. It was obvious this man was in love with Lady Johanna and was completely devoted. She would try and make sure Johanna didn't dispose of such a valuable affection so easily.

❧ ❧ ❧

Sir John was back the next day. Again, it was Claire who came to him. Of course, Johanna had plied her with questions, having watched the meeting from a window in the hospital, and Claire had patiently answered them all.

"There's been not much of a change yet, my lord. You would save yourself a fair amount of trouble if you waited to come back next week."

"I'm not one to be in the dark."

"Sometimes illnesses such as she has contracted can take a while to go away."

"I'll still be back tomorrow."

Claire could only acquiesce. "Of course. I'll tell her you were here."

He reached into his doublet.

"Another present?" she asked.

"Yes." He drew out a little parcel of brown paper wrapped with twine. "Thank you, Claire."

"Oh, your lordship, I'm only too happy to relay this to her. She's a good friend, you know."

"She speaks highly of you, too."

"I'm glad. During the past two months or so we've been spending a lot of our free time together. Lady Johanna is a most extraordinary person. It isn't any wonder you care about her so much."

She turned and walked away.

❧ ❧ ❧

"He's been here every day this week!" Claire hissed in the darkness of the hut. "With a present each day!"

Roesia was sound asleep, snoring loud enough to blow the new roof off it seemed, and Claire had snuck over to Johanna's hut only minutes before. A moonbeam fell across Claire's face, excruciatingly beautiful.

"You can't put him off forever, my lady. I'll only go out there for you for so long. The excuses are getting quite pathetic. I'm surprised he hasn't an idea of what is truly in your heart!"

"Oh, he does. And that is why he continues to come. What he doesn't know is what is truly on my face, Claire. I simply cannot bear for him to see me like this."

"Then you must tell him. Do not keep him coming back here like some simpering idiot, hoping to find you and getting only me. It's not fair to do that to him."

Johanna couldn't help but chuckle. "John could never be called a 'simpering idiot,' no matter how many times he came back without seeing me."

Claire cocked her head. "Well, you're right about that. Which leads me to my next point. How can you let a man like that go? He's a worthy gentleman, and over the past few days I feel as if I can safely say his love for you runs deeply."

"There's simply no future in our love."

"Why? Because you cannot marry or have children? Think about it, my lady. Everyone can forsake love because there's no real future in it. They'll all die, and it could be tomorrow for all they know, but they still take their chances and love while they may. It's no different with you and Sir John. You were fortunate to find each other before you got sick. I would give anything to have a comely man such as him in love with me, even now."

Johanna reached into her trunk and pulled out the small parcel he had sent to her at his second visit. She undid the twine and pulled forth a beautiful scarf of the palest blue silk, merely to stare at it.

Claire pointed at the expensive piece of cloth. "I have an idea that will enable you to see Sir John and still hide your face. You can be like the prioress and wear a veil."

"I would feel ridiculous."

"Love is like that, my lady."

Johanna looked at her thoughtfully, choosing not to speak.

Claire continued. "At least have the fortitude to tell him yourself that in light of the severity of your disease, you would rather not see him anymore. You owe the man that. His dignity deserves an explanation."

"You're right, Claire. I know you are. I'll tell him tomorrow."

❧ ❧ ❧

John's eyes saddened immediately as he saw her limping toward him. *Oh, Johanna,* he wept inwardly, *that you should have journeyed so far without me with you.*

It was all very clear now.

He recognized the scarf immediately, which covered everything but her left eye. She wore her prettiest gown, though. "Johanna."

"John. You came again."

He could tell by the way she spoke—the slurred consonants, the muffled vowels—that facial paralysis had set in. "I said I wouldn't leave you."

"Won't you have a seat?" She pointed toward the bench. So formal.

"Thank you."

"I trust your journey down was a pleasant one?"

"Yes, the rains stayed their distance the entire time."

"A blessing I am sure for both you and Gale."

Never one to enjoy pleasantries, John decided not to answer. Instead, he waited for her to say something of substance. It was at least a minute, a very uncomfortable minute, in coming.

"I'm sorry I wasn't able to come and meet you before this."

"Claire told me you were ill."

"Claire lied for me."

John focused his eyes knowingly on the veil and said nothing.

She rubbed her clawed hand with her good one. "I'm sorry, John."

He still said nothing. Inside he was feeling very gnawed. By her lack of trust in him and by her obvious suffering and mental anguish. Finally, he spoke. "I understand. As much as I can."

"I'll never show my face to you again."

"When did it happen?"

"Shortly after Christmas."

He nodded knowingly. "I knew something was amiss. The way you suddenly began trying to talk me out of coming to London was so obvious that it made me want to come even more than I did before. I knew there was a good reason you didn't want me here."

"I'm so ugly now, John."

"Your beauty was never the spark that flamed my ardor, mon amour."

"But my horrid looks affect my own feelings. I don't feel worthy of your love anymore. I don't even feel capable of the emotion anymore in this monstrous state I've found myself."

"Are you telling me that your feelings have changed?"

Johanna knew it was the time to set him free. "Yes."

"I see."

"I'm sorry."

"Then you wish for me to leave?"

She nodded. "I'm sorry."

He arose to his feet and, always the gentleman, put out his hand to help her to her own. "I don't believe you, Johanna. I know you too well. You gave me your heart, and that meant forever."

"It can never be good, John. You know that, don't you?"

He stroked her sleeve with his rough hand. "I've always known that, Johanna. I never expected rapture and ecstasy. But without you . . ."

"You must go."

"I will. Only because that is what you want. I'll still be in London. I made a promise to you to stay by you until the end, and I shall keep it."

"But—"

"I won't hear of anything else, Johanna. The day may come when you will need me, and I will be here. That will never change, nor will my love for you. It didn't matter before what you looked like, and it doesn't matter now."

Her face began to get hot as she forced down the tears. "I wish I could believe that."

"You can. You just don't want to right now. Have faith in me, my love."

"I won't chain you to a monster."

"By refusing to let me care, you will be doing just that. But the monster will not be you. It will be regret that perhaps I didn't say the right words or do the right thing to make you change your mind."

"Please, John, don't make this any more difficult than it is already. Please . . . go now."

"You turn away first, my love, for I said I will never leave you, and I always keep my word. It is you who must leave me."

Johanna took one last look at him, clad in black as usual. Looking handsome and healthy and vital. He was so strong, so gentle and unafraid of a selfless commitment. She knew as she turned that she was walking away from the last chance she would ever have for true happiness, but she couldn't help herself. *He must be free to love another. Whether he chooses to or not is up to him*, she thought, seeking to justify her actions.

Without a good-bye, she walked down the path and into the hospital, and when the door closed behind her, it sounded hollow and final, the closing of her own tomb.

THIRTY-SIX

John failed to see the filth all around him, the houses seemingly stacked on top of one another, or to notice the narrowness of the lanes and the irritable city dwellers who eyed him suspiciously.

It was incidental.

All around him at various places in the city, baptisms, weddings, and funerals were taking place. Rites of change and commitment by all the participants. Life and all its rhymes and rhythms suddenly seemed ridiculously mundane, boringly predictable, when all he wanted to do was love her.

It wasn't too much to ask, and he knew it.

He found the Church of St. Bartholomew the Great and entered the old Norman edifice. The stone felt cool to his touch as he leaned against a round pillar which supported the roof of the nave with a host of other compatriots just like it. A great organ was being played softly, and his eyes focused on the large stone baptistry with its heavy, cone-shaped iron cover, which was hoisted by a chain looped from the ceiling when the font was in use.

It was quiet here, and he needed that. Not like the Westminster Abbey these days with its army of masons, artists, carpenters, sculptors, and other workmen. Surely, God was to be found everywhere. He knew that well. But only in the still, small voice of the Creator was he to find peace. He wanted to make sure that he heard exactly what was being said.

❧ ❧ ❧

In the darkness of the hut, the parchment on the wall was only a fuzzy square of lighter hue. But Johanna knew what it said. She had already memorized the story, trying to have the same faith as those recipients of Christ's mercy. But faith was such a tenuous thing to one so new at it. And yet she clung to what infantile certitude was there, knowing that all that separated her from an abyss of utter despair was this silken cord—a scarlet line between herself and the Son of God. She couldn't feel it in her hand or see it with her eyes, but it had to be there because He promised it would be. His bleeding sacrifice made it so.

Her body was bloated and peeling, she felt feverish and warm though the April evening was still chilly. The stars hid behind a mountain of clouds as if they, too, could not bear to look upon the horrific thing she had become.

It was one thing to have leprosy when I didn't look like a leper, she thought, *but this is something altogether different.* She really was sick. She really was going to die, and that fact had finally become clear to her in all its terrible manifestations.

But for some reason, hope still burned within her breast. *I will, be thou clean.* It had to be meant for her. It had to be meant for her.

❧ ❧ ❧

It had been a comfort to know that John would come, even if she sent Claire down to see him. His presence had a rejuvenating quality. Even from the time she first saw him as Sir John, training the knights in the bailey of Castle Chauliac,

339

she had experienced a vitality that was contagious. And now he was gone . . . sent away by herself.

She felt stupid. Broken. Sore.

Weak.

There was no use trying to recall the days when she was proud and beautiful and the smartest woman for miles around. No use remembering the mane of long white hair, the stunning blue eyes, and the white smile. That Johanna was a ghost long drowned in the waters of bodily demise. Never to be recalled again, even in memory's sake, for "what I once was" was of little comfort in the here and now. Not when there was no way of returning, no matter how much she strove to do so.

She was at the bottom of a well. Alone and with no one to come to her aid from any side. The only voice she heard was the one coming from directly above, and she couldn't understand what He was saying.

☙ ☙ ☙

It was June. The nights were once again comfortable for sleeping, and the buzzing of the bugs, the chirping of the birds, and the scuffling of the forest animals kept Johanna awake long after she heard the bells of the abbey toll for Compline. She could still feel the last melodic vibration in her brain, soothing yet calling.

She could be back before anyone really missed her.

The monks would have long been in their beds by the time she roused herself sometime around 1 A.M. She put on her finest gown, donned a lighter cloak, making sure to pull the hood well up over her head. The wooden clapper remained in her trunk. She would look at no one. She would speak to no one. All she wanted was to pray in the abbey. To feel her knees grow cold on the stone floor, feel her entire body numb in the throes of prayer.

It had to be the abbey. The place from whence the sound of the bells came to comfort her each night.

She made her way quietly out the door of the hut, crept through the colony, and finally over the Tyburn and into the city of Westminster itself. The moon was full and benevolent as she limped along the way. Soon she stood at the north entrance to the great church. The stained-glass rose window above the doorway was stained black by the night, and the moon's reflection was seen in the panes, entangled now with a few stray clouds.

She entered.

The building was almost deserted, the final hymns of the day sung a few hours before, the final prayers sent heavenward. All the inhabitants of the monastery were sleeping in the dormitory not far away.

Nevertheless, now forced to use a crutch, she crept along as silently as she could. Toward the Confessor's Chapel she walked, knowing that miracles were said to have happened at the Shrine of St. Edward the Confessor. Past the graves of England's most illustrious she walked, silently noting the tombs of Edmund of Lancaster, Anne Neville, Anne of Cleaves, Edward I, and Henry III. More kings and queens would find themselves in here someday. To be crowned. To be buried. It was now the way of it.

Abbots of Westminster who long kept the faith were also in deathly repose, and she gave their graves a nod of respect. Some had devoted their lives to God, some to mammon—all had ended up here. Abbot Nicholas de Litlyngton, the present abbot, was still making many changes, and the structure grew grander and more beautiful because of him. But even his body would, in death, become the abbey's prisoner.

Soon enough she stood in front of St. Edward's tomb.

She waited, hearing only her own breathing and the occasional movement of one of the three pilgrims present who had journeyed from afar to hopefully experience a healing.

She waited more.

Expecting to feel something. She wasn't sure what… some kind of hum or something that said miracles happened here. Maybe a note of song coming from nowhere. Something supernatural or inherently spiritual. Something.

But nothing.

Feeling rather limp and out of place, she wondered if this was such a good idea. The tomb was large, an imposing shrine containing not only the body of England's last true Saxon king, but many jewels and relics as well. The base was fashioned of Purbeck marble and mosaic, built after the design of the Cosmati with interlocking circles and diamond shapes. The recesses, three on each side, in which the sick were kneeling, were also decorated with mosaic, and grooves were worn into the stone floor of each one where a pilgrim knelt in prayer. Johanna felt no inclination to follow their example. She knew little about the doctrine of saints, wanting only to go directly to the One who had healed the ten lepers.

Her eyes raised to the upper part of the tomb—the actual golden shrine which enclosed the Confessor's remains. It was decorated with small images of saints and kings, particularly Henry III, under whose auspices the shrine was built and the construction of the new abbey begun. Henry III held in his tiny golden hands a model of the shrine. His devotion to the saint was evident, having named his eldest son Edward, who would become one of the fiercest kings to ever sit upon the throne of England. Two pillars at the side supported statues of St. Edmund and St. John the Evangelist. And at the west end was the altar, its table covered with a white linen cloth and candles burning at each side. The small amount of light was of comfort not only to Johanna but to the praying pilgrims as well.

Johanna wanted to tap them on the shoulder and ask, "Why here?" She wanted to feel as they did. Wanted to kneel down in the tracks of many before her. The few that were gathered presently were from different segments of society. A poor beggar in rags, wearing no shoes, knelt beside a fine lady whom Johanna could not recognize from the back. She might have journeyed from France or Italy, but she had come for the same reason as the others. For sickness was not a respecter of class or wealth. It slipped into the bones of the rich and powerful with as much ease as it did into those who could ill afford a doctor. A young woman of the merchant class was there as well, rocking softly as she prayed. Their whispers were softer than silk, their prayers heartfelt. Johanna began to kneel. But something held her back.

Not here.

She knew that the bones of Edward did not heal. It was God. It had to be. For didn't Jesus Himself heal thousands, including the lepers? And some of those who benefited from His lovingkindness, His healing love, were not even in His presence when their sickness was overcome by His grace. *Why should it be any different now?* Johanna reasoned.

She stepped away and let out a sigh of relief, the pilgrims unaware that someone else had been among them. And she slowly traveled back around the ambulatory toward the Chapel of St. Nicholas. It was sparse and furnished with an altar and a few glittering candles. Only two graves were present here, and Johanna remembered staring at them when she was a child. It was a small tomb containing two children: Mary de Bohun who died in 1305, and her brother John, who had died in 1304. The children of the Earl of Hereford, they were also the niece and nephew of King Edward "Longshanks."

In her youth, Johanna would stare at the tombs and wonder what it was like to die so young. It seemed she would find that out. Unless there was One who still healed. One who still performed miracles though He was more silent than the night, though His love now whispered throughout men's hearts and minds, borne on the wings of the Holy Spirit and not His own voice or the ministrations of His hands. He was still present, the Christ. He was present there in the chapel, for He lived in her heart.

Johanna fell down on her knees, then her face, laying her body upon the cold stone flags of the chapel floor. She submitted in prayer with all the humility gained over the past nine months, all the faith she had garnered, all the love her heart now contained, not only for God and His Son but for her family, for her compatriots in illness, for her friend and heart's true love, Sir John.

The night passed in triumph and pain, sadness and ecstasy as the Holy Spirit descended upon her. Her mind took her back over a thousand years to a dusty road near Jerusalem, and she hobbled along with others just like her. In the distance she could see Him, so willing and ready for her to approach, His hand outstretched in love and mercy and His voice, so perfect and kind, saying "Come hither, Johanna. I've loved you with an everlasting love."

Sleep wove in and out of her consciousness, and Johanna hardly knew when she was asleep and when she awake. And as she slumbered, her spirit still cried within her, watching her Lord walk toward her on the dusty road leading to the Holy City.

"Come, Johanna, come."

The dream was vivid, and yet she was always conscious that it was a dream. She dropped her crutch and ran toward the most loving face imaginable, with eyes of tender fire and gentle hands, strong hands, marred by Roman nails.

⚜ THIRTY-SEVEN ⚜

Abbot Nicholas de Litlyngton awakened early, the dawn not yet displayed across the heavens, nor promising to do so for at least an hour. Surveying his new living quarters within the walls of the monastery, he was most pleased. Someone should have thought of it years ago.

He felt a rejuvenation of spirit and a reprise of the song his heart had sung so long ago when he had first entered the church, now that he lived here among the monks once again. Certainly his house was a goodly one, and he wanted for no creature comfort. But being here in humbler surroundings and not on one of his vast estates miles away had renewed his youth. Watching the new addition rising higher unto the heavens, not as a Babel but as a prayer worked in stone, nourished his soul and caused him to remember that the church, his religion, was all about the Christ.

He had forgotten that for much too long.

De Litlyngton lay in his bed for another minute, watching the moon dip below the horizon. He threw the bedclothes aside and rose with a great stretch, feeling the creak and pop of each joint as he extended the wires of his body to their lengthiest.

A bowl of water sat on a chest near the window and he washed, then dressed into the dark robes of the Benedictine

345

order. His days were beginning again in the way they had years ago, in prayer, on his knees before his Creator. *How could I have forgotten You?* he had asked God and himself many times over the last two weeks since coming back to the monastery to live.

But he knew it was never too late to remember.

The early summer dew moistened his shoes as he walked across the yard. The mist of the morning air, billowing off the Thames, filled his lungs.

Through the new construction he walked, unable to survey much in the darkness, but knowing precisely what strides had been taken the day before. This building was much a part of him—someone who had always loved art and architecture, but whose fingers would never have the talent of negotiating such tools which craftsmen wielded. But his mind was fertile with ideas, and they were in evidence around him.

Down the south ambulatory he walked, passing the choir, the sanctuary, the high altar, and finally the Confessor's tomb. He peered into the chapels which lined the apse. First the Chapel of St. Benedict, next the Chapel of St. Edmund, followed by the Chapel of St. Nicholas.

All of the candles had gone out during the night. He would remedy that right away. Stepping into the chapel, he suddenly stumbled over something in the middle of the floor. He caught himself before falling.

A girl was there.

Lying on the floor!

Face down, prostrate, the hood of her cloak was still pulled up over her head. Abbot Nicholas bent down on one knee, cocked an ear closer to her, stilled his own breathing, and listened.

Yes, she's breathing, he thought. *Thank God!*

His knee brushed against something hard. A crutch. He picked it up.

Reaching out, he nudged her gently on the shoulder. With a speed that caused him to startle, Johanna jumped easily to her feet and her hood fell back. "Oh!" she breathed, quickly replacing the hood. "I'm sorry. I came to pray, and I must have fallen asleep."

The abbot stood to his feet and lit a few more candles. "It's all right. It happens quite frequently. The way you were lying there, I thought it might be something more serious."

"I must go!" Johanna suddenly remembered her condition, that she was putting this man in danger by being so close. Quickly she turned and ran for the door.

"Wait!" the abbot cried, holding forth her crutch. "You forgot your crutch!"

Lady Johanna stopped still and did not move. She couldn't. Several seconds passed, and she failed to turn to him.

"My child? Are you all right?" He came to her side and held out the crutch. "Here you are then. Although I don't know why you use such a thing."

Eyes round with unsurety, she reached forward with her right hand and grasped the wooden crutch, pulling it toward her. When she saw her hand curl itself strongly around it, it became a molten thing—hot, perplexing, almost frightening—and immediately she let go, the implement clattering onto the floor.

She threw back her hood, eyes still wide with shock, and yet it was as if a veil were slowly receding. "My . . . my hand!"

"Is something wrong?" he took her hand. "The light is most dim, but it looks fine to me."

"My foot . . . my . . ." she lifted her hands to pull down her hood, "face."

The abbot grabbed a candle and held it closer to her features. "All I can see is a birthmark of some sort. But you've probably always known that was there."

Johanna reached up. The mouth no longer drooped, her cheek was taut and firm, no slackness, no weakness. The paralysis was gone. She could say nothing.

"My child. Come sit down over here. I don't understand what's happening, and I have a feeling you don't either. Come rest and gather your wits about you."

Reason suddenly returned to her. The events of the night . . . a seeming dream. It was true. It was all true. A soundness of mind was hers as well, the veil of confusion gone. Joy replacing it. "No, Father. I know what has happened. I came in here last night looking for the Christ who walked the shores of Galilee, who trod the streets of Jerusalem, and I found Him. He healed me, Father. I came in here last night diseased with leprosy!"

Nicholas's first reaction was to shrink back at the cursed word, but he held himself in check.

"Don't you remember me? I took the vows last autumn. I was accompanied by Sir John Alden."

Amazement joyously transformed him. "Show yourself to me then, my child, after the sun has risen and the light of day illumines your face. And if indeed it is as you say, I would love nothing so well as to declare you whole."

తేళ తేళ తేళ

Sir John received an urgent message from the prioress of St. James the Less.

"Lady Johanna is missing. Come right away. Please."

Within the half hour he was dismounting from his horse in the courtyard of the hospital. Sister Magdalena met him there, and one of the servants took his horse. She led him into the prioress's private apartment.

"What happened?"

"Roesia awakened this morning to find her gone. The cloak you gave her was missing, and she had changed from one of the standard dresses the bishop gives the girls into one of her own fine gowns."

"Did she take anything else?"

"I don't think so. Her hood and her clapper were lying on her bed. Can you find her?"

John's mouth set into a line of determination. "Yes."

"Then go, Sir John. I'll await your return, no matter how long it takes."

❧ ❧ ❧

Be thou clean.
I am clean.
Be thou clean.
I am clean!
I AM CLEAN!

Nicholas de Litlyngton could find no evidence of leprosy. Only scars remained on her face, her arm, and her leg. No longer raised patches, just areas of shiny skin, slick with healing, and pinker than the rest of her fair skin. They were noticeable, and they marred the beauty she had claimed in the past. But she would not complain. It was a small price, she knew.

Johanna received the abbot's blessing as she knelt in thankful humility and departed with a joy that was so great it could not have been described by even the pen of Dante himself. She floated through the streets of Westminster, then of London, not realizing how swiftly time was passing as she cherished the feel of each stone beneath her feet: the hot, the cold, the rough. The wind on her new skin.

And the sun . . . it was shining and golden and warm with the pleasure of the Almighty. The sky was bluer than it had ever been, and its essence touched her eyes as they once again received that spark of liveliness that had been a gift from God at her birth.

Johanna!

Johanna again.

But more.

For surely God was now living in her heart.

Before she even realized it, the morning had slipped away. She hurried toward the small parish church near the hospital. It was easy to find Father Clement. He was praying inside.

"Father Clement?"

He knew her voice immediately. "Johanna? I was just praying for your safety, and here you are! Where have you been, child?"

"The abbey. And God has heard your prayer."

She helped him to his feet and told him the tale, both of them in tears by the end of the miraculous story. "And so, just as He healed the lepers, He healed me, Father Clement. His mercy does not fail; I've learned it well, not because I deserve what has happened to me, but because He chose to heal me for reasons I may never know."

"It is truly a miracle!" He lifted his hands heavenward, his nearly blind eyes raising as well, seeing the glory of God's unknown purpose. "Praise be to God!"

"Yes, Father Clement! Yes. To Him be all the glory!"

The aged priest pulled his charge into a warm embrace, overcome with joy. "It is as you say, Lady Johanna, to Him be the glory."

They knelt together, hand in hand, thanking God for what had occurred, neither quite believing the words which came forth. God had healed. It was so. Finally, they rose to their feet.

"You must tell the prioress, my lady. She's consumed with worry. Sir John left several hours ago in search of you."

"Not yet, Father. I must go back to the abbey to pray. If I can prostrate myself for a night for the cause of my healing, I can prostrate myself in gratitude. Please send word for me, though. Tell her the news. I want her to know. I want the world to know."

"With pleasure, my child. But you will go to her as soon as you are finished?"

"Yes, Father. I promise. Father, would you please relay a message for me to Claire?"

"Yes, of course. What is it?"

"When Sir John returns, have her tell him to meet me by the north side of the Confessor's shrine as soon as he can. I'll be waiting for him there. Tell her to keep the matter of my healing a secret. I want to tell him myself."

"All right, my lady. Let's hope he returns soon, then."

"Yes. Let us hope he does. Oh, Father! Can you believe what has happened to me? He healed me. I don't know why. But I know it's true."

She ran from the church and back to the abbey. Back to the Chapel of St. Nicholas.

❧ ❧ ❧

That afternoon several horsemen rode onto the hospital grounds. One jumped quickly down and would have hurried inside, but he was detained by Claire, who was running breathlessly toward him.

"Sir John! Wait!"

She came up close, her voice, very soft, letting him know something was afoot. "I'm sworn to secrecy and am bid to tell you only this. Lady Johanna has sent word that as soon as you receive this message you are to meet her at the north side of the Shrine of the Confessor at the abbey."

John made no reply, running to Gale, mounting and riding from the hospital with all the speed he could command of the great horse.

THIRTY-EIGHT

He recognized his cloak immediately, and the stray lock of straight blond hair which had escaped from the side of the hood and now draped over her shoulder. His relief overwhelmed him for just a moment, and he stopped to inhale widely.

Then he went on.

"Johanna." He put a hand on her shoulder.

She didn't turn to face him. "I knew you would come soon."

"Claire just gave me your message. Come back with me to the hospital, mon amour. They're all worried about you."

She was speaking so softly he had to crane his head forward over her shoulder to hear her. "They needn't be. For all is well."

"Why did you leave? Why didn't you tell anyone where you were going?"

"I didn't know I would be gone so long. A few hours was all I had originally planned."

"Let's get you back."

"Not yet. I wanted you to come here because I've something to ask you, John."

"As you wish."

"Do you still love me?"

"More than ever before."

"And would you forsake the world and come to me, be my husband, living in a poor hut, away from all mankind?"

He didn't hesitate. "These past few months without you have been worse lived than what you describe, my Johanna. In fact, what you speak of sounds like the life I have always been looking for. To care for you. To be by your side day and night. 'Tis all I want."

"Then kiss me. Close your eyes and kiss me soundly, my love, knowing that as you do you may share more than a hut with me."

Again there was no hesitation. He turned her to face him, closed his eyes, and pushed back her hood, his lips finding hers with ease. It was the moment they had both been yearning for but had dared not hope to find. He was claiming her, even as she claimed him. And in receiving the pleasure of being close to her, he was completely giving himself away.

He opened his eyes and pulled away, seeing before him a woman whose joyful expression reflected the beauty of the sun itself. She took his hands in hers, squeezed them tightly, and raised them to where he could see them.

"Do you see my hand?"

She held it out and flexed the fingers.

"My face? My foot?" She lifted the hem of her gown several inches and made circles with her ankle. "It happened, my love. God gave us that miracle."

He could say nothing. His joy was overwhelming. John dropped to his knees and wept for the first time since he had buried his family at Seforth. It was true, then, what he had said in the cave. And the truth of it surprised him, for in the loneliness of the past several months he had forgotten that truly, miracles still happened even now.

꧁ ꧁ ꧁

The glow of the sunset much later that day cast a reddish hue over the courtyard of the hospital. Near the garden a pile of wood was growing, each of the inhabitants who were yet mobile walking in and out of the woods with bundles of sticks and laying them down.

Ida, carried out on her cot by some of the others, threw on the last stick. Agnes lit a piece of kindling held by Claire, who then threw it on the pile. The fire took hold, its breath of flame exhaling like a soft wind through the pockets of air and igniting the dry branches.

Limping forward on her crutch came the prioress. Her free hand clutched two objects. All watched in anticipation, including John and Johanna, who stood nearby, her hand held firmly in his.

The prioress drew back her arm and flung the objects into the fire. The wooden clapper landed first on the pile, its wooden tablets sounding forth a final shudder. And through the air, as though on wings of its own, the leper's hood took flight, the updraft of the fire catching it underneath and bringing it to settle softly upon the blaze.

The inhabitants of St. James the Less stared silently as the objects burned, their eyes glittering with the reflection of the fire. And when all was consumed, a cry of joy such as never was heard in their ranks was issued forth in such a hearty din that no one would have been surprised if the very angels of heaven had been momentarily distracted from their glorious praises.

John put an arm around her. "Let's go home."

❧ ❧ ❧

Under the stars they rode away from London, just the two of them, on the back of Gale.

John's arm was warm around her. "I thought you said you would never ride a horse."

"I'm only riding him because you are at the reins."

"I like that."

"What?"

"Your trust in me."

" 'Tis well deserved. You've never failed me, my love. Never once."

He said nothing, and they rode on a bit further.

"Johanna?"

"Yes?"

"Do you recall just this morning in the abbey when you asked me if I would forsake the world and live in a hut with you?"

"How could I forget that so soon? Just as I thought, your response failed to disappoint me."

"Then may I consider that a proposal?"

She turned around in surprise. He was laughing. Sir John Alden was actually laughing! It was melodic and pure and so very contagious.

"Well, 'tis a bit backward, but if you must know, I want nothing so much in the world as to marry you."

He stopped Gale, jumped down, and pulled Johanna into his arms.

"Then I accept," he said, laughing once more and pulling her even closer to him, with a kiss that told of a heart filled with love and a future filled with the promises of joys innumerable.

He pulled his head up to stare into her eyes, but Johanna would have none of it. "I've waited almost 19 years to be kissed like that, and if you stop now, I swear I'll take back my offer!"

He willingly complied with her demand, and their love for each other flowered yet more under the meeting of their lips.

"You will soon be mine," he said hoarsely against her mouth.

"I always have been, my darling knight. We've always known each other, remember?"

She held her warrior-poet, the man she had dreamed of since she had first seen Prince Edward, and she kissed him soundly, giving all she had, loving with every part that made her Johanna. And he knew that they belonged to one another, together, for the rest of their lives.

She was healed. And so was he. Together. And God had made it thus.

A ray of cool sunlight lay luxuriously across their bed. Johanna awakened, rubbed the sleep from her eyes, and turned to the side, supporting herself on her left elbow. John held a finger up to his lips and looked down at the little bundle which lay next to him.

She whispered with a laugh. "You'll spoil that child beyond repair, mon amour."

His return smile was quiet and joyful. "I still can't believe she's ours."

"Well, you had better get used to the idea, for she's the first of many if last night was any indication." She still blushed when she spoke like that. John loved both the words and the blushing.

A knock sounded at the door, and a maid came in with a bucket of hot water. "It must be time to get up, eh, Mary?" Sir John said with an eyebrow raised. " 'Tis a good thing I hadn't risen out of the bed a moment sooner!"

"Oh, get on with you, milord. I watched you come into the world, and believe me, you were nothing to look at then either!"

Mary had served John's parents. Slowly, many of the old servants were returning to Seforth Castle, but today two more would be arriving—special people whose coming was eagerly awaited by Johanna.

"What time are Margery and Henry to arrive?" John asked.

"I imagine before dinner. Their wedding was only a week ago. I'm sure the journey has been a leisurely one. I still can't believe Maman was willing to part with Henry!"

"Just when middle age is settling upon me, along comes a cook whose food I cannot resist!"

"You're the most handsome man around, John Alden, and you always will be, no matter how old you are."

He leaned across, making sure not to cover baby Bridget with his weight, and he kissed her, long and luxuriously. Not the hurried kiss of a youth, but the relaxed, slow kiss of a mature man. Johanna delighted in the hair which was turning more gray and the wrinkles around his eyes and mouth which had deepened since their marriage a year before. He blamed them on Johanna, saying he laughed and smiled more in their first year of marriage than he had in his entire life.

Mary came into the room again. "My lady, will you allow me to take little Bridget now? It's almost time for prayers anyway, and I don't want her bathwater to get cold."

"Of course, Mary. Thank you." Johanna quickly arose and began to dress for the day with the help of a younger girl they had hired as her lady's maid. Sir John donned his normal black clothing in the far corner of the room. Soon she was ready for the trek to the Chapel of Christ's Hospital, a lazar house she had founded about a mile from the castle. Even with a new child and a loving husband, Johanna purposed never to forget. John supported her work completely. The hospital had received its first patients only a month before.

"Will you accompany me to prayers down at the hospital, my husband," she asked, "or do you have some training to do?"

"The men should be gathering in the courtyard now. They'll be most disappointed if they don't get to joust today.

Let us convene for prayers after supper this evening, my lady, just you and I in the chapel."

"That, my lord, will be a pleasure I shall greatly look forward to."

She took the cloak the maid held forward, leaned down to kiss the baby, smiled fondly at Mary, and then placed her hand in John's. "Come, my soldier, I'll walk you to the courtyard."

"Thank you, my lady, for the way is quite fraught with danger, and I'll need your strength and wits to keep me alive."

She laughed. "Never fear. I'll always be here to protect you!"

He joined in her laughter, and they walked together, their steps as one, out into the crisp December air. In the pocket of her gown a scrap of parchment was tucked. She reached inside and felt the paper now grown soft with years, the words of a leper, and she remembered a day long ago when she was only 12. She kept it with her always, so she would never forget from whence she came, would never forget the God who showed her mercy. The God who healed both body and soul. The God who had blessed her with a miracle.

In the hall, Duncan played softly on his lyre, as he always did. Another day had begun in the home of the warrior and his bride.

❧ ❧ ❧

Spring 1478

"How many more children did they have?" Maggie asked, disappointed to see that the lively little figure of the Black Prince on horseback was never finished.

"Four more: three boys and one girl."

"Did they always love each other?"

"Until the day they died. They died together, out on the sea. A storm came suddenly, and they couldn't get back to shore."

"I'm sure they would have wanted it that way."

"Oh yes. It would have been impossible for one to have lived without the other."

Maggie ran her fingers over the unfinished figure of the Black Prince. "So she never finished the tapestry?"

"No. There was no need. She had found her very own knight."

"The knight of the cave."

"Yes. Her knight."

"And she found God amidst it all, didn't she, Grandmama?"

"Oh yes, child. And to we who know Him, too, we realize that this was the greatest miracle of them all."

"Of course, Grandmama. Of course."